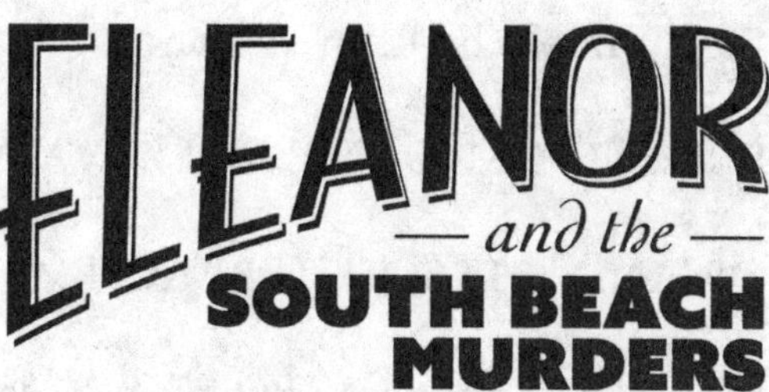
ELEANOR
and the
SOUTH BEACH
MURDERS

Books by Ellen Yardley

ELEANOR AND THE COLD WAR

ELEANOR AND THE SOUTH BEACH MURDERS

Published by Kensington Publishing Corp.

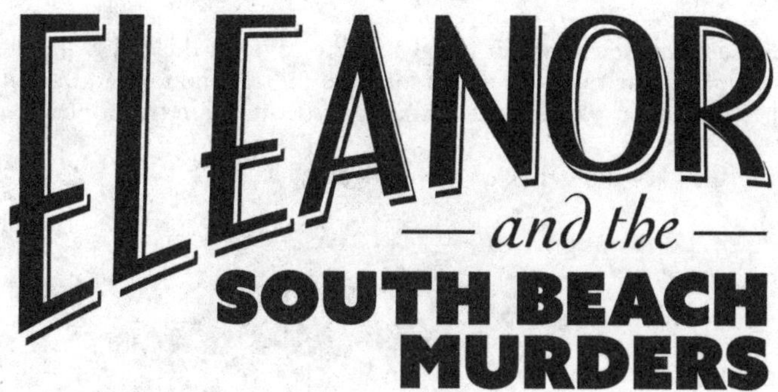

ELLEN YARDLEY

kensingtonbooks.com

This book is a work of fiction. Names, characters, businesses, organizations, places, events, and incidents either are the product of the author's imagination or are used fictitiously. Any resemblance to actual persons, living or dead, events, or locales is entirely coincidental.

To the extent that the image or images on the cover of this book depict a person or persons, such person or persons are merely models, and are not intended to portray any character or characters featured in the book.

KENSINGTON BOOKS are published by

Kensington Publishing Corp.
900 Third Ave.
New York, NY 10022

All Kensington titles, imprints, and distributed lines are available at special quantity discounts for bulk purchases for sales promotion, premiums, fund-raising, educational, or institutional use. Special book excerpts or customized printings can also be created to fit specific needs. For details, write or phone the office of the Kensington Special Sales Manager: Attn. Special Sales Department. Kensington Publishing Corp., 900 Third Ave., New York, NY 10022. Phone: 1-800-221-2647.

Library of Congress Control Number: On file

KENSINGTON and the K with book logo Reg. US Pat. & TM Off.

ISBN: 978-1-4967-5010-5
First Kensington Hardcover Edition: March 2026

ISBN: 978-1-4967-5012-9 (ebook)

10 9 8 7 6 5 4 3 2 1

Printed in the United States of America

The authorized representative in the EU for product safety and compliance
is eucomply OU, Parnu mnt 139b-14, Apt 123
Tallinn, Berlin 11317, hello@eucompliancepartner.com

ACKNOWLEDGMENTS

I want to thank the team at Kensington Publishing for all their support, especially my editor John Scognamiglio. Many thanks to my agent, Evan Marshall, for his help and encouragement. As always, I am indebted to my many writer friends for their words of wisdom and their judicious critiquing.

Finally, many, many thanks to my readers. I couldn't do this without you. I hope you enjoy sleuthing alongside Eleanor Roosevelt and Kay Thompson.

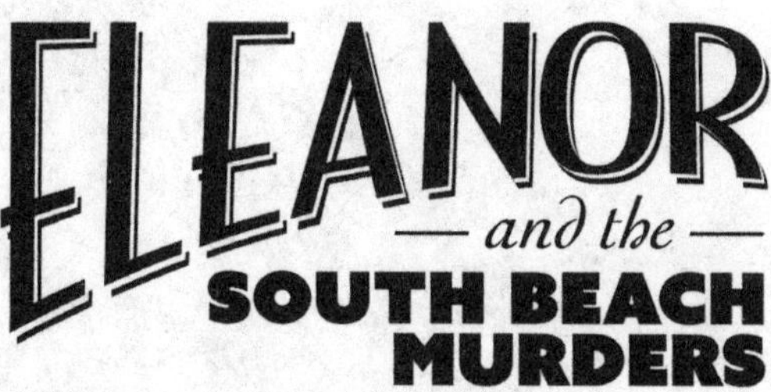
ELEANOR
and the
SOUTH BEACH
MURDERS

CHAPTER 1

The life you live is your own.
—Eleanor Roosevelt

Late December 1951
Miami Beach, Florida

Marilyn Monroe's candy-cane-striped bikini lay in Kay Thompson's suitcase, waiting to be worn on South Beach.

It didn't really belong to Marilyn, but it was a match for the strapless, two-piece bathing suit that Marilyn wore in a famous photo shoot. It was the skimpiest thing Kay had ever considered wearing in public.

She had planned to wear it today. As she sleepily pushed aside the bikini and searched for her girdle, Kay knew she would not make it to the beach today. Her job came first.

A soft knock sounded on the connecting door between her room and Mrs. Eleanor Roosevelt's suite. "Are you awake, Kay? If you wish, I could meet Tim's flight."

Despite the early hour—not quite four o'clock in the morning—the former First Lady sounded refreshed, alert, ready for her day. Kay went to the door and opened it. "It's okay, Mrs. Roosevelt. I should go. You have a packed agenda today."

"I was worried it might be awkward," Mrs. Roosevelt said.

She was dressed for the day in a light blue dress with three-quarter length sleeves, her hair arranged in a smooth chignon. Kay was still wrapped in her bathrobe. "After what happened."

"I won't let it be awkward," Kay said. She knew the first of Mrs. Roosevelt's requirements for herself was inner calm. ER, as she had been known at the White House, said: "One of the secrets of using your time well is to gain a certain ability to maintain peace within yourself so that much can go on around you and you can stay calm inside."

Kay loved her job with Mrs. Roosevelt. She wanted to keep it. That meant not allowing her personal life (a breakup on Christmas Eve day) to interfere with her job (Mrs. Eleanor Roosevelt's temporary secretary).

"I'll be ready in just a moment," Kay said. "I just need to use the bathroom."

She closed the door behind her. She snapped on the light and groaned at her reflection. Her red hair looked like a bird's nest and her eyes and cheeks were puffy from sleep. She had no idea why. It wasn't as if she'd slept. She had tossed and turned all night.

Kay turned on the tap and doused her face with cold water. Her bathroom in her room in the Delano Hotel had the same Art Deco styling as the hotel's famous exterior. Chromium fixtures, a geometric mirror, lots of white marble.

She heard a soft creak. The sound of the balcony door opening. Mrs. Roosevelt must be looking outside while she waited for Kay.

The sun wasn't up yet, but the breeze wafting in was already warm. Suddenly, Kay could smell the salty tang of the ocean. It was so quiet at this hour, she heard the soft roar of the waves.

Mrs. Roosevelt's suite and Kay's adjoining room were at the back of the Delano, overlooking the gardens, the dazzling swimming pool, and the endless stretch of the azure ocean beyond.

Kay had begged Mrs. Roosevelt not to wake up so early. With

her packed agenda, Mrs. Roosevelt needed her sleep. At eight a.m. Mrs. Roosevelt was to give an important speech at the conference for the AAUN, the American Association for the United Nations, being held downstairs in the ballroom.

But she should have known Mrs. Roosevelt would be concerned that she had asked Kay to wake up before four.

Even so early, Kay had planned to put on her makeup. From giving her skin a porcelain look with her new Revlon Touch-and-Glow in Creamy Ivory, to drawing on Elizabeth Taylor eyebrows with Revlon's tortoiseshell-plastic swivel-stick eye pencil. She was not going to meet Tim without "her face on." But she didn't want to make Mrs. R (as Mrs. Roosevelt was known) wait.

She yanked a brush through her hair. And decided she should put on her eyelashes. Wouldn't Tim notice if she suddenly had short, stubby lashes instead of the long sweeping ones he thought she possessed?

With tweezers, she picked up one long false eyelash.

Peering close to the vanity mirror, she directed the flimsy thing toward her eye. It would only take a second—

Loud pounding sounded on the door of Mrs. R's suite.

"Eleanor! Are you awake?"

Kay jerked her hand. The eyelash was gone. She held a set of empty tweezers.

"I need you!" the woman exclaimed.

Kay recognized the voice. It belonged to Josephine Baker, the famous singer. Four hours earlier, Kay and Mrs. Roosevelt had returned from a private party in Josephine's dressing room at the Copa City Club.

Why was Josephine at Mrs. Roosevelt's door?

Kay heard the door open.

"Eleanor!" Josephine cried. "I need your help. There is a dead man in my dressing room. And when the police found a dead white man in a locked room with a Black woman and a gun, the first thing they did was arrest the Black woman!"

CHAPTER 2

Dear God, please make Eleanor a little tired.
—Franklin D. Roosevelt

Two days earlier
Miami, Florida

Kay peered out of the tiny window as the airplane approached the Miami International Airport. Below she could see a stretch of sparkling lights, a patch of darkness, then a strip of more lights that ended abruptly at an endless expanse of velvety darkness that had to be the Atlantic Ocean.

The airplane made a steep bank. Kay clutched her armrests. "What's happening?"

"I believe the pilot is circling toward the runway to land," Mrs. Roosevelt stated.

Kay could not even fake inner calm. Her heart raced, she heard roaring in her ears—either from pressure or the fear of an inevitable crash.

Kay tried to twist the armrests, as if she could override the pilot and level the plane herself.

Captain Dan Williams and his copilot had been seated in the cockpit when she and Mrs. Roosevelt boarded the plane in New York. Both pilots had cut very attractive figures in their uniforms. Captain Williams's voice over the intercom had sounded deep and reassuring.

Now that they were almost *vertical*, Kay feared that calm and reassurance was for show.

She could see the city below—a grid of twinkling lights in the inky black—through the window *across* the aisle.

In the seat beside her, Mrs. Roosevelt calmly secured her paperwork in place on the small tray table. She had spent the flight carefully studying paperwork in preparation for the AAUN conference.

Kay wished she could be like ER. If these really were the last moments of her life, shouldn't she be thinking about important things? Her big regret right now was that she had eschewed a pair of adorable scarlet sandals with three-inch heels and had bought a staid, demure white pair instead.

"Oooh," she gasped as they seemed to tilt even more.

Just when she was certain the airplane would spiral to the ground, Captain Williams straightened them out.

Turbulence jostled them. Suddenly the plane lifted and fell, then shuddered side to side, like a toy kite being thrown around in the wind. Or marbles rattled in a tin can.

Kay stopped breathing.

Mrs. Roosevelt laid her hand lightly and reassuringly over Kay's. "Not to worry. I have flown many times. Pilots are experts at handling turbulence."

"Th-thank you, Mrs. Roosevelt," Kay stuttered. "I'm fine. Really."

Mrs. R patted her hand. "I know you are very courageous, Kay. Many people are troubled by flying."

How Kay wished she could have impressed Mrs. Roosevelt right now with strength and stoicism. She was working as Mrs. R's temporary secretary, accompanying her to Miami because Aunt Tommy, Mrs. R's regular secretary, was not well.

Then, by a miracle, the shuddering stopped. They began to drop in a gentle descent.

With a crackle, the loudspeaker came on. "This is your captain. I apologize for the last few minutes. We hit some unexpected turbulence on the approach. Smooth sailing now, folks. We should be on the ground in Miami in a few minutes. Local time is 4:05 a.m. Weather today will be clear and sunny with a high of seventy-five degrees."

Seventy-five degrees? In December? This time of year, Kay usually trudged to work through snow and sleet.

Now that she knew she would live to wear her sandals and bikini, Kay's faith in handsome Captain Williams was restored.

And she could admire Captain Williams. After all, she was single again.

With a jolt, the wheels touched ground. Captain Williams hit the brakes. The deceleration made her gasp.

"Safe and sound," Mrs. Roosevelt said, sliding her papers into her attaché case. Knowing they would arrive at four in the morning, she had sensibly slept before reviewing her notes.

Kay had been too excited to sleep, despite having nothing else to do for several hours.

She was going to Miami. She would be staying at the glamorous Delano Hotel on South Beach.

The airplane taxied to the terminal. Men in uniforms hastened toward it, pulling the rollaway stairs. People began to stand.

From the airplane's rounded window, Kay could see the runways with a half dozen airplanes lined up for takeoff. Ahead was a sprawling yellow building that must be the main terminal. Now Kay's job would begin in earnest. As secretary, she would collect the luggage. Hail a taxi. Ensure Mrs. R made it safely to her suite at the Delano Hotel in South Beach.

It was her job to ensure everything went smoothly.

They emerged out of the airplane into the dark.

It was not even five o'clock in the morning, but as Kay stepped out onto the stairs, warm and humid air wrapped around her. Much nicer than the frosty cold she'd left behind but instantly, she was perspiring in her wool skirt and sweater, the clothes she had needed to brave the New York winter on the way to the airport.

"I will help retrieve the luggage," Mrs. Roosevelt said, as they reached the metal shelves where airport employees manually placed the bags.

"No, no," Kay said quickly. "It's my job."

"Mine too." Mrs. R smiled.

True to her word, Mrs. R grasped the first case. Kay took the second and the typewriter case. They piled the baggage on a wheeled cart. Mrs. Roosevelt led the way to the taxi stand.

"Of course," Kay said, "you have been to Miami Beach before."

"Oh yes. Most recently in March of this year, for my son Elliott's wedding. I came during the war to visit hospitals. Franklin survived an assassination attempt here, in 1933."

"What?" Kay had no idea. She had been a child in 1933. And she had only begun working for Mrs. Roosevelt in the autumn.

"Yes, a disturbed man attempted to shoot him," Mrs. R said, her voice controlled and unflustered. "It was February, just over two weeks before his inauguration."

Kay stared in shock. "And you weren't afraid to return?"

"Oh no. And in March of 1934, I flew from Miami to Puerto Rico via Cuba and Port-au-Prince, Haiti. Before leaving, I met with three Miami policemen who were guarding my husband that day in Bayfront Park."

Kay was still amazed by the danger Mrs. Roosevelt had faced, and how she stood up to fear with strength, calm, and grace.

"It should be easy to get a cab," Kay said. "After all, how many people are arriving this early in the morning?"

She was wrong.

A large group of men milled around the taxi stand. There were at least two dozen of them. It must be a convention, for they almost all wore business suits and fedoras.

Kay usually noticed men. And now that she was single once more, she had every right to size up other men.

But something about this group sent a prickle of unease down her spine. The fine hairs on the nape of her neck literally stood up.

"Are they here for the AAUN conference?" Kay mused, frowning. Somehow that didn't feel right.

In a voice devoid of emotion, Mrs. Roosevelt said, "I do not believe so."

Now Kay realized why she felt apprehension.

The men's conversations had stopped as they saw Mrs. Roosevelt. Silently, they glowered in her direction. Usually, in any large group, some people would recognize Mrs. Roosevelt, approach her, and ask to shake her hand. Not this time.

"I believe those men are members of the KKK," Mrs. R murmured in a low voice. "I recognize several. That one is a senator from the South. I believe that gentleman is in politics in north Florida."

For all the members of the KKK wore hoods and cloaks that looked like they were draped in bedsheets, their membership in the organization was not all that secret. While working with Mrs. R, Kay had learned that members of the KKK were in politics and law enforcement. In fact, one of the men in the taxi lineup wore a sheriff's uniform.

The KKK had sent threats to Mrs. Roosevelt. Aunt Tommy, Mrs. R's regular secretary who now lived in Hyde Park, told how she often answered the telephone to gruff-voiced men who threatened awful things.

Aunt Tommy simply hung up on them.

"We should get out of here," Kay whispered. "We could wait and get a cab later."

But Mrs. R went to the end of the line and calmly waited. Kay joined her, but she could feel hatred emanating from the men. She tried to look unaffected as they moved along the line.

Finally, she and Mrs. Roosevelt reached the front. But as the next taxi drove up to the stand, a large man pushed in front of them.

"Excuse me!" Kay said sharply.

He scowled. "We're in a hurry, sweetheart."

"I am not your sweetheart, we are in just as much of a hurry, and we were here first," Kay said.

The man was big, broad, and built like a bull. A bull that was overweight. His white suit strained at the buttons. He was accompanied by a lean, good-looking black-haired man who was only an inch taller than Kay.

They reminded Kay of the "Fat Man" and "Mr. Cairo" from the film *The Maltese Falcon*. Kay had a girlfriend who'd had a huge crush on Humphrey Bogart, and they saw the movie six times.

The "Fat Man" shoved his way past them, whistling to the next taxi. His companion followed, but had the decency to look sheepish, but not the courage to stand up to his friend.

Kay stepped out from behind them, right to the edge of the curb. She put her leg forward to fiddle with her stocking. Just like Claudette Colbert in *It Happened One Night*. That had been a favorite movie of her mother's. Thinking about it made her miss her mother—who would never have guessed her daughter would have traveled to Paris and now to Miami with Eleanor Roosevelt.

The taxi screeched to a halt in front of her. The cab driver jumped out. He was a tall young man, tanned, with curly black hair. He flipped open the trunk, grabbed Mrs. R's big suitcase first, and placed it in with ease.

As he loaded the rest, he said cheerfully, “Where to, ladies?”

The “Fat Man” swiveled around and glared at Kay. “We were at the front of the line, young—” Then he looked at Mrs. Roosevelt as if he hadn’t noticed her. “Is that Mrs. Franklin Delano Roosevelt?”

“It is,” Kay said. She doubted he hadn’t seen Mrs. R. He was trying to save face, she thought.

“You gentlemen may have this taxi,” Mrs. Roosevelt said briskly. “We shall take the next one.”

“Ladies first for me,” the cabbie said. “Besides, I’ve got your cases loaded. All right, ladies, where are you going?”

Feeling the big man’s anger begin to boil, Kay smiled sweetly and said, “Don’t make me believe chivalry is dead with you fine gentlemen.”

The big man and “Mr. Cairo” stalked away, hailing another taxi.

Then Kay heard the words that chilled her to her bone.

“You’d better be careful, Mrs. Roosevelt,” said one of the men who remained in the group. “Wouldn’t want to see the same thing happen to you as happened to that Harry T. Moore up in Mims on Christmas Day.”

Harry T. Moore was a Black civil rights activist who had founded an NAACP chapter in Florida. A bomb had been planted under the Moores’ bedroom, and it went off on Christmas Day. A monstrous and cowardly attack. Mr. Moore had died, and Mrs. Moore was in the hospital.

Kay looked back toward the group of men, but Mrs. R said gently, “Ignore that man. He wishes to get a rise out of us.”

“Aren’t you worried? Maybe we shouldn’t be in Miami.”

“There have been several bombings in Florida,” Mrs. Roosevelt said thoughtfully. “It is being called the Florida Terror. I think it is important to be here. But I don’t want you to feel unsafe, Kay. If you would like to go home, you may return to Hyde Park. I can manage alone.”

To work for Mrs. Roosevelt meant stepping toward trouble and taking a stand, not running away. Mrs. Roosevelt had once said, "Every time we shirk making up our minds or standing up for a cause in which we believe, we weaken our character and our ability to be fearless."

"I'm staying right here," Kay said.

After three hours of sleep and a breakfast of eggs, toast, grapefruit, and coffee on the balcony, Eleanor Roosevelt was ready to tackle the opening day of the conference.

For Eleanor, this included a press conference, attendance at meetings, television and radio interviews in the afternoon, and giving a speech at the opening cocktail party.

The American Association for the United Nations was important to her. In a few days, it would be a new year. 1952. An election year. Of course, she hoped Harry Truman would win. But if the Republicans won, she expected this would be her last year as delegate to the United Nations. Governments wished to appoint people who were faithful to their party.

Her children, Anna, James, Elliott, Franklin Delano Jr., and John, might be relieved to see her retire and slow down. She was, after all, sixty-seven. Eleanor suspected the younger generation could not quite believe a woman her age had more to offer.

But Eleanor felt there was work to be done—for world peace and human rights—and she was eager to carry it out.

She had breakfasted with Kay on the balcony of her suite, enjoying the view of the ocean and the golden sunshine. Kay had asked if the Delano Hotel, where they were staying, had been named for Franklin.

The tall white hotel was famous for its distinctive geometric Art Deco façade, with beveled edges grouped in threes, topped with soaring fan-shaped finials.

"I have been told that it was," Eleanor answered.

She was pleased to see Kay had color in her face and looked in good spirits after breakfast.

Eleanor was accustomed to receiving death threats. When she toured America during Franklin's presidency, her security detail had discovered someone had strapped dynamite to her car tires.

Kay was not used to being threatened. Kay was brave—Eleanor had learned that while they had investigated the murder of beautiful Susan Meyer—but it was always shocking and frightening to discover that some people meant you harm.

As Kay helped her on with the light blue jacket that matched her linen dress, Eleanor gave an encouraging smile. "I am not worried about the threats. The most stressful part of today will be giving my speech."

Despite her years of experience, she still felt a flutter of nerves before public speaking. Even today, so many years later, she focused on the exercises Louis Howe had taught her to modulate the pitch of her voice and eliminate a nervous giggle.

Kay smiled. "You will be great. Are you sure you want me to attend the cocktail party? I am just a secretary."

"You are very important to the work I do. I feel you will find it interesting. There will be many young people your age as well."

"They will be much younger than me. The young people involved in these organizations always are. They make me feel old and make me realize I haven't accomplished very much in my life," Kay admitted.

"You are only twenty-five."

Kay winced. Eleanor smiled indulgently. Kay did not like to admit to her age, whereas to Eleanor, twenty-five was exceedingly young.

"You have accomplished a great deal," Eleanor said. "And

there is always time. I became a delegate to the United Nations at an age when many people thought I should retire from public life and slow down."

"Those people were wrong. Without you, I doubt there would be a Universal Declaration of Human Rights."

"That is very kind. But I was simply one person amongst many with hope for peace in the future," Eleanor said. "Now, let us begin our day."

The day proved as hectic as predicted. Eleanor was pleased at the way Kay kept things on schedule, confidently stepping in to remind the newspaper reporters and television interviewer of the time allotted. When things ran late, Kay got them back on track.

The favorite part of Eleanor's day came at the end, at the afternoon cocktail party when she was able to speak directly with the young members of the AAUN. Eleanor often convened youth leadership summits and listened intently when these young people expressed their ideas, hopes, and concerns.

They asked thought-provoking questions which proved very difficult to answer.

"What did you think of the Soviets with whom you worked on Committee Three at the U.N.?" asked a serious-looking young woman named Alice.

Eleanor said, "It is possible that Westerners never fully understand the complexity of the Russian character, but I have constantly kept trying to do so throughout my service with the United Nations."

A young man asked, between sucking on his pipe, "Do you think we can prevent World War Three or it is inevitable?"

"World peace is something all of us want, but none of us know the answer," Eleanor said. "Everyone knew it would be a slow process, a process of education and of gradual understanding of the world and the people among whom we live."

"How can America preach about human rights at the United Nations when segregation still exists in this country?"

The last question came as a demand from a young, attractive Black woman who wore a smart gray suit and had just joined the group gathered around Eleanor. She looked older than the others, perhaps close to thirty.

Eleanor sadly shook her head. "Yes, the Soviet delegation asked about our treatment of Black people in my country. I was asked: How about your Ku Klux Klan lynchings? I had no answer," she conceded softly. "What do you say, standing before a committee of a world organization, when you are asked about the Ku Klux Klan?

"But I, for one, will continue to work to have such laws put in place. And to end segregation and discrimination. For as long as it takes to happen."

The young woman gazed directly into her eyes. Eleanor felt as if her soul was being examined, but she did not fear giving the truth to this direct young woman.

"My name is Rosaleen Davis. I am Josephine Baker's assistant. She is staying here in the Delano. You might be surprised to hear that since Miami Beach is a segregated city. Black performers are supposed to stay in a hotel in Overtown, but Josephine wanted to stay on South Beach."

"I am pleased that she is," Eleanor said.

"She is performing at the Copa City Club," Miss Davis continued. "She insisted she would only perform if the audiences were not segregated. Josephine has enough clout to get what she wants. When Josephine heard you were staying here too, Mrs. Roosevelt, she sent me with an invitation. She would like you to attend her show tonight."

"To see Josephine Baker perform would be a wonderful opportunity," Eleanor said. "Miss Thompson and I will be happy to attend."

"Josephine Baker is hot stuff," breathed the tall young man who had asked her a question. He had introduced himself as Benny. He affected a blazer and a pipe, even though he had revealed he recently graduated high school. "She is known as 'La Baker' in Paris. Can I come as well?"

"It's a free country," Rosaleen answered. There was a cutting edge of sarcasm in her words that touched Eleanor's heart.

CHAPTER 3

. . . neither will it hurt the young people of today if they speak out their convictions and write from their hearts.
—Eleanor Roosevelt, My Day, July 4, 1944

The spot-lit marquee on one of the sleek, curved white walls of the Copa City Club announced that Josephine Baker was performing three shows a day. Palm trees lined the street, swaying gently in the warm breeze. A long queue of people waited under the awning to get in. The Copa City was on a road filled with nightclubs, known colloquially as "Swing Street."

Kay frowned but Rosaleen Davis moved with brisk confidence toward the head of the line. Miss Davis had flawless skin and ebony hair pulled back into a tight bun. She wore no makeup, not even a touch of color on her lips. Kay had touched up her makeup when she changed into a new evening dress.

Kay was still marveling that she was outdoors at night, at almost the end of December, wearing a strapless cocktail dress of white satin, a light silk shawl, and white sandals (with the too sensible heels). Back in New York, she would be freezing. And standing in ankle-deep slush.

Mrs. Roosevelt looked elegant in a blue sheath dress topped with a small bolero jacket. She wore a tiger tooth necklace, a treasured gift from her father. When Mrs. Roosevelt was a child (but still a Roosevelt), her father Elliott gave her that necklace, which was made from the teeth of a tiger he shot on a hunt in India.

Benny and two young women from the conference, Alice and Neeve, had gone ahead by taxi. Kay turned back and scanned the line to find them. But in the crush, she couldn't pick them out.

Miss Davis approached the big man who guarded the door. He was built like a bull, so large it would be impossible to push around him and get through the door. He filled the whole frame.

"This is Mrs. Eleanor Roosevelt, Hugo. She is Josephine's special guest."

Hugo nodded.

"And this is her secretary who accompanies her."

Kay winced a bit at the description. But she knew as a secretary, she was an add-on. It was an honor to be included in events with Mrs. R.

With a flourish, Hugo stepped aside. "What about Benny, Alice, and Neeve?" Kay asked.

Rosaleen Davis shrugged. "They will make their way in. Josephine wanted Mrs. Roosevelt as her guest."

But Rosaleen had a quick word with the doorman, and Kay overheard her describe Benny, Alice, and Neeve and direct him to send them to Josephine's guest table.

The theatre space was huge, with a soaring ceiling and streamlined design. Every table had a view of the stage. "The capacity is seven hundred and fifty," Rosaleen said.

There was a circular music bar, but the main attraction was the large stage. Josephine's guest table was in front of center stage.

Once seated, Kay glanced around. At the next table, a Black couple chatted excitedly. The woman wore a gorgeous deep purple dress with a glittering silver scarf, the gentleman looked elegant in a tan suit. They shared the table with a white couple, the woman in an unnecessary fur and the man in a seersucker suit. Throughout the lounge, Black and white patrons intermingled.

"I'm impressed Josephine Baker was able to insist on a nonsegregated audience," Kay said.

"She fought hard for it," Rosaleen said. "The worst part is that there is a curfew in Miami. Black people must be back in their own neighborhoods by nine p.m. Even though the Copa invited all people to come—white, Black, red, or green was what the owner said—Blacks were too afraid to be stopped by the police after curfew. In her whole tour of the U.S., Josephine has refused to perform unless it is an integrated audience."

"I am so impressed that Josephine has fought for change," Mrs. Roosevelt said. "For change begins with people of conviction and integrity."

"Her stance has cost her contracts," Miss Davis stated, ruefully. "And she needs the money to fix up the château she bought in France. She wants to turn it into an attraction that celebrates diversity. Her husband, Jo Bouillon, is beside himself because bills are coming in and Josephine's contracts are drying up because she is fighting segregation."

"About that, I am very sorry."

"She's taken on contracts to perform in South America. And Cuba," Miss Davis said, but she was interrupted as a male voice declared, "Miss Thompson, we found you!"

Kay looked up. Benny stood in front of her, beaming happily. He was flanked by dark-haired Alice, and Neeve, who sported a blond ponytail. Alice glared at Benny as he hurried to get the seat next to Kay.

She was six years older than Benny. At least. Kay motioned for Alice to sit on his other side. Each time he tried to ask her questions about herself, Kay tried to redirect him toward Alice.

She sighed. It was nice when a man found you attractive, but Benny was just a boy, and she didn't want to hurt his feelings.

There were a lot of single men in the audience. Attractive, well-dressed single men. And some who weren't good-looking but acted with a pretty cigarette girl as if they had the face of Cary Grant or handsome Gregory Peck from *David and Bathsheba*.

Then Kay caught her breath. At a table in the front row, sat the two men from the airport—the "Fat Man" and "Mr. Cairo."

She had thought they were with the group of men Mrs. Roosevelt had identified as members of the KKK. She shivered, remembering the threat spoken to Mrs. Roosevelt. Why would these men be here to see Josephine Baker?

Did it mean trouble?

She pointed them out to Mrs. Roosevelt. "Should we tell someone?"

"They have done nothing wrong, Kay," Mrs. R said calmly.

"They might," Kay said stubbornly. But in America, that was not enough reason to arrest them.

The lights lowered. The orchestra played a few opening notes, then spotlights lit up the stage.

The curtain swished back, revealing a simple set made to look like a park. Painted trees held pink fabric blossoms. A white metal bench stood along a fake white fence.

The spotlight moved to the side, and suddenly a tall Black woman festooned in soft, waving feathers came into view. Her dress was white, covered with sparkling rhinestones, and the feathered headdress she wore stood three feet high.

With grace and confidence, Josephine Baker walked sinuously to the center of the stage.

Out of the corner of her eye, Kay saw Benny drop his pipe.

Josephine Baker was lithe, with a dancer's lean, muscled form, long legs, but a curvaceous figure. Dark burgundy lipstick highlighted her glowing smile as she held out her arms as if embracing the audience. Her smile looked genuine, not staged. As if she were thrilled that people had come to see her.

The singer must be in her forties, but she was more dazzling than Kay could hope to be now, at twenty-five.

"It gives me much pleasure to be here, in Miami Beach, at the Copa City Club, with all of you. And to be performing in front of an *integrated* audience," Josephine Baker exclaimed.

Applause rippled over the packed theatre.

Kay gazed in awe.

Josephine launched into a love song. Her voice was light but rich with emotion. It filled the theatre. Kay had to close her eyes to hold in tears.

Wouldn't it be romantic to be in Miami with Tim O'Malley? To walk hand in hand on the beach at sunset? She hadn't seen the beach up close yet, she had been so busy, but she knew it would be beautiful and perfect for falling utterly in love.

Except that wasn't going to happen.

Tim had decided sharing *moments* like that was not enough. He didn't want to wait for her to return from trips with Mrs. Roosevelt. He wanted a wife who was at home every day, waiting for him with his dinner ready. In his mind, Kay could be a working woman or a wife. But not both. If she married him, she had to give up her job.

There was no compromise. No middle ground.

He said he had to let her go—as a husband he couldn't give her the kind of jet-set life she would have in her job with Mrs. Roosevelt.

She had realized he was breaking up with her. On Christmas Eve day. So, she jumped in and broke up with him first.

The song ended. The crowd erupted in applause, cheers, whistles.

"When I first performed in Paris," Josephine said into the microphone, "I received shouts and whistles. I thought I was a smash hit. Until someone explained that in France, the audience makes noise when they don't like you."

Leaving the audience laughing, Josephine slipped behind the

curtain. In mere minutes she returned in a new costume. A floor-length pale silver satin gown that was strapless on one side. A length of shimmering satin covered her other shoulder. The train of the dress was twenty feet long. On top of her three-foot long ebony chignon, a diamond headdress sparkled in the spotlights.

Kay thought if she wore that dress, the dress would wear her. But not Josephine Baker. The dress was a backdrop to her luminous personality.

Kay had never seen a true star so close. Josephine Baker exuded elegance, but she treated the audience as if they were her friends. She bantered with ease.

She revealed, "When I was little, living in East St. Louis, I danced in the streets for spare change and learned to play trumpet. I left home at age thirteen to make my living as a performer. With all my courage, I used my last money to go to New York. I slept on park benches, under newspapers, until I got my first part on Broadway."

The crowd gasped at Josephine's stories, told with humor and poignancy, of her impoverished childhood. She spoke of her love of Paris. Paris accepted her and there she became a star.

"It was a dark time when Paris was invaded," she said. "I was invited to do my part. I traveled to Lisbon, then Morocco, to help the Allies. It was such a joyous day when the war ended. But there was still much work to do. Performers were invited to sing at the Nazi death camps. Due to the fear of typhus, most refused to go. I went. I saw such horrors in those awful places. I performed for men who could not be moved. They looked like skeletons and were confined to their beds because they had no strength. They were ill and dying. It was too late for them. But they told me that my songs still brought them joy."

The stage lights glittered on a tear that fell to Josephine Baker's smooth cheek. "Never, can we allow such horror to happen again!" she exclaimed.

Kay saw Mrs. Roosevelt nod in approval.

Josephine's finale was called "J'ai Deux Amours."

Kay knew *amours* had something to do with love. Mrs. R explained it translated to "I have two loves."

"That sounds naughty."

"It is intended to," Mrs. R answered, surprising Kay. "But I believe it means to Josephine that she loves France, and she also loves America."

The song was in French. Kay didn't understand the words. But it didn't matter. She felt every note, every emotion.

As Josephine held the last note, then released it, the crowd got to its feet. Black and white, side by side, they gave a standing ovation.

Josephine bowed, glowing. Then she left the stage. The applause grew louder—a plea for an encore.

As Josephine returned and the clapping ceased, Rosaleen Davis appeared at their table. She approached Mrs. Roosevelt, crouching down so she didn't block anyone's view of Josephine.

She still wore the trim gray suit she had worn when inviting Kay and Mrs. R to the performance.

"Josephine wondered if you would join her for cocktails after the performance in her dressing room. She didn't want to impose, but she said she would be honored to meet you personally."

"I will be delighted," Mrs. R said.

"Good. I'll take you backstage when Josephine is finished. It's a rabbit warren back there." Miss Davis paused. "Just to warn you, Josephine has received death threats. You are a former First Lady and maybe you won't feel safe meeting Josephine."

Kay shivered. It made sense—Josephine's insistence on an integrated audience, in defiance of the segregation laws, must have made herself a target.

"I am not afraid of threats," Mrs. R said, as Kay expected. "I am honored to meet Josephine Baker."

* * *

"Josephine has three dressing rooms," Miss Davis explained as she led them to the back dressing rooms. Giggles from the chorus-line dancers and the two young female backup singers echoed down the hallway. "Jo needs one for her costumes, one where she can get dressed and do her makeup, and she likes to have a room solely for socializing."

Kay gasped as they passed the dressing room filled with costumes. The colorful sight dazzled her eyes. Pink, peacock blue, royal purple, silver, fire-engine red, and midnight black. Sequins and jewels sparkled. Airy tulle and fluffy feathers adorned many gowns. There were three metal racks packed tight with gorgeous dresses. It was like a rainbow had been captured in the room.

"Josephine's costumes are worth about a quarter of a million dollars," Miss Davis said. "They come from designers like Christian Dior and Jean Dessès. You can see why she needs more rooms—nothing but the clothes can fit in that one."

Kay had worked for Mrs. Roosevelt for several months and she had met many people. But the thought of greeting Josephine Baker left her tongue-tied.

The star was reclining on one of two pale blue sofas in a large room. A drinks cart stood in the corner. On the table, two champagne bottles stood in silver ice buckets.

Vases of flowers covered every surface and when there were no more surfaces, they stood on the floor. The scent made it hard to breathe. There were a dozen vases of long-stem roses. Colors from blush pink to dark crimson. There were chrysanthemums, large white lilies, and more baby's breath than you would find at a florist's.

Josephine Baker swept to her feet, holding out her hands. She had changed into an off-white pleated dress that only looked simple. She had tossed a mink wrap casually around her shoulders and looked every inch a world-famous star.

Rosaleen Davis whispered, "The House of Dior whipped that dress up in two days when Josephine's husband, Jo Bouillon, requested that they make it for Josephine. She sent him to fetch her clothes for Josephine Baker Day."

Kay couldn't believe it. The dress was exquisite.

Mrs. R extended her hand. "Madame Bouillon, it is an honor to meet you."

"Mrs. Roosevelt, the honor is mine. I've always admired you—and there aren't many politicians I have admired. They like to play it safe. That's something you don't do," Josephine Baker said. "And I am impressed that you didn't refer to me as Mrs. Baker. But you must call me Josephine."

Before Mrs. Roosevelt met someone, she did research, Kay had discovered. She was interested in people. She wanted to know about them.

"I was very happy to learn of Josephine Baker Day on May twentieth, Josephine. I was in Geneva at the time," Mrs. R said.

"A day named after me! Here, in America, where they didn't want me. And I think they still don't." Josephine lifted the champagne from its ice bath. "Fetch some glasses, Rosaleen, please."

With practiced aplomb, Josephine flicked a silver dinner knife against the cork and sent it flying with a pop. She took a glass from Rosaleen and expertly let the foam slide into the crystal glass.

"I had House Montaudon, in Rheims, supply their 'First Class Champagne' to my cabaret clubs in Paris, but no matter how sweetly I ask, the Copa City Club won't bring it in. But this Moët and Chandon deserves to be drunk. You know, at the end of 'forty-three, the Nazis deported Paul Chandon-Moët to Auschwitz. And Robert-Jean de Vogüé, who was also in charge at the house, was condemned to death and locked up in fortress. He narrowly escaped execution. When I drink this, I think about freedom."

"That is a very good thing to think of," Mrs. Roosevelt agreed.

Josephine was about to hand the glass to Mrs. R, then she paused. "But I have forgotten. I have heard that you do not indulge, Mrs. Roosevelt."

"Not often. But a glass of champagne will be fine."

Kay saw the soft shadow come to Mrs. R's eyes. She knew Mrs. R had lost her father and brother to the disease of alcoholism.

"But you must call me Eleanor," Mrs. R said.

"I will, Eleanor."

Josephine filled another flute and handed it to Kay. Her voice trembling a little, Kay said, "Thank you."

"Did you enjoy the show?" Josephine asked, as she served Rosaleen. She took the last flute for herself and settled back on the sofa. Her skirt spread out and she let the mink fall carelessly over the back of the seat.

"Very much," Mrs. R said. "You are a remarkable talent."

"My hands sting from clapping," Kay said. "Oh, that was because I loved it." She feared she had just put her foot in it.

Josephine laughed, a rich one that tripped over a few octaves. "But it was true that in France they made a lot of noise for me because they *hated* the performance."

"I can't believe they could have hated *you*," Kay said.

"I like you, Miss Thompson." Josephine smiled but shrugged. "They did hate me. At first. I had to learn what a Parisian audience wanted to see."

"A banana skirt and savage dances," Rosaleen Davis said. "Parisians aren't as sophisticated as they want to believe."

Josephine flashed her beautiful smile. "La Danse Sauvage. I made it artistic. But I did know that a lot of those men in the audience . . . admired me."

Kay knew what she meant. She sipped her champagne. The

flavor remarkable—like drinking silk. The bubbles tickled her nose.

"Josephine received a thousand marriage proposals," Miss Davis said. "Those men in the audience seriously believed that a few roses and a desperate proposal might win a woman like Josephine Baker."

"That is more legend than fact," Josephine said. "Though there were many proposals. I was happy. My success let me open my own club. After my other shows finished, I would go to my club in the wee hours of the morning. It was a place to have fun. My menagerie roamed freely, and I enjoyed dancing with the patrons."

Kay wondered about Rosaleen Davis's relationship with Josephine. Miss Davis seemed as outspoken as Kay used to be with her male employers. That always got her fired.

Josephine turned her smile to Mrs. Roosevelt. "It is a great honor to be in the presence of the woman who wrote the Universal Declaration of Human Rights. And you have done much work to end segregation and racism, and to give opportunity to all, regardless of color."

"The declaration was created by a committee of delegates, but thank you," Mrs. R said. "I have long admired your courageous stand against racial discrimination."

"And I have always admired you, Eleanor. I heard you attended a conference on human welfare in Birmingham, Alabama. I read about it before the war, when I saw the horror of Nazi Fascism growing closer. The audience was told to separate their seating according to race, or they would be arrested. You sat down with the African Americans. When a policeman told you to move, you placed your chair between the white and Black sections. You have such courage."

Kay saw Mrs. R blush. Kay added, "I heard from my aunt that Mrs. Roosevelt asked for a ruler to measure the distance between the sides so she could sit exactly in the middle."

"Bravo," Josephine said. "In Paris, I was accepted. When I sailed over from New York to France, I was in steerage because our ship was American, which meant it was segregated. There weren't enough lifeboats for all the people on board, and you knew it meant that you weren't getting on a lifeboat. Which became very clear when the captain feared we might hit a mine left over from the war."

"That is terrible," Kay exclaimed.

Josephine nodded. "Fortunately, the disaster was averted. A shock awaited me though. When we got on the train to travel from the coast into Paris, we all ate in the same dining car at the same time. I couldn't believe it at first. Then, I got used to it. I began to expect that was the way it should be.

"In the late 1920s, I performed in Berlin. It was said that I conquered the city as the 'Black Venus.' Two years later I returned, and everything had changed. I was called 'subhuman,' my very existence was said to be an insult to the Nazi cause. I was scheduled to perform for six months, but after three weeks of harassment, I was forced to flee.

"It was like St. Louis, when I was a little girl. Some rich business owners were hiring Blacks for less money. Instead of fighting for better pay for everyone, the whites turned on the people of East St. Louis. They burned neighborhoods to the ground. I remember running from the mob."

Josephine spoke calmly, but Kay saw her hand tighten around the champagne flute.

"We fought the Nazis and their terrible ideology. We won. Then I came home, here to America, and I was told where I could eat and where I could spend the night."

"Things must change," Mrs. R said. "Segregation is our shame on the world stage."

"Josephine's vocal stance has made her a target," Rosaleen Davis said. She frowned, worriedly. "She has been receiving threats—"

"We don't need to bother Mrs. Roosevelt with those threats. I am not afraid of them."

Rosaleen Davis took a sip of her champagne. She had barely touched it. "I think you need to stop performing, Josephine."

"I'm not afraid. Even if they kill me, they can't silence all of *us*."

Mrs. Roosevelt added thoughtfully, "My experience is that when people really mean business, they don't notify you beforehand. But that is how I feel, and I would not ask you to feel the same."

"I agree," Josephine said. "I performed during the war on a makeshift stage of planks strung between two vehicles. I was brought off the stage to take cover as bombs were dropped on us. I am not afraid of risk. And I agree: If this person really wanted to kill me, he would do it, not just talk about it."

Kay saw Mrs. R and Josephine share a look.

CHAPTER 4

It seems so easy for many people to express their enmity and so difficult to express their pleasure and friendship.
—Eleanor Roosevelt, My Day, August 3, 1945

In her hotel room, Kay shimmied into her bikini. The vanity mirror reflected her gyrations. She gave a little gulp when she saw herself in nothing but the candy-striped bathing suit—a strapless top and tiny bottoms. It was one thing to look at Marilyn's cheesecake photograph and think she could look the same. Another thing to show all that skin in public. Her bra, undies, and girdle covered much more.

Josephine had performed topless in front of the audience in Paris wearing only a skirt of rubber bananas and some ropes of gold jewelry. She had been younger than Kay, only nineteen.

Kay knew she couldn't have done that.

She would have died of embarrassment.

Josephine had grown up in severe poverty. Dancing gave her the chance to earn a good living and take care of her family. Kay admired Josephine Baker's bravery.

It was almost two a.m. Kay knew she should be in bed, sleeping in preparation for the busy day ahead. But it was so hot. The rippling azure water of the pool looked so tempting.

After taking the elevator down, Kay crossed the quiet lobby and pushed open the door with a sign that read To the Pool.

She followed the path through the garden. Kay knew an expensive bouquet of red roses when she saw one, but horticulture was not her forte. Flowering shrubs filled the garden and smelled heavenly, but she had no idea what they were.

As she neared the edge of the pool deck, where tall lights ran along the pool, interspersed with slender, graceful palm trees, a female voice called out, "Who's there?"

Kay moved forward until she was at the edge of the tile surrounding the pool deck. Palm trees lined the deck, fronds swaying. White chaise longues flanked the pool. When she saw Rosaleen sitting on the edge of the pool, dangling her bare legs in the water, Kay breathed a sigh of relief.

Rosaleen scrambled up to her feet and glared at Kay. "Oh, it's you. Why didn't you answer?"

Rosaleen had taken off the gray jacket, revealing a white short-sleeve blouse. She had a lovely figure, trim but with a curvy bosom. She was beautiful enough to be on the stage herself.

"I thought it was easier to just appear," Kay said. "I wanted a midnight swim."

"You're two hours too late," Rosaleen observed.

Rosaleen was prickly. Usually when someone was short and curt with Kay, she gave a smart answer right back. But Rosaleen looked sad, not angry. Sad people lashed out.

"I couldn't sleep," Kay said in a friendly tone. "Is that why you are down here?"

Rosaleen shrugged. She stared at the water. Her eyes were a deep brown, her lashes long and natural.

"I'd kill for your eyelashes," Kay said impetuously.

"I can see you care about looks. You touched up your lipstick to come swimming."

"Don't you care about looks? I think a woman who says she doesn't isn't being completely honest."

"I don't care. And I *am* being honest."

"That blouse and the suit fit you perfectly and are cut to flatter your figure," Kay observed.

Finally, a smile came to Rosaleen's lips. "I guess you're right. I guess secretly I'm as vain as the next woman. You understand that, but my fiancé doesn't. He thinks I really don't care about girlish things."

"You're going to be married? You aren't wearing a ring."

Rosaleen ducked her head, shyly. "My fiancé wanted to save up to buy one. I really would like to have a big sparkly ring on my finger, but I told him not to buy one since it would make more sense to save to buy a house. He says I'm the first girl he met who would choose saving over a ring, and thought I was fibbing to make him feel better. He was hurt he couldn't buy me what I wanted, and he doesn't understand that I would love to have a diamond, but I care about other things *more*."

Kay kicked off her sandals and sat down beside Rosaleen at the pool edge. She kept her wrap on and dangled her bare feet in the water. She bit back a cry of shock. The air was warm, the pool water freezing.

After a few seconds, she either was used to the water, or her feet were numb. She lightly kicked the water and asked, "What do you care about?"

"The law. I was going to be a lawyer. I studied for a year at Howard University."

"Like Pauli Murray," Kay commented.

Rosaleen's dark, perfect brows shot up in surprise. "How do you know Pauli Murray?"

"Miss Murray and Mrs. Roosevelt correspond regularly. She has visited Mrs. Roosevelt at her apartment in New York."

"I really admire Pauli Murray," Rosaleen said. "Thurgood Marshall called her book *States' Laws on Race and Color* the 'bible' of the movement for civil rights."

"If you studied for only one year, why did you leave?" Kay asked.

"Why do you think? I just didn't have any money to pay the fees. My mother raised me on her own. I never knew my father and he never gave my mother a dime to help with the bills. I grew up poor. I managed to save enough for one year's tuition."

Kay nodded. "My mother raised me on her own too after my father left. She passed away."

Kay saw that her simple statement had startled Rosaleen.

"I'm sorry you lost your mother, Miss Thompson."

"Please call me Kay."

Rosaleen treated everything like a fight, Kay thought. Was that because she had lost her dream?

"When Josephine hired me, she insisted she would pay for my room and board on top of my salary so I could save up for school."

"That is awfully generous," Kay said, impressed.

"Josephine is generous," Rosaleen said passionately. "When she became successful, Josephine tried to give money to her mother, Carrie. She offered to buy Carrie a house for twenty thousand dollars. But Jo said her mother refused because she couldn't imagine anyone earning that kind of money honestly. Josephine also paid for her siblings to attend school."

"Your mother must be pleased you will be able to go back to school," Kay said.

Rosaleen shrugged again. "My mother used to warn me that dreams don't come true."

"I guess raising a child alone and working dead-end jobs makes a woman jaded," Kay said wryly. "That happened to my mother. What does your mother do?"

"She works in the kind of job that traps a woman, especially when she has a child to raise on her own. She can never get ahead."

Rosaleen looked uncomfortable, so Kay changed the subject. "Josephine's amazing career is proof that a woman can fulfill her dreams."

"Except when she got back here, to America, she was treated like dirt. When Jo Bouillon was in America with her, hotels wouldn't rent them rooms because she is Black and he's white."

Rosaleen kicked the water too. A spray flew across the pool, sparkling like a string of diamonds under the lights. "That's why I wanted to be a lawyer. I want to fight against segregation. I want to fight the Jim Crow laws in the courts. And win. I'm tired of waiting," she said. "Look at what happened to Harry T. Moore and his wife. A bomb planted in their own home to go off on Christmas Day. The KKK makes my blood boil. That was vicious murder, and they'll get away with it."

Her words felt inadequate for the sadistic and vicious attack, but Kay said, "Mrs. Roosevelt wrote about the attack for her upcoming My Day column. I finished typing it up and sent it by wire before we came to Josephine's show. Mrs. Roosevelt wrote that she was grieving for Harry T. Moore and his widow. She condemned the violence. She said it does us untold harm amongst the people of the world."

"But nothing *changes*," Rosaleen said. "Josephine decided to come back to Miami Beach this December to send a message of hope and strength in the face of the 'Florida Terror.' Since we've been here, she has received a threat each day."

"When we arrived early this morning, there were a group of men waiting for taxis who Mrs. Roosevelt believed are members of the KKK. One of them warned her to be careful in case the same thing happened to her as to Mr. Moore. Mrs. Roosevelt endured assassination attempts when she was the First Lady. She takes it in stride."

Rosaleen nodded. "Josephine has a lot of courage too. Even though she tells stories to her audience so lightheartedly, I think she was plenty scared when she was fourteen and spent her last money on a train ticket, then slept on a bench in New York City because she had no money and nowhere to stay. She got on the chorus line, even though they said she was too young and too skinny, because she could make funny faces and make the audience laugh. She said traveling to Paris when she was nineteen was exciting, but she tried to back out of her contract at first because she was so scared to go to another country."

"But she went through with it," said Kay, awed by the strength Josephine had displayed. Could she have slept on a park bench? Could she have survived that and fought to become successful?

"I wish I had some of Josephine's courage," Rosaleen continued. "She walks into the Delano's dining room with her head held high. I can't help but look at the floor. I feel all the stares of the white patrons and I feel embarrassed. I'm scared someone is going to have a confrontation with me. Josephine has had confrontations, and she doesn't back down. Like when she went to the Stork Club in Manhattan, one of the most prestigious supper clubs in the world, to celebrate her last show at the Roxy with shrimp cocktail and steak. She saw other tables receiving food, but service to her table had stopped. When she realized what was happening, she called Deputy Police Commissioner Rowe and Walter White, the executive secretary of the NAACP. Josephine said, 'I have no intention of suffering deliberate humiliation without striking back.' "

Kay nodded, filled with admiration.

"I get so angry at being abused because of my skin color that I see red," Rosaleen said. "Then I get even madder at myself when I feel scared to confront people. Maybe it means I *shouldn't* be a lawyer. How am I going to fight cases if I feel scared walking into a dining room?"

"I think you'll find you have plenty of courage. You will

surprise yourself." Kay remembered how, when they solved the murder of Susan Meyer, Kay had stood in front of a gun to protect Mrs. Roosevelt. She never dreamed she was that brave. But when the time came, she didn't hesitate.

Rosaleen was silent for a while. "I believe you're right. You must fight to get what you want. You must be willing to pay the price. If I fight for civil rights and the KKK murders me, I want to inspire some other young woman to take up the mantle."

"I don't think you'll be murdered," Kay said, but her words felt foolish. Weightless.

For Rosaleen, that was a reality. If you tried to fight, people threatened you. They might actually kill you.

Kay didn't know why, but she asked, "Does your fiancé want you to become a lawyer?"

"Yes. Even though he works for the CIA and says defense lawyers get under his skin."

Kay had thought it logical that a lawyer and a lawman would gravitate together. Rosaleen's comment surprised her. She said, wistfully, "You are lucky. A lot of men don't want their wives to do anything more than iron their shirts."

That made Rosaleen laugh. "I would never go from being Josephine's assistant to a man's assistant. I hate ironing."

"So do I."

Rosaleen got to her feet. "I should go to bed. Josephine doesn't wake up early, as she needs to rest for her performances, but I do. Thank you, Kay. I apologize. I've been rude to you, and you've been nothing but friendly to me."

Kay was happy she had offered friendship to Rosaleen.

But as she watched Rosaleen put on her shoes and grab her gray suit jacket, Kay felt a stab of envy.

She and Rosaleen had the same job. They were both assistants. But Rosaleen saw her job as temporary. Something she had to do before she achieved her dream of a big, important career. The big, important career her fiancé supported.

But not having a supportive fiancé or achieving her dreams wasn't Kay's problem, she realized.

Not having big dreams was her problem.

CHAPTER 5

... the fact that it was sent shows that these elements in our population think they have great strength and cannot be punished for their actions.

—Eleanor Roosevelt, My Day, November 30, 1960

Breakfast began with a huge glass of orange juice and one half of a grapefruit on a plate. The grapefruit was cut with a serrated edge and topped with a maraschino cherry. Tea came with a slice of lemon and toast came with a pot of orange marmalade.

"Florida is known for citrus fruit," Mrs. R observed.

"They've covered all the bases for breakfast," Kay said, wryly.

She yawned as she spooned orange marmalade onto her toast.

For the rest of the night, after returning to her room, she had tossed and turned. Haunted by her realization that she'd never had a dream for herself other than marriage. But marriage clearly wasn't her only plan, because she had refused to put Tim O'Malley ahead of her job.

What did she really want?

Once she thought that if she met a rich, handsome, eligible bachelor while working for Mrs. Roosevelt, a head of state like Prince Rainier of Monaco, the answer would be easy.

But being surrounded by strong women with meaningful careers had made her think.

Josephine Baker had overcome terrible poverty to become a star. She used her wealth and fame to help others.

Mrs. Roosevelt worked at the United Nations for human rights and world peace. She worked ceaselessly to create a better world.

Rosaleen wanted to get her law degree and end discriminatory laws.

What, Kay thought, was she going to do with her life?

Kay was spreading marmalade to the edges of her toast, when she heard a frantic knock on the door. "I'll answer it."

But as she gripped the doorknob, she paused. What if it was someone who intended to kill Mrs. Roosevelt? She could open the door to find a man standing there with a gun.

What was she going to do? Stop opening doors?

She saw the reality of FDR's words, spoken when she was six years old. *The only thing we have to fear is fear itself.*

Taking a deep breath, Kay opened the door.

And almost laughed at her needless fears.

Rosaleen stood on the other side, a sheaf of papers in her hand. She wore a black suit and a white blouse. Lines of strain crossed Rosaleen's forehead. Her hand trembled on the papers.

"I need to talk to Mrs. Roosevelt."

Kay's relief fled. "Come in. What is it?"

"Letters. Josephine receives a half dozen threats by telephone every day. But these letters have been shoved under her dressing room door, one each day. Normally Josephine refuses to be frightened, but I saw that these letters truly scared her. She won't tell me *why*."

Swiftly, Kay mentally reviewed Mrs. Roosevelt's jam-packed schedule. She could turn Rosaleen away, but she also knew her boss always helped someone in need—Aunt Tommy said sometimes Mrs. Roosevelt was too giving of herself. And she knew Mrs. Roosevelt loved a mental puzzle. "Yes, I think you should show them to Mrs. Roosevelt. But it will have to be quick, I'm afraid. She has a half hour before she must go downstairs to the conference."

Rosaleen lifted her beautiful arched brow—a natural arch and shape that Kay envied. But she said simply, "Thanks."

Kay led Rosaleen out to the balcony and explained to Mrs. Roosevelt what Rosaleen wanted. Then asked, "Would you like coffee?"

Rosaleen rolled her eyes. "Josephine has received these crazy letters. I think she is in real danger and the police won't do anything about a threat to a Black woman. I don't care about *coffee*. A secretary doesn't need to serve everyone who shows up."

Kay felt stung. The friendliness they shared last night seemed to have disappeared in the light of day.

But she grabbed the coffee urn and poured Rosaleen a cup anyway. Partly in defiance, and partly because she suspected that Rosaleen would discover she wanted a coffee.

Mrs. Roosevelt drew one of the chairs closer to her, so Rosaleen could sit beside her.

Rosaleen spread the letters out in front of her. She ignored the cup of coffee Kay set on the table.

"These came after Jo's first performance at the Copa City Club," Rosaleen said. "Each day, I found a letter shoved under the door of her dressing room."

A breeze fluttered the letters. Kay quickly used a plate and the jar of marmalade to pin them down.

There were four of them, made from pasted-on letters cut from the glossy pages of a magazine.

The colors reminded her of something . . . something she had seen recently.

She frowned. "That letter is blue on a turquoise background. That one is black on pink. They were cut from a magazine but it sure wasn't *Time*."

Mrs. Roosevelt picked one up by its edge, using her napkin to ensure her fingers did not touch it.

"Don't worry about fingerprints. Josephine and I have put our fingerprints all over them. Believe me, the police aren't going to check them for that."

"You said the police wouldn't do anything," Kay pointed out.

"That's right," Rosaleen said, bitterly. "After the second one came, I took them to the Miami police. A detective told me it wasn't a surprise that Josephine received these kinds of letters after being so outspoken about discrimination. He said that maybe if she kept quiet and didn't rock the boat, people wouldn't want to hurt her."

"You're kidding," Kay gasped. Then regretted the words. "Obviously you aren't."

"I was so angry I wanted to spit in his smug face. But he would have arrested me if I did. He made it clear the police won't do a thing—they sure won't be dusting the paper for fingerprints."

"But Josephine Baker is an internationally famous woman," Kay exclaimed. "Any threat against her should be taken seriously. If the world knew how she was being treated—" Kay stopped.

She looked to Mrs. Roosevelt. "The world does know. This is exactly what you experience at the United Nations, when other countries condemn us for our discrimination."

"We are not alone in discrimination—it occurs in many countries. The Soviet Union, under Stalin, engineered the deaths of millions of people in its satellite countries," Mrs. R said sadly. "But we could be the most progressive in bringing forward change. Now, let us examine these letters closely."

"I laid them out in order," Rosaleen said. "The one you are holding is the first one, Mrs. Roosevelt."

Mrs. R read the letter, then set it down on the table, in front of Kay. "Would you read it too, Kay?"

Rosaleen shrugged. As if it was fine for Kay to read it, but she didn't expect that would help. The letter read:

> *You arrested a man in a restaurant. You tarnished that good man's name. You will pay.*

"Did Josephine arrest a man? How?" Kay asked. That was a stronger action than even telephoning Walter White of the NAACP and the police commissioner.

"It was a citizen's arrest, and it was in the newspapers," Rosaleen said, scornful in her amazement. "In July."

"I wasn't working for Mrs. Roosevelt in the summer," Kay said.

"And you didn't read the paper? But I guess you read fashion magazines, not newspapers."

The comment wasn't true, and it hurt. "I do read fashion magazines but I also do read the paper. In the summer, I was looking for a job and spending most of my day poring over the want ads and pounding the pavement— " Kay stopped. "That's not important."

The second letter read:

> *Willie McGee. Sentenced to death for raping a white woman. You tried to stop the execution. The death sentence is on you.*

"These are crazy," Kay muttered. She looked at the third one.

> *You seduced men carelessly. One shot himself for you. Before you leave Miami, you will pay.*

"How much longer is Josephine performing?" Kay asked. Rosaleen had not told her last night.

"She is leaving in early January for Cuba. Her decision to tour in Cuba has not helped rumors that she is a Communist. Though, I don't see how anyone can seriously believe that. You saw her wardrobe. Josephine is the last woman one could suspect of being a Communist," Rosaleen said. "But the CIA came to investigate her."

"The CIA thought Josephine was a Communist, but Rosaleen's fiancé works for them." That seemed ironic. But Kay tried to home in on the important detail. "You fear someone is going to attack Josephine in the next few days."

"That is what the letter says."

"Sometimes we have to state what appears to be obvious to gather thoughts," Mrs. Roosevelt said. "That letter is quite horrible."

"There was a man in Paris who proposed to Josephine. The rumor was that he shot himself in front of her when she refused him. Jo says that wasn't true, that it was a vile rumor. It hurt her to read it, though. But not as much as the fourth letter hurt her."

The fourth letter filled the entire page. It had been created from individual letters and entire words, of different colors and sizes.

> *Josephine Baker should be shot as a traitor. She was a double agent in the Second World War. She profiteered off her concerts. She was the lover of a Nazi commandant in Morocco.*

Kay drew in a sharp breath. It was an awful accusation.

"When did you receive the letter?" Mrs. Roosevelt asked.

"Yesterday. It was there, under the door when we arrived at Josephine's dressing room."

Kay remembered Josephine speaking of the horrors she saw when she performed at Buchenwald. That letter must have made her furious.

"The KKK's threats are usually blunt," Mrs. R remarked. "They simply threaten to kill you. These read as more . . . intellectual."

"They know a lot about Josephine's life," Kay said.

"These are based on rumors and newspaper stories," Rosaleen said. "Anyone could know about them."

"What about the accusation that she was a double agent?" Kay asked.

"She wasn't," Rosaleen said. "But Walter Winchell launched an attack on Josephine in his column when he was accused of ignoring how she was discriminated against at the Stork Club."

"I remember," Mrs. Roosevelt said.

"Winchell reported that Josephine declared in 1935 that she would recruit an army of Black soldiers to help Italy for Mussolini. He painted her as both pro-Fascist and a Communist sympathizer. Josephine felt deeply betrayed," Rosaleen continued. "Winchell had acted as her friend. But when his rear end was in the hot seat, he didn't support her. He turned on her."

"Would someone have to know Josephine well to know how much these particular incidents and threats would disturb her?" Mrs. Roosevelt asked.

"I-I don't know," Rosaleen admitted.

Rosaleen suddenly looked uncertain. "Josephine didn't want me to tell you about this, Mrs. Roosevelt. She says you are too important to be bothered. But I know these letters have gotten under her skin and her health is delicate. She was hospitalized in Morocco for three years during the war and she almost died. I'm scared that the fear will make her sick again. After all these attacks in Florida, I check Josephine's dressing room for sticks of dynamite planted courtesy of the KKK."

"You should not be doing such a thing," Mrs. Roosevelt said.

Rosaleen gave a bitter laugh. "If I don't, Josephine and I get blown up. Not looking for a bomb doesn't protect me from danger."

Kay felt a surge of anger and understood how Rosaleen felt, why she was bitter and prickly.

"Has Josephine thought of having someone to provide security?" Mrs. Roosevelt asked.

Kay was surprised. When she was First Lady and toured the country with her friend Lorena "Hick" Hickok, a reporter, ER (as she was known in the White House, to match her husband's FDR) had insisted she didn't want the Secret Service trailing them around.

"I never thought of that. If my fiancé were here . . . well, he isn't. He is working on an assignment. I don't even have a telephone number for him."

"I have someone in mind who would fit the bill," Mrs. Roosevelt said. "His name is Tim O'Malley. He is a private investigator now, and was a police detective in Washington, D.C."

Kay gaped in surprise as Mrs. R continued. "I could ask him to come to Miami."

"You can't," Rosaleen said quickly. "Then Josephine would know I told you about the letters."

Another loud knock sounded at the door.

Rosaleen sucked in a fast breath. "That must be Josephine. She is going to be furious with me for bringing these to you."

"She shouldn't be," Kay said. "Mrs. Roosevelt is very good about helping people."

"Thank you, Kay," Mrs. Roosevelt said. "We will support your decision to include us, Miss Davis. There is always strength in numbers."

"Th-thanks," Rosaleen stammered.

Kay went to the door. She expected to see Josephine Baker

swathed in silk. Instead, the beautiful singer wore shorts and a halter top with a pattern of daisies. Simple white sandals adorned her feet.

Kay must have shown her surprise. Josephine smiled. "I remember when I first met the intelligence agent who recruited me for the war effort. I was coming from my garden at Les Milandes, dressed as I am now, after collecting snails to feed to my ducks. He wore the same look of astonishment."

"Les Milandes?" Kay echoed.

"Experiencing heartbreak after my marriage to Jean Lion ended, I had left Paris for the countryside and discovered the Château des Milandes in the enchanting Dordogne region. It was available for rent and I took it." Josephine's smile widened. "I took the agent, Jacques Abtey, into my home and all the snails escaped while he told me he wanted to make me into a spy."

"You've had such an exciting life," Kay said. It was awful to think someone wanted to cut it short.

"Did Rosaleen come here and bother Mrs. Roosevelt with those silly letters?" Josephine asked directly.

"Yes. But Rosaleen is worried for you," Kay said. "It's not a bother. Maybe Mrs. Roosevelt can protect you. She was surprised that the KKK would send such detailed threats."

Josephine's face became shadowed. "That's exactly what I thought. I don't believe they are behind this. And that is what truly frightens me."

Kay led Josephine out to the balcony. She poured coffee for Josephine, who sipped it as she stared down at the letters.

"Perhaps you could tell us more about these incidents, Josephine," ER asked calmly. "There might be a clue as to who sent them."

Josephine picked up the first threatening letter. "This was July seventeenth. I was in Los Angeles, making my last appearance of my tour before returning home to Les Milandes in France. One evening, I was dining in the Biltmore. I remember choosing my dress with care and styling my hair in a long chignon with diamond combs. I wanted to look like a star. That didn't stop a Texan from announcing that he wouldn't eat in the same dining room as me. He used that word to describe Black people. Almost a quarter century ago, when I heard that, I cowered. Not now.

"I went to the nearest telephone and called the police, asking that they arrest the man. The police told me they couldn't because they hadn't heard his remark. They did tell me that California had a law that empowered me to carry out a citizen's arrest. I told them to send an officer tout de suite because I was going to do just that. I told the man he was under arrest. He was forty-five years old, from Dallas, and he didn't like being arrested by me. He was steaming when a judge found him guilty and sentenced him to ten days in jail for disturbing the peace or a hundred-dollar fine. He paid the fine. I was interviewed by the press, who seemed awfully surprised that I would stand up for my rights."

The second letter brought a soft sigh to her lips. "You would understand how I feel about this, Eleanor."

"Mr. McGee's wife is named Rosalee," Rosaleen added. "Mrs. McGee told me that when Josephine's tour reached Detroit in June, where Rosalee lives, Josephine spent a lot of time with her, consoling her. Josephine paid for return airfare for Mrs. McGee to visit her husband in prison."

"He was executed when I was appearing in Detroit at the Fox Theatre," Josephine Baker said.

"Josephine walked out and announced to the audience she would perform but her heart wasn't in it. When Josephine learned that the McGee family didn't have the money for a funeral, she arranged through her lawyer to pay," Rosaleen said.

Rosaleen's voice grew angry as she added, "Many people protested, including Albert Einstein. He wrote a letter that said,

'In the face of the evidence, any unprejudiced human being must find it difficult to believe this man really committed the rape of which he has been accused.' He added that the 'punishment must appear unnaturally harsh to anyone with any sense of justice.' "

Rosaleen looked to Mrs. Roosevelt. "Did you protest his conviction?"

"I wrote about it in My Day," Mrs. Roosevelt said. "In March, I received appeals about his case and the feeling was that he was not getting a fair trial. All I was able to do was forward the protests to the attorney general. Yet I realized that there may be nothing that he can do since I imagined the case was controlled by the courts of the state. But justice is indivisible and must be the same for all in our nation, regardless of race or creed or color." She added softly, "That was all I could do. I had no influence other than to ask for equality in justice. And that punishments be reasonable and fair."

"The execution of Willie McGee was wrong," Rosaleen said. She pointed at the letter. "The person who wrote this letter is condemning Josephine for her kindness to his family and her belief in justice."

"People see things the way they want to see them," Josephine said. "I was public about my support for Willie McGee, and I fought loud and long to stop his execution. All of America knew about that. I don't think it helps us figure out who sent the threatening letter."

"You weren't the only one who protested," Kay observed. "Why should this person think you should be executed?"

Josephine shrugged. "I guess no one wants to murder Albert Einstein."

"It's mad," Kay breathed.

"The third letter. There was a man who asked me to marry him and when I turned him down, he did take his own life. But I had a thousand marriage proposals from men in Europe, before the war. Any man I rejected I treated as sweetly as I could. *Il faut.* I couldn't have accepted every proposal."

"It is interesting that the first two letters touch on recent events—events of this year," Mrs. Roosevelt said. "The third letter is about a tragedy from the nineteen twenties, and the last letter is about the Second World War. Someone is interested in your entire life, I believe."

Josephine shook the last letter. "This makes me furious. I am no traitor. And I was no double agent.

"I was recruited by Jacques Abtey, a friend of my theatrical agent's older brother. When he came to Les Milandes to meet me, I expected a man who was short and fat, with an unappealing mustache. A bad dresser who smelled of cigarettes. Monsieur Abtey was introduced to me as Mr. Fox. He was in his early thirties, the same age as I. He was blond, blue-eyed, handsome and from Alsace. I took the two men inside, put them in chairs in front of the fire, and served them champagne. I assured them that France made me what I am. I was prepared to give her my life."

Kay felt her heart soaring. It was like a movie.

"The next time I saw Jacques, his name was Sanders, and he sported a perfect American accent. He worked at my side, traveling with me. I carried messages written in invisible ink on my sheet music into Lisbon, which was filled with spies from the Allies and the Nazis because it was neutral. I had to pass through occupied areas by train to do so. I pinned notes inside my underwear because I knew no one would dare strip Josephine Baker to her underwear to search her. I was loyal to France. And to the Allies."

Kay wanted to applaud. It sounded so exciting.

"The horrors I saw at Buchenwald, when I went to perform . . ." Josephine's hand trembled. She sipped her coffee. "When I arrived at the camp, I saw skeletal figures all along the barbed wire fence. I was told they had dragged themselves there, clinging to the barbed wire and looking out at freedom. They died there, and the weight of their bodies ripped their hands apart as they fell, sightless eyes looking outside the fence. I was filled with revulsion. I sang to raise spirits and to share joy. But deep in my heart, rage burned."

Kay shuddered.

"Never would I have collaborated. Never would I have helped the Nazis." Defiantly, Josephine added, "These messages make me angry, but I'm not scared."

"I am still concerned," Mrs. Roosevelt said. "I mentioned to Rosaleen that I have an idea."

Kay fought to look expressionless as Mrs. R suggested that Tim O'Malley act as Josephine's bodyguard. She forced herself not to think of Tim coming to Miami Beach. That, if he had not been pig-headed, they could have strolled the beach in the moonlight.

That. Was. Over.

"How can we trust a former policeman when they are ignoring us?" Rosaleen asked.

"Tim is different," Kay said.

"He is young and has a great deal of integrity. He left the Washington police because he spoke out about corruption," Mrs. R said.

"Is he handsome too?" Josephine asked. She turned to Kay. "Do you think he is?"

Kay lifted her coffee cup to hide any hint of a blush. Her heart pounded strangely fast as she lowered it. "I suppose he is good-looking."

"If I'm to be protected by someone, a handsome young man of integrity would be perfect. I'm happy to pay him. Would you telephone him, Eleanor. Or should I?"

"I'll call him," Mrs. R said. "I will ask him to book on the flight from New York tonight. He should arrive in the early morning."

"Then we just have to get through tonight," Rosaleen murmured. "Maybe you should cancel the performance, Josephine. To be safe."

"Nonsense. And Eleanor, you are invited to the party I'm holding in my dressing room tonight."

"You can't have a party!" Rosaleen exclaimed. "It's too dangerous."

"Perhaps for tonight you should not follow your normal practice of admitting guests to your dressing room after the performance," Mrs. Roosevelt said thoughtfully.

"This part is important," Josephine insisted. "You wouldn't give in to fear, Eleanor, and I won't either." She stood. "We've taken enough of your time. I know you will have a busy schedule. But you must come to the party tonight. I would very much like you to be there."

Once they were alone, Mrs. R turned to Kay. "I fear this party is a mistake. But I could not dispute Josephine's comment."

"There are few women as fearless as both you and Josephine Baker," Kay said loyally. She took a deep breath. "I will phone Tim O'Malley."

"No. I understand that would be awkward for you." Mrs. Roosevelt entered the suite and picked up the telephone. She requested the switchboard to dial a number that Kay knew by heart.

Kay was returning the dishes to the tray provided by room service when she almost dropped the coffee mug used by Rosaleen. Mrs. R was asking, "Is Mr. O'Malley in the office?"

Who other than Tim would answer the phone?

Kay had her answer minutes later. Mrs. Roosevelt came out onto the balcony. "Tim has hired a secretary," she said.

"Good for him," Kay answered, as if she wasn't the least concerned. "He hated to do his correspondence. And his typing was painful to watch."

"I'm very sorry you two ended your relationship," Mrs. Roosevelt said.

"Mrs. R, you aren't thinking . . . of being a matchmaker, are you?" Kay knew she was blushing. "It would never work. Tim wants a woman who stays at home. And I love working for you."

CHAPTER 6

I'd step in front of him, of course.
—Eleanor Roosevelt circa 1933, on what she would do if someone attacked FDR

That evening

The waiter at the Copa City Club, wearing a white jacket and neat black bow tie, glided between the tables. He brought tea for Mrs. Roosevelt and a Cuba Libre for Kay. He had suggested the drink, promising she would adore the combination of special white rum, Coca-Cola, and tart lime juice with a half lime shell muddled in the bottom to release the oils.

Kay had been suspicious. It sounded like ordinary rum and Coke. But as she took a sip, she knew he was right. The lime made the difference.

The lights went down, the velvet curtains opened, revealing Josephine Baker in her feathered gown with the formfitting slit skirt. She wore elbow-length white satin gloves and the stunning, tall, feathered headdress.

Josephine greeted the audience with delight. No one would guess that someone was threatening her life. When she sang, she exuded joy. She sang every song as if she was performing it for you alone.

Kay had seen Josephine sing just last night, but she was still holding her breath, awestruck. The ice melted in her Cuba Libre, because she forgot to drink it.

"This is my last song this evening," Josephine said, sounding truly sad. "It is called 'J'ai Deux Amours.'"

Kay had never heard anything so achingly full of love as this rendition of Josephine Baker's famous song. It was even more moving than last night's performance.

As the final note rang throughout the lounge, the audience jumped collectively to their feet with a roar of applause.

As she stepped away from the microphone stand, people shouted, "Encore! Encore!"

Josephine hesitated. Then she held up her hands, laughing. "One more! This one is for my wonderful assistant. The daughter of a dear friend of mine, who was on the chorus line with me. She is engaged to be married. The song is 'Begin the Beguine.'"

Kay was startled. Rosaleen had never mentioned her mother was a performer, or a friend of Josephine Baker.

It was strange Rosaleen kept quiet about it. It seemed a natural thing to say.

The crowd called out for another encore, but after holding up her hands to show that she loved her audience but could sing no more, Josephine did not return from behind the curtain. The lights came up. People rose from their seats and began to exit.

Rosaleen came out from backstage, wearing her black suit and low heels. She hurried to Mrs. Roosevelt. "Josephine's party is starting."

"You look gravely worried, Rosaleen," Mrs. Roosevelt observed.

"I think this party is a mistake. But at least I don't think the KKK will plant a bomb in the theatre. Too many rich white people would be killed," Rosaleen said, with her dark sarcasm.

* * *

With Mrs. Roosevelt, Kay followed Rosaleen backstage to the dressing room.

"Do you think Josephine has invited these people because she suspects one of them has sent the threatening letters?" Mrs. Roosevelt asked.

Rosaleen paused. Fear leapt to her eyes. "I never thought of that. Maybe she did." Rosaleen's hand rose to her lips. "I just wish Josephine would give up on performing in Miami Beach. Could you try to convince her, Mrs. Roosevelt?"

"I don't believe I would have any success."

Rosaleen looked really scared, Kay thought. When solving the murder of Susan Meyer, daughter of atomic scientist Elsa Meyer, Kay learned Mrs. R possessed extraordinary powers of observation. Mrs. R claimed that it was simply that she was interested in people. Kay was going to hone her skills and try to figure out who sent those letters.

Near the door to Josephine's dressing room, they passed a middle-aged Black woman pushing a cleaning cart. She wore horn-rimmed glasses that dominated her face, a simple plain navy-blue dress and low-heeled, scuffed black shoes. Kay had the strangest feeling she had seen the woman before, but last night, when they came backstage, no one was cleaning.

Bent over the cart, the woman stared at Mrs. Roosevelt through her glasses. Keys hung from a red string on the cart.

"Hello," Mrs. Roosevelt said. "I'm Eleanor Roosevelt. So delighted to meet you. What is your name?"

"F-Flora," the woman stammered. "I'd better get back to work." She pushed the cart hurriedly down the hall.

Most people wanted to shake Mrs. Roosevelt's hand and talk to her. Sometimes they wanted an autograph. It was sad that this woman felt such pressure in her work that she couldn't stop for a moment.

Mrs. Roosevelt watched Flora hurry away with a thoughtful expression.

"It's a backbreaking job," Rosaleen said suddenly. "And you'll notice that none of the cleaning ladies here are white. That's why I am going to return to school. So I don't have to serve meals or clean floors."

The door to the dressing room stood open. "There are only four people in there," Rosaleen said. "Usually, it's full and there is no place left to sit down."

"I guess Josephine decided a smaller crowd would be safer?" Kay asked.

"I don't know . . ." Rosaleen looked around her, plucking at the lapel of her jacket. The first nervous tick she had displayed.

"I didn't know how fearless Josephine is," Rosaleen continued. "I do now. Josephine excelled as a spy in the war. She isn't afraid to take risks. She will be in as soon as her dresser helps her out of her costume. I don't know how she can stand those tall, feathered headdresses. They weigh a ton." Rosaleen grimaced.

She added, "Josephine likes to make an entrance. In Paris she would arrive with Chiquita, her cheetah, on a leash. Josephine loved him, but I'm glad I don't need to look after a cheetah." Rosaleen sighed. "My job is to mix drinks and keep the champagne flutes topped up."

Rosaleen had to serve people when she vowed she wouldn't. Did that explain the bitterness she displayed?

Fresh flowers filled the room again. In the center sat a crystal vase—it hadn't been there last night. Two dozen perfect, crimson, long-stemmed roses filled the vase.

One man was laying it on thick, Kay thought.

As they walked into the dressing/sitting room, Kay saw two men helping themselves from the glass-and-chromium bar cart.

Kay grasped Rosaleen's arm to stop her. "Those two men, the ones at the bar cart— "

"I didn't even need to tell them to help themselves. They figured it out," Rosaleen said with a sneer.

"No, they were at the airport with a group that included men that Mrs. Roosevelt knows belong to the KKK."

"They look like the two characters from *The Maltese Falcon*," Rosaleen said.

Kay's Aunt Tommy, Mrs. Roosevelt's usual secretary who now lived at Hyde Park, often told her that her mind was too full of movies. She felt vindicated.

"That is exactly what I thought," Kay exclaimed in a whisper. "But why would they be here? They can't be fans of Josephine."

"I-I don't know." Rosaleen's tough sarcasm was gone. She sounded scared. "I've never seen the big man before. But the short one is Claude Mains. He has attended Jo's performances every night. He told Josephine that he was meeting a business acquaintance at the airport—and his acquaintance was desperate to meet Josephine Baker. Why would he do that if he is a racist?"

"The big man couldn't have sent the letters," Kay said. "He just arrived in Miami this morning. The other man, Claude Mains, must have been at the airport to meet him. But if he has come to every performance, Claude Mains could have sent the letters."

Rosaleen looked uneasy. "I don't think we should try to find out who sent them. I think Josephine should play it safe and stay off the stage."

"I think we *should* find out who sent them," Kay said. "We could uncover their plan. Maybe they would finally pay for these attacks."

"It's too dangerous," Rosaleen said stubbornly. "Like this party—it's a bad idea. But Jo won't listen to me. I should get you drinks. What would you like, Mrs. Roosevelt?"

"Tonic water would be lovely."

"That's all?"

"FDR enjoyed his cocktail hour," Mrs. R said with a twinkle. "But not I."

The "Fat Man" and "Mr. Cairo" had moved away from the bar cart. Rosaleen took the opportunity to pour a tonic water for Mrs. Roosevelt. Kay joined her. She was concocting a martini for herself when she almost dropped the shaker—Mrs. Roosevelt was calmly introducing herself to Claude Mains and his associate, the "Fat Man."

"I saw you gentlemen at the Miami International Airport this morning," ER said.

"That's right," the "Fat Man" exclaimed. "Didn't expect to see you at a club like this."

He held out a beefy hand. He had a pronounced gut and moved like a man who felt his bulk signified his success.

ER firmly shook his hand.

"I was a big supporter of your husband," he said, with so much joviality it read like an act. "FDR appreciated the power of politicians from the South."

If a man could be arrested for his suit, this man should be Public Enemy Number 1. It strained at the seams and the light blue and green check pattern made him look like an inflated tablecloth. He had thinning light brown hair, combed over his balding pate. His brows were dark brown and bushy. His face was fleshy, which made his eyes look like small, dark pits.

Though her assessment of him could be prejudiced by her suspicion he was a member of the KKK.

He took the tonic out of Mrs. Roosevelt's hand. "Let me add some gin to that. You gotta want something stronger."

"No, thank you," Mrs. Roosevelt said.

He had set her glass on the cart and was opening a gin bottle regardless.

Kay definitely did not like him. His assumption that Mrs. Roosevelt didn't know what she wanted proved her right.

"No, thank you," Mrs. Roosevelt repeated. "Tonic water is sufficient." She held out her hand.

Kay admired her cool, determined refusal.

The big man shrugged, handing the glass back to Mrs. Roosevelt. "The name is Reynolds. Eulie Reynolds."

"What do you do, Mr. Reynolds?"

Kay doubted his answer would be, "Assassinate famous Black stars like Josephine Baker," but she strained to hear as she poured her drink from the shaker into a martini glass.

"I'm a big success. Car dealerships. All over Alabama and Mississippi. Could have run for governor of my home state if I wasn't so busy building an empire. No rest for the wicked, isn't that right?"

"That is the saying," Mrs. Roosevelt said.

Was that a big hint? Was he boldly telling Mrs. R that he had something wicked to carry out?

Mrs. Roosevelt asked, "Have you been a longtime fan of Josephine Baker?"

Kay watched his face.

He showed nothing but admiration. "Josephine is a dazzling little lady."

Were they wrong? Was he not with the KKK? Or was he lying through his teeth?

"I've followed her exploits for a long time," he added.

Was he admitting to stalking her? Did he get angry over her exploits or admire them? Kay couldn't tell and it was frustrating. Normally, she could almost read men's minds. But not this time.

Eulie Reynolds was telling Mrs. Roosevelt all about his successful business of car dealerships. In his loud, blustering voice he told her that he was known for making honest deals.

He gave Kay the impression that when he insisted he was honest, he was anything but.

Picking up her glass, she looked over the other men in the room.

Time to think like a detective . . .

Alternate Suspect Number One: Claude Mains. Black hair slicked back into a pompadour and brooding dark eyes under neat black brows. Looked like a suspicious movie character. (All right, that was not a valid reason to suspect him.) Rosaleen said he had attended every performance. Was seen with a group of KKK men at the airport.

Those were valid reasons.

Alternate Suspect Number Two: a tall man, over six feet tall. He was the only man in the room wearing a dark suit—it was charcoal gray—and he wore it like a uniform. He stood with his chest out, his shoulders back, as if he never relaxed for a moment. His hair was white, neatly plastered down in a side parting. Eyes that were too perfectly blue. Sky blue, not ice blue like those of Dmitri Petrov, the Soviet aide she had met in Washington while she was investigating Susan Meyer's murder.

Alternate Suspect Number Two gazed coldly around the room. He wasn't going to liven up the party. He looked like he wanted to arrest everyone. She would typecast him as a Hollywood villain. Icy and condescending.

Alternate Suspect Number Three: a slender man with very fair hair, gray eyes, and a complexion that looked as if he never went out in the sun. He wore a pale gray suit, which was exquisitely tailored. A peach-colored handkerchief was neatly folded in the breast pocket. He looked around the room as if in a daze. Kay had no idea what he was drinking but he held a gimlet glass in his hand. He wore white gloves. Unusual, but was it suspicious?

The door opened. Kay swiveled around, expecting to see Josephine.

It was a woman, but not Josephine. She looked like . . . Greta Garbo. A stunning face with extravagant cheekbones, enormous eyes, a delicate nose, made movie-star perfect with porcelain foundation, plucked dark brows and lavish eyeliner. Pale blond hair fell around her shoulders in soft waves. She walked with her head almost motionless. As if she had been forced to balance a book on her head since she'd learned to walk.

The Greta Garbo look-alike lifted a pair of glasses with dark frames and put them on, blinking owlishly. The movie star allure vanished.

The woman moved hastily toward the white-haired man with the military bearing. "Mr. Miller," she said in a voice that made Kay cringe, "can I refresh your drink?"

She looked like an angel. She sounded like a road accident.

"Thank you, Miss Lane. My drink is satisfactory." His tone was curt, but it didn't sound like anger. He had a trace of an accent, but Kay couldn't identify it.

Miss Lane wasn't a date. She must be a secretary.

Would a man planning to kill Josephine Baker bring his secretary?

Maybe, Kay thought. If she was good with details.

Then she shook her head. This was gravely serious. She shouldn't make jokes. Sarcasm did make her feel safer. Calmer. Less touched by fear.

Maybe that was why Rosaleen used sarcasm and biting humor.

The bar cart held everything, including a jar of large green olives. Kay skewered one with a toothpick and dropped it in her martini as Mrs. Roosevelt left the two men and rejoined her.

"It was a challenge to escape his conversation," Mrs. Roosevelt said, glancing toward Eulie Reynolds. He was now talking to the slender blond man.

Kay had to bite back a laugh. "Do you think he was telling the truth?"

"I believe he does sell cars, though I suspect he exaggerated his sales record. As for his admiration of Josephine . . . he told me he bought two bouquets for her. The chrysanthemums."

"Never trust a man who gives you cheap flowers," Kay said.

"I will keep that in mind." Then Mrs. Roosevelt said, "I will chat with the other guests."

Kay nodded. "You solved the murder of Susan Meyer because nothing escaped your powers of observation. It is like a superpower. Like Superman's X-ray vision."

Mrs. Roosevelt put her hand to her chest and blushed lightly. "Thank you for your kind words about my powers of observation. I never thought of myself as Superman."

"If there was a Superwoman, she should be you."

"I suppose I should put those powers to use and meet more of the guests."

As Mrs. Roosevelt moved away, the pale, blond gentleman approached Kay. Up close, he was younger than she thought. About forty years old. Something in his eyes made him look closer to sixty.

"I am Isaac Gros. This night is such an honor for me. To meet Josephine Baker. And Mrs. Eleanor Roosevelt!"

He shook her hand. His fingers were long and white.

"I take it you are a fan," Kay said.

"Of both ladies. It was an honor to be invited by Mrs. Baker to her soiree. And now, to meet Mrs. Roosevelt—I could not have imagined such a privilege. Mrs. Roosevelt told me that you are her assistant. You must find the work very interesting."

"It definitely is," Kay said.

It was. She had helped Mrs. Roosevelt catch a killer in Washington in the fall. She had traveled to Paris and had sat in on meetings that would change the world.

But she had learned it was not easy to identify a villain. Could this gushing man have sent threats to Josephine? He looked as if he was floating on a cloud. Was he an Oscar-statuette-worthy actor?

"Do you live in Miami?" Kay asked.

"No. I live in New Jersey."

"Is this a vacation?"

"It is a purpose," he said.

That sent a shiver through Kay. "What is your purpose?" she asked. She sipped her martini, trying to pretend she was not unnerved.

But when he peered at her intensely, she choked on her drink. "S-strong," she muttered.

"My purpose . . ." He blinked at her, like an owl. His eyes were unusually pale. Almost light gray. His nose was beaklike. Weren't owls supposed to be dangerous birds?

"My purpose is to bring an end to the horrible attacks in Florida. I have come to join in protests. We must hold these murderers accountable. The organization to which they belong must be dismantled and destroyed. Such a group cannot be allowed to flourish. It is dying everywhere else in the country, but it survives here. Such hatred, such violence cannot be tolerated."

"I agree. But can the KKK be stopped?"

"It must be." He hung his head. "You see, I know where this leads."

He pushed up the sleeve of his pale gray suit jacket. Kay glimpsed a black pattern tattooed on his pale skin, half hidden by his white shirtsleeve. She suddenly realized it was a number.

Horrified, she looked up at Mr. Gros.

"We cannot allow this to happen in America," he said.

"We can't," she managed to say.

"I never saw my family again," he said.

"I'm so sorry. What happened?" Then she regretted her words.

With his face utterly devoid of expression, Mr. Gros said, "They were made into soap."

Kay felt her martini splash on her skirt. She had tipped her glass.

"I am sorry," he said. "That is not what you wish to hear at a party."

"I don't want to be afraid to hear truths," she said. She knew Mrs. Roosevelt would not be.

"That is good. For many of the young, they want to forget. They want to forge a new world without remembering the lessons of the old one."

"Good evening, *mes chers*!"

Josephine strode into the room, clad in a white satin sheath dress under a peach-pink robe trimmed with light pink feathers. Her long chignon reached the small of her back.

She opened her arms wide in welcome and bestowed her guests with a glowing smile.

The star had arrived. The star in danger.

CHAPTER 7

The world cannot be understood from a single point of view.
—Eleanor Roosevelt, *Tomorrow Is Now*, circa 1963

The next morning

"Eleanor!" Josephine was exclaiming. "I need your help. There is a dead man in my dressing room. And when the police found a dead white man in a locked room with a Black woman and a gun, the first thing they did was arrest the Black woman!"

Kay pulled open the connecting door between her room and Mrs. Roosevelt's suite. Mrs. Roosevelt opened her door to the corridor, then wrapped her arm around Josephine's slender shoulders and drew her into the room. With her slipper-shod foot, Mrs. Roosevelt nudged the door closed behind her.

"What has happened?" Mrs. R asked, and Kay could not imagine how she was so collected. "Who is dead?"

Kay leaped to the first conclusion she could. "You mean a man *attacked* you? Are you all right? Why were *you* arrested? How are you *here* and not in jail?"

Josephine's large, expressive dark eyes opened wider. "I wasn't arrested. Rosaleen was arrested. She went back to my dressing room because she forgot her purse. I heard a shot. I went running as fast as I could in these shoes—"

Josephine pointed at her satin pumps with a two-inch heel, then continued, "When I got there, the security guard of the club was banging on the door. It was locked. And a dead man was in the room with Rosaleen! The police didn't listen to a word I said. They slapped handcuffs on Rosaleen, pushed her into a squad car, and took her away!"

Kay's mouth dropped open.

She realized Josephine was staring at her. "There is a crawly bug on your hair."

Kay put her hand up and brushed the soft curl of the false eyelash. That was where it went.

"We should go to the police station," Josephine cried, but as she took a hurried step back toward the door, she swayed on her feet.

"Your health is delicate," Mrs. Roosevelt said. "I know you were very ill during the war. I remember reading about it. Come and sit down."

"Yes. I had an infection. Septicemia. Usually, it is fatal. But I am perfectly fine—"

Firmly, Mrs. R led Josephine to the sofa and sat down with her.

Kay picked up Josephine's fur wrap. It had fallen to the floor and Josephine appeared to have forgotten about it even though it must be worth thousands.

Kay followed them toward the chairs, then stopped. "Tim! I need to go and meet his flight."

"Join us for a moment, Kay," Mrs. Roosevelt said. "I believe there is enough time."

"You're right." Kay felt a surge of relief. She didn't want to walk out without knowing what had happened. Anyway, Tim would wait.

With a twist in her stomach, she thought: His job was to protect. They had been too late . . .

Except Josephine was safe and sound. It was a man who was dead.

At Mrs. R's direction, Josephine sank down onto the sofa. Kay laid the beautiful wrap on the sofa beside her. Josephine gathered it up, cradling it.

"Would you make coffee, Kay?" Mrs. R asked quietly.

"Right away." Their suite included a coffee percolator, one that plugged into the wall. The most modern convenience for making coffee at home.

As she carried it to the washroom to fill it with water, she heard Mrs. Roosevelt say to Josephine, "Go over everything that has happened, step by step." Her voice was gentle and modulated.

Kay was struggling to be calm. She wanted all the information at once. Questions rushed through her head.

Had Rosaleen been attacked in the dressing room? Why did she have a gun? Who did she shoot? Was it the person who threatened Josephine? Nothing made sense. The threats were against Josephine. How was the attacker dead? Why did he attack Rosaleen and not Josephine? Why was Rosaleen in *jail*?

"I can't tell you what happened," Josephine said. Her shoulders slumped with dejection. "I don't know what happened. Rosaleen wouldn't talk to the police, which is sensible. But she also won't tell me a thing!"

The coffee began to make a bubbling sound.

"This is my fault!" Josephine exclaimed again. Tears streaked down her cheeks. "I was certain I knew who was behind those letters. That's why I insisted on that party, and it led to this! Rosaleen could be *executed*!"

"Josephine, stop fearing the worst," Mrs. Roosevelt said calmly. "That has not happened yet. But I would like you to tell me clearly what *you* know. For a start, who was the victim?"

"The handsome silver-haired land developer from my party, Monsieur Frank Miller. The one who sent me all those long-stemmed red roses."

"The one who stood at attention like a former soldier and

looked as if he wasn't having fun?" Kay asked, as she checked the progress of the coffee.

From the sofa, Josephine looked over to Kay. "You guessed that from his bearing? That was very astute. I believe he was a soldier in the war. Miller is not his real name. I recognized him—I saw him at the Buchenwald concentration camp, when I traveled there and performed for the men who were still in that horrible camp because they were too weak to be moved."

Josephine paused and her eyes flared with anger. "Monsieur Miller was a Nazi death camp commandant."

"*What?*" Kay gasped. Her hand hit the percolator. She grabbed it fast before she watered the rug with coffee.

Josephine was no longer shaking, and she had brushed away her tears. She sat with Mrs. Roosevelt's hand resting comfortingly over hers.

"*Mon Dieu*, this isn't like me," the singer said. "Falling apart isn't going to help. I faced customs officials without a tremor of nerves during the war when I carried secret documents. I was in an airplane that almost crashed. As a child, I had to flee the burning of East St. Louis. But this—this is terrifying."

Kay brought in two cups of coffee for Josephine and Mrs. Roosevelt. "Thank you, Kay," Mrs. Roosevelt said, and she urged, "Take a few sips, Josephine."

"I am in control of my emotions now. I want to scream in anger but that's not going to help anyone." But she sipped her coffee. She cradled the cup in her hands, the fingernails polished a dark, glossy plum color.

"You said you recognized Mr. Miller," ER prompted. "Are you quite certain it is the same man?"

Josephine nodded. "I am certain. I will never forget those cold eyes, though he is heavier set now than he was then, in 1946. His hair was more blond then and not silver, as it is now."

"If he was at the camp at the end of the war, wasn't he arrested as a war criminal?" Kay asked.

Josephine set down her coffee cup and said, with heavy sadness, "Our troops liberated the camps, but the generals did not just open the gates and tell people to leave. The former prisoners had been starved and abused and were too weak to go. Many were dying. In the interim, while our generals decided what to do, the camps had to continue to operate, providing food and shelter for the victims. Our soldiers were needed elsewhere. It was said that our generals had to keep some Nazi officers there to help operate the camp."

"That can't be true!" Kay exclaimed.

Josephine lifted her hands in despair. "I found it outrageous, but I was told it is true."

Kay's stomach felt ill. "But how even then, how could Miller have come here to America?"

She realized Mrs. R had not interjected; she was listening with a thoughtful expression.

"I don't know," Josephine said. "I couldn't believe my eyes at first. The first night at the Copa City Club, I spotted him in the audience, seated at the very front. Watching me. That was why I invited Mr. Gros to my party. Mr. Gros had come backstage on the first night and told me his story—that he had been a prisoner at Buchenwald. He had remained and was helping to care for the dying when I came to perform. If I was right, Isaac Gros would recognize him too. I did not have a chance to find out if Mr. Gros could confirm my suspicion. Monsieur Miller ensured he was always in earshot of our conversation."

Kay sank down in the armchair, still holding the coffeepot. "I would have thought a former Nazi officer would have murdered Rosaleen. Not the other way around. I mean, I am happy that didn't happen, but— "

"That was probably his intent," Josephine declared. "I know what such a man could have done to a woman he found alone. Rosaleen was fortunate she saved her own life."

"But how could a slender young woman like Rosaleen have

wrested a gun away from a Nazi war criminal?" Kay asked, frowning. "Miller was older, obviously in his fifties, but not an *old* man. He looked strong and powerful."

Josephine nodded. "Yes. I don't know how Rosaleen could have done it."

She gently squeezed Mrs. Roosevelt's hand. "At the party, I thought I had made a—well, I thought he must have been the person who sent those letters. I thought he did it to frighten me into silence. Or to murder me and make it look like the KKK was responsible."

"Did you have specific reasons to invite the other guests to the party?" Mrs. Roosevelt asked.

"I invited Mr. Gros because he is a charming man, and I believed he would recognize Monsieur Miller. I invited Monsieur Mains . . . because he came to my performances every night, and visited my dressing room with flowers each night, yet I sensed he was nervous and hiding something. As for his friend, Monsieur Reynolds, I have never seen him before. But Reynolds looks like a Klansman to me, which makes Monsieur Mains suspect."

"Reynolds arrived at the airport when we did," Kay said.

"Would you tell me everything that happened up to Rosaleen's arrest, Josephine?" Mrs. Roosevelt asked.

Josephine nodded. She sipped her coffee, then began. "Rosaleen and I were leaving the Copa City Club after the party. Rosaleen had ushered the guests out after two a.m. I had hoped to speak to Mr. Gros alone, but he left before the others.

"We were about to leave the building when Rosaleen realized she left her handbag in my dressing room. She said she would go and get it. I said I would go with her, but she told me not to bother—she would sprint down and hurry back.

"Then I heard a *bang*. The moment I realized it was a *shot*, my legs almost collapsed beneath me. But I gathered my composure and raced back to my dressing room. I reached the hallway as the security guard was banging on the door. It appeared to be locked. I arrived just as the guard opened it. The moment he did, the guard drew his gun and pointed it at her. I begged him to lower his weapon, but he refused to listen to my plea. He marched us to his office, at gunpoint, and called the Miami police. They took one look at the body in my dressing room, learned that she had been in the locked room with the victim, and arrested Rosaleen."

"Did you see inside your dressing room when Rosaleen opened the door?" Mrs. Roosevelt asked.

"*Un peu*," Josephine said. At Kay's confusion, she said, "A little."

"Where was Mr. Miller's body? Was he lying near the door, as if he had surprised Rosaleen in the dressing room?"

"He had fallen by the drinks cart. He lay face down. A large pool of blood had soaked into the white carpet."

Mrs. R looked thoughtful. "The drinks cart was in the middle of the room. I had wondered if he had followed Rosaleen into the dressing room and cornered her in there. But then he would have been near the door, would he not?"

"Maybe he followed Rosaleen but walked right into the room."

"How was his body positioned? Was his head closer to the door than his feet?" Mrs. R asked.

"Yes, that is right."

"If he was facing the person who shot him, that person was closer to the door than he was."

Josephine blinked. "If he did not follow Rosaleen into the room, then *Rosaleen* was closer to the door. But that could not be, for it would mean she was not trapped. She could have run away to safety. Monsieur Miller *must* have trapped her in the room." She put her hand to her mouth. "While the guard telephoned the police, I whispered to her that she should tell the truth."

"What did Rosaleen say?" Mrs. Roosevelt asked.

Kay held her breath, waiting.

"She asked, 'What do you mean?' I whispered that she obviously had to shoot the man in self-defense. That he must have attacked her. Rosaleen looked at me with utter despair. 'I didn't touch the gun,' she said. 'Someone else shot him and I'm innocent. But even you don't believe me.' I promised her I did. I said, 'Then tell me what happened.' But she wouldn't say another word."

"Rosaleen needs a lawyer," Mrs. R said firmly. "Would she have money for a good lawyer to protect and advise her?"

"She was saving up to return to school. I will pay for the lawyer. I will hire the best in Miami!" Josephine declared. But then, her voice shaking, she said, "I fear that won't help. The police officers ignored me when I explained that I had recognized Miller. One officer said that Miller was an important man in Miami. He is rich and has hidden his past under a new name. They will find a white jury. All that jury will see is that a white man is the victim, and a Black woman has been accused of the crime. No one will believe Rosaleen's story that Frank Miller was shot in a locked room by *someone else*!"

Mrs. Roosevelt touched Josephine's hand gently, calming her.

"Rosaleen said she did not touch the gun—that can be proven," Mrs. R said. "Her fingerprints can be checked against those on the weapon. Tim O'Malley will be helpful there. He knows the procedure the police will follow. Once it is shown that Rosaleen did not handle the gun, she should be released at once."

Josephine looked worried. Then she said, "You believe she is innocent, Eleanor? Despite the evidence against her?"

"So far, I have not heard that there is any real evidence against her. Rosaleen struck me as a decent, law-abiding young woman."

"I want you to talk to her, Eleanor. An influential woman like you would make those police officers take notice. They would know they can't get away with shifty business."

"Shifty business?" Mrs. R repeated.

"They had to transport Willie McGee under guard in case some white mob kidnapped him and killed him. What if the police let a mob get hold of her and kill her?"

"Her lawyer will ensure the police follow the rule of law," Mrs. Roosevelt said.

But Kay saw Mrs. R looked concerned.

Josephine shook her head. "I don't trust the police. You know yourself that members of the police force have belonged to the KKK in the past. But if the police think you are on Rosaleen's side, they will be careful. I think Rosaleen was hurt when I assumed she shot the man, and she will not speak to me now. She admires and respects you, Eleanor, and she will tell you the truth."

"I will talk to her." Mrs. Roosevelt looked at Kay. "I intended to go to the conference, but this is dire. Kay, you had best take a taxi and meet Tim O'Malley at the airport. If you would kindly bring him to the station, I would appreciate it. Then perhaps you would attend the conference and take notes for me."

"Of course." Kay jumped up. "Right away."

CHAPTER 8

To be happy, two people must need each other in everything they do.

—Eleanor Roosevelt, "Should Wives Work?"
Good Housekeeping, December 1937

At Miami airport, Kay paced in the domestic arrivals area. She was going to be cool, businesslike. Mrs. R had gone to the police station with Josephine, and Kay was to bring Tim to meet her.

Kay could tell that deep inside, Josephine feared Rosaleen had shot Frank Miller in self- defense. Mrs. R believed the police could prove if Rosaleen had fired the gun.

Tim would know if that was true.

Two men strode out of the glass doors. One was Tim, wearing a dark gray overcoat that enhanced his broad shoulders and tall, lean build. Slung over his shoulder was a duffel bag.

Her heart gave a small lilt as she took in his coal-black hair, smoothed down with Brylcreem; his dimpled, casual grin; his eyes framed with thick, black lashes. She couldn't see it from here, but she knew his irises were as green as Ireland was reputed to be.

She wondered how Tim's suits were surviving being manhandled in the duffel bag. Though why should she care? That was what a wife would worry about.

Her gaze settled on the man beside Tim.

Tall, pale blond hair slicked down, handsome sculpted features—

Kay's heart gave a leap of shock and excitement . . .

No, it wasn't *him*. This man was a stranger to her.

But not to Tim because the two men were deep in conversation as they walked. Then Tim saw her.

She had wondered how he would react. Would he apologize? Drop to one knee to clasp her hand and beg forgiveness?

He shifted his duffel to the other side so he could shake hands with the blond man.

Well, really! His emotions should be in turmoil. He should not be casually lifting his hand in the abbreviated wave men gave each other as the blond man passed under the sign that pointed to the taxi stand.

Kay stepped out, right in front of Tim. He stopped, looking her in the eye. They stood almost toe-to-toe.

"Hello, Kay," he said, his voice gruff.

Throngs of people hurried around them, but all other sounds faded to a blur. The only thing she could hear was Tim's voice and screaming infants, because that was a piercing sound that never dulled.

"Hello," she said, and even that one word sounded so stiff and awkward, it was as if she had just shouted: *You hurt me*. Even though she had been the one to say she wanted to break up.

She'd done it to save face.

"I'm surprised you came to meet me," he said, sounding casual. Though he was perspiring.

"You're sweating in that wool overcoat. Surprise—Miami is a lot warmer than New York. But you're going to have to suffer longer. We need to take a taxi to the police station. Mrs. Roosevelt is there."

"The police station?" His black eyebrows shot up. "I was

supposed to provide protection for Josephine Baker. Did I get here too late?"

"Josephine isn't hurt."

He almost staggered. "Mrs. R?"

She shook her head quickly. She realized she needed to fill him in on details or they would stand there all day while he listed possibilities.

"Mrs. Roosevelt isn't hurt either. The victim is a man. He was shot in a locked room—in Josephine Baker's dressing room. Mrs. R is at the police station because they have arrested a young woman who is innocent. We can't waste time standing here talking about it. Let's go."

Kay strode toward the taxi stand. Her heels clicked over several feet of hard tile flooring before she knew Tim wasn't following. She assumed he was still confused.

But he nodded toward a sign that pointed the opposite way. "I planned to rent a car."

Kay had to admit that having a car at Mrs. R's disposal made sense.

Shouldering his duffel, Tim started walking in the other direction. "The Hertz counter is supposed to be down there. Come with me to the desk. Tell me exactly what's going on."

Walking by his side, she explained. She told him about the threatening letters directed at Josephine. "That's why Mrs. R called you. We thought someone might try to kill Josephine."

"But they didn't—"

"Let me explain. Last night, Josephine insisted on having a party in her dressing room after her performance. Mrs. R was nervous about it. So was Rosaleen."

"Mrs. Baker's assistant."

"Mrs. Bouillon," Kay corrected. "Josephine is married to Jo Bouillon, a French citizen. And yes, Rosaleen Davis is her assistant. After the party, Rosaleen discovered she left her purse behind." She told Tim about Rosaleen returning to the dressing room. About Frank Miller's murder. About Josephine's belief about his identity.

"He can't be a Nazi death camp commandant. That's not possible," Tim muttered. "But if he was hanging around after the party and went to Mrs. Bouillion's dressing room, he must have been the guy who sent the letters."

"I guess so," Kay said. But it felt wrong. She remembered Frank Miller's erect bearing. The only emotion he had displayed all evening was condescension.

Kay could not picture him cutting up magazine pages and stooping to push an envelope under the dressing room door.

She thought of the lovely blond secretary with the grating voice. She could almost believe he had tasked his secretary with threatening Josephine.

"This is a locked room murder," Kay said. "Like in *The Murder of Roger Ackroyd*, Agatha Christie's story. I did not see the end of that book coming."

"Huh?"

Tim didn't read Christie.

Moving down the long airport hallway, she added, "In a locked room mystery, there was usually just a body. And no way for the killer to have gotten in and out. That is the trick. To make the impossible possible."

"In this case, it sounds like the killer could walk out the door."

"With a key, what makes it impossible is that this time, in the locked dressing room, there was one other person. There was Rosaleen—a witness."

"So why isn't she talking?" Tim asked. "Why would she keep quiet and get arrested?"

"I don't know. I don't understand it either." She tried to describe what she saw in Rosaleen. "She has a lot of anger simmering in her over segregation and racism. Sometimes her anger just erupts."

"What do you mean?"

Kay had never been discriminated against like that, but she understood, just a little. The pats on her derriere from male bosses, the way they called her "Skirt," the assumption that because she had cleavage, she was easy, the assumption that because she was female, she didn't have a brain. It wasn't anywhere near as bad as racism, but it gave her a glimpse into Rosaleen's hunger for change.

"I wondered if Rosaleen got angry when white police officers assumed she was guilty. I thought she might have decided to be wrongfully arrested to make a point. To show how bad the system is."

"What point would she be proving?"

"Maybe she felt a wrongful arrest would make people rise up against the violence that's been happening in Florida."

They had reached the counter. Tim didn't have a chance to respond before a blonde in a trim uniform gave him a big smile.

"Can I help you, sir?" she purred.

Her blond was from a bottle, but her Veronica Lake peek-a-boo gave her a femme fatale look, even in her modest dress. Her lips were carmine red. She looked twenty-two, curvy with "puppy fat." Her name tag read MAISIE.

As Tim smiled back at her, Maisie looked dumbstruck.

Tim's slightly lopsided smile could make a woman melt.

Kay hadn't seen that smile for a long time.

After she went to Paris with Mrs. Roosevelt for the U.N. session in the fall, she hadn't returned to the U.S. until a few days before Christmas. Over the months, she wrote to Tim and called him each week. She was so excited to see him in person again. They planned a date when she and Mrs. Roosevelt passed through New York on the way to Hyde Park—Kay to see Aunt Tommy and Mrs. R to host a Christmas celebration for her children and grandchildren.

On that one evening she had spent with Tim in New York,

he hadn't smiled. Not once. She had talked about her experiences onboard the SS *America* en route to Paris. She had been so excited to talk about Paris, their side trip to Holland where they stayed in the palace under the auspices of Queen Juliana, then trips to Brussels and London. While she had tried to share all the thrilling experiences with Tim, he nursed one whiskey sour with a grim expression.

"Here is your paperwork, sir," Maisie trilled. Maisie watched Tim sign his name to the paperwork, as if she was already changing her last name to his.

He handed back the contract, grabbed the keys.

"Could you give me directions to the police station that would be nearest to the Copa City Club?"

The young woman's face had fallen. Kay suspected he had broken her heart by not asking for her number.

"I have no idea. Why not look it up in a phone book in a telephone booth? There are some in the airport." With a sniff, Maisie turned to the next customer.

Tim didn't appear to notice. He grabbed his duffel, led Kay toward the rental car parking lot. "If this victim was the crackpot who wrote the letters threatening Josephine Baker's life, why would he attack her assistant? Why wouldn't he wait until he could get to Josphine Baker? From what you said, he either was there to kill Josephine Baker because he was a racist or because she recognized him."

Tim's argument made sense. But Kay suddenly saw another angle. "What if Rosaleen caught him in the dressing room and accused him of writing the letters?"

Tim held the door for her to go out onto the car lot. "How did he end up dead and she ended up holding the gun?"

"She wasn't holding the gun. Rosaleen said she never touched the gun. Mrs. Roosevelt believes that once the police determine Rosaleen's fingerprints aren't on the gun, she will be released."

Tim was quiet.

"Isn't that right?" Kay prompted.

"I hope so," Tim said. "I hope they find fingerprints on it."

Kay frowned. They were passing by rows and rows of cars. Why did his car have to be so far from the door? "What do you mean?"

"If it was wiped clean, that doesn't necessarily exonerate her. And she was the only other person in a locked room with the victim."

"But if she shot him," Kay said, "wouldn't she have unlocked the door and run for it?"

"Did she lock the door when she went in? How did this guy follow her in?"

"I don't know because Rosaleen isn't talking," she repeated. And thought of the conversation with Josephine and Mrs. R. Maybe Miller had *not* followed Rosaleen in. Maybe Rosaleen had opened the door and found him already there.

Tim didn't say anything, but from the way he looked at her, she knew he thought there was one reason Rosaleen wasn't talking.

She was guilty.

He pointed. "That's the car."

"A dark blue sedan. Original."

"Nondescript. Habit of the trade," Tim said.

He opened her door, and she slid in. He started the engine and gracefully backed out, his strong arm slung over the seat back. He had briefly studied the map in the glovebox and now confidently negotiated his way as if he had lived in Miami for years. It was impressive.

They drove over the causeway from the mainland. Silence descended. She kept thinking: Was Tim right? Was Rosaleen quiet because she had shot Frank Miller?

But Mrs. Roosevelt seemed to believe Rosaleen was as innocent as she claimed.

Tim was tapping his fingers on the steering wheel. He

cleared his throat twice. Couldn't he just say something? But he didn't.

Finally, she broke the silence. "Who was the blond man you were talking to at the airport? It looked like you two are friends."

He didn't answer and she turned to him. Tim was studying her. He looked back at the road. "I met him on the flight from New York. Name's Stephen Roberts. He had the aisle seat beside me. Turned out he was in the army in the war. Landed on Omaha Beach, same as I did."

Kay thought about two handsome young men wading out into machine-gun fire. So many didn't make it. It was such a . . . pointless waste. It was why Mrs. Roosevelt believed that peace was worth the work, even if achieving peace could feel hopeless and frustrating.

Mrs. R always warned that you didn't achieve peace and never worry again. Peace took hard work.

Silence stretched again. What was it going to be like working with Tim, while she tried to act like their breakup didn't matter?

"Sometimes you go away into your thoughts. I know you aren't thinking about me," he said suddenly. "It happened when you telephoned me from Paris."

"I have a job. It requires thought." She didn't say she *was* just thinking about him. "What do you expect from a woman? That she stares vapidly at you, hanging on your every word?"

"I wondered if you were interested in someone else," he muttered. "You were in Paris, amongst men from all over the world. Educated, successful men."

Her mouth dropped open. "I barely had time to sleep, much less go on dates with United Nations delegates or aides. Do you have any idea how busy Mrs. R's schedule is? We were up at dawn to prepare Mrs. R for the day's committee meetings. They run all day and into the evening. She would have informal meetings afterward in her suite. Mrs. R wants to accomplish real change, and those meetings gave her the chance to discuss policies with delegates like those from the Soviet Union. In the formal meetings, they must parrot the Communist Party line, but informally, in her suite, they could speak more freely. My eyes were opened to so much."

"I know you like traveling," he said. "It was obvious you didn't want to be tied down in New York. You want to see the world. Mrs. R has opened your eyes to a jet-set lifestyle. I can't give you that kind of life."

"You told me on our last date that you wanted a girlfriend who would give up her work to get married."

"I thought that was what you wanted. It's what I want."

"I—I can't do that," she said.

"Yeah, I got that."

"But why did you have to do it at Christmas?" She hated the hurt tone of her voice.

He shifted in his seat. "I know I can't give you the future you want. I thought it would be better for you to be free for the holidays."

"That's what you thought?" She sighed. "Couldn't we have made a compromise?"

"You mean, couldn't I wait for the few days I would get to see you each year?" He shook his head.

"My job with Mrs. Roosevelt is temporary," Kay began, but Tim shook his head.

"From what Mrs. R has told me, your Aunt Tommy doesn't want to travel much anymore. And Mrs. R likes your work. I think you'll be offered a permanent job."

Kay was startled. And happy.

"When I fall in love with a woman, I want to be with her. I want to get married and wake up to my wife every morning."

Had Tim just said he loved her? She had been falling in love with him until he had jerked the rug out from under her. "When you love someone, you support their dreams," Kay said. Even though she didn't know exactly what her dream was.

Rosaleen's fiancé supported her dream of becoming a lawyer . . . Rosaleen's fiancé! Kay realized he would have to be told she was in jail. So would Rosaleen's mother.

"A wife of mine won't need to work," Tim said stubbornly.

"It isn't about need," she declared. "My work has opened my mind. If you had to travel for your work as a private investigator, you would expect your wife to put up with it. You would expect her to wait happily and have your dinner ready when you finally returned."

"That's different. A man must provide for his family."

"Why shouldn't a woman provide too?" she demanded.

"What about when you have children?"

She was so annoyed she said, "Why couldn't the man look after the children, and the woman have the job?"

"What?"

He almost drove through a red light.

"Well, why not?" Kay demanded. "Look at Princess Elizabeth in England. She becomes Queen. I don't think her husband becomes King."

"Her husband isn't going to be babysitting the children," he said.

They were arguing in circles. He stubbornly believed there was no compromise that allowed her to date him and pursue her exciting work with Mrs. R. She believed there was. Except she supposed she was asking him to make the compromise instead of her making it.

"Do you want to go by the Delano Hotel?" Kay said, changing the subject. "Drop off your bag and change your clothes?"

"That's it?"

"According to you, it is," she snapped.

"If Mrs. R is involved in another murder, I want to find out what's going on," he said. "Changing my clothes can wait."

They sat in silence again until Tim pulled up at a large building bearing the words MIAMI BEACH POLICE DEPARTMENT. Palm trees lined the street, swaying in the breeze.

At the front desk, Kay asked the officer for Mrs. Roosevelt.

"She's with a prisoner," the officer said, talking to Tim, not her. "The Black girl who shot Mr. Miller."

"She did not shoot Mr. Miller," Kay said, feeling heated.

Tim shook his head gently, implying this was a battle she did not need to have. She disagreed, but before she could argue, Tim asked, "Who is the lead detective on the case?"

The desk sergeant looked up. "Detective Harry Tomlins. His partner is Detective Mike Connor," he said.

Tim grinned. "I know Mike. A good cop." To the sergeant, he said, "I'm formerly with the Washington P.D. I was a homicide detective. Mike Connor is an old friend. Do you mind if I go in and say hi?"

"Not at all." The desk sergeant pointed the way.

"Wait here," Tim said. "I'll be back soon." Then he was gone.

Kay found herself stuck, waiting by the desk. It hadn't even occurred to Tim to invite her to join him.

CHAPTER 9

The fight in the world is against evil, and not against people because of their difference in race or creed.
—Eleanor Roosevelt, My Day, July 14, 1945

Earlier

"Now that Kay has left to meet Mr. O'Malley at the airport," Eleanor said to Josephine, rising from the sofa in her suite, "will you allow me five minutes to finish getting dressed? Then we will go to the police station to see Rosaleen."

"Five minutes? I am impressed, Eleanor," Josephine said. She paced on the carpet. "When I am at home in Les Milandes, and I dress simply to garden and collect snails for my ducks, it takes me a few minutes to dress. I thought I was unusual in dressing so swiftly."

Josephine wore an off-white exquisitely cut dress with a fur wrap thrown across her shoulders.

"It is hard to picture you looking anything less than a glamorous star, Josephine."

Josephine waved her hand carelessly. "*Il faut.* When I was a teenager, I learned from Clara Smith, the singer, that you should always go out in public looking like a star. If you look like a star, people will believe that is what you are.

"In truth," Josephine added, "I am much simpler than people believe. Of course, I am happy to have my beautiful château—though it was left in a terrible mess after the Nazis occupied Paris. They took my home, and when they fled, they stole and destroyed things in their wake . . ."

Josephine paused. "I'm sorry. I am nervous and that is making me talkative. I used to be quiet when I was growing up. At my early jobs, before I was thirteen, I was a maid. In some of those houses, I was punished if I spoke."

"I understand." Eleanor poured more coffee for her friend Josephine, then headed to her room. "I was quiet too, when I was a child." Her mother had called her "Granny" because she was a solemn, serious child and was not pretty.

Eleanor managed to be ready in four minutes. The two women hastened downstairs to summon a cab.

Josephine sighed. "I miss my convertible. Taxis are expensive. And too often, when I try to summon a cab, they whiz past."

"I am sorry about the narrow-mindedness of people," Eleanor said.

A cab stopped for them. The driver muttered, "A white woman and a Black one together. I'll take you, but I'd better not get myself pulled over by the police."

Eleanor felt a surge of frustration. She could not abide the foolishness of segregation. It had to end throughout America. A civilized country should not accept anything less.

In the cab, Eleanor decided not to discuss matters in front of the driver. But when they reached the sand-beige stucco Miami Beach Police Station, Josephine stopped her on the front steps.

"I want to believe Rosaleen is innocent, Eleanor," she whispered passionately. "Rosaleen is honest. I know she would never cheat me out of one dime. But I do believe that if a white man threatened her life, she might have shot him to protect herself. If she was protecting herself, she was justified."

"But where did she get a gun? Did she have her own?"

Josephine shook her head.

"Did you have a gun? Did you obtain one because of the threats you received?" Eleanor asked.

"I didn't. I've never handled a gun except for hunting at home. I never used a weapon during the war, even when I carried secret messages. My wits were my weapon."

"But you think Rosaleen might have had a gun," Eleanor said.

"I don't know, but I wonder if her fiancé could have given one to her. For her protection. He is with the CIA, after all. He might have been afraid that something would happen to us down here."

"Kay said he is with the CIA," Eleanor said.

"They met when he came questioning me about whether I am a Communist. Do *I* look like a Communist? The Soviet Union puts its women in drab, gray dresses. The material is less pleasant than old flour sacks. Rosaleen was afraid Stephen would make up lies about me to please his bosses. But Stephen also turned out to be as honest as the day is long. Even though it got him in trouble with his bosses and with the director of the FBI, J. Edgar Hoover, Stephen insisted there was no evidence that I was a Communist."

Josephine gave a dreamy smile. "It was an unusual way for lovers to meet. He comes to the door believing you are assisting an enemy of the state but ends up falling in love with you, and you with him."

"He must be told that Rosaleen is in trouble."

"Yes, I wished to tell him at once, but I do not know how to reach him." Josephine looked resolutely toward the door. "*Premièrement*, let us get Rosaleen out of jail."

Eleanor warned, "Josephine, I fear it won't be that easy. But we must get the true story from Rosaleen to help her."

* * *

Eleanor admired how Josephine strode into the police station like a star walking out on stage. Confident, proud, her head held high. To the desk sergeant, she requested, in firm but sweet tones, for her assistant to be released.

The desk sergeant was staring at her. "Aren't you Miss Josephine Baker?"

"I am."

"You're the one who does the banana dance in Gay Paree. I've seen pictures."

Eleanor wondered if Josephine would be offended. The desk sergeant was a beefy man, barely able to wedge between his chair and the counter. As he spoke, his gaze dropped, landing on Josephine's bosom. Often, when Josephine danced in the 1920s, she had been almost or entirely bare-breasted. No doubt that was the picture he had seen.

Josephine did not take offense. She gave a dazzling smile. "Yes, I did do La Danse Sauvage in Paris. Now, I am a singer. This, as you must have observed, is Mrs. Roosevelt. I am here to take my assistant, Rosaleen Davis, back to the Delano Hotel with me."

The desk sergeant nodded to Eleanor. "Rosaleen Davis? That the one who shot Mr. Miller at the Copa City Club?" he asked. "She's under arrest, ma'am. She's not going anywhere."

"If she is under arrest," Eleanor said, "she has the right to be represented by a lawyer. Has she contacted one?"

"Dunno. I heard she's not talking."

"Then may we speak with her? We must get her direction for hiring a lawyer."

"You want to speak to her," he repeated, uncertain.

"Mrs. Bouillon is her employer. I am her friend," Eleanor said.

"You're Mrs. Roosevelt and you're her friend?" The desk sergeant frowned. He picked up his telephone and asked to be put through to the captain. He explained, then spent several minutes saying nothing more than "Uh-huh." Finally, he hung up.

"You can see her in one of the interview rooms. Wait here."

An hour passed before Eleanor was led to the room by a young officer. A cold, oppressive room, not much larger than a cell. The room felt devoid of hope—gray and institutional and foreboding.

Eleanor took a seat and began to wait again.

This was the second time Eleanor had spoken to a person being held behind bars. The first time, it was a young man from the Soviet Union who had been wrongfully arrested.

Eleanor was not going to leap to conclusions.

The door opened and two officers led in Rosaleen. Their holsters were prominently displayed.

Eleanor's heart sank. Rosaleen was dressed in a prison uniform, also drab and gray. Her face was bare of makeup, which made her look very young and vulnerable. Her hair was free of her usual tidy bun. But what made Eleanor gasp in dismay were the iron shackles on Rosaleen's ankles and around her wrists.

"Surely that is not necessary," she said.

"Standard procedure. She's a prisoner," growled a guard.

He pressed his hand on Rosaleen's slender shoulder to force her down in the chair. Rosaleen submitted to being jostled by the two large men. She docilely held her hands in place while the officer locked her handcuffs to the metal loop on the table.

Eleanor waited until the two men left.

Once they were alone, Rosaleen faced Eleanor. Her cool, emotionless mask dropped. Her eyes were wide with fear.

"Mrs. Roosevelt, when they said you had come for me, I couldn't believe it."

"How are you, Rosaleen?" Eleanor asked. "Are you . . . safe in here? Have you been harmed in any way?"

"I've been shoved around, prodded with a baton, and spat on

by the officers," Rosaleen said. "But I guess that isn't serious harm."

A spark of her familiar pride and anger flared in her dark eyes for a moment but quickly went out.

"Josephine is also here," Eleanor said. "She is going to find a lawyer for you. Do you have any direction regarding retaining a lawyer that you wish for me to tell her?"

"Do you think I am guilty?" Rosaleen asked bluntly.

"No, I do not."

"Then you are probably the only person in Miami Beach who doesn't. I saw Josephine's face when she came into the dressing room. She told me to plead self-defense. I told her I was innocent. I never touched the gun. They can test it. I told them that. My fingerprints are not on that gun."

"How was Mr. Miller shot, Rosaleen?"

When Rosaleen stayed silent, Eleanor frowned.

"Please tell me what happened, Rosaleen. If you speak up, I believe we can get you out of jail. You were in the room with Mr. Miller. Surely you saw who shot him."

Rosaleen shook her head. "I didn't see who did it." She scowled. "Because I can't say who did it, the police—and Josephine—think I must be guilty."

"I know you are frightened and angry," Eleanor said gently, "but your resentful attitude is not helping. It is as if you want people to think you guilty, even though you are innocent."

"The police think I grabbed his gun and killed him because I changed my mind about allowing him intimacies. The officers said I must have 'encouraged' him and he expected to have some 'fun' with me in the dressing room. They told me I would be executed for killing a good white man. They made it clear that if Miller wanted to rape me, they didn't see it as a crime."

Eleanor had faced such heinous views before, but it still turned her stomach. "That is terrible. Did Mr. Miller try to force himself on you?"

Rosaleen shook her head. But she didn't speak.

"I don't understand your silence," Eleanor said, her tone brisk instead of soothing. "But I wish to deal with this logically. Firstly, was anyone else in the room at any time?"

"No. It was just me and him."

Eleanor nodded with satisfaction. At least Rosaleen was not going to be completely silent.

"You went back to retrieve your purse. How did you come to forget it?"

Rosaleen blinked. "Oh! I—I didn't expect you to ask that." She frowned, thinking. "I don't know. I guess I was so worried about the party. I suspected some of those men were KKK and I was worried about Josephine. It is my job to keep track of Josephine's things—her coat, her purse, her plans. I was so worried, I ensured she had her belongings, but I forgot mine."

"When you and Josephine left the dressing room, I presume you left it empty. Mr. Miller had left. Or you believed he had."

"Yes."

"Please go through what happened, step by step, after Kay and I left the party."

"Once you and Kay had gone, I quietly told Josephine she should end the party and go to bed. She wasn't happy. She likes parties and thrives on the adulation of her fans. I pointed out quietly that one of those fans might want to kill her. At first, she discounted my fears, but finally she agreed. We hustled everyone out of the dressing room by two a.m."

"Who was the last to leave?"

"Not Frank Miller. It was Mr. Gros. I was worried about going outside to get a taxi on our own. But Josephine was confident we would be safe."

Rosaleen took a breath. "When I realized, outside on the sidewalk, that I was missing my purse, I went to the stage door."

"Alone?"

"Yes. I told Josephine to stay. Josephine wanted to come with me, but I told her to stay. That I would be very quick."

Eleanor nodded. "And then?"

"The stage door was locked. I had to hammer on it until one of the cleaning ladies let me in."

"A cleaning lady? What did she look like?"

Rosaleen shrugged. "She was Black, like me. All the cleaning staff of the Copa City Club are Black. It's not a surprise. Segregated schools and segregated lives force Black women into menial jobs."

Eleanor nodded. "I am pleased that you are working hard to become a lawyer. Did you not notice anything more about the cleaning lady?"

Rosaleen looked down at her hands. "I guess I didn't really look at her. But not because she was just a cleaning lady. I wanted to hurry and get my purse."

"What happened after that?"

"The lights were on, which made it easy to go to Josephine's dressing room. I had the key, and I unlocked the door."

"The door was definitely locked?"

"Yes. I mean, I think so. I used my key without trying the handle. Because I had locked the door."

"You opened the door?"

"Yes. I walked into the room. He was there. Mr. Miller. Standing by the drinks cart. I hadn't even noticed the light was on in the room. I had turned the lights out when we left."

"He was in the dressing room that you had locked?"

Rosaleen nodded.

"Was he holding a gun?"

"No, he didn't have a gun. He was just standing there. So I went in—"

"Why?"

"What?"

"Why did you go into the room? After the threats Josephine received, you must have been quite startled to see Mr. Miller in the room when he was not supposed to be. Did you not worry about danger?"

Rosaleen looked confused. "I guess I was so shocked and angry I didn't think properly. I was going to demand that he tell me what he was doing in there and how he got in. But as I stormed into the room, he looked behind me, over my shoulder. He looked shocked. I started to turn, but the deafening explosion of a shot rang out. It came from behind me. From the doorway. My heart almost stopped, and my ears rang with the intensity of it. I thought I was shot, and I couldn't understand why I didn't feel it. I stood there, frozen, as Miller fell forward.

"I thought I would be next. Fear broke my body free of the icy grip of shock. I turned toward the door. If I was going to be shot, I refused to be shot in the back. My legs shook and I was sucking in sobbing breaths.

"But as I turned, the gun came sailing into the room and hit the carpet with a thud. I stared at it, trying to understand why someone had thrown it, when the door slammed shut. I heard the key turn in the lock—I must have left it in the lock. Then I turned back to Mr. Miller, but he was face down on the floor and he wasn't moving. There was a lake of blood under him, getting bigger and bigger.

"I ran to the door. It wouldn't turn—"

"You did not see the person who shot Mr. Miller when you turned toward the door?"

"No! I saw a shadow in the hallway, that's all. Then the gun came flying at me, so I flinched. Right after that, the murderer slammed the door shut." Rosaleen trembled. The chains securing her hands to the table rattled.

Eleanor respected the police but felt impatience with the handcuffs. Such precautions were ridiculous.

"Could you not unlock the door from the inside?"

Rosaleen shook her head. Her hands shook. "The lock can only be opened with the key. On both sides.

"I knew I should check if he was still alive, but I couldn't make myself touch him," Rosaleen went on, shivering. "I was a coward. I took a few steps toward him. His face was turned to the side. I could see his right eye was wide-open but not seeing a thing. I knew he was dead. I ran back to the door and rattled it again. I desperately turned the handle. I think I banged on the door."

"Were you trying to run away?"

Rosaleen shook her head. "No. I was going to call the police. But I couldn't stay locked in with a dead man. I just couldn't!"

"I understand."

"I was standing there, trying to figure out what to do when I heard a man shouting for me to open the door. It was the security guard. I shouted that I could not open it without the key. He used his master keys to open the door.

"I thought I was safe!" Rosaleen stared at her shackled hands, her eyes blazing with anger. "Instead, he pulled a gun on me. He told me to get on my knees with my hands on my head. He was shaking and waving the gun at me, and I thought he would shoot me by accident."

"Is that when Josephine found you?"

"I think so," Rosaleen said. "Josephine argued with the security guard. The fact he was pointing his gun at me made Josephine spit fire. She told him to put the thing away before he hurt someone."

"Josephine said the guard marched you to his office at gunpoint so he could call the police."

Rosaleen nodded. "He told her I was under arrest. Jo said he couldn't do that. He said something smart, like, 'If Josephine Baker can make a citizen's arrest of a man in a restaurant, I can arrest a murderer.'"

Rosaleen took a shaky breath. Tears welled in her eyes. "I'm not a murderer. I didn't shoot Frank Miller." She tried to lift her hands to brush at the tears and when she couldn't, she snapped, "The police don't believe I could possibly be innocent. The security guard told them he discovered a locked room with two people inside—and one person was dead. The police figure the other person *must* be the killer. Mrs. Roosevelt, what am I going to do? I want to be a lawyer. I never figured I'd need one!"

The door to the interview room opened. "Time's up. We gotta take the prisoner back to her cell."

Eleanor saw Rosaleen's face change. Saw it become hard and emotionless. She was refusing to show fear or sorrow in front of the white police officer.

Eleanor remembered something. "Your fiancé. Josephine said she wanted to tell him what has happened to you, but she does not know how to reach him."

"Stephen," Rosaleen whispered. "He was flying to Miami this morning so we could spend some time together on the beach. He must have already arrived. I don't want him to see me like this. Please don't tell him. Not yet. Not until I know for certain I'm going to be tried for a crime I didn't commit!"

CHAPTER 10

Every American soldier I see is a friend from home.
—Eleanor Roosevelt, My Day, November 6, 1942

A group of police officers gathered in the corner of the waiting area. From the desk, Kay watched them curiously. There was no coffee machine there so why were they crowded in a circle?

One officer wearing a uniform complete with peaked cap, turned away from the group. He wore a big smile. Young and baby-faced, he clutched a piece of paper as if it were a one-hundred-dollar bill. Red lipstick graced his cheek. He floated away as if on cloud nine.

Kay saw what the fuss was about.

Josephine Baker sat on the wooden bench, signing autographs on anything the officers shoved in front of her. Half of the officers were young, tall, and well-built, like Baby Face. The others were older and portly, but they were all awestruck by Josephine's star presence. She sat on the bench with careless elegance, her long legs crossed, her fur casually falling off her shoulders. When she signed her name and wrote a saucy, personalized message for each man, the young ones blushed.

"Miss Thompson!" Josephine waved. She shooed the officers

away. "I must sit with my friend. If one of you handsome men would bring us coffees . . . *très merveilleux*. I would be so grateful."

The officers hurried away, the young ones running like it was an Olympic dash. Obviously, each was determined to get to the coffee machine first.

Josephine motioned to the space on the bench beside her. As Kay sat down, she said, "I knew that would work. Their competition will make the job of fetching coffee go much slower."

Josephine added in a whisper, "Eleanor is speaking with Rosaleen. I hope she learns who did this and then Rosaleen can get out of this place. She *must* know."

"If Rosaleen knows, why didn't she say at once?" Kay asked. But she thought of the last murder she was involved in with Mrs. Roosevelt. Sometimes people had reasons to stay quiet.

Josephine shook her head. "I don't understand why she refused to speak." She added thoughtfully, "All the police officers here are white. The Black police officers have their own precinct, in Overtown. I fear that is why Rosaleen isn't talking. She believes they won't listen."

One of the young officers sprinted back with a brimming cup of coffee, careful not to spill it.

Another brought milk and sugar packets. "Miss Josephine, how do you like your coffee?" he asked breathlessly.

Kay frowned. None of the men had brought coffee for her. When she was beside Josephine Baker, no one noticed her. With her curves and her red hair, she was not accustomed to that.

She stood up. "There is coffee somewhere and I really need some. I'm too worried about Rosaleen to sit still."

Josephine nodded. "I will stay here. Eleanor has been with Rosaleen for almost an hour. That must be a sign that Rosaleen is talking to her. That Rosaleen is telling her what happened."

"I hope so," Kay said. She walked in the direction the young officer carrying the coffee had come from. Her heels clicked on the floor.

"Dollface, would you get me a cup of coffee?"

Kay swiveled to look at the man in a rumpled shirt, cigarette butts mashed in an ashtray by his hand. A detective wearing plain clothes, she guessed.

"I don't work here," Kay said. "How would you like to get me a cup?"

"I got work to do, sweetheart."

"So do I," Kay said, and she kept walking.

At the coffee machine, which smelled as if it was burning what was in the pot, she saw Tim O'Malley. This was where he'd gone. He was drinking from a cup and talking to a tall, red-haired man in a black suit.

As a redhead herself, Kay had never been drawn to a red-haired man before, but this man was astonishingly good-looking. His hair was auburn, his brows were dark, his eyes large and brown with long lashes. Freckles covered the bridge of his nose. He had a nice mouth—wide and well shaped.

Tim motioned her over. "Mike, this is Miss Kay Thompson, secretary to Eleanor Roosevelt. Kay, this is Detective Mike Connor."

Detective Connor turned and his jaw dropped. He spilled some coffee on his trousers and shoe. He didn't notice.

"Miss Thompson. Wow. You aren't—" He broke off. Like most redheads (her included) when he blushed, the color covered his face fast and there was no hiding it.

Kay knew what he was going to say. She beat him to it. "You aren't what I expected." She reached out her hand.

He took it and shook her hand. "What did you expect, Miss Thompson?" he asked, giving a smile.

She liked the way he timed his smile to start slowly and then light up fast. "Call me Kay." But she had backed herself into a corner. She couldn't say she hadn't expected Tim's friend to be so good-looking. "I guess I didn't expect Tim to have friends in the Miami Beach Police Department."

"Kay is a friend of Josephine Baker," Tim put in.

"And Kay needs a coffee, I bet," Detective Connor said. He shoved his mug onto the counter. He grabbed a fresh one and filled it from the carafe. "Cream and sugar?"

"Black," Kay said. She added, "I'm also a friend of Rosaleen Davis, the young woman wrongfully arrested."

"The officers didn't have a choice," Connor said. "She was in a locked room with the victim. She was the only other person in the room."

"That is circumstantial. It doesn't make her guilty," Kay said.

Tim nodded toward Mike. "Mike is on the case."

"But not lead detective," Mike Connor said.

"Oh." Kay looked him over as she sipped her strong coffee. Rosaleen's future was partly in this man's hands. "So that means you can't talk about it."

"You can talk about the victim, Frank Miller, can't you?" Tim asked. "We want to know who he was. Someone shot him and that person had to have a reason."

Mike picked up his coffee cup. "Miller is a wealthy developer. He came to Miami about four years ago. Once he started building tall hotels, he got in the newspapers. He built the first one with an underground parking garage. I hear he's a millionaire about fifty times over."

"He is also likely a former Nazi," Kay muttered.

That startled Connor. "Here, in Miami? That can't be possible."

"Josephine Baker believes she recognized him from the war. Do you know if Frank Miller was a member of the KKK?" Kay asked.

Connor suddenly noticed he had a lot less coffee and was frowning at his cup. He looked up at her question. "No idea, Miss Thompson. Why?"

"The KKK contains members who have sent death threats to Josephine Baker." Kay worried about his mild response. Law enforcement officers in various cities were members of the KKK.

Wasn't the KKK a likely place for a former Nazi officer to end up?

But at the party, she hadn't noticed any friendship between Frank Miller and Claude Mains and Eulie Reynolds. He did not speak to them.

"Did Miller threaten Miss Baker?" Connor asked.

"Someone did. But we don't know who."

"We?" the detective prompted.

Kay paused to decide how to answer the question. Keeping Mrs. Roosevelt's involvement quiet would make William "Sandy" Sandiston of the State Department happy. A longtime friend of Mrs. R's, he wanted to ensure the United States Senate approved Mrs. Roosevelt as a United Nations delegate. He would not want to see her name in the newspaper linked to this murder.

But Mrs. Roosevelt had already come into the police station to talk to Rosaleen.

There was no way to keep that quiet.

In fact, Mrs. Roosevelt was walking toward them, answering Mike's question. Mike looked startled.

"Mrs. Roosevelt," Tim said. He approached her and they shook hands. "It's good to see you again, ma'am."

"Good to see you, Tim."

"Let me get you a coffee, ma'am," Tim said. Kay sensed he was watching what he said to Mrs. R in front of the detective. "This is Detective Mike Connor, Mrs. Roosevelt. We served in the same unit in the war. Mike's a great detective, but he is the secondary in this case."

Mrs. Roosevelt, who was a few inches shorter than tall Detective Connor, firmly shook his hand. She thanked him for his service, both as a soldier, and now in law enforcement.

Connor went red-faced to the roots of his short-cut red hair.

Mrs. R turned to Tim. "Rosaleen told me that she did not handle the gun. It was thrown into the dressing room by the person who shot Mr. Miller from *outside* the room. I hoped to meet with the detectives on the case to ask them if they tested the weapon for fingerprints. I believe that is possible, isn't it, Tim?"

"It is. Mike, you guys must have pulled prints from the weapon and compared them to Miss Davis's prints?" Tim looked to Detective Connor.

Kay saw Detective Connor shift uncomfortably. "Harry Tomlins is the lead detective on the case. I don't think he's run a comparison."

"I would suggest the police do so," Mrs. Roosevelt said.

Kay watched Mike Connor's face. She was surprised it hadn't already been done. Would the detectives refuse to find evidence that exonerated Rosaleen?

Was it to ensure there was no other solution to the crime than Rosaleen?

Was it racism?

"You should do it, Mike," Tim said. "It would be expected, given Rosaleen's story. A defense lawyer would tear into that."

Kay frowned. Wasn't he on Rosaleen's side?

"It helps you and it helps Miss Davis to do things fair, by the book," Tim added.

Tim glanced at her, and she understood. He was giving Mike a reason to argue to his superiors that the fingerprints should be tested.

"It will be done, Tim," Mike Connor promised. "And I will get the results."

A burly man came up to the coffee counter. "What's going on, Connor?" he demanded.

The man was short with a big stomach that made him look like a sphere. His bald head was startlingly round. The only straight line on him was his mustache, trimmed to pencil thinness.

Detective Connor made introductions. The round man with the glowering expression was Detective Tomlins, the lead detective on Rosaleen's case. Mike Connor said, "I'm going to run a fingerprint check on the gun. Compare it to Rosaleen Davis's prints."

Tomlins glared. "Who else's prints would be on it?"

"If her story is true, someone else's," Connor said.

"Mrs. Roosevelt, you may be an important person, but the Miami Police Department doesn't play political favorites."

"I respect that, Detective Tomlins," Mrs. R said. "But I also respect the due process of the law."

"We need to get to work, Connor," Tomlins snapped.

"We will leave you to get on," Mrs. R said. "Josephine Baker will be returning with a lawyer for Miss Davis."

They walked out to the waiting room. Josephine shooed away her admirers. "I must contact a lawyer. Rosaleen cannot remain locked up. These ridiculous charges must be dropped."

"I don't know if they will do that," Kay said warily.

"Then she should be allowed out on bail!" Josephine exclaimed as they walked outside.

The sun shone, as bright and round as a Florida grapefruit, and the sky was azure. It was a perfect warm day. It seemed terrible after what had happened.

Tim paused on the steps. "Your point about the fingerprints was correct, Mrs. Roosevelt. I can't believe the lead detective hadn't already sent the gun to the laboratory to be tested."

"Unless he doesn't want any evidence that points to Rosaleen's innocence," Kay breathed.

Josephine looked mystified. Kay quickly explained.

"Do you think Detective Connor will test the gun?" Josephine asked.

"He will. He owes me," Tim said firmly.

Kay could imagine why, when the two men had been to war together. "You're sure he will be honest with the results?"

"I am. As for Tomlins . . . he worries me. If they test the gun and don't find Rosaleen's fingerprints, their case against Rosaleen takes a serious blow."

"I think it destroys their so-called case against her," Kay declared.

Tim shook his head. "They could argue she wiped the weapon clean. Since she didn't, and she says the gun was thrown into the room right after the shot, it means there should be fingerprints. If the shooter didn't wear gloves."

He looked grim. "But if someone in the department wants to see Rosaleen Davis get charged with murder, he knows to wipe the prints off the gun. Or plant one of Rosaleen's prints, which is harder to do, but not impossible. Connor could get the test results done in good faith, but they've had a heads-up." He shook his head. "I guess I'll know what kind of trouble we're facing when I get information from Mike Connor."

"Rosaleen could be in danger here," Josephine cried. "Grave danger. I need to get her out of here!"

CHAPTER 11

. . . there is one great thing which we must learn—that humanity is all one.

—Eleanor Roosevelt, My Day, June 18, 1946

After arriving back at the Delano, Eleanor attended the rest of the morning's events at the AAUN conference, as was her duty, but extended her regrets for the luncheon. She decided to have lunch in her room, where she could discuss Rosaleen's story with Kay.

Josephine was in her suite, telephoning law offices. Eleanor had been pleased when Kay immediately offered to help make telephone calls, but Josephine had been adamant about handling it herself.

Despite her fame, Josephine was strong and down-to-earth, qualities Eleanor greatly admired.

As she left the conference room, Benny, the young man who sported the tweed coat and a pipe, approached her. Blushing fiercely, he asked hopefully about Kay. "Is she coming to the cocktail party this evening?"

"I do not think we will be able to attend," Eleanor answered truthfully. Not with a woman wrongfully accused of murder. Eleanor knew Sandy Sandiston would want her to keep out of this, but she could not.

Benny looked crestfallen. Obviously, he thought Kay attractive. But he was too young, hardly a good match for Kay. Eleanor knew she had no right to play matchmaker, but she had felt that Tim and Kay were right for each other. Yet it appeared she had been wrong. Tim had been stubborn and hardheaded about Kay's job. Eleanor could not approve of that!

Returning to the suite, Eleanor found Kay diligently typing correspondence. Even while she was away, Eleanor could not take a pause from answering the hundreds of letters she received.

"Would you order lunch, Kay?" she asked. "We can eat out on the balcony. I would like your thoughts on what has happened. Also order enough for Tim."

She saw Kay hesitate, then say, "Of course."

Was she wrong, pushing Kay and Tim together? Well, not really pushing. Engineering opportunities.

But when Kay telephoned Tim's room to invite him to lunch, there was no answer. Kay frowned at the phone as if it had delivered a personal insult. She then dialed room service.

Eleanor overheard Kay's half of the conversation. "Egg salad sandwiches, with pickles and potato chips on the side. Two large glasses of orange juice. A pot of tea . . . no, not iced tea. Hot tea. You know, with hot water. Not lemon. With milk. No . . . not milk and lemon!"

Eleanor smiled.

As she slipped into a light cardigan and comfortable slippers, a knock sounded on the door. Kay opened it, and the bellboy rolled in the room service cart. Kay took the plates and drinks out to the small table on the balcony looking out over the ocean.

As they ate, Eleanor paused to say, "You and I both believe Rosaleen is innocent. Since she is, that means someone else shot Frank Miller. The question is: Who?"

"You want to find the murderer?" Kay looked hopeful.

Even after the danger they had encountered last time, Kay wanted to investigate.

Eleanor understood. She had never felt such a rush of emotion as when she had unmasked Susan Meyer's killer. But she said, "That is best left to the police."

"Can we trust the police?"

"I do trust Detective Mike Connor," Eleanor said. "I was impressed when he stated he would ensure the weapon was tested. And he is a friend of Tim's. I sense they trusted each other during the war."

"But can one decent man fight for justice if his superiors want to pin the crime on Rosaleen?" Kay wondered. She looked up, her delicately drawn brows arched and excitement in her dark blue eyes. "If we could figure out who did it, we could prove Rosaleen is innocent."

"It is too dangerous, Kay. Especially if the KKK is involved."

"But we can speculate," Kay said hopefully. "It must be one of the people at the party."

Eleanor sipped her tea. The view over the vast ocean was very pleasant. Being able to sit outside in late December and feel warm was intriguing. Franklin had discovered this joy many years ago when he traveled south to Warm Springs, Georgia, in 1924. He hoped to find a cure for the polio that had paralyzed and weakened his legs. He swam daily in the pool. She remembered his delight when he discovered he could stand in four feet of water. He opened a therapeutic polio treatment center there and built a cottage. He had enjoyed his time there.

Eleanor gave a soft smile. Her thoughts turned bittersweet. Franklin had died at Warm Springs on April 12, 1945. She allowed herself a wistful moment, then got back to the business at hand. She had serious issues to consider.

"We cannot say for certain that someone else, completely unknown to us, did not obtain access to the Copa City Club. Another audience member could have remained hidden."

"That's true. But how could that person know Mr. Miller would go to the dressing room?" Kay asked.

Eleanor nodded her head approvingly. "Correct. If Josephine was to be the victim, any audience member could have hidden and waited for the opportunity. But that is not what happened."

"Do you think the killer shot Miller by accident? Maybe he was aiming for Rosaleen, thinking she was Josephine?"

After asking the question, Kay blushed. "No one would make a mistake identifying Josephine Baker."

"Mr. Miller was shot from the doorway and hit in the chest, which meant he was facing his killer. The killer saw him. The choice of Mr. Miller as victim appears intentional. We were considering who might have a motive to harm Josephine. But who would have a motive to shoot Frank Miller?"

Kay's expression turned sad. "That nice, gentle man, Mr. Gros, had a motive. He showed me the tattooed number on his arm. He said the Nazis made his family into soap. Josephine said that Isaac Gros would also recognize Frank Miller as a Nazi. *He* would want revenge."

The telephone in the room rang.

Kay got up from the table. She had kicked off her shoes and Eleanor watched her sprint back into the suite in bare feet and snatch up the receiver.

Kay listened, set the receiver down and came outside. "It's Josephine," she said quietly. "She wants you to go to her room at once, Mrs. Roosevelt. Should I tell Josephine you have to attend the conference after lunch?"

"I will speak to her," Eleanor said, rising. She went into the suite and picked up the receiver.

The moment she said hello, Josephine said urgently, "Eleanor, I must speak to you. You must come to my suite right away!"

Eleanor was not offended by the almost imperious summons. She knew Josephine was deeply worried. Her thoughts were entirely focused on helping Rosaleen.

"I have an hour before the conference meetings begin. I can come to your suite for a short while," Eleanor promised.

Josephine opened the door dramatically. Kay noticed Josephine now wore a simple yellow sundress.

"Thank you for coming. And thank you for this morning—for coaxing Rosaleen to talk!" Josephine declared.

Josephine embraced Mrs. Roosevelt. Then Kay was swept into Josephine's hug and enveloped by the singer's fragrance, as if she had been plunged into an exotic garden. Kay remembered reading that Josephine's magical scent was Guerlain Sous Le Vent, which blended bergamot and lavender with the anise-like note of tarragon and sweetgrass.

Kay loved scents. Her knowledge of men's cologne proved useful before. Kay's perfume, Coty's L'Aimant, came from Woolworth.

Josephine waved her hand elegantly, her long, dark plum nails flashing. "Come, Stephen. You must meet Eleanor Roosevelt. And her assistant, the very pretty Miss Kay Thompson."

The door to the balcony was open, and the billowing curtains screened a man's tall silhouette. A strong hand pulled the fabric aside and the man stepped through. Over six feet tall, his head almost grazed the door frame. Kay drank in the blond hair, slicked down, the dark brows, and the sharply honed features.

She gasped in surprise.

The man moved to Mrs. Roosevelt and shook her hand. "Mrs. Roosevelt. A privilege to meet you."

"You were on the flight this morning," Kay exclaimed. She remembered how, in the first moment she saw him, she had felt a jolt to her heart. He reminded her of Dmitri Petrov, the U.N.

aide from the Soviet Union. She had met Dmitri while she helped Mrs. Roosevelt investigate the murder of Susan Meyer.

Josephine's expressive brows lifted in surprise. "Are you clairvoyant? Do you have the sight?"

"No, I saw him when I met Tim at the airport. They sat together on the flight."

"That's right. I met Tim O'Malley on the plane. A former Washington P.D. detective."

"This is Stephen Roberts. Rosaleen's fiancé," Josephine said. "I've told him everything. I know Rosaleen doesn't want Stephen to see her in prison, but I'm certain he can help. Stephen is with the CIA."

A faint blush colored his high cheekbones at Josephine's certainty. "I want to get Rosaleen out of jail right away. But it's not that simple. I don't have jurisdiction. I can't just walk in and demand they release her."

"Then use your pull, darling," Josephine urged. "Contact your superiors."

"I don't have 'pull,' Josephine," Stephen said ruefully.

"You know she is innocent, don't you, Stephen?" Josephine asked, placing her hand gently on his arm.

But Stephen hesitated. Kay watched him in surprise.

"If her life was in danger, what choice did she have?" Stephen asked huskily.

"Rosaleen insists she is innocent," Mrs. Roosevelt said.

"She acted in self-defense," Stephen said. "It's extenuating circumstances."

"Why do you believe it was self-defense?" Mrs. Roosevelt asked.

Stephen's brows knitted. "Rosaleen must have walked in on the guy who was sending threats to Josephine. Are you saying you think she deliberately murdered this man?"

"I believe Rosaleen's story," Mrs. Roosevelt said. She related to Stephen what Rosaleen told her in prison.

Stephen groaned. "Rosaleen doesn't lie. But she must be so scared, she's made up this story." He looked to Mrs. Roosevelt. "Josephine thinks that Rosie and I are playing with fire. That we are crazy to even think of getting married. This isn't France where Josephine and Jo Bouillon could marry and find a life of acceptance."

"You and Rosaleen could come to Les Milandes with me, dear boy," Josephine said. "When this is over."

"I appreciate it, Josephine. We both do. Getting Rosaleen out of jail is my first mission," he said. "But Rosaleen and I don't want to run away. We want to work to end discrimination here."

Kay squirmed guiltily. She had been shocked when Stephen Roberts was introduced as Rosaleen's fiancé. He was a stunningly handsome man. Well built, which was expected for a young CIA agent, she supposed, with platinum-blond hair and vivid sky-blue eyes.

She admitted to herself that she hadn't expected Rosaleen's fiancé to be white.

"There are so many places that will not accept you," Josephine warned. "I have lived through this with my husband Jo. You will not be able to enter hotels and restaurants. In some states, your marriage will be a crime. Rosaleen could work with me at the château. I can pull strings and find work for you."

"You are kind and generous, Josephine," Stephen said. "But Rosie and I will be okay. Once she is released from jail."

He looked around. "If you think our engagement made Rosie a target with the KKK—that this guy followed her to punish her for seeing a white man—you're wrong. We kept the engagement a secret from everyone but Josephine. Rosaleen wanted it that way. Now, I'd like to go down to the station and see her."

Josephine looked worried. Mrs. Roosevelt shared a look with her. "Rosaleen specifically said she did not want you to see her in jail, Stephen," Josephine said.

"But I can't just sit here while Rosaleen is in trouble. I *need* to see her."

"And she does not want that. Upsetting Rosaleen isn't going to help," Josephine declared. "I expect you have not eaten. I shall order breakfast."

"I'm not relaxing over breakfast while Rosaleen is in *jail*," Stephen said, heading toward the door.

Josephine touched his arm, and he stopped at once.

"You must eat," Josephine insisted.

"I will order some food and coffee," Kay said, wanting to be useful.

At Josephine's nod, she put in the order by the room telephone. The moment she hung up, Josephine took the phone and spent the next while contacting law firms in Miami.

When the food arrived, Josephine piled eggs, bacon, and toast on a plate and pushed it into Stephen's hands. "Sit there, on the sofa."

Despite his protests, Stephen sank down and began forking his food in his mouth hastily, wolfing it down.

"After you eat, you can come with me to speak to the lawyer. I believe I have found the right one. But if he can't deliver the goods, or I suspect he's not a fighter, I'm firing him in a heartbeat," she declared.

"Very wise," Mrs. R said.

"I told Eleanor and Kay how you met Rosaleen because you had to find proof that I am a Communist."

"Laughable," Stephen said, between mouthfuls. "But, yes, it gave me the chance to meet Rosaleen, and I fell in love."

"It's proof that America could be—and should be—an accepting place for all kinds of love," Josephine declared.

Stephen blushed again. He was a good-looking man, but he had that air of being unaware of how handsome he was. One of the most charming attributes about a man.

"Now I juggle the fine line of obeying my superiors while

trying to convince them that women like Josephine and Rosaleen, who fight for the freedoms and rights of all Americans, are not Communists."

Josephine picked up a bundle of folded papers from the side of the room-service cart. "I also telephoned and requested that they bring all the papers available in Miami. I am worried about what the press is saying about Rosaleen."

She unfolded the newspaper. A large photograph of Frank Miller filled the top half of the page, black and white, and grainy. A picture of Rosaleen, in handcuffs, was below.

"They describe Rosaleen as the only suspect. Taken into custody, they write. They are all but convicting her in the news."

Stephen reached out for the newspaper with his left hand. As Josephine handed it to him, he reared back onto his chair and dropped his fork. "This guy—this is the guy who was shot?"

"Yes, that is Monsieur Frank Miller."

Stephen stared at Josephine in disbelief. "You didn't tell me the victim's name."

"Did I not?" Josephine said. "I am thinking only of Rosaleen, I guess."

"Do you know this man, Stephen?" Mrs. Roosevelt asked calmly.

"Yeah, I do. This man is my stepfather."

CHAPTER 12

For where there is no vision the people perish.
—Eleanor Roosevelt, *Tomorrow Is Now*, 1963

Stephen's strong hands clenched around the newspaper. Eleanor saw the shock on his face as he raised his gaze from the grainy picture of Frank Miller.

"I don't get it. How was my stepfather in your dressing room?" he asked Josephine.

"How was this man your stepfather?" Josephine demanded. "Rosaleen did not tell me this."

Stephen groaned. "Rosaleen didn't know."

"What do you mean, Rosaleen does not know?" Josephine demanded, hands on her hips.

"Exactly that," the young man answered.

"Monsieur Miller sent me flowers each night of my performance. Exquisite red roses. In return, I invited him to my small party."

"That doesn't sound like my stepfather. He has the money, but— " Stephen broke off. Agony flashed across his expression. "This means . . . this has to mean . . ."

"Do not panic, young man," Eleanor said firmly. "Let us assess carefully what you believe this means. You might be quite wrong."

Eleanor put her hand on his forearm, and she could feel the rock-hard strength even through his shirtsleeve. Perspiration sprinkled his forehead. The heat had not done that. It was shock—and fearing the worst.

Josephine stared at Stephen in concern. When a large, tough man was felled with shock, it was concerning.

The coffee Kay suggested they order was perfect. As Stephen took a cup, he said in hard tones, "I'd rather have whiskey."

Eleanor lightly patted his knee. "A clear head would be preferable."

"Your stepfather did not know of your engagement, is that correct?" she continued.

"Yes. He didn't know." Stephen hung his head. The sunlight glinted on his slicked-down white-blond hair. "Rosaleen didn't know who he was, and he didn't know about her."

"Your stepfather was wealthy. Is that why you kept it secret? You feared he would disinherit you because you were engaged to a Black woman?" Josephine asked.

"No. I never expected to inherit a dime. My stepfather and I never got along. We had a big fight three years ago. I haven't seen him or spoken to him since. I always figured I would support myself with my own career."

"You never thought you would have a share of his millions?" Josephine asked, in disbelief.

Stephen shook his head. "I walked out. Refused to work in his business. Got the job with the CIA." He sucked in a deep breath.

"I couldn't tell my stepfather about Rosaleen because he was a racist," he continued. "I had to protect Rosaleen. My stepfather's empire was built on corruption, intimidation, and violence. Two years ago, I discovered he was a member of the KKK. I put forward to my boss that he might have been involved in the Carver Village bombing."

"Heavens. Was he investigated?" Eleanor asked.

"I don't know. The FBI took over the case. I wanted to be part of the investigation. I could get the dirt on him better than anyone. But the guys at the Bureau said I was too close to him, so I couldn't be on the case."

He looked up at Josephine imploringly. "You see why I had to keep Rosaleen a secret, don't you? I was afraid Miller would have her hurt. Or worse."

"Yes, I understand," Josephine said.

Eleanor believed she did. She saw the deep pain etched on Stephen's face as, hollowly, he said, "The old man must have found out Rosaleen is my fiancée. That's why he went to your dressing room. He followed Rosaleen there. He was going to attack her to drive her away from the family. Or he planned to kill her. Usually, he got other people to do his dirty work, so it was hard to pin a crime on him. Maybe this time he wanted to do it himself—"

Stephen let out a low, pained moan, like a wounded animal. "Rosaleen *must* have shot him," he said, his deep voice breaking. "But she did it to save her own life."

"You are not looking at the facts, young man," Eleanor said firmly. "Your stepfather was already in the dressing room when Rosaleen returned to find her purse. He did not follow her. And if you were estranged, why should he want to harm your fiancée?"

"Even if I never spoke to him again, he would never accept a Black woman in the family." Stephen fell back against the sofa cushions. "Are you sure I can't have that whiskey?"

"I can order some sent up for him," Josephine said.

"I do not think it is a good idea," Eleanor said. "Drinking is not the answer. Thinking is."

"No one is going to believe Rosaleen is innocent," Stephen said. "Not when the cops find out the victim was the man who would do anything to stop the wedding."

"You need to believe in her," Eleanor exclaimed. Usually, she kept her voice modulated. But Stephen was sunk in a mire of depression, and she needed to pull him out of it. "Rosaleen needs you to fight for her."

"Like I told Jo, there's nothing I can do. I have no influence."

"But you have information. Rosaleen is innocent, which means someone else murdered your stepfather. You said he built his business on corruption—that usually means there are people who wish him harm. Would you tell me more about your stepfather? Did you grow up with him here, in Miami?"

Josephine was about to speak, but Eleanor shook her head slightly. Josephine, who Eleanor now knew was usually strong-willed and outspoken, remained quiet.

"My stepfather isn't just a racist. As I said, he's a crook." He stopped. "I mean, he was a crook. Rosaleen planned to be a lawyer. She wanted to work with the NAACP. All she ever wanted to do was defend people. I kept our engagement a secret to protect her from him, but also because I didn't want to taint her by introducing her into his world."

Kay refreshed Stephen's coffee. He glanced up, thanks in his eyes. The hurt, vulnerable look he wore twisted Eleanor's heart.

Eleanor suspected that Josephine had been ready to reveal to Stephen that his stepfather was a Nazi death camp officer.

"Tell me everything you know about Frank Miller's past," Eleanor said. "When did he become your stepfather?"

"I don't know much. My mother met Miller early in 1947 when she came with a friend for a vacation in Miami. They got married a few months later. She was widowed just after I was born. I don't remember my real father," Stephen said. "My mother worked hard to support us. I went overseas, and she struggled to survive. I was sending my army pay home to her, but they didn't pay us a lot to stand in the line of Nazi machine-gun fire."

"So she was not married to Monsieur Miller before the war?" Josephine asked. Eleanor heard the eagerness in her voice. She wanted to know she had been right.

"That's right," Stephen said. "Miller offered me a job with his company, but I knew he wasn't on the up-and-up. I took a job with the CIA in 1948. I would have supported my mother, but she felt it was better to have a husband. Any husband."

"What do you mean?" Josephine frowned.

"Was he abusive, Stephen?" Eleanor asked.

"He didn't like being questioned and he sure didn't like being made to look a fool. She had bruises sometimes, but mostly he liked to shout her down."

"Did you live with them?" Eleanor asked.

"Nah, I worked in Washington."

"Your mother must be notified of Mr. Miller's death," Kay said.

"My mother is dead," he said curtly.

Kay blushed. "I'm so sorry. I guess I just assumed . . ."

"My mother died in a car accident a year after they were married."

Eleanor saw Kay become alert at that news. Kay was a lover of mysteries and thriller movies, that sort of information would pique her suspicions.

"What did your stepfather do in the war?" Josephine asked suddenly.

"I don't know. He said he owned factories, so he made a lot of money producing parts for airplanes."

"Where?"

Stephen looked confused.

"I mean, in what country?" Josephine asked.

"Here. In America. My stepfather told me that he sold the

factories near the end of the war. He sold them for a pile of money, then the Nazis surrendered. Once Japan surrendered, there was no more fortune to be made selling airplane fuselages. He got out at the right time. He moved to Miami and socked that money into land and construction. Made his fortune in under five years."

"Your stepfather remained in America through the war?" Eleanor asked.

"I guess so. His factories were essential. And he was in his late forties. Too old to be called up."

Josephine wore a frown. Eleanor could tell she was certain that Frank Miller was a Nazi. She could see Josephine could not keep quiet anymore. "But you see, *cher* Stephen, I believe I saw Monsieur Miller before."

Eleanor said quickly, "We should be quite certain before we speak about that. Another shock would not be helpful. Especially if there is any doubt."

Josephine bit her lip. "Yes, I understand. For me there was no doubt, but from what Stephen has just told us, perhaps I *was* wrong after all."

"Would you mind telling me what you are talking about?" Stephen asked.

"As Eleanor said, I may have been mistaken. It is not important right now. Getting Rosaleen released from prison is important."

Stephen set down his coffee cup. "You said my stepfather was already in the dressing room. What if he had found out about our engagement? Maybe that was the reason for the flowers—to get close to you and Rosaleen. What if he made an appointment to meet Rosaleen?"

"But why would she not tell me?" Josephine asked. She paced in a circle. "Rosaleen was going to leave with me. She returned to the dressing room because she forgot her purse."

"Maybe that was a ruse. He arranged to meet her and told her to keep it secret. All along he planned to murder her in your dressing room. He probably planned to pin the crime on you, Josephine. But Rosaleen outsmarted him—" Stephen's voice broke. "But she couldn't admit to shooting him, so she came up with a crazy story."

"No!" Josephine cried expressively. "Rosaleen told Eleanor that she did not do it. Rosaleen respected Eleanor as a former First Lady. She would not lie to Eleanor Roosevelt."

Eleanor hoped that was the case. She believed Rosaleen, but had the young woman been completely truthful with her?

Josephine wagged her finger at Stephen. "Rosaleen says she is innocent. Eleanor believes she is innocent. You must have faith in the woman you love! I intend to save Rosaleen, even if you intend to sit around, pining for a bottle of whiskey."

Josephine stood. "Eleanor, would you come out to the balcony with me? I am excited and I must cool off."

Once outside, out of Stephen's earshot, Josephine declared, "I believe the story Miller told Stephen was lies. He met Stephen's mother *after* the war. He could have been at Buchenwald and pretended he was a factory owner in America."

Eleanor frowned. "It is true that what Stephen knows about Frank Miller's past was told to him by Mr. Miller himself. But could Frank Miller have entered the U.S.? How did he have millions of dollars, if he even managed to escape justice?"

"The Nazis stole things. Art. Gold. I am sure the officers at the camps stripped anything of value from their victims," Josephine said. "They ensured their nests were feathered. And not everything was recovered after the war."

"That is true," Eleanor said. "There are organizations trying to track down artwork and jewelry that were stolen by the Nazis."

"I am certain that man was a Nazi," Josephine declared. "I am a forthright person. I must tell Stephen. It makes sense, does it not, that a Nazi would then join the KKK? There is a person who can corroborate my memories. Mr. Isaac Gros."

Eleanor knew Josephine was forthright. Honest. But she warned, "It would be a great shock to Stephen to know his mother married a Nazi. It would be heartbreaking on top of the many shocks he has just received. I believe we must wait until we are certain without a doubt."

"If Monsieur Miller was indeed a Nazi, he may have guessed I could expose him as a Nazi to Stephen and Rosaleen. What if he came to my dressing room to prevent me from doing so? But I was not there, then Rosaleen came . . . No! Rosaleen is innocent and Miller was murdered by someone else. What if Mr. Gros saw Miller hang around and return to my dressing room?"

Eleanor thought of how Kay had pointed out he had a strong motive. Revenge.

"I do not want to think it of Mr. Gros," Josephine said. "He was a kind man. Despite being starved and almost skeletal himself, he risked death from typhus to care for his fellow men."

Eleanor nodded. Mr. Gros had seemed kind. He was so admiring of Josephine. Eleanor couldn't picture him shooting anyone. But the Nazis had murdered his family. The need for revenge could turn the heart of a good man dark with rage.

"I will telephone my friend Sandy Sandiston in the State Department," Eleanor said. "I want to learn if it was at all possible for Miller to have escaped custody at Buchenwald, and then, with no papers or passport, for him to have entered the U.S."

"That is a good plan." Josephine waved her hand flamboyantly. "There must be many other suspects! Stephen said his father was crooked. Such a man must have enemies. The police must be forced to look for suspects other than Rosaleen."

"In normal circumstances," Eleanor said thoughtfully, "Stephen himself would be a suspect. But since he flew into Miami just this morning, he must be innocent."

"That is a blessing, at least," Josephine declared. "I want those two to be married and live happily ever after. I am going to the lawyer's office. I will then personally escort him to the police station, and we are going to free Rosaleen. I must bid you adieu, Eleanor. *Il faut*—I must dress befitting a star and frighten this lawyer into performing for me."

Eleanor smiled. If anyone could do that, it was Josephine.

CHAPTER 13

Democracy will have to prove its worth with an equal belief in itself and a deeper sacrificial devotion to its standards.

—Eleanor Roosevelt, My Day, January 21, 1947

To Eleanor's surprise, Kay knew Sandy's telephone number by heart.

Using the telephone in the room, Eleanor called down to the hotel's switchboard and they dialed Sandy's office at the State Department, connecting her call. As Eleanor waited, listening to the curious clicking sounds, she asked Kay, "How can you remember that number? I haven't had to call Sandy that often."

Eleanor found people interesting. One could learn so much by simply talking to people and asking them questions.

"I remember telephone numbers. Lots of them. When I worked at other companies, and there was a handsome single client, I always remembered his number. I guess I developed the skill," Kay said.

The clicking stopped and Sandy's secretary, Joan, answered. "The office of William Sandiston."

"This is Mrs. Eleanor Roosevelt." Once she would have introduced herself as "Mrs. Franklin Roosevelt" for that was how a woman was once identified, but now she realized people recognized her more readily by her own name.

"Good morning, Mrs. Roosevelt," Joan trilled. "Mr. Sandiston is in his office. I will put you through."

In a moment Sandy Sandiston answered the telephone with a soft groan—the sound of a man shouldering the many troubles of the world. "Mrs. R, I saw the headlines in Miami. How can you be involved in another murder?"

"I didn't ask for it to happen, Sandy, it simply did. I am calling you with a question."

"Okay—just a moment, Mrs. R— "

She gave him a moment. In her mind's eye, Eleanor could picture Sandy. In his early forties, he possessed a barrel chest—his upper body was solid and broad with muscle, evident even beneath his tailored suits. A pugilist in college, he still sparred at a local gym for exercise; though, with his hectic life in the State Department, he had put on some weight. It was a struggle not to, with dinners and drinking happening almost daily. But with his sandy blond hair and blue eyes, he was an attractive man.

When he met Kay, he had been flirtatious with her. Eleanor did not believe he would stray from his wife, Letitia, but like many men, he flirted because he wanted to feel vital and masculine. To prove to himself that he "still had it."

Eleanor had not been surprised. Kay was a beautiful young woman. Her bright dresses showcased her hourglass figure. Kay's Aunt Tommy had feared Kay was man-mad, interested only in marriage.

Eleanor knew there was more to Kay. She was pleased that their work together was opening Kay's eyes to that fact.

There had been quite a long pause. Sandy apologized. "Sorry. Joan brought me fresh coffee. She knows when I need it before I do. Late night last night. Pounding headache. So, Mrs. Roosevelt, what do you need to know?"

"It was not in the newspapers, but Josephine Baker believes she recognized Frank Miller as a Nazi officer at the Buchenwald concentration camp. She performed there after the camp was liberated by our forces."

"And she remembers him after six years?"

"Yes. I am calling you to find out if it was possible that a Nazi officer could have escaped to the United States. He would have been under arrest, surely. I was told that because the American army did not have experience in operating the camps, which they had to do while the former prisoners were nursed to health or cared for in their final days, our army used the Nazi officers to run them." Eleanor paused. "Is that possible?"

"Very possible. Our generals oversaw the liberation of the camps. But our forces didn't have the men to manage them, and it was reasoned that the Nazi officers knew how to run the camps."

"Oh dear." Eleanor felt deeply troubled. "How could that be? Was it not cruel to have these men in charge of the people they had tormented? How could the inmates of the camps feel that they were now truly safe and free?"

"The Nazis knew their funny stuff was over. They toed the line."

Funny stuff. What a horrible expression. But then, Eleanor had found that many people could not voice what had truly happened. She thought of the image Josephine had seen when she first arrived at the camp.

"Josephine told me that she first saw skeletal figures dangling from the barbed wire. People who dragged themselves to the fence surrounding the camp, looking out at blessed freedom. But they were not to find it. They died there, clinging to the barbed wire. As their bodies drooped, their eyes glassy and empty, the wire tore through their hands. The officers responsible for that were the men that were left in charge."

"I don't make the rules, Mrs. R."

She sighed. "I know, Sandy. I should not be angry with you. Misplaced anger is not the solution. I wrote that in My Day, five years ago. It expressed what I hoped I had learned." She remembered the words. *When will our consciences grow so tender that we will act to prevent human misery rather than avenge it?*

"I'll give you the truth, Mrs. R. But you aren't going to like it. You're not going to approve of it, that's for sure."

She waited. Her fingers twisted the telephone cord.

"Frank Miller is German, born Franz Müller. Müller didn't have to sneak into America. He and thousands more came in with the help of our intelligence agencies. We gave visas to Nazi officers, bringing them here to work with the CIA to hunt Communists."

"You are telling me that a known Nazi officer of a concentration camp was in America with the approval of the government?"

"That's the size of it, Mrs. R."

It turned her stomach. It was horrifying. Müller had not received justice—he had received a good life. A reward for what he did. To hunt Communists.

"Their records where cleaned. Even Intelligence could see that senior-level Nazis wouldn't get through U.S. immigration. So that information disappeared."

"That is shocking." Such an understatement.

"Communism was considered the active threat. The red-level danger."

"Then Mr. Müller's past was kept hidden. Perhaps from his wife. And very likely from his stepson."

"Dunno. I don't think putting starving humans into gas chambers and brick ovens is the kind of pillow talk a woman wants to hear."

Eleanor winced, but she was accustomed to the bluntness of men in government.

"That was the idea," Sandy continued. "They could come here, have the American dream, and live out their lives in anonymity in return for their spy work."

What spy work? Eleanor wondered. Had the results been worth such a bargain?

"If you know about Franz Müller's identity, then you must know of his marriage to Stephen's mother," Eleanor said.

"Yeah. I made a few telephone calls about Müller when I saw the newspapers. He got married in Miami. His wife was Austrian but came to the United States with a small child in 1919. She entered alone with the child. The boy's father had died of illness before they were traveling. No birth certificate for either of them—a lot of records were destroyed or lost after the first war. Why do you think the dame is innocent?" Sandy asked suddenly. "The papers said she was locked in the room with the victim. There was just the two of them. He was rich and white. Maybe he tried something on, and she got uppity."

"You do not shoot a man because you are 'uppity,'" Eleanor said, disapprovingly. "It comes from a place of great fear—or fury—to take a life. This young woman planned to become a lawyer and defend people."

Sandy paused. "You think someone shot Müller because he was a Nazi."

"I do not yet know," Eleanor said. "It is a possibility. According to Stephen, Mr. Müller's business dealings were also not strictly honest."

"Some guys in construction end up in concrete footings," Sandy said.

Sandy could be colorful, she thought.

"Also, what do you mean by 'yet'?" he asked. "I don't like you messing around in this. Last time you were almost shot. I don't want you involved with another person who takes potshots at people."

"Sandy, I was the First Lady. I became well accustomed to people taking potshots. I remember the impromptu speech my husband made a fortnight before his inauguration, right here in Miami, and Mr. Zagara attempted to shoot him. My husband was unharmed, but Mr. Zagara hit five people as he shot wildly while people struggled with him."

"You may be used to it, Mrs. Roosevelt, but I don't like it," he repeated. "From the way you are talking, it sounds like you are going to be involved."

He had not called her "Mrs. R" and Sandy was one of the people in Washington who used that nickname for her. This was Sandy trying to put his foot down.

"There is concern that the police might not look further than Rosaleen Davis. Mr. Miller's work in development and his past as a Nazi indicate there are other suspects."

"I'm sure a fancy defense lawyer will put that out there. You don't need to," Sandy said.

"Well, thank you for the information about Frank Miller, Sandy. I believe Stephen does not know about his stepfather. The question is, should he be told?"

"Dunno. Everyone worries about people being sensitive these days. Don't see why he shouldn't know. From what you said, he hated his stepfather anyway. Bet he liked the money though."

"He did not receive money from his stepfather."

"Question is, does he get it now that the man is dead?" Sandy mused. "Follow the money."

Eleanor could see many motives for the demise of Frank Miller. His horrible Nazi past. His current illegal business practices, if they were indeed illegal as Stephen conjectured. His money.

"You know," Sandy added, "I can't see a Nazi officer being happy that his stepson was going to marry a Black woman. Maybe she did shoot him. To protect herself. Or maybe she realized her fiancé would be disinherited. This way she gets to marry a millionaire. If he is the heir, I mean."

Oh dear. It came back to Rosaleen. The prosecution could find many motives to attach to Rosaleen. Would anyone believe the poor young woman?

"I will let you go, Sandy. I know you have a busy schedule."

Sandy snorted. "My schedule is usually nothing on yours,

Mrs. R. But listen to me. Keep out of this. Someone picked up a gun and shot this guy. Sounds like he deserved it. But murderers don't always just shoot people who deserve it. Though I know you won't listen."

"Sandy, I do listen to you. But I cannot stand by while such a miscarriage of justice occurs."

"I knew it," Sandy muttered, and his voice sounded once more like that of a man shouldering a great many troubles.

CHAPTER 14

We should always be scrupulously fair and just.
—Eleanor Roosevelt, My Day, December 29, 1951

"Would you come out to the pool with me? I feel I have kept you cooped up with work all afternoon," Mrs. R said.

Kay set down the finished typed copy of Mrs. R's My Day column, which mentioned the new American ambassador to Moscow. Mrs. R wrote that "we should always be scrupulously fair and just."

Simple but powerful words, Kay thought.

Mrs. R had just returned from the afternoon sessions of the AAUN conference. Ever since her conversation with Sandy Sandifer, Mrs. R had looked gravely worried.

"I would love to go to the pool," Kay said.

In her bedroom, once again, Kay struggled out of her undergarments and slipped into her small bikini. She tied her wrap firmly around her waist and went into the suite to join Mrs. Roosevelt, who wore a pale beige skirt topped with a blouse patterned with colorful flowers. Kay had never seen Mrs. R wear anything so bright.

"I enjoy your bright and cheerful colors," Mrs. Roosevelt said to her. "I thought I would try it too."

Kay was astonished. When she had started her job in the fall,

Kay wore dowdy colors and grandmotherly cardigans to look serious. Mrs. R had advised her to dress how she liked instead. But Kay had no idea Mrs. R would ever be influenced by her fashion tastes.

"I am concerned that Josephine and the lawyer have not yet returned with Rosaleen," Mrs. R said as they took the elevator downstairs.

"Maybe it takes time," Kay said hopefully.

But she realized Mrs. R feared Rosaleen would not be treated in a way that was fair and just.

Kay opened the door to the garden for Mrs. R and they stepped out in the golden light of the setting sun.

Two rows of cushioned chaise longues flanked the sides of the pool, but at this time of day, guests were preparing to go for dinner and the pool was deserted.

To Kay's surprise, Mrs. R said, "Shall we sit at the edge? I have a great desire to paddle my feet in the water."

"Yes. Of course."

Kay could barely believe her eyes as Mrs. R removed her shoes, then discarded her knee-high stockings. With astonishingly nimble movements, despite being sixty-seven years old, Mrs. R sat on the pool edge. As she dipped her bare feet in the water, she gave a sigh. "Very refreshing."

Kay joined Mrs. R and gave a happy sigh as she slid her feet in the water. She had spent the day in heels and even sensible ones hurt after so many hours. She loved towering shoes but also loved taking them off.

Kay had fallen in love with the pool on the night she sat on its edge with Rosaleen. It looked exotic and glamorous, flanked by tall palm trees, with a view of lush, fragrant gardens, and the ocean beyond. The setting sun painted a glittering gold path across the water. Kay could hear the crashing of the surf on South Beach and the whisper of the palm leaves as they undulated in the breeze.

It was hard to believe it was almost twenty-four hours since the murder.

"Can you tell me about your telephone call with Mr. Sandiston, Mrs. Roosevelt?"

Mrs. Roosevelt gently kicked her feet in the water. "Sandy wanted me to promise I would keep out of it, but I ended the conversation by advising him that I could not stand by while a miscarriage of justice was carried out. He warned me of the danger. I warned him that I am quite accustomed to danger. But here is what I learned from him . . ."

With her usual efficiency of words, Mrs. Roosevelt relayed the conversation.

Kay listened, her shock and horror increasing.

At the end, Mrs. R summarized, "Josephine is correct, Kay. Frank Miller, formerly known as Franz Müller, was a Nazi. Worse, our own intelligence service may have provided him the paperwork to resettle in America and build a new life. We might have enabled a man who committed heinous war crimes to become a millionaire. And to continue his spread of hatred here, in our country."

Kay wanted to kick the water in the pool in fury. "I can't believe our intelligence agency *invited* a Nazi to come into this country. Then helped Miller slip through immigration."

"He was not the only one," Mrs. R said sadly. "Sandy intimated there were several."

Mrs. R added, "Though Sandy confirmed it, there may be no proof that Mr. Miller was at Buchenwald. Sandy warned that any official record was probably destroyed, cleansed by the intelligence agency."

"In the name of fighting communism, Nazis are rewarded with freedom. It's insane," Kay exclaimed. Then she put her hand over her mouth.

But Mrs. R looked sympathetic at her outburst.

Kay felt a stab of horror. "The most likely reason Miller

was in Josephine's dressing room was because he knew she had recognized him. Maybe he hoped to find her there and silence her."

"Rosaleen said the door was locked. Once Mr. Miller discovered the locked door, he would know Josephine had left."

"Maybe he wanted to plant something. Like a bomb."

Mrs. R shook her head. "The police said nothing about an explosive device. I believe Detective Connor would have mentioned it."

"The terrible thing is that the police could twist this to give Rosaleen yet another motive. She caught Müller in the dressing room, and he felt he had to silence her. She gets the gun and shoots him. Poor Rosaleen has too many motives. It would make so much more sense if Müller was the villain," Kay said. "But he is the victim."

"That is an interesting observation," Mrs. Roosevelt said.

Kay swirled the water with her feet. "I'm sorry to say it, but I think Mr. Gros is the most likely suspect. It must have made him furious to see Müller alive and successful in the United States."

She found her throat was tight. "Should we tell this to the police? I want Rosaleen to be freed but I—I really don't want it to be Mr. Gros. He was so happy to meet Josephine. I don't want to think of him being arrested, after all that he had endured . . . oh!"

Mrs. R looked at her questioningly.

"What if Mr. Gros did it to protect Josephine?"

"Josephine suggested that perhaps Mr. Gros saw Franz Müller return to her dressing room and followed him."

Kay frowned. "I could imagine Mr. Gros shooting a man, but would he be ruthless enough to pin the blame on Rosaleen?"

"That part is confusing. But we do not really know him," Mrs. R said.

Kay nodded. "I remember how blank and expressionless Mr. Gros was when he told me about his family's fate. He reflected no emotion at all. That had to mean there was a lot of emotion seething inside him, emotion he was keeping hidden . . ."

"That is very interesting, Kay."

"I want to like Mr. Gros, but— "

"But?" Mrs. R prompted.

"It would be a better solution than Rosaleen," she admitted.

"For us, yes. I am sure the police will question all the guests at the party that night."

Kay wasn't so sure. "We haven't been questioned. No one has asked for my statement."

"That is true. We were not there at the time of the murder, but we did attend the party," Mrs. Roosevelt mused.

"Is it because the police don't think we could possibly be guilty or because they don't think Rosaleen could possibly be innocent?" Kay asked, then added, "Sorry, Mrs. Roosevelt. You don't know the answer to that either."

"I understand, though," Mrs. Roosevelt said.

A shadow fell across the water of the pool. Kay looked up in surprise and noticed Mrs. R did so too.

Tim O'Malley stood at the end of the pool. He looked grim. Then he looked shocked as he realized she and Mrs. R had their skirts pulled up to their knees and their bare legs in the water.

Eleanor had heard the soft crunch of footsteps and looked back to see Tim O'Malley approaching. The tall lights around the pool lit up his face. The starkness of light and shadow enhanced his handsome appearance.

But the look on his face tore at her heart. Haggard did not begin to describe it. He looked as if he was in great pain.

Then his brows shot up. "I never expected to see you ladies sitting on the edge of the pool."

"It's very refreshing," Eleanor said. "But you look as if you have bad news."

"There's some good news. And some serious bad news," he said, his voice deep and soft. He sat down on the pool deck, but kept his trouser-clad legs—and shoe-clad feet—out of the water.

"I believe we are ready to hear it, Tim," Eleanor said.

"I know you feared that Mike Connor wouldn't check the fingerprints on the gun, Kay, but he did. He pulled a favor and had the police's expert expedite it. I just talked to him about the results. This is off the record. He would lose his job if his superiors found out he gave me this information."

"I understand. I will never reveal that Detective Connor gave you this information. What did he learn?" Kay asked. Eleanor heard the hope in her voice, but it was wary.

"Rosaleen's fingerprints were not on the gun."

Kay let out a sigh, then swiftly asked, "Were there any fingerprints? I hope there were! It is the only thing that will exonerate Rosaleen."

"There were prints. Not Rosaleen's. Problem is that the ones on the grip were smudged. Connor agreed with me—that likely means someone wearing gloves fired the shot."

"Oh dear. Was Rosaleen wearing gloves?" Eleanor asked.

"She had a pair of small white gloves. But she didn't have them on when she was brought in. Mike Connor remembers that. He found them in Rosaleen's handbag, which is in evidence. Problem is that his superiors say she was likely wearing them and took them off after firing the shot."

"Oh no," Kay whispered.

"Is there not a test that can be done on the gloves to determine if they were worn when the gun was fired?" Eleanor asked. She had heard something of this.

"There is," Tim agreed. "It is a test for gunshot residue. It's called a GSR test."

"Is it definitive?" Eleanor asked.

"I can explain how it works."

Eleanor watched Kay prop her chin on her fist. When a technical explanation was introduced, Kay was fascinated.

"When a gun fires and the primer mix burns, it forms a blast plume that escapes all available openings on the gun," Tim explained. "It solidifies on surfaces around it. The compound includes particles from the primer and the propellant. Trace amounts of the compound can be found on the hands or clothing of a person in the vicinity of a discharged weapon."

"How is it tested?"

"Chemistry. The hand or clothing is covered with a thin layer of paraffin. When the paraffin cools, it is broken off, and it's treated with an acid solution that contains a reagent that detects nitrates or nitrites. If the result is positive, it appears as blue flecks on the wax."

"Very clever," Eleanor murmured. "Is it a trustworthy test?"

"It's been used in the U.S. since the early nineteen thirties. But the lab man at my old precinct said it can react to nitrates present on the skin or clothes for other reasons. Nitrates can come from fertilizers, wastewater, sewers."

"I don't think Rosaleen stopped to clean the toilet," Kay said.

"But it means a false positive is possible. That is worrisome," Eleanor said. "When did Detective Connor think he could have results?"

"He's going to push to have the test run tomorrow. His argument is that if Rosaleen Davis is cleared of suspicion, it means someone else is guilty. Time wasted is time that allows evidence from the real shooter to degrade. And by now, the shooter will have washed his or her hands and clothes."

"Do you think it will be a fair and legitimate test?" Eleanor asked.

"They seem to be grasping at straws to *make* her guilty," Kay added fiercely.

"Mike Connor will be on the straight and narrow," Tim said. "Mike gave me more details at lunch. A lot of this information will end up in the newspapers, but he'd still like to keep it under wraps that he is the source."

"Of course," Eleanor said, and Kay echoed her words.

"The victim was shot at a range of about fifteen feet. Mike figures Frank Miller was in the dressing room, standing near the drinks cart. He was facing the door, so he was facing Rosaleen when she walked in."

Eleanor nodded. She had been correct in that conjecture.

Tim leaned over and dipped his finger in the water of the pool. He made a wet dot on the white-painted surround of the pool. Then a second dot at a short distance away, and a few inches toward Kay from the first dot. "From the position of Miller's body, Mike figures he was not standing in line of sight of the hallway. Mike thinks that was why Rosaleen Davis continued into the room. She wouldn't have seen Miller when she first opened the door. She had to step in to see him. The angle also means the killer had to be in the doorway to take the shot. The killer had to be close behind Rosaleen when the trigger was pulled. The loudness of the shot would have left her ears ringing. It would have shocked her. Mike says her statement that she was frozen makes sense. The loud sound and pain to her ears would have immobilized her.

"Since she was in the room, it was possible for the door to be slammed shut behind her. She said she left the key in the lock as she stepped in because she intended to grab her handbag, relock the door, and run up to meet Josephine outside. The killer could easily turn the key, locking her in the room, after tossing the gun in there."

"Her story makes sense," Eleanor mused.

"Mike thinks it does. But the thing is, Rosaleen isn't being released."

"What?" Kay cried.

"Mike told me that Josephine went with Stephen Roberts and the lawyer to try to get Rosaleen out."

"Stephen went too?" Eleanor asked, surprised.

"Mike said he was really shaken up and it sounded like he had insisted on going along."

"The serious bad news is that they refused to release her. No bail hearing. The lawyer's fuming, but they aren't letting her go yet."

"I was afraid of this," Eleanor murmured.

"I ran into Josephine right now," Tim said. "She isn't performing tonight since the Copa City Club will be closed as a crime scene for tonight."

"I wonder what will happen," Kay said. "Maybe her show will be canceled?"

"I doubt it. The manager told Josephine that ticket sales are going through the roof. She asked me to pass along a request. Would we join her for dinner tonight? Here at the Delano."

"An excellent idea," Eleanor said.

"She suggested we meet at her suite for cocktails first, in an hour."

"I must go upstairs and change," Eleanor said.

Eleanor smiled as Tim jumped to his feet, then gallantly held out his hand to help her up. Once on her feet, she knew Tim would assist Kay. She slipped her shoes on, not bothering with her stockings.

Blithely she said, "I will head up to the suite quickly. I wish to jot down some of my thoughts from this evening. You two can be . . . more leisurely."

Then she added, "Do you know what I think is curious? Why Rosaleen did not feel worried about leaving Josephine alone outside. She did not insist Josephine come with her. She hurried away, alone, to the dressing room."

Kay gazed upward. "I hadn't thought of that," she said.

"It is something to ponder."

"Mrs. Roosevelt, you told Sandy that you can't stand by while there is a miscarriage of justice taking place. I think we need to find the killer," Kay said passionately.

Eleanor saw Tim's expression. He looked worried. But then, last time, he had saved Kay's life.

Yet Kay was right. Eleanor was gravely worried that a proper investigation by the police would not take place.

But first . . .

"I should hurry upstairs and make some notes," Eleanor said. "Jot down what we have learned. And record several points of curiosity."

Eleanor almost broke into a run. It was a lovely evening. Though there was a great strain upon them all, she wanted to give Kay and Tim time together.

She had been on her own for six years, but she had good friends who were men. There was Earl Miller, who had been her bodyguard while Franklin was the governor of New York and they lived in Albany. He had become a longtime friend. And there was David Gurewitsch, her personal physician who was also a dear and close friend.

Kay needed such a friend. Tim, Eleanor felt, was the perfect choice.

Eleanor paused at the door to the lobby. She smiled as she saw Tim help Kay to her feet.

CHAPTER 15

It seems to me important that there be no greater stress laid on our divisions, but that we stress as much as possible our agreements.

—Eleanor Roosevelt, *Courage in a Dangerous World*

"I know why Rosaleen isn't being released!"

Her voice ringing out passionately, Josephine paced angrily on the carpet in her hotel suite. She wore an off-white Dior gown, fitted perfectly to her figure.

The dress left Kay awestruck. She wasn't proud of feeling a stab of envy.

After leaving the pool, Kay had changed in her room into an emerald-green satin cocktail dress. Tim had met her and Mrs. R in Mrs. R's suite. Tim wore a dark gray suit suitable for the Delano's restaurant and Kay consciously ignored how attractive he looked wearing it.

"I know Josephine will want to hear the details of my conversation with Sandy," Mrs. R prophesied. "I don't want to shock Stephen with the truth about his stepfather just yet. I think that should be handled with more delicacy. Tim, would you go to Stephen's room and give me a few minutes to speak with Josephine before you men come to her suite?"

Tim agreed. "I'll talk with him while you talk with Josephine, then we'll come to Josephine's suite and go to dinner from there."

Tim left, and Kay accompanied Mrs. Roosevelt to Josephine's suite. The minute Mrs. Roosevelt explained what she learned from Mr. Sandiston of the State Department, Josephine had erupted out of the armchair in which she had been curled up.

"I knew it," she declared. "At first, I thought it was because the police weren't going to look any further once they could pin the murder on a Black person," she said. "There is a mob down at the police station with placards, demanding that Rosaleen be executed. I just thought it was racism, pure and simple. But this is worse!"

Kay couldn't see what was worse, but Josephine explained, "The government won't want the American people to know they brought Nazis into the country. If Müller was murdered because he was a Nazi, that's why Rosaleen isn't being released. The government is using her as a scapegoat. If a Black woman is executed for the murder, then no one finds out the government helped a death camp commandant."

Josephine flung her arms wide. "Maybe the government got rid of him. And must hide their crime."

"I do not think the government would murder a man on American soil," Mrs. Roosevelt said. "And they would not pin the crime on Rosaleen. If there were such clandestine actions, Miller could have been killed in an 'accident.'"

"Well, I fired that pricey Miami lawyer and his silly seersucker suit," Josephine said. "I could tell right away that he thought Rosaleen was guilty. He talked about her making a plea bargain. What I need is a scrappy lawyer who believes in his heart and soul that Rosaleen is innocent and will fight to the end to set her free!"

Josephine took a breath. "I'm worried about Stephen. White as a sheet with worry, he said, 'Maybe Rosaleen should take a plea bargain.'"

Kay was shocked, "Stephen suggested she actually go to jail?"

"He fears she will be found guilty. I said, 'When the police have the results of the GSR test, they will be forced to admit she is innocent and release her.' "

"What did Stephen say?"

"He poured himself a stiff drink."

Kay shook her head. Stephen worked for the CIA. Shouldn't he be mentally tough and strong?

The room telephone rang. Kay was going to answer it, acting as a secretary, but Josephine swept up the receiver.

"You must come to dinner, Stephen," Josephine exclaimed into the telephone. "Starving yourself helps no one. Neither does nursing your pain with a bottle of whiskey. Put that darling Mr. O'Malley on the telephone and I will insist to him that he make you come, even if he must knock you out and carry you over his shoulder."

Kay was impressed when Tim and Stephen arrived at the door mere minutes later. Stephen had relented and come to Josephine's suite. He had not forced Tim to knock him out and carry him in the elevator, fireman style.

They went down in the elevator to the lobby. But as they entered the restaurant, Kay heard murmurs rush over the room.

Kay was walking beside Josephine Baker, and she saw the singer stiffen and lift her head high. Josephine waved at several patrons, wearing a confident smile. But Kay knew something was wrong.

The maître d' led them toward a table at the back.

"We would prefer a table that is not by the kitchen," Stephen said coolly. "Josephine Baker and Mrs. Franklin D. Roosevelt do not belong at the back of the restaurant."

"Of course not, sir." The maître d' changed course and threaded them between the tables to one with a view of something other than the kitchen doors.

The two very famous women said nothing. The maître d' held

out a chair for Mrs. Roosevelt. Stephen did the same for Josephine Baker.

Tim held out a chair for her.

Stephen tapped his foot as waiters hurried to and fro, but not one came to take their order.

Josephine's smile disappeared. "Is this going to be like the Stork Club again?" she murmured. "Though I was allowed to order food there. It just wasn't going to come."

Tim frowned. "I can't believe they would treat you and Mrs. Roosevelt badly."

"Miami Beach is segregated. I am not oblivious to the way people are looking at me. I am willing to make another citizen's arrest, if I must," Josephine said, with pride. "Of course, I wouldn't want to ruin your evening, Eleanor."

"You would not. I would be happy to help you."

Stephen gave a small, impatient wave, and a waiter came, profuse with apologies. Orders were taken. Drinks came quickly.

But then the nightmare began.

"Is she gonna eat in here?" a man demanded loudly. He sat two tables away. "Her kind belongs in the kitchen," he snapped.

Kay cringed, horrified. Josephine did not react. She kept her head up, and her smile did not waver.

"They can't mean to serve her," his wife added. Kay noted that his blond wife was tanned a coppery color. Tanning was becoming a sign that one had money and leisure. How ridiculous to make her skin brown while complaining about the color of someone else's skin.

Another man, seated across the room, stated in a booming voice, "What is she doing in here? Miami is a segregated city. Maître d'!" He continued to shout until the maître d' glided over. Kay saw the sweat on the hotel employee's brow.

"You're breaking the law here," the man bellowed.

"I will bring the manager, sir."

"You'd better. Or I'm calling the cops."

Josephine sipped her cocktail. She was speaking to ER, and Kay saw how desperately she was trying to ignore the commotion.

Kay began to rise to her feet. She was going to tell them all to shut up. Tim put his hand on her arm. "You should leave it."

"I won't. I *can't.*" She launched to her feet. All eyes turned to her now—angry eyes, hate-filled eyes. She tried to hold her head as high as Josephine's. "Mrs. Bouillon is a guest of the hotel, with every right to eat in the restaurant. She is a great talent. You should be honored she is here."

She sat back down.

Chairs scraped. "We aren't going to stay in here," a man declared loudly, as if he wanted everyone's attention. Overweight, balding, and pasty-faced, he got to his feet. Instead of pulling out his wife's chair, he let her fend for herself while he glowered at Josephine and ER.

Grasping a knitted shawl, the wife scurried to her husband.

"We don't have to eat with people who shouldn't be in this restaurant by law," he snapped.

The couple had to pass by them. He said something terrible—and the way he did it, believing he had every right to insult Josephine and ER, made Kay see red.

She jumped to her feet again. "You can't speak that way to an international star and to a former First Lady of the United States. You should apologize!" she cried.

She saw a look of panic on Tim's face.

This was what usually cost her a job—speaking out.

But then Tim began to applaud. Softly, but loud enough that everyone could hear.

Stephen got to his feet. "I agree. You owe these fine ladies an apology," he said.

The couple hurried toward the entrance. "You are running away like cowards," Kay declared. "We can see what you are made of. Both women at this table are courageous. You aren't!"

The couple scurried out as fast as they could. Two other couples slunk away, quietly, hugging the back of the restaurant, as if trying to disappear.

"I'm sorry for the display I just made," Kay said as she sat down. She feared the confrontation had spoiled the meal.

"Don't be sorry," Josephine said huskily. "Thank you, Miss Thompson, for standing up."

"I couldn't sit in silence," Kay said, awkwardly.

"Your courage to speak up is admirable," Mrs. Roosevelt said. "You are right. We cannot be silent."

Josephine sighed deeply. "Despite the small-mindedness of some of the diners, I wish Rosaleen were here to dine with us. I cannot think the food she is being served is good. I remember what it was like to have very little to eat. I cannot rest until she is free from prison. Firstly, I am going to hire another lawyer. One that doesn't automatically believe Rosaleen is guilty."

"Yes, you need a lawyer who believes in his client," Mrs. Roosevelt said. "Rosaleen impressed me greatly. She is a very intelligent young woman. Women admitted to law school at Howard University are amongst the best scholars."

Josephine beamed with pride. "That is true. Rosaleen was one of two women in her freshman class. Her female classmate was a Wac major."

"You were a Wac also, Josephine," Stephen noted.

"A second lieutenant of the French women's air force corps. It is the role of which I am most proud," she said.

"Rosaleen's mother must be very worried about her daughter. I believe you said she used to perform with you on the chorus line," Mrs. R said.

Josephine lifted her hands in a helpless gesture. "I have not seen her for many years—since we were both nineteen. I do not know where she is. Rosaleen came to me when I was performing here, at the Copa City Club, last December. Her mother was known as Florence Willis back then. Willis was her maiden name, and everyone called her 'Flossie.' I don't know her married name and Rosaleen never told me where she lived. Rosaleen told me that Florence's marriage was unhappy, and her father left while Florence was pregnant. A lot of times that means good riddance to bad rubbish."

Kay nodded.

"But it is heart-wrenching that this man turned his back on his infant daughter," Josephine added. "I asked Rosaleen to let me contact her mother, but Rosaleen refused. She doesn't want her mother to see her in jail. I told Rosaleen that her mother will read about her arrest in the newspaper—it is national news. But Rosaleen refused to budge. She can be stubborn."

"I am sure her mother would want to give her support," ER said. "A mother can bear anything to provide support and love."

Kay knew Mrs. Roosevelt must be thinking as a mother—her four adult boys served in World War Two.

"I'm sorry I lost touch with Flossie," Josephine admitted. "We parted ways when I left for Paris. I sent some letters back to her, but I guess she moved on, because they were returned to me unopened."

"Did you compete with her to go to Paris?" Kay asked.

"You think that is why she didn't write to me? That she was jealous? We didn't try out for the part. Caroline Dudley Reagan, the producer, asked me to be part of the show. She liked my 'comedy girl' routine, and I went along because I was fed up with segregated America. I wanted to bring Flossie. Having a friend with me would have made the adventure more fun.

"Flossie was beautiful. I thought she had a better singing voice than me, back when we were teenagers. I had to learn to project my voice. When I started singing, my voice was high-pitched and not very strong. But I got laughs and the applause. Caroline said people came to see me, and that was why she wanted me in the show. There was only room in her budget for one, she said, so Flossie couldn't come."

Josephine sighed softly. "Seeing Rosaleen made me happy. I missed my old friend. Rosaleen looks just like her mother."

"It is so unfortunate Rosaleen had to stop her studies at Howard," Mrs. R said.

"She had run out of money. On the spot, I offered her a job as my assistant. I offered a good salary because I need to work with someone I trust. Even so, it was my hope Rosaleen would eventually go back to Howard and complete her studies. But I don't know if I can hope for that now, unless she is proven innocent."

"Rosaleen's arrest has been in the newspapers. It makes one wonder why Rosaleen's mother has not come to see her," Mrs. R said.

"It is strange," Josephine agreed.

"It can't be that her mother doesn't care," Kay said. "Rosaleen told me that her mother was working in a terrible job. Perhaps she has no money to travel."

"If she needed to travel, I would help her," Josephine said. "She would need only to ask."

"Maybe she is too proud," Kay added.

"*Peut-être*," Josephine said. "My mother was like that. After I was a success in Paris, I bought her a house and she refused it! At least she let me contribute so my siblings could go to school. It was the saddest day for me when my youngest sister, Willie Mae, died in December of 1932. She was twenty-two."

"I am so sorry," Mrs. R said.

Stephen signaled the waiter for another drink.

Josephine said to him, "You have hope, don't you? No more nonsense about accepting a plea bargain! I will fight for what is right and true—Rosaleen's complete exoneration."

Kay wanted to applaud.

Stephen looked abashed. "You're right, Jo. That's what I want."

Kay turned toward the entrance. In the innate way she had,

Kay sensed that a handsome man had just entered the dining room. Her gaze riveted on him.

Tall, blond, with a blade of a nose, piercing eyes, handsome features, the man wore a well-cut dark blue suit tailored to enhance his broad shoulders and trim waist. He was too old for her—in his forties. But he was the sort of man who was even more appealing with a few years of experience behind him. He looked . . . intriguing.

He was in conversation with the maître d'. She supposed he was asking for a table. Curiously, he was on his own.

Kay's fork fell to the plate with a clatter as the man came toward them with determined strides. Panic made her shoulders rigid. What if he meant harm?

Tim and Stephen noticed. In unison, they were pushing back their chairs, ready for a confrontation, when Josephine exclaimed, "*Jacques est arrivé!*"

CHAPTER 16

I remember the determination of the younger people that the war just won should really be "a war to end war."

—Eleanor Roosevelt, My Day, November 13, 1946

The handsome man's blue eyes glowed with delight as he bent over Josephine's hand. He bestowed a gallant kiss that made Kay sigh. Josephine laughed and wrapped him in her embrace.

As she released him, she told the table, "This is Monsieur Jacques Abtey. I suppose it is safe now to say he was my handler in the war. We carried out many missions together for *le* Deuxième Bureau."

"Jacques, this is Mrs. Eleanor Roosevelt, Kay Thompson, Tim O'Malley, and Stephen Roberts, Rosaleen's fiancé."

Jacques Abtey gave a nod toward the two men, though Stephen had lifted his glass and was draining it, the glass obscuring his face as he drew in the last drop. Mr. Abtey shook Mrs. Roosevelt's hand. He bent over Kay's hand and when he murmured the words, "*Enchanté, mademoiselle*," it took her breath away.

"Jacques recruited me as an 'honorable correspondent' at the beginning of the war. A fancy name for work as an unpaid spy." Josephine motioned to a waiter. "I will have the waiter bring another chair. Jacques, will you join us?"

Stephen had stood, and was looking away from them, toward the door—and the bar, Kay noted.

"Have my seat. Thanks for getting me out of my room, Jo, but I don't feel up to dinner and conversation right now. I need some time alone," Stephen said.

"You are not going to go and drink, are you?"

"To be honest, I want to make a few telephone calls from my room."

As Jacques Abtey went to thank him for the seat, Stephen was already walking away, his shoulders hunched. He looked like a man under great strain.

"I am sorry. He did not mean to be rude," Josephine said.

"This can't be easy for him, knowing his fiancée is in jail," Jacques said. "You told me he was a soldier. He's seen hell. Now he must feel like he is living through it again—and so is the woman he loves."

Josephine nodded. "I will save them both."

Taking the seat, the handsome Jacques Abtey smiled, gazing at Josephine with admiration and respect. "You will. I know you. And I remember that when I met you, you were judging me even as I was assessing your suitability."

The waiter hurried forward, producing a menu for Mr. Abtey. Josephine requested another bottle of champagne and a glass for Monsieur Abtey. After the waiter departed, she said, "*You* surprised me. I expected a secret service agent would look like . . . Inspector Maigret, the character in the novels written by my friend Georges Simenon. Or be short, paunchy, with a smelly cigar, a bowler hat, and jowls. I did not expect to be faced with a young, blond, athletic man, bursting with life."

Kay watched Mr. Abtey blush.

"I thought your first impression of me was not so favorable," Josephine teased.

"That was not true. I knew the dangers of the work—a misstep could lead to death. The first time I saw Josephine," he said to the table, "was at Beau Chêne, a grand villa in Le Vésinet, a suburb cradled by a bend in the Seine, where the wealthy of Paris lived. I thought she would be reclining on a chaise in a designer gown, weighed down with jewels. Instead, she emerged from her garden in trousers and a battered felt hat, clutching a tin full of snails for her ducks. But when I explained what would be expected of you as an honorable correspondent, I was left speechless when you said that you were prepared to give your life for France. As you spoke, I could not look away from your beautiful, misty eyes."

Josephine laughed, delighted.

Jacques nodded. "She convinced me at once," Jacques said. "But then her dangerous life began. Traveling to Lisbon, Josephine carried important secret information written in invisible ink on her sheet music."

"I pinned scraps of paper containing information to my underclothes." Josephine finished her glass of champagne. "No customs official had the courage to strip me to my underclothes to search me."

"Her work was vital to the war. Even when she took ill and was in hospital for many, many months, close to death, her concern was for victory. For freedom. She held meetings in her hospital room."

The waiter returned and took Mr. Abtey's order. He promised that Mr. Abtey's dish would be prepared swiftly. The other meals would be out in minutes; the chef would ensure the wait for Mr. Abtey would not be long.

"Thank you," Josephine said. The waiter hastened to refill her champagne flute. Then he refilled Kay's. She sipped slowly. Bubbles did go to her head.

There was a deep, powerful relationship between Josephine and Jacques Abtey. When they gazed at each other, wearing soft smiles, Kay knew they shared a history. But Josephine married Monsieur Bouillon after the war. A simple gold wedding ring adorned the appropriate finger of Mr. Abtey's left hand.

Why had these two people not married? They obviously cared about each other deeply.

"I have been in America for several months, staying close to Josephine on her tour. I remained in New York for a few days and arrived today."

"On the flight?" Mrs. R asked.

He nodded.

Tim looked surprised. But would Tim have noticed this man? Kay thought. She would have—in a heartbeat. But a man might not.

"Jacques flew to New York from Paris, because I asked him to come. I need his support in my fight against segregation. And Stephen arranged for him to testify to clear my name of accusations of being a Communist. He did so admirably. He told them of my work for the Allies in the war."

"I told them about your commitment to justice, no matter what the cost might be."

Josephine laughingly said, "Many presumed Jacques would ask to marry me after the war. But he did not believe he could live as 'Mr. Baker.' He has found a wife to make him happy. They have a child, and they live in a house on my estate at Les Milandes."

That was the answer to the puzzle. Kay was astonished at how friendly Josephine was with the man who had refused to marry her despite the closeness that had blossomed through the war.

"I'd love to hear about your wartime adventures," Tim said. "If you are allowed to talk about them," he added.

"When I first arrived in Algiers, in North Africa, I was arrested at once," Josephine said. Abtey refilled her champagne.

"As a spy?" Kay gasped.

"No. The managers of the Opéra de Marseille, who had claimed they would let me out of my contract, decided to sue me for 400,000 francs for breach of contract."

"That's terrible." To Kay, 400,000 of anything sounded like a lot.

"It took eight days to straighten it out, then I was able to set out for Casablanca. We traveled by train," Josephine said.

"During which your menagerie was running wild on the train," Abtey said with a soft smile.

"We lost a few of them. The white mice disappeared on the train. I felt it was a bad omen. And indeed, Jacques was blocked from traveling from Casablanca to Lisbon. No amount of buttering up would help. I had to go alone."

"Your first solo mission. And when we were reunited in Casablanca, you were exhausted."

The tales thrilled Kay. Josephine went alone to Marrakesh, known as "the Red City." She befriended Si Thami El Glaoui, the governor of Marrakesh, and stayed as a guest at his brother-in-law's villa. "Si" was a term of respect, equivalent to chief.

"It was a residence worthy of *One Thousand and One Nights*," Josephine said. "It had a courtyard that held an enchanted garden with a fountain and orange trees and exotic birds."

"Josephine went on clandestine missions of mercy, wrangling Spanish Moroccan passports for refugees from Europe fleeing the death camps. She went in for a medical test and after that, she developed peritonitis." Jacques's expression grew grave. "We didn't know. Josephine had crippling pain. I took the first train to Casablanca to find a clinic, and returned to her, fraught with worry. I could not find an ambulance available for the drive into Casablanca. Josephine had to lie on a large inflatable inner tube in the back of a car, as the car jolted over potholed roads and dirt tracks. Dr. Henri Comte, of the Comte Clinic, took us in. So began our struggle with death. The rage with which we said no to death, and our unshakeable will and faith was all that could save Josephine. As she became better, her room in the clinic became a safe meeting place for clandestine operations."

"While I was in the hospital, Jacques could not always be with me. He had missions to carry out. He made pacts with the dangerous smugglers of Tangier."

Jacques looked surprised. "How do you know about those times? I couldn't tell you."

"I found out."

Jacques gave a rueful grin that was charming. "I expect you asked some of the men who came to visit you, men of the Bureau, or the SAS or OSS." He explained to Kay that the OSS was the Office of Strategic Services, the intelligence agency created by the United States in the second world war, the precursor to the CIA. The SAS were British forces operating in North Africa. Mrs. R knew about these, of course, but Kay was fascinated to learn more.

"Those men were supposed to keep secrets, but I suspect you proved irresistible."

Josephine merely smiled. Kay saw the power Josephine had—the power to enthrall.

"Those were dark times. As Josephine said, I was working with smugglers," Jacques said. "With their help, the Bodden system was destroyed." When he saw they didn't know about it, Jacques Abtey explained, "The Bodden was the code name for an infrared surveillance device. If it hadn't been sabotaged in an explosion set by the SOE, it would have used infrared beams to detect any ships passing through the Strait of Gibraltar at night. A potential disaster for the planned Allied landings to liberate North Africa and move into Europe."

He took a long sip of his champagne. His expression became haunted. "The Abwehr retaliated. The Abwehr was the Nazi's military intelligence, also carrying out sabotage. They planted a diplomatic bag filled with explosives aboard the Tangier-Gibraltar ferry, killing twenty-nine people. I believe it was the work of an Abwehr saboteur known as the 'Ghost.' Despite the moniker, that person was no wraith, but a flesh-and-blood person who was ruthless, and who savored death."

He paused. "I tried to track down the Ghost in Tangier, but I had no luck. My allies in the world of smuggling had colorful names. The right-hand man to the 'King of all Smugglers' had the evocative code name 'Subhumanity,' for example. But no one could lead me to the Ghost."

Kay thought how fortunate they were that people such as Mr. Abtey, Josephine, Tim, and Stephen had fought in the war.

"You were arrested by the Gestapo, Jacques," Josephine said.

Kay gave a gasp.

Jacques turned to her. "You wonder how I am here now? I had to play for time. Little did I know I was placed in *Zelle Null*, which meant Cell Zero. No one came out of Cell Zero alive. But one night my jailer, one of the Amazigh people whom the French called 'Berbers,' opened my cell door. He had not exchanged a word with me, but he threw a bundle of clothes at me. I put on the traditional women's Berber robe and face veil. Even a pair of lady's slippers. We escaped by pretending I was one of the cooks and I accompanied Abderrahman out of the prison. We escaped into a forest of evergreen oaks, where I changed into the dress of a Berber male, complete with a curved dagger. Two mules in riding gear were tethered, waiting for us. The escape was arranged by the great and powerful sherif, a man whose influence extended across the tribes of the Rif mountains. That is the strip of rugged coast where Morocco meets the Mediterranean. The allegiance of the tribes was key, as control of the coast was vital to a successful landing. For either the Allies or the Axis forces.

"That the sherif helped me escape was a good sign that they would help us. But as I was making for a remote mountain farmstead to hide, I asked Abderrahman what he thought of the

Germans. 'They are lions,' he said. 'Do you think they will win this war?' I asked. 'Yes,' he said. He believed they would."

There was silence for several seconds.

Jacques Abtey reached for Josephine's hand.

"But men like you . . . and you, Monsieur O'Malley . . . and Stephen. They ensured it was not to end that way," Josephine said.

"So did women like you," Abtey said.

The food arrived and conversation halted while each person received their plates.

Kay glanced at Jacques Abtey beneath her lashes, pretending to be absorbed in her food.

This man was a French spy, she thought. He said he just arrived in Miami. But what if that wasn't true? What if he had come on an earlier flight, perhaps the day before. What if he was already here on the night of Josephine's party, and he wanted revenge on a Nazi killer?

"I have not spoken to Jacques in many weeks," Josephine said to Mrs. R as they were leaving the restaurant. "But when I asked him to travel here to support me in my fight against segregation, he did not hesitate."

"Did you tell Monsieur Abtey about the letters?" Mrs. R asked.

"Yes. I telephoned him after I received the third letter. I wished to warn him in case he was afraid of the risk and decided not to travel. But that was not necessary. Jacques is fearless."

"Did you mention Mr. Miller?" Mrs. R asked.

Kay was startled. Was Mrs. Roosevelt wondering if Jacques Abtey was the murderer, hunting down a Nazi criminal, just as she had wondered?

"I spoke of the men who had sent me many flowers and clamored to come to my dressing room since I believed one of them could be a suspect."

"I see," Mrs. Roosevelt said.

She could not say more, because many young members of the AAUN marched into the lobby, all talking at once. Alice, Benny, and Neeve were at the front of the crowd, carrying placards that read FREE ROSALEEN DAVIS.

They all stopped, gazing in surprise at Josephine Baker, who stood beside Jacques Abtey, her hand resting on his arm.

"Mrs. Baker," dark-haired Alice said. "You are staying here? At the Delano?"

"I am. What is your name?"

"Alice."

Josephine took Alice's hand. "You are fighting to free my assistant, Rosaleen. How good of you."

"We protested at the police station until they sent officers out. One grabbed Benny's sign from him and hit him with it."

Benny pointed to his forehead. There was a cut, a smear of blood and a growing bruise.

"Oh dear," Mrs. Roosevelt said. "I don't want you to get hurt."

"They started it," Alice said. "We were peaceful, just marching and chanting."

Benny had his pipe clenched between his teeth. Around it, he said, "I bet the KKK is behind it. Maybe they killed the guy to railroad Rosaleen Davis." He looked to Josephine and blushed. "Maybe they did it to hurt you, ma'am."

"That is a good theory," Alice said.

Benny preened. He puffed out his chest.

"But don't you think it's kind of convoluted?" Kay pointed out. "It would be easier to make Josephine the victim. Getting Rosaleen Davis arrested for murder hasn't made Josephine back down. This has made her more determined to fight."

"Yes," Josephine declared.

Benny looked crestfallen that his theory did not hold water.

In her clear, dulcet tones, ER advised, "We will work within the law to free Rosaleen. We must not incite violence."

"We should be willing to do whatever it takes to get the cops to listen," Benny said, stubbornly.

Benny was filled with bravado. Kay knew the type. She suspected he had been scared when he first felt blood after being struck, but she did admire his willingness to fight for Rosaleen.

"That is not wise," Mrs. Roosevelt said firmly. "The protest must be peaceful."

Blond-haired Neeve said, "If we don't stop it, Rosaleen Davis will be wrongfully convicted. Maybe executed. I agree with Benny. Whatever it takes."

Mrs. Roosevelt suggested they gather in her suite for drinks and discussion. They excitedly agreed. This was something Mrs. R loved, Kay had learned. She loved to sit with a group of young people and listen to their ideas.

As they headed to the elevators, Kay felt sick to her stomach. She said to Mrs. Roosevelt, "What if Rosaleen is convicted? What if she is sentenced to be executed?" She wanted to believe that could not happen to an innocent person.

But she thought of Josephine, fighting for Willie McGee. Who had been executed. Even Josephine, an international star, hadn't been able to stop it.

An instinct made her look up and gaze across the lobby. Tim was approaching them, his expression cold, grim, carved of stone. There was no glitter in his green eyes, they looked empty.

"What is it?" Kay asked impulsively.

"Mike Connor left a message for me," he said in a low voice. Josephine moved closer with Jacques Abtey. Mrs. Roosevelt exchanged a glance with him, then herded the group of young people onto the elevator with her. The door closed behind them, and they went up toward Mrs. R's floor.

Tim said, "I used the phone at the reception desk to call Mike right back, at his home. Rosaleen Davis's clothes, hands, and the gloves in her purse tested negative for gunshot residue."

"*Mon Dieu!* Of course they did!" Josephine exclaimed. "We must go and collect her at once."

Tim shook his head. "They aren't releasing her yet. Her skin and clothing were tested more than eight hours after the shooting. The police are considering the test inconclusive. GSR tests are no good after eight hours. Residue degrades quickly. There isn't enough left to show up."

As Kay was about to protest, Tim said, "Mike wanted to let her out on bail anyway, but it wasn't his call to make. Once the cops found out about Rosaleen's engagement to the victim's stepson, and Miller's objection to the relationship, Mike's chief figured she had a powerful motive to shoot him."

"What of his past? As a Nazi commandant?" Josephine said.

"The department chief said there was no proof Miller was a Nazi. And if he was, all the more reason he would disown his stepson for marrying Miss Davis. They don't think it was self-defense. The theory is that she arranged to meet Miller at the dressing room to kill him."

"But he was in the room when she returned for her purse," Kay said.

"Only her word for that. Mike said his chief figures she's lying. She set it up to get rid of Miller before his disinherited his stepson."

"I am horrified," Josephine said.

"But aren't people supposed to be able to post bail?" Kay asked. "Why can't she?" Kay had one brush with the law when she was arrested for taking part in a protest. She had been released, so she didn't know the intricacies.

"The DA argued that Miss Davis should remain in jail for her own protection."

"What?" Kay cried.

"He figures that if she is released, some mob might decide to carry out justice itself."

"Inspired by the KKK," Josephine said sourly. "So Rosaleen

must stay in prison, even though the negative test proves she did not shoot him!" Josephine threw up her hands.

"I guess they feel it doesn't prove anything," Kay said, mournfully.

She saw the truth now.

The only way Rosaleen would be released was if the real murderer was delivered to the police on a silver platter.

CHAPTER 17

There is a price to pay for love, for the more happiness we derive from the existence and companionship of other human beings, the more vulnerable we are when there is any cause for apprehension.

—Eleanor Roosevelt, My Day, April 1, 1939

At midnight, Kay got out of bed.

The connecting door between her hotel room and the sitting room of Mrs. Roosevelt's suite was closed but not locked. Carefully cracking it open, Kay peered into the dark of Mrs. Roosevelt's suite. It was utterly silent. Retiring before midnight was early for Mrs. Roosevelt, whose work often kept her up to one a.m. Tonight, Mrs. Roosevelt suggested an early sleep. Kay had agreed, almost crossing her fingers behind her back. She'd had an idea. A daring one. But it was worth a try.

Quietly, she closed the door between the two rooms. She wriggled into slim-fitting capri pants and pulled on a cotton blouse. Slipping her feet into sensible sneakers, she knew she didn't look glamorous. But that wasn't the point.

The knock on her door almost stopped her heart.

It wasn't on the connecting door between her room and the suite. It was on the door to the hallway.

Kay approached and looked out the peephole. Tim leaned against the door, wearing his dark gray suit.

Bringing her handbag, she wrenched open the door. "What is it?"

In a low voice, he said, "I had an idea. I wanted to go to the Copa City Club tonight."

"The club is closed."

"I'll see if I can bribe someone to let us in. The cops searched the place, but their thoroughness might have been colored by their point of view that Rosaleen is guilty."

"I had the same idea," she admitted, realizing they were thinking the same.

"I was afraid you did. And given what you are wearing, it looks like I got here just in time. You were planning to go yourself, weren't you? That would have been a foolish move. Don't you remember last time you were involved in a murder you almost got shot? You can't chase killers on your own."

She had been planning to go to his room and convince him to take her. But she didn't tell him that. "I'm not now. Since you are now here, you can drive."

She locked her door, grasped Tim's wrist and pulled him toward the elevator. "The good thing with the club being closed is that clues the police missed might still be there. We need to figure out who really shot Miller." She explained her theory that the police could not ignore a murderer delivered on the proverbial silver platter.

He nodded as the door elevators opened. He held the lobby doors open, and they stepped out into the soft, warm air of the night. Kay expected it would be still and quiet, but vehicles zipped down the main artery. There was something about heat at night that made you want to be active.

The young valet who fetched cars was still on duty. He had unruly blond hair, a sunburn, and he barely looked old enough to drive.

They waited for him to bring the sedan around front. Kay gazed up at the sky—inky black and dotted with stars. She was anxious to get to the Copa and it seemed like hours before the sedan pulled up at the curb and the valet hopped out. Tim handed him a dollar bill for a tip. The valet held her door for her while Tim hopped in the driver's side and turned over the engine. Lifting his cap, the young man closed her door.

Now that she was alone with Tim, Kay itched to talk. "I thought Mr. Gros, who was a prisoner at Buchenwald, had the best motive to shoot Franz Müller. Müller ran the death camp where he was a prisoner. His family were murdered. He must want vengeance," she said to Tim. Then added, "But at dinner, I began to think of another person who hated the Nazis. Jacques Abtey."

"He said he arrived this morning."

"And you didn't see him on the flight."

"That doesn't mean he wasn't there," Tim said. "Keep an open mind while we look at the Copa City Club. If we can get in."

Kay stayed quiet until they reached the Copa City Club. Lights shone from other popular night spots, but the Copa, being closed, was deserted.

"Last night the line stretched down the block," Kay murmured, as Tim pulled up at the curb out in front. "Spotlights illuminated the night sky. You could hear the music outside. It looks eerie."

Kay felt her hair curling in the humid, warm air, ruining her smooth chignon. She ran her hand over her slightly damp neck as Tim turned off the engine.

"It is December twenty-ninth. It's hot and sultry in Miami Beach. My partner's Tim O'Malley; the boss is Mrs. Eleanor Roosevelt. My name's Thompson. It was 12:25 a.m. when we reached the deserted parking lot of the Copa City Club—" Kay broke off, feeling Tim's stare.

"Are you imitating *Dragnet*?"

"Sort of."

"Uh-huh." He paused. "Kay, you aren't Joe Friday. And he's fiction. This 'bad guy' is real."

"I know that. I wanted to cut the tension," Kay said. She had succeeded in layering it on. Tim was watching her with a wary expression. When he got out of the car, she followed immediately, before he could insist that she stay put. They shut their doors together, the soft slam echoing in the quiet.

"It's not hot and sultry tonight. Warm, I guess. But not sultry," he said.

"Sounds better," she threw back as they walked to the club.

Tim knocked on the stage door. He rattled the handle. They could see the glow of light under the door. "The cleaners must be here, getting ready to reopen. Why isn't anyone opening the door?"

"Probably because a man got shot there last night and you are now banging on the door," Kay pointed out.

Finally, the door was thrown open. It opened outward and Tim had to jump back to avoid having his nose broken. A sweating security guard glared, his hand on his gun holster.

"What do ya want? If yer a reporter, we're not talking."

Reporters. They must have swarmed the club.

"We are— " Kay began.

"We are with Rosaleen Davis's defense team," Tim said, leaning against the door frame, so the guard could not close the door. His other hand was in the pocket of his suit jacket. "We would like to look around the scene of the crime."

"Get lost," the guard snarled. He pulled the door back. At the last moment, Tim jumped out of the way.

The door shut, but there was no click. Tim put his finger to his lips. After several moments, he grasped the handle and pulled the door open. A small piece of silver fell out.

"Piece of chewing gum. I managed to slip it in. Kept the latch from engaging. I was praying 'Sweaty Boy' wouldn't notice. But we had better be careful. He catches us, he'll call the police." He paused. "I thought about telling you to wait in the car. But you know the layout of the place. You were in the dressing room. I want you to look around. But if 'Sweaty Boy' shows, I'll keep him busy, and you get out."

"You know perfectly well I would not stay in the car," she said. She wondered if he knew that also meant she would not run and leave him to get in trouble alone.

Tim opened the door enough for Kay to slip through. He followed. As she took a step, he looked down. "Sneakers. Good. I thought you would be wearing your heels."

Sneakers had been the perfect choice, even if they did make her legs look stubby.

Keeping her voice whisper soft, Kay asked, "Why wouldn't he let us in? Was it because we are trying to prove Rosaleen innocent?"

"We don't have any official authorization to look at the place. I tried the line that we are part of the defense, but he didn't buy it."

Kay stared at the hallway. "Uh-oh. I came from the other direction."

"Maybe I should have made you stay in the car."

"Give me a minute." She reconstructed the walk from the theatre to Josephine's dressing room, then flipped it around in her head. She led Tim to the dressing room. He slipped on gloves and tried the handle. "Locked."

"I suppose it's not surprising," Kay said.

She crossed the corridor and tried the door there. Did someone hide in this room, behind this door, then shoot Miller? It swung outward, revealing a supply closet. The shelves were crammed with cleaning products, but there was enough room for a person to fit inside.

Kay stepped in. It was a tight space, and she ensured the door couldn't slam shut on her.

A glint of gold caught her eye. She crouched down, recognizing the slim, gold, tubelike shape. A woman's lipstick. It was a color she knew well. Revlon's Love That Red.

It wasn't Josephine's color.

But a man wasn't hiding in here with his lipstick.

"Why are you in a closet?"

Kay jumped. She bumped into a bucket. "Looking for clues," she gasped. She held out the lipstick.

"Does it belong to Mrs. Baker?"

"Mrs. Bouillon. I don't know, but I haven't seen her wear this color."

"Guess we'll ask."

Kay put her finger to her lips. She heard voices. "Security guard?" she whispered.

"The voices sound female," Tim said.

"The cleaning staff. Perfect. One of those ladies was outside Josephine's dressing room that night. Maybe she saw something." Kay went off, and Tim, caught by surprise, had to lope after her. With her boring flat shoes, she could move quickly.

One woman was sweeping the floor, leaning over her broom. The other was talking. The second woman was clearly no cleaning lady—a Black woman, she wore a red dress that hugged her curvaceous figure. Her black hair was straightened and secured with a red satin headband.

She gaped at Tim. "Hello, handsome, are you with the police?"

"You were on stage," Kay said. "One of Josephine's backup singers."

"I am a singer," the woman said airily. "My name is Stella Hilton." She extended her hand, and the motion threw off glittering reflections. Rings adorned every finger. Even her thumb. Tim took her hand, more of a soft squeeze, then Kay shook it firmly, as a man would.

"Were you there that night?" Tim asked.

"Are you the police?" Miss Hilton repeated.

"No. We're helping Rosaleen Davis. Trying to get the truth," Tim said. "You must have had admirers come to see you that evening, after the show. Lots of them?"

Kay admired his technique. Stella Hilton preened. "Several. But I let one stay. A good-looking man. But we were enjoying a drink when I heard a big pop. I said, 'That's champagne,' but the man said, 'That's a gunshot.' He was going to the door, the fool of a man. I said, 'What are you doing? We should stay here.' But he opened the door, and I was standing behind him."

"What did you see?" Tim asked.

"There was a man running down the hallway."

"What did he look like?"

"Tall. He wore a trench coat. A fedora. Like Humphrey Bogart."

"He looked like Humphrey Bogart?" Tim asked.

Kay felt an affinity to Miss Hilton, using movies as a reference, because everyone knew Humphrey Bogart. "He was dressed like Bogart, you mean. Did you see his face?" she asked.

"No. Just his back. I pulled the fool of a man I was with back into the room. 'Maybe Josephine Baker got assassinated,' I said. The man looked scared as a rabbit and he sputtered, 'I'm not hanging around for someone to shoot us. I've got a wife.' That was the first I'd heard about that! But he was right, I didn't want to hang around. And I figured I was safer with him than without him, even if he was a lying, two-timing swine, so I grabbed his hand and we hightailed it out of there."

"Where did the man go?" Tim asked.

"Back to his wife," Miss Hilton said sourly.

"No, I mean the man in the trench coat who you saw in the hallway."

"I don't know what happened to him. I was too busy not getting shot," Stella Hilton said.

"What about you?" he asked the cleaning lady.

"This is Flora," Kay said.

"You remembered," Flora said. Her voice was low, throaty, very attractive. Despite Flora's drab uniform dress and unflattering horn-rimmed glasses, Kay saw Flora was younger than she had thought. Stella Hilton was close in age to Rosaleen, she guessed. Flora was close to Josephine.

Hanging from the handle of Flora's cart was a colored string with a bunch of keys. "You have keys to all the dressing rooms?" Kay asked.

Flora looked down. "Yes, so I can clean them."

Kay remembered the keys swaying on the cart as Flora had pushed it away. "The string holding them all together—the one you had last night was red. This one is blue. It's a different set of keys."

Flora blinked. Her tongue ran over her lips. "Don't tell the manager, please. I lost my keys. I had to borrow another set tonight. I could lose my job."

"When did you lose them?" Kay asked excitedly.

"After I met Mrs. Roosevelt, I moved my cart down the hall and kept cleaning the dressing rooms. When I finished the last room and came back to my cart, the keys were gone."

"What time was that?"

"I don't know. But all the people had left Josephine Baker's party."

Kay rolled her eyes in frustration. Of course it had been then. Anyone leaving the party could have seen the keys dangling and grabbed them quickly as they left the dressing room.

But "anyone" didn't need the keys. Frank Miller did—because Rosaleen had walked in on him in Josephine's dressing room. But Frank Miller was the victim . . .

"I'd better get to work," Flora said.

"Before you go, Flora, did you see a man in a trench coat?" Kay asked.

"I did. I don't know who he is. Or what he was doing here."

"Can you describe him more?" Tim asked.

Flora shook her head. "I didn't see anything more than Miss Hilton did."

"Did you hear the shot, Flora?"

Flora nodded in answer to Tim's question.

"What did you do?"

"Hid myself in the supply closet."

Kay looked at the lipstick in her hand. "Is this yours?"

"Lipstick in a fancy case like that? No, miss. I don't wear any makeup when I work."

Kay turned to Miss Hilton. "Does the lipstick belong to you?"

"Not mine. I never wear that color. Now, I gotta get home," Miss Hilton said. "I'm in Overtown. Supposed to be home by the curfew, but this job doesn't allow for that."

"How do you get away with it?" Tim asked.

Stella Hilton rolled her large, beautiful eyes. "Bribes, dear boy. A few dollars in the right hand go a long way. But it sure makes it hard to get ahead." With that, she walked off down the hallway, head high, hips rolling from side to side.

"I saw they arrested a young woman for the murder," Flora ventured, after Stella Hilton had gone. "She isn't guilty, is she? She can't be. She looks like a nice young lady."

"It isn't looking good for her unless we can track down this man. If he was here, in the hallway after closing hours, he might be the killer."

"I wish I could help you more," Flora said. "I really, really wish I could."

She turned her back to them and pushed her cart down the hallway.

"A tall man in a trench coat and a fedora."

"Does it eliminate many people from the party?"

"Women, of course. And maybe Claude Mains. He is only a few inches taller than me," Kay said.

"Flora, pardon me," Tim called out.

Flora stopped and turned to face Tim.

"Are there other people cleaning tonight?" he asked.

"Two other women, Maisie and Lily," she said. She pointed in the other direction. "I think they are down there. But they had already gone home that night. I don't think they can help you."

Flora proved to be right, and with the club closed, there was no one else on site. No members of the orchestra, and not the second backup singer.

"We should head back," Tim said finally. "It's almost two a.m."

They left the building, avoiding the security guard. The night was still warm.

"What did we learn?" Tim asked, leaning back against the seat.

The streetlights barely illuminated him and the lights from the dash cast shadows on his handsome features.

"We learned that Flora and Stella Hilton both saw a tall man in a trench coat. Which could be Mr. Gros. Or even possibly Mr. Abtey," Kay said. "Mains is not tall."

"What about Reynolds?" Tim asked.

"Reynolds has a large stomach and looks like The Fatman in the *Maltese Falcon*, but he is tall. Neither woman mentioned his girth, but maybe he looked trimmer in a trench coat."

"Both women are shorter than you. Maybe to her, Mains is tall."

"True. I hadn't thought of that." She added, "You're smart. You don't jump to conclusions. At least when you investigate."

Tim started the car. He drove away from the club, tapping his fingers on the steering wheel. "I can talk to Mike Connor. Suggest that he confirm what flight Abtey took."

"Couldn't we find out? What if we went by the airport and talked to the check-in desk attendants?" Kay asked. Excitement stirred at the chance to do more investigation.

"I used to flash a badge when I was a cop," he said. "That opened people up pretty quick."

"Now you flash your smile. I saw how you had that simpering Hertz counter girl hanging on your every word. I bet your smile is more effective. Women will spill everything to a good-looking man to keep him hanging around. I bet they don't talk as much to a police detective."

"Only the good-looking ones," he said.

"You're modest, aren't you?"

"I'm joking." He flashed her his grin. Her heart gave a flip. How she had missed having that devastating smile directed at her.

She was proven wrong as they reached the airport and approached the National Airlines counter. The counter girl was a counter man. Tim's devastating smile wasn't going to work. But when Kay went up to the desk and gave a sweet smile, she got everything they needed from the young man. National Airlines had their headquarters in Miami, and he was able to search paper files for the manifests for the last few days.

Jacques Abtey had flown into Miami two days earlier than he claimed.

"Aha!" she exclaimed.

"It doesn't mean anything yet," Tim warned. "But you were right."

"I like it when you say that," she teased. She missed this. Teasing Tim. She liked investigating with him.

CHAPTER 18

Every woman wants to be first to someone sometime in her life . . .

—Eleanor Roosevelt, letter to Joseph P. Lash, January 21, 1944

It was after three a.m. when they pulled up at the front entrance of the Delano. Tim got out and handed the rental car keys to the sleepy young valet, along with a couple of dollar bills. He opened Kay's door. He reached to take her hand, but she ignored it, getting out by herself.

"What should we do?" she asked. "Confront Jacques Abtey?"

"No. We don't have proof he murdered Franz Müller. He is a war hero, like Josephine."

"And that is why he is a suspect," Kay said stubbornly. "If he eliminated Franz Müller, it could have been to protect Josephine. He cares about her."

Tim shook his head. "Think about it, Kay. How did Abtey know Müller would be at the Copa City Club?"

"Müller had attended Josephine's performances for days," Kay argued. "She must have told Abtey by telephone the first time she recognized Müller."

"There could be a lot of other reasons he came early."

"Then why didn't he tell Josephine the truth?"

"She doesn't have security clearance anymore," Tim threw

back. Then he said, "Or maybe he did tell her when he arrived and—"

"And she is backing up his story to us," Kay finished.

She had *more* than missed this. Talking things through with Tim. She felt like they were partners, like on *Dragnet*. She really *loved* it. Except talking about murder was where their partnership ended because Tim couldn't compromise.

"We can't talk about it out here." Tim nodded toward the front entry of the Delano. "We should sleep on it."

"Sleep? He could disappear by the morning."

"He won't do that. Not after he just arrived. It would look suspicious."

Reluctantly she said, "I guess you're right."

"I like the sound of that."

She threw him a withering look. But then, she liked it when he had to admit she was right.

The doorman opened the door for them. The concierge saw her and immediately sent a bellboy toward her. The bellboy handed her a note.

Kay looked at it warily. Was it from Mrs. Roosevelt or from one of their suspects? Abtey? Mr. Gros? One of the KKK men?

"Aren't you going to read it?" Tim asked.

Kay sighed. He was right—it was silly to speculate when all she had to do was read it, but she couldn't help it.

She suddenly thought about fingerprints. But there were prints on the paper, the concierge, the bellboy, and she had destroyed them.

She expected to see cut-out letters pasted to the page. Instead, this note was handwritten in black ink.

> *Kay, I will never forget martinis and orange soda. Before you, I thought heaven was hot dogs at baseball with yellow condiment. I will try to see you.*

There was only one person who could have written the note. One man with whom she had drank martinis in Washington, D.C. One man who had grinned like a little boy as he revealed how much he liked American hot dogs and soda pop.

"Who is it from?"

"No one."

It was from Dmitri Petrov. Former aide to the Soviet delegation from the United Nations. She had met him in Washington when she went investigating on her own. At the time, he was a suspect in the murder.

Sandy Sandiston had made it a condition of Dmitri's defection from the Soviet Union that he change his identity and never contact Mrs. Roosevelt or Kay again. Kay had wondered where Dmitri ended up. She thought she would never know.

But he was here now. In Miami Beach.

She looked up. Tim was staring at her. "*No one* wrote you a note?" he asked.

Uh-oh. *Hardly quick thinking*, she chided herself. "I mean, it is for Mrs. Roosevelt. From . . . Benny. Thanking her for the meeting in her hotel suite."

She met Tim's gaze. She tried not to wince at the clumsy lie. But then she looked beyond Tim, and she gasped.

"What?" He whipped around.

A distraction! she thought. She had a clear view into the Delano's bar and lounge. A blond man was slumped over the highly polished bar. "That's Stephen. He did go drinking, after all."

Tim followed her gaze. "He looks in bad shape."

"How is getting drunk helping Rosaleen?" Kay said.

"He's scared, Kay," Tim began.

But Kay marched across the lobby. Quicker than usual in her flat sneakers.

Stephen was bowed over the bar, supported on his elbows, his head in his hands. His hat and coat were tossed over the stool beside him, and he wore white shirtsleeves. His pale blond hair was no longer smoothed into place but hung over his eyes.

Kay reeled from the strong alcohol scent clinging to him. An open whiskey bottle stood in front of him. She had worked for enough male bosses to recognize an expensive whiskey. Almost the entire bottle was gone, but whether that was all in Stephen's gut, she didn't know.

Kay grasped the bottle to move it away, but drunks sense one thing with lightning speed—when their liquor is being confiscated.

Stephen's hand snaked out so fast she squealed. His strong fingers wrapped around the bottle's neck. "I'm not finished with that."

"You should be. This isn't helping Rosaleen."

Tim intervened. He got the bottle away from them both. Then he sat on Stephen's other side.

"What would you do, Miss Thompson," Stephen muttered, "if you learned your stepfather was a monster?"

Her heart sank. "You know?"

"Jo told me. Sh-she thought she was helping. Showed me that my stepfather was worth shooting. But hell, I knew that already."

"Getting drunk doesn't change that," Kay said, even though she was not averse to a martini herself in times of stress. Mrs. Roosevelt, who lost her father to the disease of alcoholism, did not drink. Knowing that and seeing Stephen like this made her realize that her martini didn't actually help.

"It doesn't make it any better," she went on, gently. "It just means you will wake up tomorrow knowing your stepfather was a monster and you'll have a colossal headache on top of it."

He stared at her with his sky-blue eyes. He barked out a laugh. "True enough. But I've already drunk enough to have a hangover. Might as well keep going."

"No," she cried. "Doing that could kill you."

"Kay is right," Tim said softly. He asked the bartender for a soda water.

"I'd prefer a beer," Stephen muttered. "In fact, I'd prefer more whiskey."

"Would you like a cocktail, miss?" the bartender asked. He was a young, handsome man with dark, curly hair and very dark eyes. "I'm closing soon. I'd recommend a daiquiri. In Santiago, men would meet at the Venus bar at eight a.m. and drink three of them in the morning," the bartender said. "It is a healthy cocktail."

"It's morning now, but I think I'd better set a good example. I'll have soda water."

"I can make them without the rum," the bartender said.

"Two daiquiris without the rum," Tim ordered.

When they arrived, Stephen watched her take her first sip. "Looks good. I'll have one. With rum."

"Without rum," she said.

"Without the liquor it's just sugar, lemon juice, and mineral water," Stephen scoffed.

"Don't worry. It will mix with all the whiskey in your stomach," Kay returned.

The waiter set down a cocktail napkin and placed the glass on top. Stephen grimaced. He downed the nonalcoholic drink with a quick bolt of his wrist.

"I knew it would be hard for Rosie and I," he said, grimly. His brow furrowed as he focused hard on each word. "I knew the old man—I mean, uh, my stepfather—would be furious. Knew he would disinherit me. Didn't care. I loved Rosie . . . love Rosie . . ." He swung his arms wide as if demonstrating an embrace.

He was very drunk, it appeared.

"You wanted Rosaleen to go to school and become a lawyer?" Kay asked.

"Yeah . . . wanted her to have her dream."

Kay felt a pang in her heart. She had been annoyed Stephen didn't have more faith in Rosaleen. But he cared about her dream and she admired him for that.

He looked down at his watch. "Funny. I can't tell what time it is."

Kay looked down at Stephen's battered watch. It had a black face with simple white numbers and hands, a silver case, and a green canvas strap. "It's so plain," she said, surprised.

"That's an A-11 watch. Issued to American soldiers," Tim noted. "I still have mine. It still runs."

"It . . . saved my life," Stephen slurred. But he didn't explain how. "My lucky charm, I thought."

He groaned. Rubbed his forehead. "When my stepfather met and married my widowed mother in America . . . his story was bullshit. Bullshit!"

Kay flinched. Men didn't swear in front of women. Unless they were drunk. Or wanted to scare a woman.

"If Jo-Josephine's right . . . my s-stepfather was a sadistic killer. I brought him into Rosaleen's life. He was gonna kill her. She grabbed the gun and—"

"How?" Kay asked suddenly.

The two men, one drunk and one sober, stared at her.

"How could Rosaleen disarm a larger man, one with military training?"

"Taught her," Stephen said, miserably. "I did. Taught her how to protect herself . . . worried when she was coming down here with Josephine."

"Why are you so *convinced* Rosaleen shot him?" Kay asked.

"No other solution. Locked in the room with him. He's dead and she's in prison. It's my fault. She never had a chance . . ."

"Maybe she really is innocent," Kay snapped. "I believe it."

Stephen looked at her with sorrowful eyes. "I know her," he muttered.

"Her fingerprints aren't on the gun. The GSR test was negative," Kay said.

Stephen shook his head. "It was my fault," he said as if Kay hadn't spoken. "I should be the one in jail."

"You need to sober up and think of how to help your fiancée. A good place to start is to figure out who really pulled the trigger," Kay said briskly. "You said your stepfather had business enemies. Who were they?"

But Stephen tilted over. Like a chopped-down tree, he fell sideways. Tim caught him before he fell off the stool, and redirected his toppling body so Stephen lay on the bar.

"Wonderful," Kay groaned. "He passed out when I wanted to get names from him. Why is he being such an ass? He isn't helping Rosaleen at all."

"I guess her arrest and learning his stepfather was a Nazi has shaken him up. Why are you being unsympathetic?" Tim asked. "Look, he knows Rosaleen best. Maybe he's right."

Shock made her mouth drop open. Then she snapped, "Rosaleen told Mrs. Roosevelt she is innocent. That is what I am going to believe."

"Maybe you just want to play detective again."

"Maybe you *should* play detective," she said. If eyes could blaze, hers were.

"I'd better get him to his room."

Tim lifted Stephen over his shoulder, taking him in an impressive fireman carry. He had to take a break and lean Stephen against the wall while they waited for the elevator.

The elevator dinged and Stephen woke up. Blearily he muttered, "Where am I?" as the door rolled open.

"Elevator. Almost at your room," Tim said. He didn't say anything more to Kay. He was breathing hard as he staggered, supporting Stephen's weight as he helped him out on his floor.

Tim turned back, but Kay hit the "door close" button.

The floor for her room was lit up. Impetuously, she selected

Josephine's floor. She knew it was late, so she rapped lightly on the door. It was wrenched open at once. Josephine stood there, dressed in a belted robe of periwinkle-blue silk.

"It's Stephen," Kay began.

"What happened? Has he been shot?" Josephine exclaimed.

"Oh no," Kay said. "He's drunk."

Josephine tut-tutted. "The poor boy. Come in."

Kay followed Josephine to the sitting room of her suite. But neither she nor Josephine took a seat. "It was learning about his stepfather on top of Rosaleen's arrest," Kay said.

"You think I should not have told him. He needed to know the truth. Now that he has indulged his shock and sense of betrayal with a good drunk, he will be able to be strong about it."

"I believe Josephine did the right thing," a male voice added.

Kay turned. Jacques Abtey had come in from the balcony.

"Jacques and I have been speaking about old times," Josephine said. "And strategizing what to do."

"Stephen thinks Rosaleen did it," Kay said suddenly.

"And you fear he is right because he knows her well? So do I, and I believe she is innocent."

"Don't hold his words against him," Abtey said. "In the morning, he will hate himself for what he said—if he remembers it."

"Mr. Abtey . . ." Kay hesitated. Tim said they needed a plan. But maybe she just needed to get Jacques Abtey off guard. "You didn't tell the truth. You arrived two days ago."

Kay heard a little gasp. Josephine had not known.

"I am working again," he said. "Sometimes we are told to be clandestine for no good reason at all."

"Did you come here for Franz Müller?"

"For revenge on a Nazi?" Jacques looked offended. "*Non*, and if I had, mademoiselle, I would not have been so clumsy, nor would I have implicated an innocent woman."

Kay felt her cheeks flame. "I'm sorry. I just—I had to ask."

"Be careful, mademoiselle," Abtey said. "This is not a game."

"I should go," Kay began.

"How did you learn about Jacques's arrival?" Josephine asked. She was frowning, her delicately plucked eyebrows drawn together.

"We visited the National Airlines counter. After going to the Copa City Club."

"We?"

"Tim O'Malley and I."

"The manager has told me the club will reopen tomorrow," Josephine said. "He asked me if I would be able to perform. I have decided to do it. I have a special reason now to perform."

"Josephine received a threat by telephone today," Jacques Abtey said, his face grim. "The man on the phone warned she could be killed if she goes up on stage."

"I am not afraid. Jacques, you know that I performed for the troops in North Africa in 1943 on a stage of makeshift boards strung across the hoods of two jeeps. Bombers flew over and as the bombs came whistling down, soldiers hastened to get me off the stage to take cover. Several bombs exploded around us. But I got back on the stage and continued to sing. An artist cannot abandon the stage.

"I will sing tomorrow night," she vowed. "But first, Miss Thompson, I presume you and Mr. O'Malley went to the Copa City Club to investigate. Did you learn anything other than the time of Jacques's flight?"

Kay felt a blush heat her cheeks. She pulled out the lipstick tube. "I found this. It had rolled into the supply closet across from your dressing room door. Is it yours?"

"I use darker colors with plum tones," Josephine said. "This is too red for me."

"Rosaleen doesn't wear lipstick," Kay said.

"No. She wears no makeup at all. Is this a clue?"

"I don't know," Kay admitted. "There are other singers and

the cleaning ladies who go backstage. One of the cleaning ladies admitted her keys had gone missing."

"That could explain how Monsieur Müller entered the dressing room," Josephine said. "It is evidence that Rosaleen was not lying when she said she found him in the room that she had locked."

Though Kay did wonder what had happened to the keys. And did it help Rosaleen?

"Flora—the cleaning lady—claimed she saw a tall man wearing a trench coat and a fedora," Kay said. "So did one of your backup singers, Stella Hilton. Stella had a male admirer in her dressing room when Miller was shot. She said she grabbed the man's hand, and they hightailed it out of there. Before they did, they saw that man running down the corridor," Kay said.

"Perhaps it was one of the KKK men," Josephine said excitedly. "And you see—it was probably this man, not Jacques."

But there is a possibility it was Mr. Abtey in a trench coat, Kay thought. "I tried to ask Stephen about his father's business enemies, but he passed out."

"He will be no use now," Josephine said, thoughtfully. "In the morning, we will rouse him with coffee, and we will say, '*Il faut*, you must tell us all about Monsieur Müller's enemies!' "

Kay hesitated. "We . . . uh . . . should start early. Rosaleen told me that you sleep late when you are performing since you must stay up so late— "

"Tomorrow I will wake up with the dawn."

"It's almost that time now, Jo," Jacques pointed out gently.

"We will rouse Stephen at nine. Does that suit you, Miss Thompson?"

Kay nodded. "Thank you."

Josephine walked her to the door. And said quietly, "Miss Thompson, I am shocked you would make an accusation against Jacques. I trust him with my life. In the war, he saved my life, by risking his own to take me to the Comte Clinic."

Kay said helplessly, "I didn't really suspect Mr. Abtey—"

"In detective stories, the sleuth is supposed to suspect everyone. But in real life, there are some people who are above suspicion."

But were there? Kay thought. Still, she had annoyed Josephine by being impulsive. What would happen when Mrs. Roosevelt found out?

In the morning, she would tell Mrs. R about the club and Jacques Abtey's arrival. She had not discussed it with Mrs. R. Was her impulsiveness going to get her in trouble?

Feeling abashed—and worried—Kay took the elevator to her floor. She opened her handbag to take out her room key. It was hidden by the jumble of cosmetics . . .

And the folded note from Dmitri.

He wanted to see her.

She couldn't.

If she saw him, she was risking Dmitri's life and her own. Sandy Sandiston had warned that the Soviets might threaten Dmitri by harming one of his friends. Her or Mrs. Roosevelt.

She should tear up the note and throw it away.

Instead, Kay opened her door and left the note in her handbag.

CHAPTER 19

If you are somebody's secretary it isn't just for your good looks that you are being taken to dinner and offered opportunities to obtain things at special prices, etc. Sometime or other you are going to be asked to do a favor—and one perhaps that you will find very unpalatable.

—Eleanor Roosevelt, My Day, December 28, 1951

As Stephen opened his door at nine a.m., Kay noted his eyes were bloodshot. The other clue to his hangover was the bag of ice he held against his head.

Mrs. Roosevelt's day had begun early. Kay had told her everything—her investigation of the Copa City Club with Tim, their discovery about Mr. Abtey's arrival, and her clumsy accusation, which had offended Mr. Abtey.

"Since you were with Tim, I feel assured you were safe," Mrs. R said. "I am pleased you planned to have him accompany you."

"He does have the car," she said. She added, feeling her cheeks heat, "I trust him."

"I must attend the conference today," Mrs. Roosevelt said. "Perhaps you and Josephine will speak to Stephen. I trust you to get the information we need."

Now, here at Stephen's door, with Josephine, she felt proud that Mrs. Roosevelt trusted her to investigate.

Josephine immediately sashayed into his room. "I have ordered coffee, silly boy."

Josephine led Stephen to his bed in the modest-sized room and pushed him down to sit on its edge, while she took the armchair.

Kay remained standing. "Getting drunk is a waste of time," she said.

"You know nothing about how I feel," Stephen snapped. He slapped the ice bag onto the bedside table. The explosive sound made Kay jump. The bag of ice had burst, soaking Stephen's sleeve, the table, and the carpet.

Stephen looked sheepish. "Sorry. I scared you and made a mess. Stupid thing to do." He rubbed his forehead. "Not to mention, the noise made my brain feel like it wants to explode."

Kay folded her arms in front of her chest. She wore a cap-sleeve dress in pale pink. It was supposed to be wrong for redheads, but she liked light pink.

"Last night I tried to ask about your stepfather's enemies, but you passed out."

Stephen sighed heavily. "Yeah, it was not my finest hour. I think you told me it was a stupid idea because I'd wake up with a hangover and Rosie would still be in jail. Exactly what happened."

He acknowledged she was right, but he didn't sound like he appreciated it.

"I should have realized my stepfather would do something violent, even before I knew he was Nazi scum." He rubbed his temple, wincing. "That explains so much. My mother denied it, but I was sure he was hitting her. The man was evil, through and through."

"What about enemies?"

Stephen said, "You told me he was a Nazi. When I started at the CIA, I heard rumors that we had brought Nazis into the country for programs like Operation Paperclip. Our government wanted scientific knowledge from the scientists behind Germany's advancements in weapons. And they wanted Nazis to help hunt Communists. On the other hand, there are men who have made it a mission to hunt Nazis. Maybe a Nazi hunter shot my stepfather."

"Jacques told me about Nazi hunters. They locate them and reveal their crimes to prosecute them in court," Josephine said. "Mrs. Roosevelt found it of interest. But they don't assassinate former Nazis."

"Maybe some do."

"What about any *other* enemies?" Kay repeated. "You said he was a ruthless businessman. Could he have other enemies in Miami?"

"Any small building company that he bankrupted. Anyone whose land he got cheap because he paid off city officials or used threats to get the sale."

"Could you give me a list of the names?"

"Go to the Yellow Pages and find a list of businesses that do electrical work, or carpentry, or supply building materials, and write all the names down. My stepfather tried to rip off every one of them."

"That isn't helpful, Stephen," Josephine said.

"Did you know of anyone angry enough to kill him?" Kay asked.

"I don't know. But I bet someone in his office knows. They would be there when people stormed in to threaten him."

Kay was about to ask more about Miller's office staff when the knock came on the door. Josephine answered and brought in the room service cart set with a coffee service.

As Josephine poured a cup for Stephen, she said, "I telephoned the lawyer, and I have fired him. I am hunting for a lawyer from New York. A fighter who is driven to win the fight for Rosaleen, even if only for the publicity. I don't care what it costs."

"I should help pay, Jo."

Josephine shook her head. "I will cover the costs."

There was something in the way she looked at Stephen. Kay sensed Josephine did not want to relinquish control. It would be better if Josephine was in charge, as opposed to Stephen, who had suggested Rosaleen take a plea bargain.

Kay suddenly thought of one person who must know a lot about Frank Miller.

Why hadn't she thought of it before?

If she played her cards right, she could learn about his enemies at lunchtime.

Leaving Josephine with Stephen, Kay put her plan in motion.

She returned to Mrs. Roosevelt's suite, where she telephoned the hotel switchboard and asked the operator to connect her call.

After kicking off her heels, Kay paced the floor, barefoot on the rug as the telephone rang. The call was picked up and the nasal-toned voice announced, "White Star Developments. This is the personal secretary to Mr. Miller. Can I assist you?"

"This is Kay Thompson, Mrs. Roosevelt's secretary. Is this Miss Lane?"

"Mrs. Roosevelt!" The secretary's voice dropped in volume, which only made it flatter, more nasal, and painful to the ears. "This is Anna Lane. I want to talk with Mrs. Roosevelt. There are things I know that I didn't tell anyone. In the newspaper, it sounded like she is involved in that girl's defense."

"She is," said Kay. Even if not officially.

"I need to tell her that she is in the company of a killer, and she has no idea."

"Who?" Kay demanded.

"I want to tell her in person."

Of course she did, Kay thought. It was like a movie. Anna Lane would refuse to give a name, then die before she could.

"Can she come here, to the offices of Mr. Miller? It is here that I have evidence to show her."

"She is busy today, but as her secretary, I could speak with you."

This was not at all what Kay expected. She had planned to lure the secretary out to lunch and question her, while picking up the tab for food.

Anna Lane hesitated.

Kay added, "She is attending a conference. She cannot miss the sessions this afternoon."

"You will tell her everything I tell you?"

"Yes. That is my job," Kay answered.

"Come to the office." The woman relayed the address. No directions, just the number and street name. "I await you," she said, and hung up.

Kay grabbed her purse and a white bolero jacket, which she swung on over her shoulders. The Delano's doorman hailed her a cab.

As the car traveled down the sun-drenched street, Kay realized that though Müller was dead, someone had to be running the office. What secretary would show up for work and answer the phone, if she didn't know if her salary would be paid?

That was an angle Kay hadn't thought of before. A motive for murder.

Control of Frank Miller's business.

The cab pulled up. "Here you are, miss."

Kay gazed out the window as she paid for the taxi. Miller's offices were in a building with the Art Deco styling of the 1930s. But instead of the soaring angular shape of the Delano, the office building had rounded corners, the softened shape emphasized by horizontal bands of dark windows. It was tiered like a wedding cake.

Inside, the streamlined design continued. A security guard directed Kay to the top floor. Müller had the top-floor office, the one just below the stylized "WS" for "White Star." As Kay crossed the marble floor, her heels echoing, she looked around in disgust. The walls were either marble or mirrored. Large plushy armchairs were placed in the lobby. The building was a symbol of success. As she rode up in the elevator, it made Kay sick to think Müller had all this after his past as a Nazi.

The elevator door opened. Kay stepped out. She faced a large oak double-door stained a rich, dark brown. Wood paneling, elaborate moldings, and wainscotting ran along the walls. Along with beautiful artwork. The subtle lighting glowed on the brush-strokes of the oils.

The lobby had been an austere modern design. This felt like the drawing room of a Newport mansion. Not that Kay had ever been in one, but she had seen magazine photos.

She could knock, but she tried the handle of the right-hand door. It opened and Kay faced a beautiful office filled with polished wood and extravagant artwork, the space dominated by a large mahogany desk.

Miller's secretary, Anna Lane, who today looked more like Lana Turner than Greta Garbo, stood up from behind the desk. She was almost the same height as Mrs. Roosevelt. Her white-blond hair was smoothed into a swirled bun, tightly pinned to the back of her head. Her black dress clung to her figure. She wore perfect cat-eye eyeliner, and her lipstick was Revlon's Fire and Ice, a warmer red than Love That Red.

She held out her hand. "Miss Thompson, I thank you for making the trip to see me."

Kay hid the wince she felt at the voice.

Miss Lane pointed to the side, where a square of leather sofas was arranged. "Let us speak there."

"I was planning to take you out for lunch, Miss Lane," Kay said.

"I have ordered in. Sandwiches from the delicatessen. I do not often eat lunch." Anna Lane took a seat, tucking her form-fitting skirt beneath her trim posterior. She poured coffee into two gold-rimmed china cups. "When I go out, I prefer Embers or the Park Avenue restaurant. Mr. Miller liked to take me there and have me make notes of his development ideas over dinner."

Kay did not know Miami restaurants, but she sensed the food in both places came with high prices.

Kay did not think Mr. Miller's thoughts had been on work.

"The office is empty now," Miss Lane said. "Police removed many of his papers. I protested. Mr. Miller left instructions for me to carry on the business until his successor takes over. How can I do business if the files are gone? But the police all but shoved me aside to take the boxes."

"You were to carry on the business?"

"Temporarily. I know everything about the work: the projects, the schedules, the costs, the clients. Mr. Miller trusted me implicitly." Anna offered the sandwiches.

"Who is his successor?" Kay took one.

"His stepson, of course."

Kay frowned. "I thought they were estranged."

Anna Lane bit her lip. She did it carefully without ruining her soft, creamy lip color. "That is what I want to tell Mrs. Roosevelt about the murder." Her words came quickly, her voice had gone from grating to whiny. "It was *Stephen*."

"What was Stephen?"

"He shot his stepfather. It *must* have been Stephen. He knew of his stepfather's fascination with Josephine Baker. I will show you Mr. Miller's office. The walls are covered with exquisite art, but one framed picture. A signed photograph of Josephine Baker. He called it a 'treasure.'"

How could an ex-Nazi be fascinated by Josephine Baker? "Could I see that picture?"

"Of course. I will show you before you leave. Stephen's

stepfather had found out about his engagement. Stephen tried to keep it secret, but all secrets come out, in the end."

"How did he find out?"

Miss Lane smiled smugly. "I told him."

"Why?"

"He had to find out eventually. And Stephen did not like me. He once called me a 'gold digger.'"

Kay sensed Anna Lane had *enjoyed* revealing her information and hurting Stephen.

"When Mr. Miller learned Josephine was returning to Miami, he was delighted. It would have been easy for Stephen to arrange to meet with his stepfather, promising him the chance to be backstage with Miss Baker. Stephen knew that if he did not act quickly, Mr. Miller's will would be changed. Stephen would be disinherited."

"Do you know how much the company is worth?" Kay asked.

"Yes. As I said, Mr. Miller trusted me in every way. All the documents of this business I have reviewed. I took the job as his secretary, but I acted as his advisor. His recent acquisitions of buildings and land were my suggestions. They have made him a great deal of money. Stephen stands to inherit fifty million dollars in assets."

"I thought Stephen butted heads with his stepfather right from the beginning. Why was he the heir?"

"To please his wife, Mr. Miller wanted to make a place in his company for his stepson. He was impressed that Stephen has risen in the American law enforcement world. But he soon saw that Stephen wanted only money. It ran through his fingers like water. Cars. Women. Gambling."

"Women? He is engaged to be married," Kay said.

"Before he became engaged, he had a different woman on his arm each week. He is a man who knows he is desirable to women, and he uses it to his advantage. To put a notch in his bedpost. Is that the expression?"

"It is. But I am sure he has changed now that he has found the woman he intends to marry."

Anna Lane shrugged. "Some men never change."

Kay did not know if Stephen was one of those men, but she had met several.

"His father did not like the engagement. He wanted to stop Stephen. He intended to change his will. His wealth would go into a trust."

"Who was the beneficiary of this trust?"

Kay expected Miss Lane to smugly declare it was she. But she said, "An organization in which Mr. Müller was called a Grand Dragon."

Kay blinked. "Do you mean the KKK? He was leaving all that money to them?" Despite his ridiculous title, she was horrified.

"That is what I believe. I did not see his actual will."

"He didn't have a chance to change the will?"

"He did not. He hesitated. He put the papers away. He decided he would send them this week. But he was murdered."

"Then Stephen Roberts inherits his stepfather's estate."

"Yes. And the papers are gone. I went to retrieve them, to show them to the police, but they are missing."

Kay knew what Anna Lane was implying, as she sat with perfect posture, looking demure. But Kay didn't want to jump to assumptions, to put words in Miss Lane's mouth. "Who took them?"

"It must have been Stephen. He had every reason to hide this information from the police. Mr. Miller warned him that the will was to be changed. I saw Stephen as he left his stepfather's office. His face was purple with fury. In that moment he was no longer a secure and wealthy man. He was a desperate man."

"Did he have access to the office?"

"He works for an agency of spies. Would a locked door be a deterrent to such a man? Those papers are gone now. Torn to pieces. Or burned."

Anna Lane lifted a handkerchief to her eye. "Mr. Miller was kind to me. I came here from Europe after the war. I was only twenty-one. I had nothing. I wore cast-off clothes given to me by charity. Mr. Miller gave me work.

"He was married when I came. To Stephen's mother. She was a beautiful woman. She was forty-five years old—I thought she was very old, and I was surprised when Mr. Miller said he wished to sire his own children. I thought she was too old for children. Then there was a car accident. The brakes did not work in her car, and she had a crash. It was very tragic. Stephen—I think he blamed his stepfather."

"For the accident?"

"I thought he meant that his stepfather did not ensure her automobile was safe. But I overheard their argument. They began shouting. Stephen accused Mr. Miller of causing the brakes to fail. Mr. Miller threw him out."

Anna lifted her hands in a graceful shrug. "You see? I am certain it was Stephen."

"Stephen could not have shot his stepfather. He was traveling by air from New York," Kay said. "There are witnesses to that."

"Then it was his fiancée. They were in it together. To gain fifty million dollars."

"There are other suspects," Kay said. "You said Mr. Miller was going to create a trust to fund the KKK's horrible activities." She thought of Eulie Reynolds and Claude Mains. "Maybe they didn't know the will hadn't been changed. Maybe one of them murdered Mr. Miller. Or one of his business enemies."

Anna's forehead puckered in a frown.

Kay could see Anna did not like Stephen. Maybe Anna Lane had fallen for Stephen, and resented Rosaleen. She didn't need Miss Lane's vitriol, she needed information. What would Mrs. Roosevelt do?

"Is there anyone else who could have wanted to harm Mr. Miller? Perhaps a client? A small contractor who worked for Mr. Miller?" Kay asked. "If Stephen and his fiancée, Miss Davis, are guilty, eliminating other suspects will help strengthen the case against them." She was grasping at straws.

"That is the business of the company. I should not say."

"If it can be shown that Stephen and Rosaleen have the only real motive, it would help convict them," Kay said. She was playing on the other side of what she truly believed. "Stephen said his stepfather was ruthless in business. That he had destroyed smaller companies and bullied people out of their land."

"That is not true! Mr. Miller was an honorable man. A successful man because he was very smart."

In business, Kay had learned that smart meant a man was better at taking advantage of other men—and had less of a conscience.

"You were at Josephine Baker's party with him. How did he end up in the dressing room alone? You went to the Copa City Club with him, you were at the party. Where were you?"

"He sent me home in a taxi. Usually, he accompanied me. He would 'walk me to my door'—is that the expression? But not that night. He said he had to meet with someone. I thought it was Mrs. Baker."

Anna got up. "Come with me." She pushed open the door to Müller's office. The wood paneled walls held paintings in heavy frames.

Were they plundered treasure? Or had Müller bought them with stolen gold?

Anna Lane walked to the smallest piece. The framed and signed photograph of Josephine Baker.

Anna crossed her arms over her chest. "I now believe he arranged to meet with Miss Davis."

"Did he keep an agenda? Maybe he recorded it— "

"There was nothing written down for that day. The police took it anyway. Now, you must go. I have work to do."

Kay threw in one last question. "Did you know who Mr. Miller really was?"

Anna Lane gazed at her blankly.

"His name was really Franz Müller. The man who you believe was generous and good was a Nazi death camp commandant."

"You are right. I knew Mr. Miller as a good man." Anna Lane lifted her head defiantly. "I want you to leave now."

Anna led her to the elevator as if to ensure Kay got on and left the office.

"Goodbye," Anna said, as the door opened, and she moved away with the grace of a model.

Kay rode down to the lobby. Due to Anna Lane's stubborn loyalty, she had learned nothing about his business enemies. Still, she had the nagging feeling she had missed something.

If only every piece of evidence *didn't* point to Rosaleen Davis.

CHAPTER 20

An old woman knelt on the ground, grasping my knees. I lifted her up, but could not speak. What could one say at the end of a life which had brought her such complete despair?

—Eleanor Roosevelt, My Day, February 16, 1946

"Where have you been?" Tim jumped up from one of the comfy leather 1930s-style armchairs in the Delano Hotel's lobby. His fedora lay at his feet. A big dent had collapsed the crown. He must have accidentally put his foot on it. "I was worried about you."

"Don't be," Kay said lightly, but she meant it. It was not his business. She had wanted to investigate by his side last night, but she was still horrified that he wanted to accept Rosaleen's guilt. Did he listen to Stephen simply because Stephen was a man? But saving Rosaleen was more important than her shock and annoyance. She explained, "I met with Frank Miller's secretary."

"Miller's *secretary*?"

"I contacted her, and she told me that she had information for Mrs. Roosevelt."

"You went to the office of the *murder victim*?"

"That's where you find secretaries. I telephoned her and she invited me there because she wanted to speak to Mrs. R. I thought it would be useful because if there is one woman who knows a man, it's a man's secretary."

That made him look at her uneasily.

"I hear you have a secretary."

"She's fifty-five years old. She makes me peanut butter sandwiches when I forget my lunch."

"I guess she knows what you like."

"I hate peanut butter sandwiches."

Kay started to walk toward the elevators. She wanted to record what she had learned before Mrs. Roosevelt returned.

Tim moved quickly to get in step. "What did you find out?"

"She told me Stephen was going to be disinherited. She thinks Stephen is guilty."

"You told her—"

"That he was traveling by air from New York at that time? Yes. But she wouldn't give up. She said Rosaleen and Stephen must be in it together."

Tim was quiet, looking up, watching the floor numbers light up as the elevator came down.

Did he believe that? After what he said last night . . .

"If Rosaleen was guilty, wouldn't she have run instead of locking herself in a room with her victim?" Kay demanded. "She could have run back to Josephine and said she heard a shot. She could have locked Miller in the dressing room with the gun. She could have claimed he was dead before she even got to the dressing room. There were any number of better stories she could have invented."

Tim looked away from the display of floor numbers. His green eyes held hers. "Those are good points. You believe Rosaleen is innocent and I believe in you, Kay."

"Sure," she said. Was he trying to make her less irritated with him, or did he truly mean it? That he believed in her?

"If all she told you is that Stephen and Rosaleen must be guilty, I guess it was a waste of time."

"Not exactly."

The elevator door slid open. She stepped in, and he followed. She pressed her floor number. Then his.

"I learned Frank Miller planned to set up a trust for his money to go to an organization in which he was a Grand Dragon. That was obviously the KKK. They would have all those millions for their campaign of terror. Claude Mains and Eulie Reynolds, who we believe are Klansmen, were at the party. Maybe one of them killed him."

"The KKK will get the millions?" Tim asked.

"No. Anna Lane—Mr. Miller's secretary—said that he intended to change his will but didn't go through with it. His money goes to Stephen. I also learned that Frank Miller used to take Anna Lane to nice restaurants. I think she hoped to become the next Mrs. Miller. There was no love lost between her and Stephen, so once he takes over, he'll probably fire her."

"If she hoped to marry Miller, she had no motive to kill him."

Kay shook her head. "She had no obvious motive. That makes her the most likely suspect."

Tim gave a short laugh. "In your beloved Alfred Hitchcock movies, maybe."

"You liked *Strangers on a Train*."

"I also liked *The Day the Earth Stood Still*. Doesn't mean I am expecting an alien invasion."

"We kind of had one," Kay retorted drily, "when we let Nazis like Müller escape justice and flourish in our country."

Tim's lashes dipped over his green eyes. "You're right about that."

"Anna Lane was at the Copa City Club with Müller. I asked her why he went to the dressing room alone. She said he sent her home in a taxi. He said he had to 'meet with someone.' At first, she thought he meant Josephine. Now she believes it was Rosaleen. Miss Lane told Müller about Stephen's engagement."

"She hoped to see Stephen get disinherited, I guess," Tim said. "But if she killed him, she did it too early. Besides, I thought secretaries were hardworking, honest, and above suspicion."

"*I* am," she answered. "But not every secretary is like me."

"I won't argue with that."

She narrowed her eyes at his overly cheerful tone when the elevator stopped with a disconcerting shudder. Kay gasped. Instinctively she reached out. Her fingers grazed Tim's arm. She pulled them back.

"It's okay," he said.

She held her breath until the doors rolled open. "I suppose I will see you later. What I need to do is contact the men who were at the party—"

"No, you don't. You are not questioning a couple of KKK members. I forbid it."

"You aren't married to me," she threw back. "I'm going to start by finding Mr. Gros."

Tim put his hand over the door to keep it open. "How do you plan to do that?"

She turned back. "The hard way. I'm going to call every possible hotel and ask to speak to him."

"What if they won't reveal that he is staying there?"

"When you say you work for Mrs. Roosevelt, people think it's official. I know, not exactly playing fair, but this is murder."

"There's something I need to tell you. Something I found out today."

His hand was still over the elevator door, preventing it from sliding shut. An alarm began to sound.

He knew how to tempt her. "Okay," she said. "Tell me quick before the elevator breaks down."

He looked crestfallen, as if he'd hoped she would invite him into the suite.

But he relented. "While you were out, I hunted down a cab driver who picked up a fare a block from the Copa City Club at two a.m. on the night of the murder."

"How did you do that?"

"You ask around and you make it worth their while to give you information," Tim said. "The cabbie described his fare as a tall, slender man wearing a trench coat and a fedora pulled low. The man wore a black silk scarf and held a handkerchief up to his face. He spoke gruffly, but the voice was not deep."

"That sounds like a perfect description of Mr. Gros. Reynolds is not slender." Kay felt sick with disappointment. "I had better start making those telephone calls. I must prove that Stephen and Rosaleen did not cook up the murder together."

"Kay, you can't chase a murderer."

"Conversation never harmed anyone."

"It can," Tim said grimly. "I don't like this idea."

"Maybe you don't. But I decide what I do. Besides, I will be with Mrs. Roosevelt."

"That does not make me feel any better."

As she finally turned to leave, he said, "The cab driver was a short man. To him, Mains could be tall."

"Good to know another suspect isn't eliminated," she said.

Through the afternoon, Kay telephoned the reception desks of various South Beach hotels. She told them that Mrs. Roosevelt met Isaac Gros at an event and wished to speak with him.

Some hotels pointed out they did not "prefer" Jewish guests. Kay told those people that their policies were biased and their behavior inexcusable, then quickly added she was speaking personally. Though she thought Mrs. R would agree.

Finally, she found the hotel where Mr. Gros was staying and left a message for him.

He telephoned back within fifteen minutes. "Miss Thompson! I was told Mrs. Roosevelt wishes to speak to me. Such an honor. Mrs. Roosevelt is a remarkable woman. Courageous, intelligent, admirable in her work for human rights—"

"Would you be available to meet with Mrs. Roosevelt?" She had to cut off the effusive praise.

"Of course. Such an honor," he repeated. "I—"

"Where shall we meet?"

"Wolfie's," Mr. Gros said. "Is there anywhere else to go?"

"I don't know," Kay answered.

Mr. Gros laughed gently. "You will like Wolfie's."

"What is Wolfie's?" Kay asked. She heard the uncertainty in her voice. She hadn't meant to let it slip in. She didn't want Gros to know he was a suspect.

"A famous diner in Miami Beach. A good, safe place to meet."

Kay got directions from Mr. Gros. After she hung up, she wondered why he had stressed that Wolfie's was a safe place to meet.

When Mrs. Roosevelt returned to the suite at the end of the afternoon, Kay swiftly relayed Tim's discovery. "A tall man caught a taxi a block away. At two o'clock in the morning. After shooting Müller and locking the door, the killer must have run. He probably thought it wouldn't be smart to catch a cab right outside the club."

Kay added, "There are four men who meet that description. One was Müller with his white hair, but he was the victim, so he wasn't hailing a taxi at two a.m. Another is Stephen, but he was on a flight from Miami. The third man is Isaac Gros. And lastly, Claude Mains. Tim said Mains was taller than the cab driver."

Mrs. Roosevelt nodded thoughtfully.

Kay set down a piece of paper. "I telephoned the reception desks of various South Beach hotels until I found the one where Isaac Gros is staying. I have arranged for us to meet for dinner."

Nervously Kay added, "If you agree, I mean. And if I may join you."

"I wish to meet with Mr. Gros. I am impressed that you tracked him down. And, of course, you must join us."

Kay nodded seriously, but inside her stomach bounced with excited nerves. She wanted to be part of the investigation.

Maybe this time she would solve the mystery. She figured out who had murdered Susan Meyer, but only after Mrs. R had already done so.

If she could use her brains to save Rosaleen, maybe she could prove to herself she was more than a secretary and typist.

The telephone rang then. Kay picked it up. She assumed it was Josephine—who would be performing tonight. But it could be Stephen. Or Tim.

"Miss Thompson?"

It was Mr. Gros. "Would Mrs. Roosevelt allow me to pick her up at the hotel tonight in my car?"

Kay looked up to see Mrs. R cock her head, asking a silent question.

Kay covered the receiver. "Mr. Gros wants to pick you up here."

"I am willing to meet him here, but is there a particular reason?"

Kay repeated the question to Mr. Gros. She moved the receiver slightly away from her head so Mrs. Roosevelt could listen to the response.

"I would like to take her on a short drive, then bring her to Wolfie's," he said. "There is something I absolutely must show Mrs. Roosevelt."

"What is it?" Kay asked.

"It will help her understand."

Kay was going to ask for more information, but Mrs. R shook her head slightly. Kay said, "That will be fine."

Mr. Gros said, "I will come at six o'clock."

Kay hung up. It sounded like a bad idea to get in a car with a suspect.

But Mrs. Roosevelt was as calm as usual. "I will ask Tim to follow us at a safe distance in that nondescript car he rented."

Boards covered the blown-out windows. A sultry breeze swayed palm trees, but Kay thought it looked like a scene from the war.

"This is the Miami Hebrew School," Mr. Gros explained. "It is awaiting repairs to the damage caused by a bombing."

Standing beside ER and Isaac Gros, Kay felt a surge of rage. A *school!* At least no children had been harmed, but the message was terrifying.

Mr. Gros said softly, "Forty-four memorial windows were shattered by dynamite. This year, from June to December, there were thirteen bombings in and around Miami. These dynamiters targeted Jewish community centers, Hebrew schools and temples, and housing developments such as Carver Village, which now houses Black Americans. Dynamite was found on the steps of Miami High School. No one has been arrested."

Kay glanced to Mrs. Roosevelt, whose expression was filled with sorrow. "It must be stopped," Mrs. Roosevelt said.

Kay stared at the school. "After what you went through, at Buchenwald, it must be terrible to experience these attacks here."

"It is," he said simply.

"Why did you come to Miami?" Mrs. Roosevelt asked.

He had told Kay it was to protest these outrageous acts. Was it more?

"I learned that Mrs. Josephine Baker was to perform. I wished to ask her to speak out against what is happening. She is an international star. Her condemnation would reach the world's stage."

"Did you talk to her about it?"

"No. I wished to, but it grew late, and the party ended. I hoped to speak to her the next night, but the murder occurred, and the Copa City Club was closed for the night."

He led them back toward his car, parked at the curb.

"You recognized Mr. Müller," Mrs. Roosevelt said, in a gentle questioning tone.

"Yes, I saw his picture in the newspaper a few months ago and I recognized him. I knew Frank Miller's real identity as Franz Müller. I began investigating him and I learned he was involved with the KKK. I believed he helped both finance and facilitate the bombings. He is a die-hard Nazi who became a millionaire. His contacts in construction could get him access to explosives. I feared he wanted to bring his regime of terror to our country," Mr. Gros said as Kay slid into the back seat, after Mrs. R had settled in the front passenger seat.

Kay tried to catch Mrs. R's eye in the mirror. Was that tantamount to a confession? Mr. Gros had strong motives to shoot Müller. In some ways, she didn't blame him. The kind of men who bombed schools needed to be stopped.

Kay glanced up to the rearview mirror. She saw a nondescript car that looked like Tim's rental car. If it was him, she was happy to see him behind them.

They took Collins Avenue southward. Mr. Gros turned into a parking lot filled with cars. A huge red and green neon sign, glowing as dusk settled, read WOLFIE'S.

"It's owned by Wilfred Cohen. Known as Wolfie, as you can see," Mr. Gros said.

A long line of customers waited at the door. Many were gray-haired men, with heavy, dark-framed glasses and short-sleeved shirts. Their wives and daughters stood with them, wearing ankle-length skirts and almost identical small white pearl necklaces. Their hair was tamed by hair spray to survive the humidity. Kay had been using hair spray since it first came in aerosol cans.

Several couples recognized Mrs. Roosevelt who, as usual, did not want to "cut" the line. Many of the patrons were ardent readers of her My Day column. Kay watched as Mrs. Roosevelt greeted everyone with genuine friendliness and interest.

As they neared the door, Mr. Gros explained, "Wolfie became a friend of mine when I met him when I came to America after my release from Buchenwald, through the Displaced Persons Act. Wolfie was born in Schenectady, New York. He was a former busboy in the Catskills and came to Miami Beach in 1940. A smart businessman, Wolfie opened the diner and kept it open twenty-four hours a day. It became a haven for people living in the beachfront rooming houses, because they don't have kitchens. Eventually he began hosting big-name performers like Milton Berle and Henny Youngman."

"A very impressive story of entrepreneurship," said Mrs. R.

The delicious smells inside made Kay hungry. A brightly colored counter filled the center of the space. Mr. Gros led them to one of the blue and red leatherette booths, the colors matching the striped tile floor.

When their orders came, the sandwiches were enormous, rye bread slices piled high with smoked meat and pastrami.

Kay knew she couldn't open her mouth wide enough for the whole thing. She took a knife and fork to it. It had a hot mustard that would have made Dmitri Petrov smile with joy.

When they were halfway through, Mr. Gros asked, "Mrs. Roosevelt, do you think I shot Franz Müller?"

Kay almost choked on her pastrami sandwich.

"Did you, Mr. Gros?" ER asked. She had eaten half her sandwich.

"Isaac, please."

"Then do call me Eleanor."

"An honor. First, let me tell you what happened in those last hours at Buchenwald."

He got a faraway look in his pale eyes as he began. "The American troops had marched up the road to us, the road they called 'the Blood Road' . . ."

Kay held her breath. *Was* he confessing?

"The Nazi officers feared what would befall them," he said.

"The tables had turned. They feared they would now be executed. Many of them, like Müller, acted in desperation. They seized the uniforms given to prisoners and dressed themselves to look like one of us. Some even demonstrated their own methods of torture in front of the American forces, pretending that they had been victims. It was sickening to see it.

"I spoke to an American soldier and I said: 'He is not one of us. We are so starved, we are skeletons. Look at him. He is fat.' They knew then that he was a Nazi, trying to escape by pretending to be a victim. I was smug because I thought he would see justice. But he did not. Somehow, he was not arrested and imprisoned, he was able to escape and come to America."

Kay was going to speak but saw the small shake of Mrs. R's head.

"When I saw him here in Miami, I saw his wealth and I saw that *he* was the one who was smug, I wished him dead. Could I have taken a gun and shot him? Should I not say to myself, 'He deserves this punishment?' This would be merciful compared to what he did."

He paused to brush at a tear. "My family were murdered in death camps. My wife and my two young daughters. Even her parents and mine."

Kay's stomach churned. What must it be like to be haunted by such memories? Was it possible to feel joy again? Mr. Gros had smiled at Josephine at the party—but she sensed his smile was hiding tears.

"I did not know of this until after I left the camp. I was still there, in the camp, when Josephine Baker came to us . . ."

His voice trailed away. He sighed. "Liberation was not what I had always hoped it would be. They opened the gates, but we did not run free. Most of us were weak and hungry. We had no strength. Many were too sick. Some were dying. I was physically able to leave, but I could not abandon those other men. I ached to leave that hellish place behind, but I stayed. I nursed the dying men. We had typhus wards. Even our liberators, the allied soldiers, feared the sick, for they did not want to catch the disease that was now ravaging the survivors. That was freedom for so many—the gates thrown open so they could say they were free for a few last days, or hours, before they died."

Kay had to pick up her napkin to stifle a sob.

He smiled kindly at her.

"Then, a car arrived bearing Josephine Baker. She came to sing for us. She sang to the men in the typhus wards. She did not hang back in fear. She said her duty was to bring us joy and hope. Her magnificent performance provided the last moments of pleasure in some men's lives—men who had known only torture and agony for years.

"I accompanied her tour of the camp. When the American generals first came to the camp, it made General Patton, who I was told was nicknamed 'Old Blood and Guts,' sick to his stomach. He had to stop and vomit.

"Josephine said to me that she *never* doubted what we were fighting for, she never doubted that fighting for France and freedom was worth risking her life. The horrors she saw have vindicated the passion she held in her heart. I asked her why she did not also become nauseous—she said she did not want the victims in the camp to believe they were a horrible sight and to be pained by her horror."

Mr. Gros continued. "She arrived in her army uniform, and it was festooned with medals attesting to her bravery and service. When she sang, her voice filled with compassion and beauty, I felt we had been visited by an angel."

Kay sniffled again, picturing the scene.

"Josephine made me realize what we must fight for. A compassionate world. How could I lift a gun and become as bad as the Nazis we defeated? I did not shoot Franz Müller."

Mrs. Roosevelt nodded. "I understand that you would never do such a thing in vengeance. But there are desperate circumstances that force us to break our moral code. Josephine Baker received death threats. Someone might have shot Franz Müller to protect Josephine."

"I would have given my life to protect Josephine Baker. But I do not believe I could take someone else's life."

"A man meeting your description was seen leaving the club after the shooting," Kay said impetuously.

A look of worry flashed over his features. "But how—?" He sighed. "I will not lie. I waited at the club. I followed Müller because I wanted to confront him. After the party hosted by Josephine, Müller returned to the theatre area. He sat at a table alone. He looked at his watch. One of the cleaning ladies told him the club was closed and that he must leave."

"What did he say?" Kay asked, excitedly. This must be a clue.

"He said that he was sorry. He said he had too much champagne and the excitement of meeting the beautiful Josephine Baker had gone to his head, but he would leave."

"And then?" Mrs. R prompted.

"I stood in the shadows, watching him. As he left the room, I followed. I stopped him by the stairs that led down to the dressing rooms. I told him that I knew who he was, and I would expose him."

Kay sucked in a breath. At that point, Müller knew Mr. Gros was a threat. "What happened?"

"He laughed at me. He said he was here with the approval of the American government. He helped catch Communists. The war was over, he said, and there was nothing to fight anymore. He survived as I had done, and the spoils of the world went to the survivors."

Mr. Gros hung his head. "I wanted to kill him at that moment. He walked past me, without fear, thinking I was weak. I wanted to bash his head in. But I did not. I thought of Josephine, and I knew I would not kill him. But I also would not cower from him. I followed him. I stopped him in the hallway backstage and told him I suspected he was involved in the bombings.

"Müller claimed he had nothing to do with the Florida Terror. He stared at me then for a long time. I almost dropped to my knees. I remembered him looking at me at the camp. I used to watch his eyes as he decided if I would live or die."

"That's terrible," Kay whispered. She could not imagine surviving such a life.

"Then Müller surprised me. He said he knew who had orchestrated the bombings. If I wanted to get the name of that man, I needed to meet with him. We were to meet here, at Wolfie's, the next day. But of course, we did not meet. He was shot that night."

"Did you leave him there, near the dressing room?" Mrs. Roosevelt asked.

Mr. Gros shook his head. "He walked out with me. I saw him get into a taxi. I thought he had left. He must have returned and reentered the club."

Did that mean *Miller* was the man who had taken the cab? But what about Mr. Gros?

"Did you tell this to the police?" Mrs. Roosevelt asked, concerned.

"Yes. But the police are convinced the young woman murdered Müller. They were not interested in other suspects that I brought to the table."

"Which other suspects, Mr. Gros?" Mrs. R asked.

"The two men at the party, Mr. Mains and Mr. Reynolds, who are members of the KKK, I believe. They try to be anonymous in those ridiculous hoods. But I have been investigating the Klansmen of Miami since the bombings began. That put me on the trail of Franz Müller. It was a shock to see two Klansmen at Josephine's party. I warned her, and she put her finger to her lips. I realized she knew . . ."

"Did you see Josephine or Rosaleen Davis after the party? Inside or outside?" Mrs. R asked.

"No, I did not."

"You do not think Rosaleen Davis is guilty?" Mrs. R asked.

"No. Segregation and discrimination angered her. She was bitter that the war changed nothing. But I do not believe she could kill Müller." Isaac Gros looked down at his half-finished sandwich. "The best solution is that one of the Klansmen killed him. It would be preferable for everyone."

"Only if it can be proven," Mrs. R said. "And then Rosaleen is exonerated."

"It is late. I have taken much of your time," Isaac Gros said. "I fear I have ruined your appetite. For that, I am sorry."

"It was more food than I could manage anyway," Mrs. Roosevelt said.

Kay nodded agreement.

"I will return you to the Delano," Mr. Gros said.

They took the remainder of their sandwiches to go. Mr. Gros drove them to their hotel. As he stopped the car, he said, "I am not a killer. It has to be Reynolds or Mains. But they are dangerous men. If there is evidence against them, it would be gravely dangerous to try to find it."

After they got out, Mrs. R asked, "You saw Frank Miller take a taxi. When did you leave the club?"

"Immediately afterward. I hailed the next taxi," he responded through his open window. "Good night, Mrs. Roosevelt. Miss Thompson."

Mrs. R bid him good night. Kay did, and then he drove away. Kay watched his car merge into the light traffic on Collins Avenue.

"I am sure he is innocent," Kay said.

She saw Tim's car come up to the entrance. The valet hurried forward to take the keys. Mrs. Roosevelt waited for him to join them.

The doorman opened the door and Mrs. R thanked him. In the elevator, Mrs. R said, "Kay believes Mr. Gros is innocent," she said to Tim. "Why are you so certain, Kay?" she added.

"I believe he wouldn't let Rosaleen pay for his crime. Also, on the night of the party, Mr. Gros revealed his tattooed number to me. If he intended to murder Miller, would he have drawn attention to himself?" Kay asked.

"Those are assumptions," Tim pointed out. "Not facts."

"I know," Kay said. "But those are the reasons I think Mr. Gros did not do it. It must be either Mains or Reynolds."

"I agree with Mr. Gros," Mrs. Roosevelt said. "Those men are far too dangerous."

"Yeah," Tim echoed. "Keep away from them."

Mrs. R looked at her watch. "It is almost nine p.m. Josephine is performing tonight. Earlier, she left me a message asking if we would all be her special guests tonight. The two of you, myself, Stephen, and Jacques. She wishes for us to meet in her suite."

CHAPTER 21

Where do human rights begin? In small places, close to home—so close and so small that they cannot be seen on any map of the world. Yet they are the world of the individual person.

—Eleanor Roosevelt, Remarks at the United Nations, March 27, 1958

Mrs. Roosevelt knocked on the door to Josephine's suite. Stephen opened the door to them, then returned to stand in front of the sofa with his arms crossed over his broad chest.

Kay bristled at the tension the moment she walked in.

"You can't go on stage tonight, Jo," Stephen growled. His pale blond hair glowed in the light of the ceiling light. He wore long white shirtsleeves and dark blue trousers, his suit jacket folded over his arm. Kay couldn't take her eyes off his gun holster.

Standing in front of him, her arms also crossed, Josephine lifted her chin defiantly. Kay knew the signal. It was a strong woman's response when a man was attempting to tell her what to do.

"I am touched that you are worried, Stephen," Josephine purred. "But I will perform tonight. I have never missed a performance unless I was deathly ill. Even in the war. *Especially* in the war."

"Someone could shoot at you the minute you go out on stage."

Josephine shrugged. "I have often performed in such circumstances."

"Not when you were the direct target. Rosaleen's arrest has people riled up," Stephen said, growing heated. "There was a clash outside the precinct this afternoon between the people demanding her release—mostly Black people and young people—and a group of white men who want her to get the death penalty—"

He broke off. "God. I can't believe that could happen to her."

"It will not! Why do you insist on giving up?" Josephine exclaimed. "She will be exonerated. People are protesting as they did for Willie McGee."

"The white jury took two and a half minutes to find McGee guilty," Stephen muttered. "The DA will put together a jury who will convict her in their minds before they hear the evidence."

Kay knew Josephine feared the same thing.

She caught the expression on Josephine's face. Josephine was furious with Stephen for giving up hope over Rosaleen.

"No!" Josephine's voice rose, ringing and strong as it would be on stage. "Tonight, I am going to make a plea to my audience. I am going to tell them the truth of what is happening."

"I'm asking you not to do that. It's going to incite a riot," Stephen snapped.

"Eleanor, what should I do?" Josephine implored.

"I have always advised patience over violence," Mrs. Roosevelt said. "I cautioned people to wait for change. To push for change with riots and protests generates fear in politicians. Such actions make politicians believe they were right to keep wrongful laws because the people they oppress are violent. I soon realized it is impossible to ask for patience from people who saw their basic human rights trampled each day. People did not want to wait years, or decades, or generations. They are right. But there must be a way other than violent clashes."

"Tell the truth, Josephine," Mrs. R continued, "but ask people to be calm. Do not incite. That will not free Rosaleen, and I very much fear it might lead to violence against her."

The two women, who came from different backgrounds but who hoped for a common future—a future of peace and equal rights—looked at each other.

Kay saw they spoke a common language.

"I will tell the truth, but I will tell people that we must free Rosaleen legally. Don't you see, Stephen?" Josephine looked over to Stephen, who looked haggard.

"I am not in danger," Josephine added. "There have been no more threatening letters. Müller is dead so the letters stopped. *Now* the threat is to Rosaleen. I will save her." Josephine walked to Stephen's side. She laid her hand gracefully on his shoulder. "I must."

Stephen touched her hand. "O'Malley and I are going to be in the wings, watching the audience. If I see any sign of trouble, I am getting you off that stage. I want to go early to the theatre to scope out possible threats."

"I'll go too," Tim offered. "Josephine, I am here to act as your bodyguard."

"You boys go ahead," Josephine said, shooing them toward the door. "I must change into clothes I can wear to go to the Copa. We will be safe. Jacques will return and accompany us."

Stephen frowned. "Where is Jacques Abtey?"

Josephine shrugged. "I do not know. He came to see me, but he has work to do as well. But he will be here as promised."

"Okay," Stephen said. "Abtey's war record shows he is a seasoned special agent."

After the two men left, and Josephine closed the door behind them, she said, "Stephen forgets I lived through a war. I lived through the occupation of my beloved Paris. Goebbels called me an enemy of the Nazi state. I lived in great danger. But freedom is always worth it."

Five minutes after the men left, Mr. Abtey had arrived. Josephine's smile could have lit up a town, Kay thought. Josephine went into her bedroom to dress, and Mrs. Roosevelt, Jacques Abtey, and Kay sat in the sitting area.

Jacques Abtey said, "Josephine is the most courageous woman I have met."

He wore a pale blue suit that made his eyes look blue as sapphires. His blond hair was slicked down. He had watched Josephine leave the room with obvious admiration.

"In her childhood, she slept with newspapers for covers and her father papered the walls with them to keep out the cold of a St. Louis winter," Jacques said. "Josephine herself told me that the random pictures on the pages, pasted over each other, would transform into exotic animals before her eyes. She thought her father was the best artist in the world. When she was a child, she stole coal from parked freight trains to sell. When the train began to move, she hung on for as long as she could to get that precious coal, because it would sell for pennies. She only jumped when she knew she would perish if she waited until it was moving faster."

"Heavens," Mrs. Roosevelt said.

"I met Josephine at Beau Chêne," Abtey continued. "She volunteered to become an honorable correspondent at once. She could fly airplanes, proudly announcing to reporters she could do a loop-the-loop. In the winter of 1939, Josephine performed for soldiers on the front lines to keep up morale. For her grand finale she wore a costume of rhinestone-studded strips that barely covered her, with plumes of feathers and tulle hanging from her hips. For the homesick soldiers manning the Maginot Line, Josephine was like a goddess or an angel."

"Monsieur Abtey—" Kay pronounced "monsieur" carefully, but it sounded nothing like Josephine's lovely accent.

"Jacques," he said, and she wondered if it was to be friendly or because he could not bear hearing his language butchered.

"Jacques . . . I am sorry I made that accusation against you."

She saw Mrs. Roosevelt lift an approving eyebrow.

Jacques smiled magnanimously. "You are doing everything you can to free Rosaleen. I appreciate that. Her freedom is the omelet, I was just an egg that you needed to crack to get there."

Kay took a deep breath. "I have another impertinent question."

Mrs. R looked curious.

Kay batted her lashes. Not flirtatiously, but to look like an innocent in the world of secrets and espionage where he was a master. Flattery worked with men.

He nodded. "Please ask. I am curious now."

"Jacques, was Franz Müller the 'Ghost'?"

"I am not at liberty to say," he responded. "But it is an interesting question."

The way he answered surely meant yes.

If Jacques had encountered the Ghost in Miami, what would he do? He couldn't hand Müller over to the authorities—that would go nowhere, as the government had brought Müller here.

Would he decide to take justice into his own hands?

Had he been forced to act quickly, never dreaming Rosaleen would be arrested?

Then she looked down, at the coffee table.

A stack of magazines had been placed on it. On top was *Harper's Bazaar*, *The Christmas Issue* for December 1951. Kay had pored over the magazine as soon as it came out. On the cover, the model wore a tiny-waisted gown by Balenciaga. The backdrop was artwork with stylized chanticleers or, as Kay knew them, roosters. The letters were a deep wine red against a soft beige background.

Roseleen had sneered about Kay reading these magazines. Apparently, Josephine did too.

It came to her. A swift realization, like a fork of lightning in her head.

The threatening letters. Kay was certain the letters and words used to make them had been cut out of fashion magazines. Specifically the Christmas issue of *Harper's Bazaar*.

Kay opened the magazine. She now remembered seeing a full-page advertisement for Coty perfume with the typeface and colors she recognized from the last letter Josephine received.

She quickly flipped the pages. That page was missing. It had been neatly torn out.

Had *Josephine* made her own threatening letters? Why?

Or was it . . . ?

Josephine's suite was very much like Mrs. R's suite. There was a connecting door that led to Rosaleen's room. It stood open.

Mr. Abtey was engaged in conversation with Mrs. R. Josephine was in her bedroom.

Kay stood. "I must use the powder room."

She moved toward the washroom, checked that no one was looking, then slipped through the open door to Rosaleen's room. The wallpaper was diamonds of gold against a deep blue background. A blue satin bedspread covered the bed.

Shouldn't she feel guilty, searching Rosaleen's room? She didn't. Instead, she felt a thrill of excitement.

Quietly, her muscles tense, she went through the drawers of the vanity table, the bedside table, the chest of drawers. She ignored Rosaleen's personal items. Even when she found nothing, instinct compelled her to keep looking.

She listened for sound. All she heard was Mr. Abtey's luscious accent and Mrs. Roosevelt's gentle tones.

She went to the closet. Rosaleen's suitcase lay in there. As Kay opened it, she noticed a small lump, under the lining. Crouching down—dratted girdle—she noticed a small slit in the lining and slipped her fingers inside. Her fingers touched smooth, glossy paper. There were several, obviously missing, pages from *Harper's Bazaar*.

Reaching further, Kay touched something rubbery and slippery. She caught the scream before the sound left her lips. Steeling herself, she pulled the weird object out. Then sighed in relief.

She held a pair of yellow rubber gloves.

Returning to the vanity table, Kay found a bottle of glue for false eyelashes. Kay had never seen Rosaleen wear false eyelashes once. The glue bottle was almost empty.

As she slipped out of Rosaleen's room, she anxiously waited for her opportunity to tell Mrs. R. It came as Josephine emerged from her bedroom in a pale gray suit, looking marvelous. As Jacques Abtey went to Josephine, Kay whispered to Mrs. Roosevelt, "There is something I have to tell you."

"You found evidence that Rosaleen created those letters. I saw the expression on your face as you looked through that magazine," Mrs. R murmured.

"You—you knew?"

"I suspected."

"But why would she do it? Josephine has been so good to her."

Mrs. R put her finger to her lips to warn her to be quiet because Josephine was approaching. "I have a theory. Once I have proof, I shall tell Josephine."

Josephine had linked her arm with Jacques. "It is time to go to the Copa," Josephine said.

Kay nodded, staying quiet. She now knew Rosaleen had

planted the threatening letters. It hadn't been Franz Müller or the KKK. But what did that mean?

Even if Rosaleen intended harm, Josephine hadn't been the murder victim.

In the theatre of the Copa City Club, the spotlight made a white-gold circle in the center of the stage. Kay watched, awe-struck, as Josephine Baker stepped into it. Her sequined white dress sparkled. Her long, black chignon reflected the light. She held her head high, like a queen.

Applause rippled across the crowd. The lineup outside the Copa City Club had been longer tonight—nothing like scandal to bring out the crowds.

Kay had felt relief knowing Rosaleen was behind the letters. It meant there was no outside person who planned to murder Josephine Baker.

But now Kay realized that didn't mean someone wouldn't try to harm Josephine tonight, to stop her helping Rosaleen.

Kay sat beside Mrs. Roosevelt at a table right beside the stage. Tim stood in the wings of the stage on the right-hand side. Stephen was on the left.

Josephine picked up the microphone. "It is difficult for me to sing and bring you joy tonight," she said, her soaring voice filling the theatre. "My heart is filled with fear and worry.

"My assistant, a young woman, is being wrongfully held by the police in Miami."

Murmurs washed over the crowd.

"Rosaleen Davis is innocent!" Josephine declared.

More murmurs. There was a dark, sharp undertone, as if some of the crowd did not agree.

"The police tested the gun for Rosaleen's fingerprints!" she cried. "Do you think they found her fingerprints on the weapon that killed Frank Miller?"

Someone in the crowd shouted, "No!"

"Exactly! Her fingerprints were not on the gun. They tested for residue left after a gun is fired. They tested her hands, her clothes, even a pair of gloves she owned. They didn't find a thing. But the police did not let her go! They claim she had a motive!"

Kay saw shock on faces. They did not expect Josephine to say words that might condemn Rosaleen.

In the audience, Kay saw Mr. Gros, who stood out with his pale coloring and fair hair.

Nearby, in the audience, a man shouted, "Where there's smoke, there's gonna be fire."

Did most people feel that way?

"Frank Miller's real name is Franz Müller, and he was a Nazi officer who ran a concentration camp during the war," Josephine exclaimed. "He deserved to face justice. He should have faced it in a court of law, but he evaded the law. A former Nazi must have many enemies. Evidence has shown Rosaleen Davis did not shoot him. Someone else murdered former Nazi Franz Müller. Rosaleen should be freed. If you believe in justice, you must help fight for her freedom!"

Josephine lifted her hands.

Several members of the audience applauded. They rose to their feet. But some people did not.

Kay scanned the crowd. Mr. Eulie Reynolds was in the audience. With his bulky body and white suit, he was hard to miss. He lifted his hand. His thumb was raised, his forefinger pointing at Josephine, as if his finger was a gun. Then he smiled and waved his hand as if he were just pointing at Josephine.

But Kay had seen the gesture. So had Mrs. R.

Josephine did not appear to feel threatened. She continued in her strong voice, "I sang this song for troops on the Maginot Line. It is called 'Mon Coeur Est un Oiseau des Îles.' In English, it means, 'My heart is a bird of the isles.'"

Kay's heart pounded as Josephine sang. It kept pounding

until they reached intermission and the lights came up. Somehow, she felt Josephine would be safe if the lights were on.

Mrs. Roosevelt rose from her seat. "Come with me, Kay. There is something I wish to confirm backstage."

Kay was curious. She expected they would go to Josephine's dressing room. But they walked past it.

Kay could hear female voices. Turning a corner in the corridor, she saw two middle-aged women. One was Flora, in her large spectacles and uniform dress, carrying a wastebasket out of a room. The other, a short woman with a broad, sturdy build, held a large garbage bag.

Mrs. Roosevelt approached Flora. "Could we speak with you, please? We met before. I am Eleanor Roosevelt."

"Yes, Mrs. Roosevelt, I know who you are. I don't know why you all want to talk to me. I just clean around here."

Kay could see that behind the glasses her eyes were large and red-rimmed, as if she had been crying. But she frowned at Mrs. Roosevelt and in that expression, Kay saw beyond the glasses and the drab dress. Kay saw the truth.

"I see the resemblance to Rosaleen," Kay said.

Draped over the handle of the cleaning cart was a pair of yellow rubber gloves.

"I don't know what you are talking about. I've got my work to do." Flora turned away, grasping the handle of her cart filled with cleaning products and buckets and rags.

But Kay could sense the woman's fear.

Mrs. Roosevelt held out a handkerchief. Sensible, white, monogrammed with ER. "For your eyes," she said kindly. "Even behind the heavy glasses, I see your eyes are red-rimmed. You must have been crying a great deal over your daughter's arrest."

Flora hesitantly accepted the handkerchief.

"I noticed the resemblance on the first night," Mrs. Roosevelt said. "After Rosaleen told us about her mother being a friend of Josephine, I was curious as to why would her mother be here, yet not acknowledge her daughter or her friend?"

Kay remembered Mrs. Roosevelt looking at the cleaning lady, who had also hurried away that night. Mrs. Roosevelt had observed something Kay had not seen.

"Josephine didn't even recognize me," Flora said, bitterly. "Not after I'd aged over twenty-five years. But I have to get to work." She began to push the cart away, down the hallway.

"I believe you didn't want Josephine to recognize you. You wanted to hide behind the glasses and the uniform," Mrs. Roosevelt said. Mrs. Roosevelt added, calmly, after Flora, "Mrs. Davis, did you let Rosaleen use your rubber gloves so that she did not leave fingerprints on those fake threatening notes?"

The woman stopped.

Mrs. R continued. "When I learned from Josephine that Rosaleen's mother was once a performer, I saw the connection. I believe Rosaleen concocted the threatening letters and planted them. The letters revealed that you knew a great deal about Josephine's past. I assume you kept tabs on her accomplishments. Josephine was chosen to go to Paris instead of you and she became a star."

"While I got left with nothing," Flora Davis said angrily. "I could barely make ends meet."

"Was your plan to harm Josephine?" Mrs. R asked.

"No!" Flora exclaimed. "And it was all my idea. Don't blame Rosaleen."

She leaned back against the wall and removed her glasses. Kay realized Flora Davis was as tall as Mrs. R. She had been stooping over the cart to appear smaller. Flora suddenly looked younger. She looked more like the chorus girl she had once been.

"I convinced Rosaleen to help me," she said. "When I learned Josephine was coming back to Miami, I got a job here at the Copa. I felt this was my chance. I never meant to harm Josephine. I wanted to frighten her away from performing so I could take her place on stage. I could convince the manager to give me a chance if he was desperate to replace Josephine. He's got back-up singers, but I'm a better singer. They can't solo but I can. I haven't performed for years, but I practice every chance I can with the musicians when they are off work."

She hung her head. "All I wanted was one chance to be in the spotlight. I thought maybe the Copa City Club would give me work as a singer if I got the chance to perform."

"But you must have known Josephine Baker is hard to scare," Mrs. Roosevelt said.

"You don't believe that I didn't plan to hurt her. I swear that is the truth. When I realized I couldn't scare her, I planned to dose her with a couple of sleeping pills before her show. I was going to tell the manager she was drunk, and I could take her place."

Flora gazed up at Mrs. Roosevelt. "Those letters had the opposite effect to what I intended. Every letter made her more determined to perform. I knew I had to try something else . . ."

"Did you go to Josephine's dressing room the night of the shooting?" Mrs. R asked.

Flora hesitated. Then admitted, "Rosaleen was going to slip the sleeping pills into Josephine's customary glass of water that she drank before a performance. I was going to hide the pills where Rosaleen could find them."

Kay's heart sank. She had liked Rosaleen. But Rosaleen had tried to trick Josephine. She lied to Mrs. Roosevelt about the letters. Rosaleen was not the honest and just woman Kay had thought she was.

"I found a tube of lipstick," Kay said. "Was it yours?"

Flora shook her head. "I don't wear any makeup when I'm cleaning. As you deducted, Mrs. Roosevelt, I wanted to look different from the Flossie that Josephine knew all those years ago."

"If you were at the dressing room, did you see Frank Miller in the dressing room with your daughter? Did he threaten her?"

"You think I shot him? To protect her?"

"Did you?"

Flora met Mrs. Roosevelt's gaze, saying nothing. Then she said, defiantly, "I don't have a gun. Where would I have gotten a gun?"

"You could have gotten a gun very easily, ma'am." Tim O'Malley stepped up from behind them. Kay hadn't realized he was there.

Flora shrank back, right against the wall. "Are you the police?"

"No, I work for Mrs. Roosevelt. I know the kind of men who run nightclubs. The owner of the club kept a handgun in his office. I learned that gun is now missing."

Kay had to admit Tim was good at his job. She had never even thought of that—that a gun might be on the premises.

"It would also have been easy for Rosaleen to take that gun," Tim said. "If it turns out to be the gun the police have in evidence."

"But she didn't!"

"The police will think she did. Or they will suspect you took it and gave it to her, with the plan to murder the rich man who wanted to stop her marriage," Tim continued.

Flora staggered. She almost slid down the wall, her head swiveling as she looked from Tim to Mrs. Roosevelt. "I know exactly what the police will think." Tears welled in her eyes. "All right! I shot Frank Miller. Take me to the police. I will confess. My daughter is innocent!"

But Mrs. R shook her head. "I am not going to telephone the police."

"I just confessed to murder. You must call the police!" Flora cried.

"You do not have to confess to a crime you did not commit, to save your daughter."

Tim said, "With all due respect, Mrs. Roosevelt, how are you so certain she is innocent?"

"I think if she was guilty, she would have turned herself in the moment Rosaleen was arrested."

"I heard Josephine say that the police proved Rosaleen couldn't have shot that man and they still won't release her," Flora said. "Maybe my confession will set her free. Better I'm wrongfully convicted than Rosaleen. The letters and the sleeping pills were my idea. It's right that I should take the blame."

"Not for a murder you didn't commit. That only means the real murderer will go free. Please, Flora, listen to me. Do not do this. The real culprit will be found," Mrs. Roosevelt said.

The two women gazed at each other.

Then Flora nodded. "I'll trust you, Mrs. Roosevelt. Please, save my daughter!"

CHAPTER 22

If we hope to be trusted, we must trust others.
—Eleanor Roosevelt, My Day, January 5, 1946

As Josephine performed the second half of her show onstage, Eleanor sat down with Flora in an empty dressing room. She sent Kay back with Tim to watch the show.

Though the mystery of the letters was solved, Eleanor wanted to ensure Josephine was safe. She felt Flora would speak more openly in a private setting. Flora looked like a different woman without the unbecoming horn-rimmed glasses.

Eleanor asked gently, "Tell me exactly what happened on the night Frank Miller was murdered, Flora. You went to Josephine's dressing room."

Flora nodded. "I waited until Rosaleen and Josephine had left. Rosaleen locked the dressing room door. I have keys to all the rooms so I can clean."

"The keys that you claimed were stolen?"

Flora looked down. She twisted her fingers together in her lap. "That wasn't true. I had to make it look like someone else could have had access to the dressing room and could have locked Rosaleen inside."

"Take me through every detail. We cannot help Rosaleen without the truth."

"You believe she is innocent?" Flora asked.

"I do believe it. I am trying to *prove* that she is," Eleanor said.

"I unlocked the dressing room door," Flora said. "I was about to go inside to plant the sleeping pills when I heard voices. Rosaleen's voice and a man's voice. I realized they were coming closer, so I panicked and ran. I hid in the supply closet."

"They were together?" Eleanor asked, surprised. This was not what Rosaleen had said. But she did not state that or confront Flora.

She listened.

"I had forgotten to relock the dressing room door," Flora said. "I opened the closet door an inch and peeked out. Rosaleen was with the tall white-haired man. Miller, the man who was shot. They were arguing. He said, 'You can't marry Stephen.' Rosaleen said, 'We are in love, and I will marry him.' Miller said, 'He's not in love with you. Anyway, he can't marry you. It's not legal.' Rosaleen responded, 'It's not legal in *Florida*, but we will go to a place where it is legal. We can marry in New York, which never had miscegenation laws.' Miller said something else, but I could not hear it. He opened the door to the dressing room. He went inside and Rosaleen followed him . . ."

"What happened then?" Eleanor prompted.

"They were in the dressing room, and I could no longer make out their words. I don't know why I continued to hide. I thought I heard footsteps, but the sound was so soft I couldn't be sure. I didn't look out. It was foolish, because I had every excuse to be in a supply closet. I could have pretended I was cleaning. Then I heard the gunshot. It was so close my ears were ringing. I had to clap my hands to them. I thought Rosaleen had been shot. I pushed open the door and I saw a tall man in a trench coat running away. Like Stella Hilton saw."

Eleanor remembered what Kay had related from Miss Hilton. "Stella Hilton told my secretary and Mr. O'Malley that she had a guest in her dressing room, and after she saw the man, she grabbed the hand of her admirer and hightailed it out of there before the police came."

Flora nodded. "Your secretary talked to both Stella and I. Stella was telling everyone about that tonight. She said she feared Josephine had been assassinated, and she didn't want to be next."

"But you knew there was not a real threat to Josephine," Eleanor said.

"I knew the letters weren't real. But I was scared. I thought maybe the KKK had decided to attack us."

"Why didn't you go to Rosaleen?" Eleanor asked.

"I saw the security guard coming so I stayed in the closet."

Eleanor frowned. "As a mother, if I feared my child had been shot, I would have rushed in, heedless of danger. Heedless of the security guard."

"I was frozen. I'm ashamed of myself, but I was so terrified and shocked, I couldn't move. I heard the security guard pounding on the door. I heard him talking to Rosaleen. I realized she was all right. But I was afraid that she had shot that man."

Tears welled in Flora's eyes.

"Why did you think that when you saw the person running away?"

Flora just shook her head. She was sobbing now.

"Did you see Stella?" Eleanor asked. "If she ran out of her dressing room, you must have seen her and her admirer. If she ran away between the shot and the arrival of the security guard."

Flora stared, tears dripping off her cheeks. "I didn't see anyone."

"Do you remember anything about this man? Anything more than a hat and trench coat?"

"He was tall, and he looked like he had a skinny build. That's all."

"Why didn't you come forward? This helps to corroborate Rosaleen's story that someone else shot Mr. Miller." But then, it revealed that Rosaleen had lied. Why had she done so? Was she simply too afraid to admit that she knew Frank Miller? Was she foolishly hoping that the police would not find out?

"Do you remember how tall he was? You and I are of a height. Was he taller than you?"

"I don't know. It was hard to tell because he was running. He didn't look unusually tall. Maybe my height," Flora said.

Mr. Gros was several inches taller than Eleanor. Mr. Mains was shorter.

But then, Flora shook her head. "I really can't be sure. When I found out that Miller was the victim, I thought the man in the trench coat might be Stephen, Rosaleen's fiancé. Maybe he shot his stepfather to protect Rosaleen. I've never met Stephen. I don't know what he looks like."

"It couldn't have been Stephen," Eleanor said, and she explained why.

"Stephen must be innocent. I'm sorry I kept quiet about everything. I didn't want the police to know that Rosaleen had walked into that dressing room with Mr. Miller. And I didn't want them to know about the letters—I feared that would make them more convinced that Rosaleen is guilty."

"Now, you must tell the truth," Eleanor said. "Rosaleen told the police she found Miller in the dressing room. That was not true. Do you know why she lied about that?"

"I don't know. But I can't talk to the police now. I can't tell them that Rosaleen lied."

"You must tell the truth."

"I won't!"

As Eleanor quietly observed her, Flora exclaimed, "Don't blame Rosaleen for sending Josephine those letters. I know she hated to do it. Rosaleen is the most honest person I've ever known and I'm proud of her. But she spent her life listening to my bitterness. She wanted to give me one more chance. It went against everything she believed in, but she did it for me."

"Will you tell Josephine the truth?" Eleanor asked.

"I can't face her," Flora said. "And I don't want her to blame Rosaleen."

"She must know that those letters are not real."

Flora nodded. "Tell her. But please, please tell her that Rosaleen meant her no harm and that blame for frightening her lies only with me."

It was midnight when Eleanor and Kay returned to the Delano. In the suite, Kay typed up the My Day column for the day and went downstairs to send it by wire. When she returned, Eleanor noted she was pale.

"Rosaleen shouldn't have created those letters, but I understand why she did it. Sometimes it is impossible to say no to someone you love. But what if we can't solve the murder before we have to return to Hyde Park?" Kay asked. "What if we can't help Rosaleen in time?"

Eleanor was somber. She had to travel to Paris for the United Nations session on the 31st of December. Kay was right. They were running out of time.

"We must try," she said.

"What did Josephine say when you told her about the letters?" Kay asked.

"With a solemn expression, she thanked me for telling her. Now, I must retire for the night."

"I'm going out on my balcony for a little while," Kay said. "Good night, Mrs. R."

"Good night, Kay. It is a lovely night to look at the stars."

The next morning, Eleanor awoke with a sense of frustration. They had many suspects: Flora, Mr. Gros, and Reynolds and Mains, if those men were members of the KKK. If Frank Miller really intended to reveal the name of the man who had engineered the bombings in Florida, as Isaac Gros had claimed, the KKK had reason to silence him.

As she put on her robe, Eleanor felt there was a vital clue that she had already learned, but try as she might, she could not think of what it was. She had first thought it curious that Flora had not seen Stella, the backup singer. But Flora had seen the man in the trench coat from the closet, and Stella saw him from her dressing room. It was possible the two women had not seen each other.

There had been the lipstick found by Kay in the supply closet. Flora claimed it was not hers. Whose was it?

No, it was something else that she had learned . . .

What if Kay was right? What if she ran out of time?

Eleanor went to the door to Kay's room and knocked on it. There was no answer. Eleanor ordered breakfast. When the food arrived, she knocked again.

After a half hour, she tried again.

When there was no answer, Eleanor tried the knob. She felt guilty simply opening Kay's door and barging in, but she had a sense of apprehension.

The door was unlocked. When she swung it open, she saw at once that the bed was neatly made. It had not been slept in. The room was empty.

Where was Kay? Where had she spent the night?

CHAPTER 23

As for the Ku Klux Klan, I fear it is one of the organizations that no democracy can long endure.
—Eleanor Roosevelt, My Day, April 6, 1949

Earlier

Kay stepped out onto her balcony, knowing she wouldn't be able to sleep. Flora Davis had admitted to murder to save her daughter. But Mrs. R believed Flora was innocent and Kay had faith in Mrs. R. It had to be one of the other suspects.

They had to solve the murder before they had to leave.

Kay looked down at the pool. Just like on the night she had sat on the edge with Rosaleen, spotlights illuminated the graceful palm trees and shimmered on the water.

This time two men sat on the chaise longues by the pool edge. They didn't look like they were swimming. Kay recognized them even from several floors up. Eulie Reynold's bulky body and his garish blue-and-green suit gave him away. The other man, who wore a gray suit and fedora, and had a lean build, was Claude Mains.

Why were they at the Delano? And why were they talking by the pool?

They were fully dressed. Obviously not planning a midnight swim.

Kay felt a surge of excitement. They had to be up to no good. Josephine—or Mrs. Roosevelt—could be at risk. Or maybe they were discussing Müller's murder.

She had to find out what they were saying.

Kay was not known for making a quick change. An outfit had to be selected. Makeup touched up. Hair rearranged and secured with a mist of hair lacquer. But she wriggled out of her foundation garments as fast as she could and yanked on her bikini.

What if Mains or Reynolds shot Müller to prevent him from talking about the bombings? Then, in the cowardly fashion of the evil KKK, did the killer try to pin the crime on Rosaleen, a Black woman?

In three minutes, Kay was in her bathing suit with a wrap thrown over it. She jammed her feet into her sandals. She was about to leave when she thought: what if she had to follow the men? She threw capri pants and a blouse into her straw beach bag because she could pull them on over her bikini. Then she raced out of her room. She jabbed desperately at the elevator's down button, as if it would come faster if she pushed it more.

Seconds later, she strode out of the elevator into the lobby.

For her plan to work, she needed to look like a woman with no thought in her head but looking glamorous at the pool.

She felt like a Hitchcock heroine. Risking her life to find out the truth.

Her stomach churned with fear. But she had never felt more alive.

It was almost two a.m. As she pushed open the door that led to the gardens and outdoor pool, Kay heard the rhythmic murmur of the ocean waves rushing up on the sand from beyond the back of the property. She didn't know if the tide was going out or coming in. The sign on the door indicated the pool was for guests only. Either Reynolds or Mains—or both—were staying at the hotel.

Right now, the pool was deserted other than Reynolds and Mains, who sat at the far end.

If only she could wear sunglasses, the perfect movie-star-style poolside accessory. Behind the dark glasses, she could secretly watch Mains and Reynolds.

But wearing sunglasses would look *ridiculous* at night. Therefore, suspicious.

Reynolds glanced over at her.

Kay tried not to stare at him. Or shake with nerves. She wanted to get close enough to listen in, but wouldn't it look suspicious if she selected a chaise beside the two men when all the other lounge chairs were empty?

She had an idea. She walked around the pool, passing the two men.

Mains noticed her now. Both men were watching openly. Kay put on an act, sighing breathlessly as she put down her bag on the empty chair beside her, then dropped the wrap on top of it. It was one thing to fantasize about wearing the Marilyn bikini on the beach. Another to do it in front of two men who could be involved with murder.

She felt . . . exposed. But she had to act as if nothing was wrong.

Kicking off her sandals, she grasped the shiny metal handrails that flanked the stairs leading into the pool. She dipped her toe in. "Oh, mercy, it's so c-cold!" she exclaimed. She had just affected the worst Southern accent. She must be the hammiest actress ever. Alfred Hitchcock wouldn't be breaking down her door and turning her into his next leading actress.

She made her way slowly down the ladder and the men turned away. They hunched down and continued to talk.

They obviously dismissed her as being dumb because she was a woman with curves in a bathing suit.

Paddling lazily in an ineffective backstroke, Kay pretended to swim, but listened in.

"What is the Klan gonna do now that Miller's gone?" Mains asked. "He was bankrolling our plans."

Kay frowned, making a supposedly lazy circle in the pool. Mains didn't sound like he had carried out the murder.

"What about the stepson, Stephen Roberts?" Mains asked. "Looks like he's getting a fat inheritance. Will he come on board?"

Reynolds stayed silent for a minute before he said, "Roberts is CIA."

Mains's knee jiggled up and down as if with nerves. "That doesn't mean he wouldn't back us."

The way the men were talking, it appeared Isaac Gros was wrong—Miller was behind the bombings.

"It was lucky for Roberts that Grand Dragon Miller died," Reynolds said slowly. "Miller is worth about fifty million dollars. That's a hell of a lot of moola."

Grand Dragon Miller.

Kay had to turn her face away as she swam past them. Anna Lane had used the title, and it made Kay want to snigger. But despite the silly title, Miller/Müller had been truly evil.

"The Grand Dragon told me he was thinking about cutting his stepson out of his will," Reynolds said.

Anna had been right. Not that Kay doubted Anna's information. A secretary knew *everything* about the boss's personal life. More than a wife.

Fifty million dollars was a powerful motive.

But Stephen was in the clear. And Kay didn't want to believe this was like Agatha Christie's *Death on the Nile*. She refused to believe Rosaleen had fired the gun while Stephen was establishing his alibi in an airplane.

Her faith in Rosaleen had wobbled when she realized Rosaleen had written the threatening letters. She had admired Rosaleen for her determination to build a career. It took brains and courage to get admitted to Howard University to study law.

Flora had wanted Mrs. Roosevelt to understand that she was the reason Rosaleen had broken her moral code.

Kay believed in Rosaleen again.

Reynolds said, "I overheard Miller tell Gros that he wasn't the architect of the bombings. But he knew who was."

He overheard? He knew Miller was going to give up a fellow KKK member . . . or maybe Reynolds was that man.

Reynolds had been at the Copa City Club, meaning he was "on the spot" of the murder, and he was tall. Maybe the trench coat made him look trimmer—

"I was sure he was," Mains said, looking surprised. "He had the money. It had to be Miller."

Kay forgot to kick and paddle with her arms. She ducked under for a second. She came up sputtering.

The men were too engrossed to notice her.

She was surprised Mains didn't know who was behind the bombings. She noticed Reynolds didn't say anything.

"Do you think Rosaleen Davis did it?" Mains asked.

Kay frowned. It sounded as if he had no idea who did it. Or was he acting?

"Our friends in the Miami Beach P.D. say she couldn't have fired the gun." Reynolds frowned. "It's a problem."

Kay couldn't believe her ears. The KKK didn't have *a* friend in the police department. They had *friends*. It was a shocking thought. But then, Tim O'Malley had been forced out of the Washington P.D. because he had been outspoken about corruption.

"Who are they? Can we trust them?" Mains asked.

"They are men loyal to a former police chief who was a Klansman," Reynolds answered.

"If she didn't do it, was it one of our brethren?" Mains asked. "Someone who knew Miller planned to talk to Isaac Gros?"

Reynolds pulled out a handkerchief. He mopped his broad forehead. "Are you accusing me?"

"No, I'm not. I'm just wondering. I don't understand why Miller would talk."

"Miller was losing his nerve."

Kay found that astounding. He had been a death camp commandant.

Mains said, "The Grand Dragon is dead. You could move into his position like you wanted."

"Yeah. Our problem is the Davis girl. We don't want her to go to trial."

Mains looked as confused as Kay felt. She glanced quickly at him as she did another partial lap of the pool. "We don't?"

"No. Fortunately, that is going to be taken care of."

"What do you mean?"

Reynolds lifted his bulk off the chaise longue with a loud grunt. "We need to go. We're meeting tonight at the fun park."

The *fun park*? Why were the KKK meeting at an amusement park in the middle of the night?

Or was "fun park" code for something else, something horrible?

"What is the plan to eliminate Davis?" Mains asked.

Reynolds hesitated. This time he looked at Kay. Suddenly he smiled at her. She froze, chilled to the bone.

"I will explain on the way. It's going to happen in the morning."

"At the park?" Mains asked.

Reynolds' answer was under his breath. Kay couldn't hear.

She ducked under the water and swam quickly back toward the end of the pool, to her towel and bag. Her heart pounded and she struggled to hold her breath, but she propelled herself with fast, clean strokes—she had grown up around boys and used to compete with them before she started thinking about dating them. But swimming was hard because her whole body was tense. Right now, Reynolds could shoot her easily.

Reynolds had known she was listening. That smirk revealed

it. He was goading her, telling her that the KKK planned to murder Rosaleen.

She came up by the ladder that led out of the pool.

The men were gone.

Then she heard footsteps crunching on the path that led to the lobby.

Kay pulled herself up the ladder and out of the water. She struggled to pull her wrap over her wet body. It cost precious seconds, but she couldn't run through the Delano in her bikini. She snatched up her bag.

Reynolds and Mains would be going to a car, which meant they had to get the valet at the front to bring it around for them.

She had to get to the hotel's entrance. Maybe she could jump in a cab and ask him to "follow that car."

She yanked open the door to the lobby and collided with a man who was about to step outside.

"Sorry," she said as she tried to move past him.

"What were you doing out here with those two men?"

She looked up at green eyes that flashed with annoyance and worry.

It was Tim.

CHAPTER 24

You must do the thing you think you cannot do.
—Eleanor Roosevelt, *You Learn By Living*, 1960

Tim stood directly in front of her. "I saw the two KKK guys come inside. Were you *spying* on them? Have you lost your mind? You think you are some kind of detective. You aren't. You are not going after those men."

He said it as if when he said no, she had to acquiesce.

Kay bristled.

"And you aren't going to do it in a wet bathing suit."

The bathing suit was under her wrap. She didn't know how he knew it was wet until she saw the damp had leached through, making the wrap cling to her hips and bosom.

Tim blushed.

"I overheard them say there is a plan to murder Rosaleen. The KKK has friends in the police. They may already have her prisoner, and they are meeting up to kill her. *We* need to follow them!"

"What?"

She threw him a withering glance. "They might be meeting up to kill Rosaleen. There isn't time to discuss this. They are probably getting away right now."

"Their cars are in valet parking. It will take a few minutes to get them out," Tim said calmly. "I learned they are both staying at the Delano."

"How did you find out?" she asked.

"Mrs. R spotted Mains in the lobby, so I gave a generous tip to the concierge for some information," he said.

"Oh. I thought it was because they were at the pool, which is only for guests."

"Huh," he said. "Good observation. My car is on the street—I didn't park it. I can be in the car and ready to follow them."

"I'm going with you."

"No."

"Yes."

"No."

"You shouldn't go alone," Kay insisted. "I can keep a lookout for their car while you're driving. If I'm in the car, I can't be in any danger, can I?"

She expected he would balk. But he said, "Maybe it's a good idea to have you with me, so I know where you are."

It annoyed her, but she said, "Exactly!" as if he was right. "You get the car. I'll wait out front."

"Shouldn't you get . . . changed?"

"I can change in the car. I brought spare clothes in my beach bag. Now, hurry up. We've wasted enough time circling around the conclusion we both knew we would reach."

He stepped aside and she swept past. She heard him mutter, "I bet I'm going to regret this."

She ignored that. Hitching her beach bag on her shoulder, Kay hurried through the lobby and out the front doors. The blond, sunburned young man on valet duty was standing under the entrance canopy. Guests were returning from night clubs.

He tipped his cap to her. "Can I get your car, miss?"

"I was going to meet my friend out here," she said innocently, "but I don't know what car he is driving. You parked it for him."

Kay knew she was about to be caught in a lie, and she had to work fast. "My friend is Mr. Mains. Your height. Dark hair. His smile isn't quite as nice as yours."

The young attendant blushed—she seemed to be able to put color in a man's cheeks. "Mr. Mains drives a red Ford coupe. But he didn't wait for you, miss. He's gone."

Bravo. The young man didn't realize she'd lied. "He . . . uh . . . didn't know I would meet him. I wanted to surprise him. I guess you don't know where he went?" she simpered. "I think he's going to a fun park."

"Yeah, he wanted directions to Whoopee."

"To what?"

"Whoopee. It's an amusement park," the young man said.

Kay fished in her tote bag for her change purse. She pushed a dollar bill into the young man's hand. "Maybe I can catch up to him. Where's the park?"

He gave her directions. She tried to remember them all.

Tim's car rolled up. She opened the back door and slid in.

"I'm the chauffeur?"

"I'm going to get changed in the back seat. Don't talk. I don't want to forget the directions that young man gave me to Whoopee."

"To what?" Tim asked, just as she had.

"It's a fun park." She gave him the address.

"Why are they going to a fun park in the middle of the night?"

"When we get there, I guess we will find out." She felt sick despite her tough talk. They had to get there in time!

She began the directions as Tim started out. He floored the accelerator. The tires squealed, and Kay realized he was going awfully fast. Fast enough to catch up to Mains.

"That could be him," Tim said abruptly. Looking out the windshield from the back, she saw a car painted dark red. "That's a 1949 club coupe." As the Ford veered off to the left, Tim said, "It looks like he's following the same route."

Tim looked up into the rearview mirror. "When we get to wherever Mains is going, you are going to stay in the car."

Kay didn't answer. She pulled her clothes out of her bag. He must know she wasn't going to agree.

Getting changed in the back seat wasn't as easy as she thought. The blouse was easy. She put it over her bikini top and buttoned it up. The challenging part was wriggling into her capri pants over her wet suit.

She lifted one bare leg in the air to pull the snug capri pant leg over her foot.

The car suddenly swerved to the left. Horns blared furiously.

"What are you doing?" Tim demanded.

"I'm trying to put clothes on over my bathing suit. What are you doing? Are you trying to crash the car?"

"I looked in the rearview mirror and your bare legs were waving around."

"One leg."

"And where is your bathing suit?"

"It's there, I promise. It's a bikini. Like Marilyn wore."

He muttered something. It sounded like "Mother Mary have mercy."

She let out a huff of breath trying to pull up her pants. "Putting my top on was simple. The challenge is wriggling into these capris. They're stuck. I'm trying to lift my hips, but it doesn't help when you—"

They shot to the right this time and the front passenger-side wheel bounced off the curb.

Kay squeaked as she slid off the back seat. She braced herself with her bare foot.

"Could you drive more carefully?"

"I'm trying."

Kay had a brainwave about the capris. Turning her back to the front seat, she managed to stand, with her back arched against the roof of the car. She was tugging them up over her backside—

"Shit!" Tim exploded.

The car lurched to a stop. Kay lost her balance but toppled forward onto the plushy back seat. "Ow," she said.

"Sorry. Almost hit the car in front of me."

"Aren't you paying attention?" she demanded.

"Not with your rear end in that scrap of fabric filling up the rearview," he muttered. "That's not a bathing suit. It looks like you tied a hankie around your hips."

"That is a bathing suit. Keep your eyes on the road—and on Main's car." Then she cried, "Look over there!"

Against the dark sky, a Ferris wheel was lit up, revolving slowly. It looked like it was filled by ghosts. She peered forward. "I can't believe it."

"What?"

"Can't you see? The Ferris wheel is full of men from the KKK, and they are wearing their white robes and pointy hoods."

Stopping in a corner of the parking lot, Tim shut off the engine.

From the back seat, Kay watched the Ferris wheel circle backward, lifting the white-hooded men in a slow revolution. The KKK must have rented out the amusement park. It was creepy.

"I'm not staying in the car," she said. "I'm coming with you. It'll be safer. For both of us."

Tim turned. She was sure he was going to argue, but he looked spooked too. As if the incongruity of the KKK on a Ferris wheel made him as nervous as she.

"Okay," he said. He pushed open his door and got out.

Kay slid out of the back seat. She heard the tinny music that accompanied fairground rides. Screeching gulls swooped through the air.

Somewhere in the amusement park a gray plume of smoke rose. The smoke curled up almost as high as the Delano Hotel.

"Is something on fire?"

"Yeah," Tim said, his expression grim. "I think it's a cross."

"Oh."

"We can't hang around and we can't blend in at the fairground," Tim said. "I didn't think to throw in a few bedsheets from the hotel."

"What if they have Rosaleen in there?" she demanded. "We have to find out!"

"I can sneak in through the fence. If they have her, it's probably where they are burning that cross."

"I'm coming too."

"No."

"Yes."

"No."

"I can just follow you."

He sighed. "I can't stop you. So come on." He took hold of her hand, startling her.

The phrase "I can look after myself" ran through her head but she didn't say it. She was trembling. As they followed a path that ran along the fence surrounding the amusement park, she appreciated having him at her side.

As they neared the back fence, the smell of smoke grew stronger.

"We fought a war against tyranny and the racism of the Nazis, but back home there are guys in hoods burning crosses and attacking people." Tim shook his head.

"I think these kinds of men were fighting to be the ones able to carry out the tyranny," Kay said.

"I think you're right," he said softly.

She heard the catch in his throat. She knew he had bad memories of the war—most men did.

At the back of the park, they were sheltered by a grove of palms. They weaved between the trees, following the back fence. Then ahead, Kay caught a glimpse of flames leaping toward the stars, yellow, orange, red. The crackling of the fire filled her ears.

Please don't let us be too late, she thought.

A gate in the fence stood open.

"All are welcome," Tim muttered very softly but sarcastically. "Guess some of the Klan tends to show up late."

Kay slipped through the opening in the gate. Tim sputtered, but then he followed her. The asphalt underfoot was cracked, with weeds pushing through. They were behind the tents that held the games, like target shooting.

At the edge of the row of tents, Tim stopped. He put his finger to his lips. Unnecessarily. Kay had no intention of making a sound.

Peeking out from around the last tent, she saw a huge burning cross erected on open space in the back of the fairground. A circle of figures in white robes and hoods surrounded it.

She couldn't see Rosaleen.

One figure raised his hands. Silence fell, except for the crackling of the fire.

The man talking praised the men who bravely orchestrated the death of Harry T. Moore. "Our source at the hospital says that Harriette Moore won't survive," he said. "Her injuries are too great."

The circle of white-sheeted men cheered.

Kay wanted to throw up.

This wasn't *human*. Or worse, maybe it very much was.

Were Reynolds and Mains out there in the circle? She couldn't tell. Several men were tall and wide. Others were short and fat, their white robes making them look like baseballs. Their anonymity let them do the most inhuman things. Cowards.

Tim took her hand again. His long, strong fingers wrapped around hers. His hand felt hot, which likely meant hers was ice-cold.

"We will destroy Rosaleen Davis. Our friends have arranged for her to be transferred from the cells at the station to a prison this morning. She will be taken when she is in transit."

These men had attacked an innocent, defenseless couple. Planted bombs on high school steps. Had blown out windows of a school for young children.

Kay didn't doubt they were serious.

"We know their plan. I need to talk to Mike Connor so we can stop it," Tim said softly. His strong hands turned her shoulders. "We need to get out of here."

He gave her a gentle push, but the heel of her right sandal caught in a fissure in the asphalt. Her ankle wrenched over. Kay bit back a scream of pain.

Trying to support her, Tim fell over the same fissure. He landed on his knee and let out an "oof." Over the chanting of the men and the crackling of the burning cross, the sound should have been undetectable.

But two men, who had their backs to Kay and Tim, watching the fire, swiveled around. They wore the same shapeless robes and pointed hats as everyone else. But one was tall and hefty and the other was shorter than her. It had to be Reynolds and Mains. They were at the back. They had arrived late, like she and Tim.

They started running toward Tim and her. Kay stared for a moment, frozen, realizing they couldn't run all that fast in the long, flapping robes.

"Go!" Tim shouted. "Get back to the car. The keys are under the visor. Get out of here."

"No, you aren't going to face the KKK alone," she snapped.

"Go!" he yelled. "They're coming."

"I can't drive," she shot back. But she ran. One of them had to try to get out, get help. She ran across the pavement, stumbling in her sandals, trying to remember how Tim had started the car. Blue squiggles danced in front of her vision as she tried to see. The flickering flames of the cross had blinded her.

Maybe Tim had the smarts to be armed. Maybe he had a gun in his car. She didn't want to touch a gun. But a woman holding a gun with shaking hands would make these hooded cowards pay attention.

Kay glanced behind her. The skinny man, probably Mains, was pursuing her. He had to hold up the hood so he could see through the eyeholes and hold up the hem of his robe to run.

Looking back, she almost stumbled. Her sandal twisted, almost falling off. With a cry of anger, she kicked it away. Her next step brought her bare foot down on a sharp crack in the tarmac. She winced and squealed.

She had to get to the car. If he'd left the keys behind the visor, Tim had left the car unlocked. At least she could lock herself in.

She could see the gate ahead—

A strong hand grabbed her by the shoulder and yanked her back.

Every woman wondered what she would do if she was walking home alone, and a man grabbed her.

Kay had walked home alone after some of her dates (before Tim), taking small steps in her high heels, because that felt safer than getting in a cab with the date.

She used to think: What if a man grabs me? Are you able to fight for your life? Would you just surrender like a coward?

For one second, she froze as the man pulled her backward. Then she swung around, planning to rake her nails on his face.

Fight dirty. Fight to escape.

But she couldn't scratch his skin with the hood over his head. As he yanked her toward him, she made a grab for the hood. She wrenched it sideways so he could only see out of the right eyehole.

With her bare foot, she kicked him, aiming for his most sensitive area. Her foot floundered in the robe. She lost her balance. So did he. They both went down on sand. His weight landing on her chest jarred the air right out of her.

Are you going to let yourself die here?

Kay hit wildly at the man's face—or at least at his hood. The heel of her hand connected with what had to be his nose. He howled. Desperately, she struggled beneath him.

She had her answer. She would fight for her life, but this was a fight she couldn't win.

"Stop hitting me!" the man growled. "I'm not your enemy."

The voice belonged to Claude Mains.

Obviously, he was her enemy. She had no weapon. No way to protect herself.

She had one hope. Surprise. "Hello, Mr. Mains."

Busting his anonymity had the effect she hoped. He dropped his grip on her wrist. "How do you know—?"

"That garb doesn't change your voice. I recognized it right away. And I recognize you by the one eye I can see. Dark. Long lashes. A bit of a hangdog look that *some* women find appealing if they aren't too smart."

Mains grabbed his hood and pulled it off, which meant he let go of her. "Damn thing. I can't even see out of it half the time."

"Complaints? Aren't you the superior race and gender? You should have gotten the hood right."

That took him aback.

Kay took advantage of his surprise. She scrambled to her feet and ran. Mains cursed and got to his feet.

"Miss Thompson, come back. I'm not going to hurt you. I want to help you."

Terrified, she bolted for the car. But Mains ran like an Olympic sprinter.

She flew out of the gate and ran along the fence to the parking lot. The car sat there, barely illuminated by the lights of the fairground. Happy music floated ironically toward her.

She had her hand on the driver's-side door handle when Mains grabbed her again. She jerked his robe up, hoping to throw it over his head and tangle him in it.

Something fell to the ground with a thud.

Moving with the speed of a viper—she hoped—she grabbed the dark lump. She thought it would be a gun, and she could use it to keep Mains at bay.

She grabbed it and jumped back. It was soft, surprisingly flexible. Her fingers touched a metal coil, and she knew what it was.

Something she had held daintily many times, her legs crossed, her fingers poised with a pencil to take shorthand dictation.

"A notebook?"

Horror raced across his face. He reached out for it, but she moved back again.

She opened it. His handwriting was a scrawl, but she was used to bad handwriting. She could read a man's handwriting even when he couldn't himself.

"Notes on the meetings? What are you? The secretary?"

"No, I'm not the secretary." Claude Mains sagged against the side of Tim's car.

She saw the names Harry and Harriette Moore, heavily underlined. Then Frank Miller. Eulie Reynolds. She saw notes:

Miller—bankrolling the bombings?
Josephine Baker—target for assassination?
Isaac Gros—claims Miller is Nazi commandant

Franz Müller. Government denies. Contact—
State Department.
Get story in by January 1.

The word *story* clicked.

"You're a reporter, Mr. Mains."

CHAPTER 25

It is inspiring to find a reporter who will stick out a story.

—Eleanor Roosevelt, My Day, January 27, 1948

"If you stop shouting the word *reporter*, I'll explain."

"I'm not shouting, Mr. Mains. And I'm not a fool—I'm not going to let you keep me here until the rest of those hooded thugs show up." She yanked on the door handle. To her relief, she heard the click of it releasing.

But Mains pushed the car door shut, jerking her with it. "Please, give me a moment to explain. I'll let you go, then I'll run back into the park and keep the rest of them busy while you get away."

What about Tim? Should she wait and see if Tim came to the car? She didn't know how to drive.

Mains didn't know that. And she didn't want him to find out.

"I don't want them to get you," Mains said.

"Neither do I," Kay said, with a calm delivery that belied the terror coursing through her. For the first time, she felt she sounded as collected as Mrs. Roosevelt.

She could die tonight. Anyone who murdered a couple on Christmas Day could end her life without a flutter of moral concern.

"You're right," Mains said. "I am a reporter. Carrying the notebook was stupid, but I also didn't want to leave it in my hotel room for the wrong people to find."

"I assume you're going to say you are infiltrating the KKK. But a reporter could be a Klan member, the same as a politician or a sheriff."

"Believe me, I don't hold with their beliefs," Mains said. "I was planning to write an exposé on them—I want to find out who is really under those hoods and who was responsible for the Florida bombings. If I could name the men behind the murder of Harry T. Moore, I'd be looking at a Pulitzer."

"Or you could meet the same fate."

Leveling his gaze on hers, he gave a terse nod. "I know that. But it's worth it. These men look like they're hiding under those white hoods, but they believe they don't need to."

"Was Miller behind the bombings? I learned that he denied being responsible for them, but he planned to reveal who was."

"Was your source Isaac Gros?"

"I can't say," Kay demurred. "But it means the KKK had a motive to kill Frank Miller. To silence him. Did the Klan do it? Did Eulie Reynolds do it?"

"You were listening in. I figured that out. So did Reynolds."

"I know. He smiled at me."

"Reynolds doesn't look all that bright, but he is a smart man. You've made yourself a target, Miss Thompson."

"Were you going to just let Rosaleen Davis be killed?"

Intense pain flashed over his face. "I didn't know what to do," Mains admitted. "If I tried to stop it, I might blow my cover, as the saying goes. But I can't let her be killed. I was going to try to stop them."

He wiped his forehead with his white hood, mopping up sweat. "I knew I couldn't go to the cops. I thought about the FBI. Then I thought I could warn Stephen Roberts. That was what I was feeling out with Reynolds. If Roberts is one of them."

Kay reared back. "You think Stephen would let his fiancée be killed? I can't believe it."

"Reynolds wasn't saying directly, but I don't think Stephen Roberts is KKK. You need to get to him at the Delano and tell him what is going on. If I leave now, they will be on to me."

Kay stared. She felt sick. She should have warned Stephen she overheard Reynolds talking about Rosaleen. Instead, she went haring off after Reynolds and Mains, dragging Tim with her.

Stephen wouldn't have had details, but he would have known to protect Rosaleen.

"I had to wonder if Stephen Roberts was working with one of the Klansmen to get rid of his stepfather. Funny thing . . . I was watching Stephen Roberts at the Delano's bar the other night. He spends a lot of time polishing the bar with his elbows. Looking at him in profile I'd say he was Miller's son, not his stepson."

Kay blinked. She hadn't seen a resemblance. But she hadn't looked, and she had never seen them together. But she shook her head. "That can't be possible. Why would Stephen call himself a stepson? I guess he might if he knew his father was a Nazi, but he didn't. He said his mother met Miller after the war. Stephen served for the U.S. military and landed at Omaha Beach in the D-Day invasion. He still wears the watch issued by the U.S. army. How could Stephen have been an American soldier while his father was a death camp officer at Buchenwald?"

"I guess I got it wrong," Mains said.

"Stephen Roberts definitely did not shoot Frank Miller," she said. "He was on a flight at the time of the murder."

"I think the KKK was behind the murder," Mains said. "Someone wanted to silence Miller. My money would be on Reynolds. With Miller gone, Reynolds wants to become Grand Dragon. Pinning the crime on a Black woman would be icing on his warped cake— "

"There. Look over there. By the car!"

Kay's heart almost stopped. A group of men in white robes had reached the edge of the parking lot. They were far enough away that she could escape. If she knew how to drive.

Mains backed away, allowing her to open the car door. "Get out of here. I'll say I couldn't stop you. I'll help you escape if you promise not to breathe a word to anyone about my real identity."

"But Mrs. Roosevelt—"

"Not even Eleanor Roosevelt. No one."

Kay suddenly realized he had no leverage. He must be as terrified as she. He couldn't turn her over to the men in the circle. If she started claiming that he was a reporter, he would be in as much danger as her.

"Please, Miss Thompson," he said.

Reluctantly, she said, "All right. No one. Not even Mrs. Roosevelt."

"Good. I'll try to slow them down. You drive out of here."

"Wait," Kay said. "No one knows who you really are?" she breathed. "Not even Frank Miller?"

He jerked in surprise. "You think I shot him because he found out I was a reporter? That's a stupid question to ask me here and now. But the truth is, I didn't kill him. If Miller had known I was a reporter, I wouldn't have lived long enough to shoot him. Now pretend to shove me and go."

Kay gave him a fierce push. Mains flailed his arms, then staggered backward.

Kay was about to jump in the car. And pray she could start it, when a voice shouted, "Kay!"

It was Tim. Taking a shortcut, he had clambered up on the wire fence surrounding the park. He jumped down and sprinted toward her, also moving like an Olympian compared to the men in robes.

Kay almost sobbed for joy. He could drive.

Tim ran to the car. He stopped at Mains, who was pretending to be tangled up in his robe, while pulling the hood back over his head. He had the eyes backward. Tim looked confused.

"Let's go!" Kay exclaimed as she jerked open the driver's-side door. She banged her knees but slid across to the passenger side. Tim jumped in, grabbed the keys, and turned the engine over.

In an instant, they were speeding out of the parking lot.

As Tim drove, Kay wrestled with her conscience. Claude Mains was risking his life to bring down the men who bombed innocent people. She couldn't jeopardize his work.

But she didn't want to be dishonest—or lie by omission—to Tim. Even though he had broken up with her.

She looked at him as he sped around a corner. Blood smeared his cheek. A trickle of red ran down from his nose to his upper lip. Bruises bloomed around his right eye.

"You're hurt."

"Just fine."

"What happened?"

"I had to subdue a few pursuers."

"Subdue?"

"Knocked them out."

Her eyes widened. "You knocked out a few men. How many?"

"Dunno. Three. Maybe four."

"I think you know how many."

"Four." He paused. "The army taught me a few skills."

"Apparently."

"It felt good to punch those racists right in their anonymous hoods." He paused. "You should learn how to drive. Mrs. R can drive."

"What happened tonight has taught me that I should." Then

her wits kicked in. "We need to get back to the Delano. I need to warn Stephen about their plan to murder Rosaleen."

"We'll get out of here and find a pay phone."

He took a corner so fast Kay heard the tires squeal. She clung to the door handle.

"Sorry."

"It's all right. Drive as fast as you can. I don't mind being tossed around."

A smile flickered on his lips, then he was serious again. "I hate what the KKK does. Dancing around a burning cross in bedsheets. They would be a laughingstock if it wasn't for the violence they perpetrate." Then he said, "If Miller was killed because he was a member of the KKK, is his murder justified? The country is better off without him."

"People can't take the law into their own hands," she protested. "That is what the KKK believes it can do. Americans will become more enlightened. We are becoming more aware. These old men, clinging to old ways, are going to be swept away," she said passionately.

"They aren't necessarily old," Tim said. "And they aren't all men."

"Both men and women, then. The way they think is old. No different than the bosses that patted my rear end and called me 'sweetheart' or 'honey' and figured that I couldn't understand that their businesses were really on the rocks or that a lot of receipts they handed over for their expense accounts had nothing to do with work. A lot of those men had power they didn't earn and didn't deserve, just because they took power away from other people."

She was warming up. "The laws will change. I believe it. Segregation will end. People will see that it is wrong and backward."

"You really think so? I thought you were cynical."

"I guess I have hope. About the things that really matter."

He nodded. "I want to feel that way too." But then he added, "It's been a long time coming," and she heard the heavy jaded tone in his voice. She remembered he had gone to war to defend people from a horrifying ideology.

Tim kept looking in his rearview mirror.

"What is it?" Kay asked.

"I think we're being followed."

"Like in a movie? Do people really *do* that?" Of course, Tim had followed Mrs. R and her when they met with Mr. Gros, but that had been at Mrs. R's request.

Tim's foot pushed down on the accelerator. Kay watched the speedometer needle wiggle a bit as though it was caught by surprise.

Then it flew to the right. To 80 mph.

She twisted to look behind them and gasped. She had never seen a car so close. The large black sedan filled the rear windshield. Squinting, she could make out a shape behind the wheel, but it was more shadow than person. The most distinctive thing was the fedora.

Tim put more distance between them.

He cornered on the road so fast, the tires shuddered, and the car seemed to lurch to the right. He jerked the wheel to make it around the bend.

Kay's stomach dropped, then rose, then tumbled around like her girdle in the washing machine.

Their car suddenly jerked forward. Tim fought the wheel as the front of the car swung wildly.

He got it back under control as Kay cried, "What happened?"

"We were deliberately hit by the car behind us."

"Why?"

"He's trying to run us off the road. But I'm not going to let that happen."

They reached a sharp corner. Kay expected Tim would have to slow, which meant the car behind could catch up.

He didn't slow down. He said a word that women were not supposed to hear.

His hands crossed each other, dragging the steering wheel in an arc.

"Slow down," she gasped.

"Can't. No brakes."

"Oh God," she whispered.

"At least Miami doesn't have hills. The highest point is twenty feet above sea level."

What was he talking about? She wanted to scream but he was so calm. "A delightful fact to know, Tim. But how does it help us?"

"It means we aren't going to go over a cliff."

"Okay," she said slowly. "You know what to do, right? You can drive without brakes? Did they teach you how to do that when you were a police detective?"

"They did not."

"Then what do you do?"

"Staying in gear helps slow the car down. What I can do is downshift and look for a safe place to pull off the road. But having that guy behind me changes things."

"Then what are you going to do?" She knew it didn't help to shriek the same question, but she couldn't help it.

The road swerved closer to a stretch of sand and grass. A road branched off toward a sand dune. Tim downshifted, then turned the steering wheel. They shot down the rougher road. The car bumped and rattled. Kay braced her hand on the door.

The road leveled out onto a stretch of beach. Sand shot up from the tires, and sprayed the windshield, but Kay felt them slowing.

Tim pulled the parking brake, the car skidded, then stopped.

Kay lurched forward, almost slamming into the wide dashboard. Tim's hand shot out, grabbing her shoulder to prevent her from impact.

"He's gone," he said. "He didn't follow us." He let go of her shoulder.

"You . . . you stopped the car. And evaded them."

He shrugged. Then he pulled up the lock button, opened his door. "We should be safe to get out of the car. He could have followed us. Stuck in the sand, we're easy prey. For some reason, he let us get away."

Kay shivered. Why? She knew Tim was thinking that. "Maybe the idea was to scare us, not hurt us."

"He cut the brakes and hit our car with his. That doesn't sound like he just wanted to scare us," Tim said. "I don't get it."

"Unless he is waiting for us to get out of the car. You should close your door, in case he starts shooting."

"If so, we're better out of the car. It's no defense against bullets."

They both stayed still. And quiet. She knew they were both listening. For the sounds of an engine. For the crunch of tires on the road. For any sign someone was watching them and waiting. All Kay could hear was the ocean.

"Do you think he's coming?"

"He's being damned slow about it. I think he took off."

Then she knew. "He ran us off the road so we couldn't protect Rosaleen."

"Maybe."

Reality crashed in like waves. "What do we do now?" she gasped. "The car is stuck in the sand. We're stranded. I don't know where we are. How can we get back to the Delano? It's miles away. Maybe they *are* out there, in the dark, waiting for us."

Tim reached across her, into the glovebox. He took out a gun. Kay swallowed hard. "You aren't with the police anymore. Can you just . . . shoot someone?"

"I have a license for it. I'd only use it in a life-threatening situation, Kay."

"What do we do now?"

"We walk."

"I don't know if you've noticed, but my sandals aren't made for walking, and I lost one already. My foot is scratched, bleeding, and sore."

"I can carry you."

"For miles?" She arched a brow. The rearview mirror showed her eyebrow makeup was intact. "Or we could do the safest and easiest thing. I can make it to a pay phone. Then we call a taxi.

"And, by the way," she added, "Thank you for getting us out of that predicament. Thank you for saving my life . . . again."

"Anytime. Every time," Tim said casually.

"I hope there aren't any other times."

"With you, I worry that there will be," he said. Then he bent down. "I can carry you piggyback."

"Not in your arms?"

"Not this time."

Kay was going to refuse but the sole of her bare foot stung, even in the sand. She kicked off her other sandal. She didn't want to just leave it on the sand, so she put it in the car.

"Okay." She half jumped onto his back. Her arms wrapped around his neck. She let her cheek rest against his neck, her skin touching soft hair and smooth skin. She smelled aftershave and Brylcreem. A new aftershave. Caswell-Massey's Jockey Club, the scent worn by John F. Kennedy. Who she'd met in Washington. The scent reminded her of meeting Tim on the Royal Blue train. It reminded her that together they had helped Mrs. Roosevelt solve Susan Meyer's murder in Washington.

They were stranded in the middle of nowhere. But with Tim, she had never felt safer.

As Tim carried her, making astonishing speed through the sand, Kay thought of what she had learned.

Mr. Gros knew Claude Mains was a reporter infiltrating

the Klan. What if he had revealed it to Franz Müller? What if Müller had pretended to be a turncoat to Mr. Gros to flush out Mains?

What if Claude Mains had discovered he had been set up—and his life was in danger?

It gave him a motive to murder Frank Miller. He did it to save his own life.

Kay knew Tim would accuse her of creating a plot worthy of a Hitchcock movie. It might seem convoluted, but it was possible.

But all that mattered was getting to Rosaleen in time.

CHAPTER 26

Courage is more exhilarating than fear and in the long run it is easier.

—Eleanor Roosevelt, *You Learn by Living: Eleven Keys for a More Fulfilling Life*

Eleanor stared in astonishment at the bedraggled figure who opened the door to the suite, then sagged against the wall.

As a mother who raised one daughter and four sons, she had learned that a sharp demand of "Where have you been? I've been worried sick!" never brought about the desired response. She had learned to listen. She did not always agree, but she listened.

Kay said, "I'm sorry I'm so late. We had to walk to find a pay phone. It felt like we walked for miles . . ."

Eleanor laid her hand on Kay's arm. "Come and sit down."

She brought Kay to the sofa. She hated giving the maids the extra work of vacuuming up sand, which was falling off Kay's clothes, but her secretary looked ready to collapse.

"I should change my clothes first," Kay said. "I'm making a mess."

Kay had stoicism. And concern for others. Both were qualities Eleanor admired.

"Tea first. Hot, strong tea," Eleanor said. "Then we will talk about what happened to you."

"No, I don't have time . . . I need to tell you . . ."

Kay was always efficient as a secretary. Her summaries of the correspondence received were always concise and clear.

But exhaustion and fear had taken their toll. Kay's story was a convoluted jumble. Eleanor knew time was of the essence. She pieced it together quickly. "The KKK have friends in the police who are planning to 'transfer' Rosaleen, but it is a ruse to allow a mob to get at her." Eleanor moved swiftly to her feet. "That will not happen."

"Tim called Detective Connor to warn him, and he went to tell Stephen. They've gone to the police station to try to stop it happening."

"They are putting themselves in danger," Eleanor said. She picked up the room telephone receiver and dialed "0" for the operator.

Eleanor did not like to use influence unless necessary. Many male politicians had resented the fact that as the president's wife, she had his ear. Of course, that did not mean she could always bend him to her will. Through the Great Depression, the war, and her belief in ending segregation, Eleanor had seen politics for what it really was—a terrible brinkmanship, a negotiation where one had to weigh unthinkable choices.

Her telephone call was to the office of President Truman.

He picked up her telephone call, knowing she would not call him on a whim.

After he greeted her warmly, she said, "Harry, there is a terrible miscarriage of justice happening in Miami Beach." She told him about Rosaleen—of course, he was aware of the story. His staff had brought him the information from the newspapers. Josephine's impassioned speech at the Copa City Club was the headline in the Miami newspapers.

Harry listened.

He could not order Rosaleen's release. She knew he would

not want to. But the police were holding a young woman in prison when evidence pointed to her innocence, and a very plausible threat on her life existed.

"Eleanor, I agree," President Harry Truman said in measured tones. "There is no real evidence against this young woman and plenty of conclusive evidence that she did not fire the gun. On the record, there is nothing I can do. I don't have any jurisdiction."

"I know that, Harry. But my concern is that many people in the country don't know that. Those people feel the president is all-powerful."

"Let me consider this problem, Eleanor."

"Just knowing it is on your mind is reassuring, Harry," she said. "But there is also a very real and serious threat to the life of Rosaleen Davis. Two young men involved in law enforcement have gone to the police station to try to thwart the plot." Briefly Eleanor explained.

"The Ku Klux Klan?" the president mused. "That is a problem . . . the Florida Terror, as they call it, is lowering our standing in the world. As you know, we can't condemn other forms of government when we have murders and acts of terror happening in our country. The death of Rosaleen Davis would be a disaster on a national scale. It would lead to violence as sure as day follows night. I will make some telephone calls."

Eleanor knew that meant Harry would exert his influence as much as possible to protect Rosaleen.

Usually, Harry would put in a ribald joke or a witty remark. Reputedly he had quipped, "If you want a friend in Washington, get a dog." Right now, he was deeply serious.

"Can you send Mrs. Bouillon and her lawyer down to the police station?" Harry asked. "I'm hoping that Rosaleen Davis will be released on bail. I'm also hoping that knowing the president of the United States has taken a direct interest may make these men stand down."

"I hope so. And Harry, I will accompany Josephine and her lawyer."

Josephine had engaged a lawyer named William Schwartz. In his late forties, wearing a neat dark blue suit, with dark hair slicked back, he stated that he never lost. Josephine had stated she did not know if that was true, but he had better win Rosaleen's case so she would believe him.

"Eleanor—" Harry broke off. "Your presence might escalate tensions. I need to ensure you're protected."

"I've been in danger before. I want to ensure Rosaleen is safe."

She extended her best wishes to Harry's wife, Bess, and their daughter, Margaret, then ended the call.

She prayed they could rescue Rosaleen.

If Rosaleen was killed, any investigation would end. A dead woman could not defend herself. Was the murderer working to ensure that happened? Was it a man involved with the KKK, either Mains or Reynolds?

Was it someone else?

Eleanor felt a surge of frustration. She had learned to possess inner calm, but she was human. She felt the answer was in her grasp. That something she had seen, or that someone had said, had been the key.

She was sixty-seven years of age. Not very old. She knew, if she concentrated, she would remember what that clue was.

Young men and women of Kay's age surrounded the steps of the police station. Kay swiftly counted over twenty people. They carried the same signs that Kay saw Benny carrying in the Delano lobby. They chanted "Free Rosaleen Davis!" She felt the same surge to be involved that led her to march on Capitol

Hill to support the Moton student strike. But she saw worry on Mrs. Roosevelt's face.

She and Mrs. R had followed Josephine and the lawyer, Mr. Schwartz, to the police station. Kay opened the door to the taxi and slid out. Just as Mrs. Roosevelt got out of the cab, uniformed police officers burst out of the building. The officers, all burly men, began pushing the young people back, shoving them hard. Truncheons were raised. Kay thought it was to scare the crowd, until one of the officers slammed his truncheon across the back of a slender, young, bearded man. It was Benny.

A cry of shock left her lips.

The officer hit him again, multiple times until Benny dropped to his knees. Some people surged forward in anger; others tried to scramble back for their own protection. A young woman fell, landing on the pavement. Kay couldn't see her for all the legs, and her heart hammered.

"She's going to be trampled." Kay took a step to run to the woman, but Mrs. Roosevelt grasped her wrist, stopping her.

Kay saw why. Tim ran into the crowd, pushing his way through. He grabbed the woman, pulling her to her feet.

A truncheon came down toward his shoulder. Kay heard her own scream. But Tim spun and his hand snapped around the officer's wrist with astonishing strength, stopping the swing.

Stephen shouted something to Tim—she couldn't hear it over the screams as people were hit, and the angry shouts of the protesters and the police.

Stephen took off toward the side of the police station. Kay had planned to now stay close to Mrs. R, but she looked to her employer and said, "I'm going to follow Stephen!"

"No, Kay," Mrs. R began, but Kay took off after him.

She reached him as he was almost all the way around the side of the building. Stephen stopped at the corner and swung around on her. "What are you doing? Keep back!" he yelled.

He sprinted around the back.

Kay didn't listen to him. She followed.

"Rosaleen," she gasped.

Two brawny police officers were dragging Rosaleen toward a dark green sedan. Stephen shouted, "Stop where you are!"

One of the officers ran at Stephen, baton raised. But as the man reached Stephen and swung at his head, Stephen moved gracefully and flipped the man onto his back. Stephen had barely seemed to expend an effort.

"I'm with law enforcement," Stephen shouted. "We know your plot. Get away from Rosaleen Davis. I'm armed and I will shoot."

The officer holding Rosaleen shouted, "She's being transferred."

Rosaleen struggled to get free of the man's grip. "Stephen, be careful," she cried.

"Shut up," the officer snarled.

"There is no transfer," Stephen barked. "We know this is a setup—"

Stephen broke off. Kay saw why. Detective Connor and another man in plainclothes had come out of the rear door. They pointed their guns at the officer and the green sedan.

A gray-haired man in uniform came out. "Release her!" he commanded.

Stephen rushed forward. The officer in uniform hesitated. Then he removed his hands from Rosaleen. The green sedan began to back up, away from the officer and Rosaleen. Detective Connor aimed his weapon. With a squeal, the car accelerated backwards. Rubber burned. The car shot away, down the drive, toward the main road. It made a backward skidding turn, then took off.

Connor lowered his gun. He glared at the officer. "Who were they?"

"Dunno," the man answered. "I'm not telling you anything."

Kay looked over to Stephen and Rosaleen. He had embraced her, and she pressed her face into his chest. Her hands were cuffed behind her. But Stephen's hands stroked Rosaleen's head gently.

Kay had been furious with Stephen for giving up on Rosaleen, for believing she might be guilty.

At this moment, she believed he was worthy of Rosaleen.

"It's so wonderful that you are released! You are here at the Delano, where you are safe and sound!" Josephine declared. "Finally, we have something to celebrate!"

With a swift movement, Josephine used a table knife to pop the cork, and she quickly filled a set of champagne flutes.

Kay saw that Rosaleen, seated on the sofa, looked confused and nervous. She looked much thinner. She had changed into a fresh, dark blue short-sleeve dress. Stephen sat beside her, holding her hand.

"And you need to eat some proper food. I have ordered room service."

"I'm all right, Jo," Rosaleen demurred.

"You have endured a terrible ordeal. You look as if you are skin and bone."

Josephine knew Rosaleen sent the threatening letters, but she was still kind and concerned.

A knock on the door signaled the arrival of the room service cart. Kay moved to open the door, but Josephine went first. The bellboy looked dazzled, as he always did. It was always the same bellboy. Kay wondered how hard he fought to be the one to serve Josephine Baker.

Mrs. R poured tea. Rosaleen set down her champagne flute and gratefully accepted the tea.

Josephine perched on the arm of the chair. Mrs. Roosevelt sat on the other armchair. Tim leaned against the wall by the patio doors, and the breeze fluttered the gauzy curtains around him.

Rosaleen gazed up under her long lashes. “I’m sorry, Mrs. Roosevelt, that I didn’t tell you the truth. Josephine told me that you know I went into the dressing room with Frank Miller.”

Mrs. R stirred her tea with a tiny spoon. “Why didn’t you tell the truth?”

“I—I was afraid. At the party, Frank Miller told me that he was Stephen’s stepfather. He said that he had to meet me afterward. He said he had something important to tell me. He said I must not tell anyone. When the police thought I was guilty, I was too afraid to tell them the truth. I am sorry. Everything else I said was true. I hope you believe me.”

“What was the important thing he wanted to tell you?” Mrs. R asked.

“I don’t know.” Rosaleen looked to Stephen. “He was killed before he could say.”

“He likely planned to threaten you into breaking up with me,” Stephen said.

“There is something else that you must know, Rosaleen,” Mrs. Roosevelt said. “We found the cut pages of the magazine.”

Rosaleen’s eyes widened. “Oh,” she said softly. Her gaze slid guiltily to Josephine.

“Kay recognized that the letters had come from *Harper’s Bazaar*, which was clever of her.”

“You searched my room?”

“We had to know the truth about the letters.”

Rosaleen hung her head. “After the murder, I guess the letters confused the issue. And it is true that I sent the threatening letters.”

Kay noticed Rosaleen made no mention of her mother. Mrs. R gently said, "We also know you worked with your mother, Flora."

Rosaleen's shoulders sagged. "You found my mother?"

Mrs. R nodded. "Flora insisted you did this for her. She wanted to confess to shooting Frank Miller so that you would be released."

Rosaleen cocked her head like a confused child. "My mother wanted to do that . . . for me?"

"Yes. I told her that it was not necessary to confess to a crime she did not commit."

"It was brave and noble of her to do it," Josephine added.

Rosaleen's dark brows drew together. "How did you know that she was innocent?"

"I do not believe she would have locked you in the room with the victim if she had been the shooter. She would have ensured you fled to safety. As a cleaner, she could have even hidden you in the building while the police came. A locked room with only the victim inside would have been more perplexing. Whoever took that action wanted the blame for the crime to fall upon you, Rosaleen."

"To cover up for the real murderer," Rosaleen said.

"Or the crime was intended to have you arrested," Mrs. R said. "If you had an enemy."

Stephen said, "That doesn't make sense. Why would someone want to pin a crime on Rosaleen?" He had downed his champagne flute and eaten half the coffee cake that had come on the room service cart. Despite living on jail food for days, Rosaleen had only nibbled at her piece.

Mrs. Roosevelt said mildly, "It is a far-fetched theory. But I like to address all theories. It is unwise to leap to conclusions."

Mrs. R was not offended by Stephen's words. And her point made sense.

"We only wanted to scare Josephine. We never intended to hurt her," Rosaleen said. She admitted what they had done. Flora had already explained their plan, but Mrs. R listened intently to Rosaleen. Kay realized Mrs. R wanted to see if Rosaleen would tell the same story.

She did.

Rosaleen gazed at Mrs. R with anguished eyes. "When my mother saw that Josephine would never be scared away from the stage, she suggested we make Josephine too sick to perform. The sleeping pills were her idea. We would pretend that the fear induced by the threats caused Josephine to take them."

"Flora told us about that. That was dangerous," Mrs. Roosevelt said, in a firm tone. Kay knew the subtext was that Rosaleen should have known better.

Rosaleen looked miserable. "I know!" she exclaimed. "But my mother believed that she could take Josephine's place. She was obsessed with the idea. You don't understand—"

"Help me to understand," Mrs. Roosevelt said. Kindly but still firm.

"My mother never got over being left behind while Josephine went to Paris and became a star. She married, but it didn't work out. Once I came along, she needed to take on menial jobs to support us both. She began to drink. Bitterness made her angry—she would scream and hit herself. Or she would become so weighed down with sadness that she would slump on the floor and sob until she ran out of tears and fell unconscious. I couldn't bear to watch her. When Josephine returned to America and I had no money for school, my mother urged me to apply to Josephine for a job. She was certain that guilt would lead Josephine to help me."

"It wasn't guilt," Josephine said. She had poured herself a cup of coffee and stood in the background quietly. "I could tell at once you are an intelligent woman. I am sorry that Flora didn't have her chance. I honestly did ask if she could come to France with me and perform in La Revue Nègre, but the producer, Caroline Dudley Reagan, didn't have the money. I was nineteen and wanted my chance to leave America and segregation."

"If my mother had been the one chosen, she would have gone and left you behind, Josephine," Rosaleen said. "She admits that now, too. I know you weren't handed your stardom on a silver platter. You worked hard for it. You used your wits. My mother let the defeat destroy her. If the same thing had happened to you, you would have fought for another opportunity. You would never accept defeat. I felt bad for Mama and when she begged me to help her . . ."

"You felt guilty," Kay said. She understood. "Your mother lost her chance, then she became pregnant. You felt you cost her her stardom."

"I guess I did," Rosaleen said.

Stephen stroked her hand.

"I think your mother has realized what she has done. She said that, if you were willing to see her, she wanted to apologize to you," Mrs. Roosevelt said.

"Yes, I want to see her," Rosaleen said.

"Then I shall invite her to stay here. A daughter needs her mother," Josephine said wistfully. "I shall pay for a room."

"Thank you," Rosaleen whispered.

Kay realized Mrs. Roosevelt made you see sense. She made you want to be a better person, because she always endeavored to give of herself to others.

"Did you fear it was your mother who shot Frank Miller?" Mrs. Roosevelt asked. "That is why you kept secret about meeting him."

"Yes." Rosaleen took a shaky breath. "I told her who he was. I told her he wanted to meet me. I was afraid she shot him so he couldn't break up my engagement to Stephen."

"Did you see her do it?"

"No. And that is the absolute truth!"

Kay wondered if it was indeed the truth.

"I don't know who shot him. I didn't see who did it. It happened just as I said—there was a gunshot, and Mr. Miller was shot in the chest. I turned to face the door, in shock, and the door got slammed in my face. I swear that is the truth."

Rosaleen gazed up at Stephen. "You do believe me, don't you?"

Kay watched him. It was back—the hesitation. Then he said, "You know I do. I love you."

Stephen reached into the pocket of his trousers. Kay knew exactly what was in his hand from the look in his eyes and the size of the small box that he cradled in his palm. She caught her breath.

"This is for you," he said to Rosaleen. "I should have done it a long time ago, when I first asked you to marry me. It's not as big or fancy as I wanted it to be, but I want you to wear it. I want everyone to know you are mine."

He opened the box. Josephine clapped happily as Stephen slipped the ring on Rosaleen's finger. It was a small diamond with a gold band. Tears dripped to Rosaleen's cheeks.

"Thank you," she whispered.

"I love you," Stephen said. Rosaleen threw her arms around his neck.

"More champagne," Josephine declared. She went to fetch a bottle from the ice bucket. Tim walked over to stand beside Kay.

"Rosaleen has been released but she is still charged with murder," Tim pointed out.

Returning with the champagne bottle, Josephine said, "But she can tell the truth. That she knows nothing. And that it must have been the KKK. Why else would they have attacked her?" Josephine said.

Rosaleen looked up from her ring. She had been gazing at it as if it was a miracle.

"I can't tell them that my mother knew I was meeting Frank Miller," Rosaleen whispered. "What if she confesses to protect me?"

"Eleanor," Josephine said passionately, "the men in that green sedan escaped and the corrupt police officer is not talking, but we know it was men from the KKK. How do we *prove* it?"

CHAPTER 27

If you believe in democracy you believe that basically there is good in the vast majority of people and, given time, education, and good leadership where people are able to express themselves freely, they will eventually arrive at wiser decisions than can be assured by the rule of a few supposedly wise individuals.

—Eleanor Roosevelt, My Day, December 10, 1952

Kay knew Mrs. Roosevelt wanted to find the murderer. But Mrs. Roosevelt warned Josephine, "If the KKK is involved, this will be dangerous. They already attempted to harm Tim and Kay by running them off the road."

After they left the suite, Mrs. R confided to Kay, "I am worried. We know Rosaleen did not see the person who shot Franz Müller, but does the killer also know Rosaleen cannot give an identification?"

Kay gulped in horror. "The murderer might try to harm Rosaleen now that she is out of jail. I didn't think of that." But it was obvious, she realized. After all, the KKK had planned to harm Rosaleen while she was in jail.

Kay settled down in Mrs. Roosevelt's suite to type up the My Day column. Mrs. Roosevelt left to attend meetings at the conference, which was ending the next day.

Kay had plucked the page from the typewriter when a loud knock came at the door of the suite. She went to the door and checked through the peephole.

A young bellboy stood on the other side. He handed her a note. She had to scurry to her purse for change to tip him. After he left, she unfolded the note, recognizing the slanted handwriting.

> *Would you meet me? I would come to escort you, but I can't come to Delano Hotel. Meet me at diner near beach. We will have hot dog with yellow. Two o'clock. Show you new life.*

Dmitri had written the address of the diner. He hadn't signed his name.

Was this message really from Dmitri? She escaped the clutches of the KKK last night. The KKK's attempt to murder Rosaleen had been thwarted.

Could that message be from Reynolds, luring her into a trap?

Think sense, Kay. How could the KKK know about Dmitri? How could they have found out about the hot dog with the yellow? Either Dmitri had forgotten that she'd explained the flamboyantly yellow condiment was called mustard, or he had used the phrase deliberately so she would know it was him.

To go was to defy the rules. But she wanted to know what he meant by his wish to "show her new life."

Kay put on a white sundress with bright blue stripes, sunglasses, and a large-brimmed white hat. She had lost one of her white sandals, so she wore her black pumps. She had to punch the hat back into shape. It was so big it had been squashed by her suitcase. But it looked glamorous.

She took a cab to the tiny diner that was across the road from a stretch of white sand beach. Getting out of the car, Kay scanned the parking lot. No sign of a blond man with pale blue eyes.

Maybe Dmitri was inside.

Maybe he decided it was too dangerous to see her.

Or maybe it was a trap after all.

Kay crossed her arms over her chest, unsure of what to do. Then she felt . . . that awareness.

In the far corner of the lot stood a new convertible. A dark blue Cadillac, polished to perfection. A big chrome bumper shone on the front, and arrows of shimmering chrome ran along the sides, reflecting the sun. The top was down. Sunlight reflected off the blond hair of the driver.

Her heart gave a jolt of shock. And happiness.

Dmitri Petrov waved at her. He slung his arm casually along the back of the bench seat in the front of the large car. Dmitri reversed with practiced ease, despite how tightly the cars were packed.

The engine purred as he glided up beside the front entrance. He waited. She knew he wanted her to get in.

She hurried to the car. The faster she got in, the less likely she would be seen.

There was no chance now she could walk away.

She grasped the smooth chrome door handle and opened the door.

Her last trip in a car with a man had been more adventure than she ever wanted again, and that man had saved her life.

"Hello, Kay. I am happy you obeyed my note."

"'Obey' might not be the right word," she said. But she had to smile. Dmitri had not changed. His fair hair was slicked down neatly, his ice-blue eyes were as stunning as she remembered. She remembered his high cheekbones and the scars he had gotten in the war.

"I am happy you have come."

The words, spoken in his deep Russian accent, awakened the

beat of her heart. But she said, "You shouldn't have done this. You aren't supposed to contact me."

"I had no choice."

"What?"

"I saw in the newspaper that you are here with Mrs. Roosevelt. I saw your picture, in pretty dress, standing beside Mrs. Roosevelt when reporters asked her about the dead man in the club."

"I still don't see what you mean by 'you had no choice.'"

"Once I knew you were in Miami Beach, I couldn't stop thinking about seeing you."

He accelerated smoothly toward the parking lot exit. The steering wheel was large, clad in tan leather. Dmitri turned it, taking them out onto the road. Palm trees waved above them. The road, sidewalk, and buildings were sun-soaked.

"Do you live in Miami?" she asked.

"Yes."

It was fate. Of all the places he had to be in America, it was here.

"I will show you." He turned to her, his boyish grin lighting up his face.

"I have a business," he said. "I sell cars."

"That's wonderful," she said, and she was thoroughly happy for him.

Dmitri put on the turn indicator, and he turned off the road onto a stretch of dark black asphalt. It was a huge lot covered in gleaming cars. The showroom was an Art Deco-styled building which had enormous glass windows. Kay could see a cherry-red convertible behind the curved glass. A large sign declared this was MIAMI'S NEWEST DEALERSHIP.

Kay had expected he owned a small car lot. After all, he had escaped the Soviet Union—it wasn't as if he had a fortune stashed away.

She was startled and impressed.

Dmitri parked and led her inside. He introduced her to three young men who were his salesmen, then took her to his office, a modern space with a metal desk and chromium chairs. After drawing back a chair for Kay, he sent his receptionist, a young dark-haired woman named Catherine, to bring coffee.

Kay saw a faint blush on his cheeks.

He suddenly looked shy. "I have success. I wish I could share it with you, Kay. Every day, I think of you." His eyes, so blue, held hers. "Do you think of me?"

"I do . . . often," she said. "But—but I was dating a man."

"Detective O'Malley?"

She nodded. "He isn't a police detective anymore."

"Are you going to marry him?"

"No. We aren't dating anymore. My job keeps me busy. I don't think I can marry anyone."

"You must. A man would be the most fortunate man to marry you."

She knew her cheeks were becoming as pink as his. "That's sweet."

They had to pause their conversation as Catherine entered the office, with two coffee mugs on a tray, a bowl of sugar cubes, and a tiny pitcher of cream.

Kay thanked her and took a mug, leaving the coffee black. It was excellent coffee. "You've done well fast."

"Mr. Sandiston is in contact with me. Often," he said. "I cannot date you, as much as I want to."

"He is? To check in on you?"

"Always he has small jobs for me. I have success. I am not dead. I am not in gulag. But there is price. Once you are owned by the government, nothing is free."

"What do you mean?"

"Your government fears Communists. They believe there are Communists in Cuba who come here to Florida. I am Russian. I am told to make friends. I am to spy on those friends. I have a business, and I can buy large house with swimming pool and patio. But I do not have all happiness. I cannot share my life with you, Kay."

"I know." She knew in her heart that while she liked Dmitri, and she was attracted to him, she wouldn't give up her job for him. He was not the man she wanted to marry.

"Your secretary, Catherine, seems very nice," she said.

"She is intelligent. Kind."

"And pretty," Kay said.

"She reminds me of you, except her hair is not red."

"You mustn't compare her to me. She seems wonderful in her own right. Wouldn't she be the right girl for you?"

"No." His face became grim. "Her father is one of my friends. I cannot marry her while I spy on her father. There are some secrets that have no place in marriage."

"I suppose that's true."

"I am happy to be with you today," he said.

Her heart gave a pang. "I am happy to be with you, too," she said. "It is very good to see you again. I am sure you will find a wife in the end. How could you not?"

"Will you find a husband?"

Kay realized she didn't know. But what was more important was finding her future.

"I wish I could take you for dinner tonight."

Kay shook her head. "That is the last thing we can do. I appreciate it, but we would both get in trouble. Dmitri, I should go. I can get a taxi."

He frowned. "I could drive you closer to the hotel— "

"It's all right. And I want to be on my own."

Dmitri telephoned for a taxi. He gave the driver money to cover her ride back to the hotel. Several folded bills.

It was growing dark when she arrived. It felt as warm as summer in New York, but the sun set before six o'clock.

As she hurried to the Delano entrance, the door opened suddenly, and she almost slammed into the bulky body of Eulie Reynolds.

"Well, Miss Thompson," Reynolds said, his joviality exaggerated. "I heard that Mrs. Roosevelt got that murdering woman out of jail."

"Mrs. Roosevelt was involved in protecting Rosaleen, who was in danger from the KKK," Kay shot back. She knew she was trembling, but she refused to fear this man. They were at the front entry of the Delano. He couldn't harm her.

"Don't know what you are talking about," Reynolds said. "But I'd advise you stop eavesdropping."

"I don't know what you are talking about. And Rosaleen Davis is innocent. She didn't murder Frank Miller."

"I know she did."

Kay stared into his fleshy face, at the bulbous eyes. "What do you mean?"

"I saw her that night. I saw her walk into the dressing room, cool as ice with Miller. I knew what she was planning to do with a rich white man." He let out a string of horrible racial and sexual slurs.

Kay's hand twitched. She almost slapped his face. But she knew that was a bad move. The politeness he had displayed to Mrs. Roosevelt that night at Josephine's party was gone.

"Did you see her shoot him?"

"Maybe I can say I did," he answered. "That would cook her goose."

"If you lie to the police, I will tell them what you have just said to me. Rosaleen is innocent. In this country, we have laws. And women like Josephine Baker and Mrs. Roosevelt will do everything to ensure those laws are respected."

Eulie Reynolds leaned so close to her, she almost gagged. She could smell the sour sweat that had soaked into his suit.

"The KKK is the law around here," he snarled. "Tell Mrs. Roosevelt to keep out of our business in the future."

He pushed past Kay, leaving her fighting the urge to shake.

A threat didn't mean anything. It was just talk. Mrs. Roosevelt wouldn't let Eulie Reynolds scare her.

But as Kay moved to go open the door to the hotel lobby, Eulie Reynolds shouted, "One more thing, Miss Thompson." He was waiting at the curb for the valet to bring his car. He smirked. "I heard her. Rosaleen Davis said, 'This is for the money.' Then she pulled the trigger."

Kay didn't believe him.

He had just revealed he had been backstage at the Copa when Franz Müller was shot. Or was his whole story just a lie?

Having taken off her large sun hat and kicked off her pumps in favor of slippers, Kay sat down at the typewriter to type up Mrs. Roosevelt's handwritten letters, but her hands were so shaky, she hit all the wrong keys. She had already typed and sent the My Day column before she went to meet Dmitri. The column included Mrs. R's intelligent, measured thoughts on important political issues. Yesterday's was about the U.S. ambassador to Moscow, the payment of ransom to Hungary for the release of four American flyers.

The hours passed. Kay changed out her sundress into a twin set and a trim-fitting skirt, worn with her slippers. Mrs. Roosevelt didn't return to the suite. Sometimes Mrs. Roosevelt got delayed at meetings, but Kay was worried.

She walked out onto the balcony, wanting some air while she waited for Tim. Moonlight glimmered on the ocean in the distance. Kay's gaze moved inward from the ocean, until she was dazzled by the lights of the pool. She blinked until she could see properly.

There was a dark shape on the pale gray pool deck.

Horror gripped her. She bolted from the balcony and ran for the door to the hallway. She yanked it open and walked right into Tim.

"There is a body down there. By the pool."

"What?"

"What if it is Mrs. R?" she cried. "She's late!"

"Did it look like Mrs. Roosevelt?"

She threw a withering glance. "I was looking from the balcony and it's dark, except for the lights by the pool. It looked like a *body*."

"It won't be Mrs. R," he said. "It can't be."

"You don't know. Come on!" Kay let the door slam behind her. It locked automatically. Then she remembered she had forgotten her key, but that didn't matter either.

"You have slippers on."

"Who cares? Let's go."

Inside the elevator car heading down, Kay slumped against the wall. "I'm so scared. What if it is Mrs. Roosevelt?"

"I doubt it's Mrs. R. I also doubt it's a body."

"You think I'm making this up?"

"You could have seen someone lying on a chaise longue."

Kay folded her arms over her chest. "You think I can't tell the difference between sunbathing and death?"

"You couldn't tell who it was. So— "

"Keep quiet," she said. "You're not helping."

"Kay." He clasped her hands. "You're cold," he said. He leaned closer. She couldn't resist looking into his green eyes. "It's going to be okay," he said.

"I don't think it is."

The elevator door rolled open. Tim stayed right at her side. She reached out and took his hand.

He let her.

Together, they reached the pool deck.

It wasn't Mrs. Roosevelt. Kay almost melted with relief. And even though the victim lay face down on the pool deck, Kay knew who it was from the girth.

"I don't think Mr. Reynolds is sunbathing," she said.

A puddle, dark and glistening, spread underneath him. Kay thought: Why does it look black in this light when it is so obviously red?

"Stay back here," Tim said.

"I don't think Reynolds is going to get up and attack me now."

But she did let Tim go first. As a former Washington P.D. detective, he was a trained investigator.

Tim crouched beside the body. "It is Eulie Reynolds. I can't touch him, but I believe he was stabbed in the chest."

A small glint of gold caught her eye. *You are like a magpie*, Kay's mother used to say. *Anything glittery catches your attention.*

It was under the chaise longue near the—the body.

Was it the—the knife? She couldn't touch it. There might be fingerprints. But she crouched down to see what it was.

"Oh no," she gasped.

"What is it?" Tim asked, his voice soft.

"A r-ring." She could barely speak. "It is the engagement ring that Stephen gave to Rosaleen today."

CHAPTER 28

You will ruin yourself as a citizen, and your own happiness and that of your family, if you do not learn to face whatever comes with courage. If you haven't got courage, make believe you have it and that will help you to acquire it.

—Eleanor Roosevelt, If You Ask Me, *Ladies' Home Journal*, October 1948

Returning from an afternoon of meetings, Eleanor encountered Detective Connor and his partner, Detective Tomlins, as she alighted from her taxi.

Detective Mike Connor doffed his fedora. "Evening, Mrs. Roosevelt. Guess you heard what happened."

Eleanor was in the dark. "I am afraid I did not, Detective."

"Your secretary, Miss Thompson, found a body by the swimming pool. She identified him as Eulie Reynolds."

Accompanying the two detectives, Eleanor hurried out to Kay at the pool. She took in the lights glittering on the water, illuminating Kay and Tim standing side by side at the pool edge, several feet from Eulie Reynolds's prone body.

Kay came to her and explained what happened. Eleanor studied Kay as she meticulously went over the details. Kay was holding up very well. Cool and collected.

The lead detective, Tomlins, said at once, "The girl did it. A white man dies the minute we must let her out of jail. Not a coincidence. Her ring is right there."

Kay exclaimed, "The ring proves nothing! Anyone could have planted it there to cast suspicion on Rosaleen Davis."

Eleanor saw the considering look in Detective Connor's dark brown eyes. He said, coolly, "We're not arresting anyone until we have statements."

Tomlins sneered. "That Black girl lured this guy out here and stabbed him."

Mike Connor sighed. "Why?"

"He's a Klansman. She wanted revenge."

"For what?" Detective Connor asked, wearily. "Are you saying you know the KKK was behind that attempt to kidnap Rosaleen Davis?"

"Uh," Detective Tomlins replied.

"Yeah. Now act like a real detective. We're going to investigate this crime scene properly and take accurate statements from Tim O'Malley and Miss Thompson." He turned back to Eleanor and said politely, "I would like to interview you in the hotel, Mrs. Roosevelt, after we wait for the medical examiner."

"Would you wish to carry out the interviews in my suite, Detective Connor?" Eleanor asked.

"That will be okay, ma'am," the detective said.

An hour later, the two detectives arrived outside her suite, with Mike Connor rapping gently on the door. Josephine and Jacques Abtey had come to Eleanor's suite, while Rosaleen had remained with Stephen and Flora, her mother. Josephine had personally fetched Flora with a taxi to reunite mother and daughter. With deep concern, Josephine explained that Rosaleen appeared to be in shock and had barely spoken a word.

Eleanor had told Kay to remain seated, and she went to the door and opened it to the two men. "You must come inside." Eleanor led the way for the two detectives.

"I will talk to Miss Thompson here," Mike Connor said. "My partner will talk to Tim O'Malley."

Eleanor cast an assessing glance over Detective Tomlins.

She trusted Mike Connor, the tall, gangly, red-haired police detective. He had shown his true colors when they went to Rosaleen's rescue. He was honest and forthright. Much like Tim in Washington, he was trying to fight corruption of justice within the police force. But it was a hard battle. The green sedan had gotten away, and the police chief of the station denied knowing about the plot to harm Rosaleen.

His shorter, round partner did not inspire the same trust. She remembered the faith she had placed in the policemen who guarded Franklin when he made his speech in Bayfront Park and Giuseppe Zangara had fired shots at him. Franklin was unharmed, but Chicago's mayor, Mr. Cermak, was fatally wounded.

Tomlins said, "I can interview O'Malley in his room."

Josephine was about to protest, but Jacques Abtey said gently, "It is customary, Josephine. We cannot be party to the questioning."

Tim stood and said calmly, "Follow me, Detective."

Monsieur Abtey led Josephine out to the balcony. He clasped her hands to reassure her. Eleanor smiled softly at the gesture. It was clear Josephine and Jacques Abtey had once been in love. That passion had matured into deep affection and caring.

But Eleanor was not naïve. Jacques Abtey had worked in military intelligence during the war. Josephine had explained that his war record had finally been accepted after the war and he was working again with the French government. Kay had told her that he had arrived earlier than he claimed.

But Jacques had protested he would never have allowed Rosaleen to take the fall for his work. Eleanor believed him. She was certain that if Monsieur Abtey had wanted to eliminate Franz Müller, it would have been done with absolute precision.

The murderer had not cared about setting up an innocent woman.

Or, as she had observed before, the murderer had deliberately incriminated Rosaleen. As the murderer had done now, by planting Rosaleen's ring.

Kay settled down in an armchair. Detective Connor sat across from her. It was obvious Detective Connor was not immune to Kay's attractiveness. A blush washed over his cheeks as Kay crossed her legs.

Eleanor was impressed as Kay recounted every detail with care. As Kay explained she had been worried about Eleanor being late, Eleanor felt a warm tug of affection. Kay had become as indispensable to her as Kay's aunt Tommy Thompson was. But there was more. Eleanor was growing to care about Kay as she would her own children.

She had been truly frightened when Kay had been gone for the night. It was strange to realize Kay had felt the same way when Eleanor's meeting had run long, and she was late.

"I looked over the balcony and saw the body," Kay explained.

"You just happened to look over the balcony?"

"Yes. I was nervous and went out on the balcony for air. I looked toward the ocean, then down at the pool. That was when I saw Mr. Reynolds. I didn't know it was him."

"Why did you decide to go downstairs?"

"From the distance, I could only guess it was a body. I thought— "

"You thought it might be me? Oh dear," Eleanor said. Kay had not explained that down by the pool.

"I didn't mean you look like him!" Kay said hurriedly. "He is so . . . large. I just saw a shadowy shape and feared the worst."

"I am sorry I caused you worry," Eleanor said. "Now you must continue your story."

Kay told the detective that she saw the glint of the ring. "I didn't touch it. Someone must have planted it under the body. Maybe you could get fingerprints."

"Not much we can get off a ring," Detective Connor said. "This ring—you said it was her engagement ring. Was it loose?"

"No," Kay said honestly. "It fit her finger very well."

"It wasn't likely that it fell off." The detective ran his fingers through his auburn hair.

"No," Kay said.

"I thought girls didn't take their engagement rings off. Ever," he said.

Eleanor saw Kay swallow hard.

"Would you take your engagement ring off?"

"That is not relevant," Eleanor pointed out. "And Kay cannot possibly know whether Rosaleen took her ring off or not. You must ask Rosaleen."

"Yeah. I'm sure that right now she will tell me she dropped it somewhere."

"You will only know that answer when you speak to Rosaleen Davis," Eleanor said.

Detective Connor nodded. He said, "How come you told us that the ring belongs to Rosaleen Davis?"

Eleanor saw Kay straighten in surprise. "That's true," Kay said. "I don't know for certain that it is Rosaleen's ring. It looks like the one that Stephen Roberts gave her. I guess I said it because that was my observation."

Kay looked worried. "Maybe I'm wrong. Maybe it isn't her ring at all. And I pointed the finger at her."

"We'll talk to Rosaleen Davis and Stephen Roberts. It gets interesting if they do not identify the ring as the one that Roberts gave to his fiancée."

Kay bit her lip.

Detective Connor moved off to the side to complete his notes. Josephine and Jacques Abtey came in from the balcony.

"I'm sorry," Kay said quietly. "I should not have offered my opinion that the ring belonged to Rosaleen. I don't want to give evidence against her. And I don't know for sure it is her ring."

Eleanor touched her hand. "You had to tell the truth. The police would have questioned us all about the ring. We could not say for certain it was the same one, but if it looked similar, we would be required to state that."

"How could someone have gotten Rosaleen's ring?" Josephine asked.

"Only Rosaleen can answer that," Mr. Abtey said.

"We will go to my suite, Eleanor. Rosaleen and Stephen are there. We will see what they say."

Jacques Abtey said he would go to Tim's suite and see what had happened during Tim's questioning and inform Connor's partner that they were in Josephine's suite.

Once there, Detective Connor put the question of the ring to Rosaleen. Without hesitation, Rosaleen identified the ring as the one given to her by Stephen. Flora gave a small gasp.

"How did it come to be with Eulie Reynolds's body?" Detective Connor asked.

"I-I took it off."

Stephen wore an expression of guilt.

Kay said suddenly, "Did you ask her to take it off?"

"No," he said. "I said something stupid, and Rosaleen took it off."

"What is he talking about, Miss Davis?" Connor asked.

"Stephen fears that I might be responsible for his stepfather's death. He thinks I was forced to act in self-defense. I am innocent, but I can see his doubt. I-I told him I could not marry him until he knew the truth about me. I took my ring off. Stephen begged me to keep it. He said he loves me and that he believes in me. I went to my room and put the ring on the bedside table."

"And—"

"It was not there when I woke up."

"Did you take it?" Connor asked Stephen.

"No. I was in the bar until it closed. Some guy I met helped me up to my room and I passed out on my bed," Stephen said. "I didn't leave my room after that."

"Did you?" he asked Flora. "I believe you are staying at the hotel."

"I am," Flora said. "And I did take—"

"You must tell the truth," Eleanor interrupted gently.

Flora sighed. "You are right. I was going to say I took the ring, that I had it, not Rosaleen. But that would not be the truth. I did not know my daughter had taken off the ring. I was so happy that they would be married despite all that has happened."

Detective Connor turned again to Rosaleen. "No one else knew you had taken the ring off."

Rosaleen shook her head.

"Did anyone see you without the ring?" Connor asked.

"I said good night to Josephine," she said. "But I didn't tell her about what happened between Stephen and me. I don't know if she noticed the ring was missing."

"I did not," Josephine said. "I noticed that Rosaleen looked weakened by her ordeal, however."

"Look, Miss Davis, Reynolds was a big-time member of the Klan," Connor said. He turned to Eleanor and Josephine. "I'm thinking of bringing in Miss Davis. She's a suspect and this is for her own protection."

Flora gave a cry of dismay.

Eleanor did not like this. "But can you ensure her safety at your police station?"

"I'm going to protect her myself," Detective Connor said.

She knew why Tim trusted this man. "I fear you cannot promise she will remain safe."

"I'm calling that lawyer, Monsieur Schwartz," Josephine said. "You have nothing on which to charge her. Other than a dropped ring. A fair and impartial judge would laugh you out of court."

Rosaleen's voice broke in. "Stephen, do you think I did it?"

"No. I mean, you couldn't have. Unless you put the ring back on like I asked you . . . and if you did, if you dropped the ring, it was only because you were protecting yourself. I know it."

Rosaleen looked at him in horror. "You think I did it. Why can't you believe me?"

Stephen didn't say anything. As Detective Connor formally arrested Rosaleen Davis on suspicion of the murder of Eulie Reynolds, Stephen just let her go.

Kay turned on him. "You should believe in the woman you love! She insists she is innocent. Why can't you listen to her?"

Fury blazed in Kay's eyes. It was as if Kay's heart was being broken, Eleanor noted.

Stephen sank down onto the sofa. "If I was accused of two murders, would you tell Rosaleen to trust me?"

Eleanor saw Kay begin to answer and then stop. Kay's cheeks went pink with a blush. "I guess I would tell her to be careful. To not take everything on faith that a man tells her. I would be afraid you were lying, and she was going to be hurt," Kay admitted.

"Yeah. You wouldn't tell her to have blind faith in me—"

Josephine interrupted. "I will get Rosaleen out of prison once more. Then you and Rosaleen must have a serious talk."

"I will. But right now, I need to go," Stephen said. "I feel like I'm considered the criminal here."

Kay began to sputter. Stephen leapt up and strode to the door. He yanked it open to reveal Jacques Abtey and Tim on the other side.

Abtey said, "Finally, we actually meet, Stephen. I didn't get a chance to talk to you on the night we had dinner. After that, we seem to keep missing each other." Abtey extended his hand. "I am sorry for what Rosaleen is enduring."

Eleanor noticed Abtey scrutinizing Stephen Roberts's face. It was subtle, but Eleanor had no doubt the former intelligence officer was searching Stephen's expression.

What was he looking for?

Then she knew. She remembered the spoken words that had piqued her curiosity. Combined with Jacques Abtey's study of Stephen's face, they made sense to her.

CHAPTER 29

It is foolish to worry, for all of us know that whatever comes we have to meet it.
—Eleanor Roosevelt, My Day, August 16, 1941

Shoving his gray fedora on his head, Stephen walked out of the door, letting it shut behind him.

Wearing a sorrowful expression, Josephine watched him go. She shook her head and tutted. "He will come back. He is confused and upset."

Kay arched a brow. "Rosaleen is having to endure more accusations and another arrest. How can he be leaving in a huff?"

"I am afraid Stephen is under a great strain," Mrs. Roosevelt said. "I do not approve of his behavior, but I do . . . understand."

"I don't," Kay said. "He rescued her from the KKK yesterday and today he is back to suspecting her! Nothing he does or says makes any sense."

"To Stephen, it does," Mrs. R said.

Kay did not understand why Mrs. R was defending him. "If Stephen was your son, I think you would tell one of your sons to buck up and be a better fiancé, I bet."

Mrs. Roosevelt was silent for a moment. Kay wondered: Had she crossed a line?

But Mrs. Roosevelt said calmly, "I have learned to not voice my opinion about the romantic lives of my children. Even my daughter Anna's divorce was fodder for critics of FDR's politics, and I hardly see how the two things connect."

"I guess everything FDR did—and you did—was scrutinized."

"Oh yes. There were stories that we accidentally left Fala on a Pacific island during the war and sent a military plane to fetch him at great expense to the public. It wasn't true, but people believed it."

Mrs. R paused. "We would never have forgotten Fala."

"I can't believe people would accept a made-up story as the truth," Kay said. It made her think—what things did she read and learn and believe were facts, that weren't true at all?

"I am not going to sit idly by while Rosaleen is dragged off by the police on the flimsiest of evidence. As if she could attack that enormous, terrible man. *Il faut*, I shall command the lawyer to demand Rosaleen's release!" Josephine declared.

Josephine picked up the telephone receiver. Within a minute, she was speaking to Rosaleen's lawyer. She exclaimed, "We must get Rosaleen released on bail! Detective Connor says Rosaleen needs protection. I have two strong, smart men here who can keep her safe. She will *not* be safe in police custody."

Kay hoped it was true that Stephen could help keep her safe, or would he be too busy drinking away his sorrows?

When she was in high school, she believed it was her duty to warn a friend against a bad boyfriend. Her mother, while she was alive, had warned that a girl who heard disparaging comments about her boyfriend from her female friends always dropped the female friends and kept the boyfriend. Until he went on to break her heart and sometimes empty her purse.

Josephine hung up. "I am going with Jacques and the lawyer to fetch her," she said with determination.

"Do you wish Kay and I to accompany you?" Mrs. Roosevelt asked.

Jacques shook his head. "It is best to keep this low-key. We can handle this."

Kay looked over to Mrs. Roosevelt, who nodded. "I agree. We do not want to inflame things."

Kay knew Mrs. R would get back to work. Keeping busy helped the time pass. It was hard to believe it was only hours ago that Kay found Eulie Reynolds' body. It was late afternoon when Jacques Abtey telephoned their suite. Kay was typing up letters and waiting for Mrs. R to return from her many meetings.

"We have returned successful," he said. "Josephine insisted on having a hearing before a judge today. She is such a force of nature that the judge could not resist the chance to meet her in person. At first, the judge leaned toward denying bail since Rosaleen is a suspect in two murders. Josephine threw herself upon his mercy. She insisted that Rosaleen was in danger in jail. And reminded him that Rosaleen has only been charged and not convicted. He agreed to her release. She is in her room, resting. Josephine has insisted Rosaleen should rest and not accompany her to the Copa City Club tonight."

"I will tell Mrs. Roosevelt," Kay said.

"I am glad she has been released," Mrs. Roosevelt said, when she had returned and Kay recounted the telephone call. "I am very worried."

"So am I," Kay said.

In the early evening, Kay and Mrs. Roosevelt took a taxi to the Copa City Club. The doorman handed Mrs. Roosevelt a note from Josephine, asking them both to come to her dressing room.

Only a few days ago, Rosaleen had walked into this room with Franz Müller, Kay thought. Then her nightmare began.

Tonight, Rosaleen was staying in her room at the Delano while Josephine performed.

A woman stood up from an armchair as Kay and Mrs. Roosevelt walked in.

"It's Miss Hilton," Kay said, surprised.

Stella wore a lavender suit trimmed with feathers. The dyed feathers rimmed the neckline of the jacket, swathing her neck like a fur boa. They fluttered on the cuffs and floated from the hem of her skirt. Her pale purple suit wasn't cut by a designer, but it was striking. She towered on stiletto heels. Rings flashed on her fingers. Big rings, and Kay guessed they weren't real jewels.

Kay remembered how Josephine had told them she learned from the singer Clara Smith that to be a star, she must project the image to her public that she was a star. Even when she was just starting out and struggling, she had to look glamorous and successful.

"This is Mrs. Eleanor Roosevelt," Josephine said. "You have met Miss Kay Thompson. Ladies, this is Stella Hilton."

Mrs. R extended her hand and clasped Stella's. Kay did the same, giving a confident handshake.

Stella wore a ring on every finger except the finger that would be graced by a wedding ring. That finger, which was to bear the most important ring in a woman's life—supposedly—was bare.

Josephine led Mrs. Roosevelt to an Art Deco-styled chromium armchair and pulled another one forward for Kay, while Stella settled back in her chair and arranged her long legs attractively.

Josephine said, "Stella came to me because she claims she saw who shot M. Miller." Josephine waved her hand at Stella. "Why don't you tell Mrs. Roosevelt what you said to me?"

Kay's brows rose. Stella had claimed to see a tall man in the hallway. After the shot, she had run away with her date for the evening.

From the look of self-importance on Stella's face, it was obvious she had more to say. Something that she hadn't felt the need to say when Kay and Tim had spoken to her.

But Kay kept quiet to let Stella talk.

"I *saw* her," Stella said, fluffing the feathers at her neck.

"Saw who, Miss Hilton?" Mrs. R prompted.

"I saw Rosaleen Davis shoot that old white man. She said he wasn't going to get away with stealing his stepson's rightful inheritance and she shot him. In cold blood."

"How did you see all that?" Kay demanded, shocked. "You said you saw a tall man running away."

"I'm telling you what I saw now. And I didn't lie. I did see a tall man. Looked like he had very pale skin."

Isaac Gros, Kay thought.

"But he wasn't the one who shot Frank Miller," Stella said.

Kay wanted to scream, but ER said calmly, "Please tell me exactly what you saw. Did Mr. Miller threaten Rosaleen?"

Miss Hilton shook her head. "He said he wanted to talk to her, but she just pulled out a gun and shot him."

"Pulled it out? From where?"

"Her purse."

Kay's eyes widened but ER simply said, "Rosaleen Davis was not carrying her purse."

Miss Hilton looked startled. "I guess she was holding the gun. Maybe hiding her hand in the folds of her skirt."

"I see," Mrs. R said. "Why did you not tell the police? This is very important, Miss Hilton."

"I've learned not to talk to the police," Stella Hilton said sourly. "My young brother, Samuel, was arrested by the Miami police. His crime was buying a nice car after saving up the money he earned playing the trumpet. They figured he had stolen that car. I was afraid that if I talked to the police, they would end up arresting me. They already had a Black woman who was guilty. They didn't need anything from me."

"Instead, Stella came to me." Josephine crossed her arms in front of her chest.

"It was time for me to do the right thing," Stella said.

Josephine's brow arched. "She asked me to pay her in exchange for keeping her mouth shut about what she saw."

"You said you wouldn't tell!" Stella cried.

"I said I would not tell the police you attempted to blackmail me."

Stella fluffed the feathers around her neck nervously. "I know that Josephine wanted Rosaleen Davis to be found innocent. I don't get paid a lot to be a backup singer. I have two other brothers who are still teenagers. They depend on me." She spoke with defiance.

"I told her I was sorry for her plight, but I don't pay blackmail. I believe in justice. I would help her family in any way I could, but I don't need threats to do that," Josephine declared.

Kay thought once more of the similarities between Mrs. R and Josephine. Both women were generous. They wanted to help those less fortunate. They wanted to give others opportunity. But they were smart and just.

"Blackmail is a serious crime," Mrs. Roosevelt said. "And dangerous. If you are a witness to a crime, you must go to the police. I will take you—I assure you that I won't let anyone arrest you or mistreat you."

Panic flashed in Stella Hilton's eyes. "I just wanted a little money to pay my bills. I'm not going to the police."

Stella pushed up from the sofa. Josephine stood in front of her, but Stella pushed past her. "You can't keep me here. I've gotta change for the show."

Josephine let her go. As Stella rushed out the door, Josephine cocked her head to the side in a childlike way. "Is she telling the truth now?" Josephine asked. "She very definitely doesn't want to speak to the police."

Mrs. R nodded. "Is that because she is truly afraid of them? Or because she is not speaking the truth?"

"I think she's lying. She made up a story to extort money from me," Josephine said. "She knows that if she talks to the police, they will tear her story apart."

"I'm worried," Mrs. Roosevelt said, pensively.

"I don't think she will take her lies to the police," Josephine said.

"That isn't what frightens me," Mrs. R said. "I am going to have Tim watch over that young woman."

Kay knew then what Mrs. R feared.

The knock came early the next morning.

It meant something bad. Kay knew it as she opened her hotel room door. Tim stood there. A blood-soaked bandage was taped to his temple.

"What happened?" she exclaimed, her voice so shocked and sharp, she was surprised her window didn't shatter.

He winced in pain. "Can't take loud noises yet. I just got out of the hospital. They wanted me to stick around, but I needed to get here."

"Come in." Kay opened the door wide.

He looked at her and she knew the pain went deeper than physical. He did not step inside.

"I failed, Kay," he said.

"No, you couldn't have—"

"I did. I need to tell Mrs. Roosevelt," Tim said. "She wanted me to watch over that singer, Stella. I caught up with Stella as she was waiting for a taxi and offered her a ride. Once she was home, I planned to set up in the car, like a stakeout, watching over her apartment."

"And Stella slugged you over the head?"

"I wish." He groaned.

"Someone slugged you over the head," she pointed out.

"Someone did. The same person who murdered Stella." He slumped against the doorframe. "I was supposed to protect the singer. Instead, I got clobbered and she was killed."

Kay closed her hand gently around his wrist. "You are coming inside. I'll get some ice. They patched you up, but you must have an awful headache."

"I do."

She thought he would resist. But he let her lead him into the suite. "Mrs. R is in the washroom."

"She's up this early?"

"When she has a busy day. Which is almost always. Sit." She pointed at the sofa. "I'll come back with ice."

She paused before leaving, ensuring he did take her advice and sit.

"Was she shot?" she asked.

He hesitated. She guessed that he wanted to be chivalrous and spare her. No deal. "Tell me."

"The killer used a knife."

"Stabbed her? Tim, I've seen a stabbing victim. I won't faint. Since the very first time, I've gained a lot of sangfroid. My knees won't even wobble."

"Not stabbed. Her throat was cut. Cleanly and efficiently. It was someone who knew what he was doing."

Someone who knew how to cut a throat. Kay thought of Josephine's espionage work. Not Josephine . . . but secret agents in the war received that kind of training.

"The Overtown police are investigating."

"Which means there is no place for Mrs. R or me in the investigation."

"Yeah, but I was the one who found the body. When I came

to, I raced up to Miss Hilton's apartment. The door was unlocked. I studied the crime scene before notifying the cops. There are a few things I want to describe to Mrs. R."

"Such as?"

"There was a gold bracelet near the bed. It looked like it had been dropped there. There was blood on it. I didn't touch it, but I could see it was inscribed on the inside from Josephine. It said, TO MY WONDERFUL ASSISTANT R, FROM J. I guess it must have been a gift."

"Rosaleen said Josephine was generous," Kay murmured.

"I had to tell the police I believed the bracelet might belong to Rosaleen and the 'J' might stand for Josephine. It looks like they are going to question Rosaleen for the murder of Stella Hilton."

"They think she was released from jail and went out and stabbed Stella Hilton skillfully? That makes no sense."

"To the cops, especially Mike Connor's partner, it makes all the sense they need."

After Tim told Mrs. Roosevelt about the murder, he left. Kay could see he blamed himself. Mrs. Roosevelt picked up the telephone receiver to call Josephine and Kay asked, "Would you mind if I went down to the pool for a minute? I feel I need to go outside."

"Of course you may."

To her surprise, she found Stephen at the pool. Sitting on the edge like Kay had done with Rosaleen.

She kicked off her shoes, peeled off her stockings, and sat on the edge a few feet from him.

"I wanted to go to the bar," he admitted to her. "I convinced myself to come here instead." He looked at her, his eyes filled with sorrow. "I don't want to believe she did it. But what other explanation is there? She was wearing the bracelet last night, at

Jo's performance. She told me she was innocent. But three murders?" He groaned, rubbing his temple. "I asked her how she could prove it."

"You asked her *that*?"

"She can't prove it," he said. "She doesn't know how her bracelet went missing. Or her ring. But Josephine told her that Stella Hilton claimed to see her shoot my stepfather. Rosaleen had a motive to kill her."

Kay waited. She had learned this while working for male bosses—if a man needed to talk, let him. There was no point in adding to the conversation because he was listening only to the words coming out of his mouth, not yours.

"I've got to accept the facts. She did it. She's been lying to me. I know she is scared and desperate. I love her. I want to help her. But I don't know what to do."

"I'm afraid that you don't love her," Kay said bluntly.

Stephen frowned at her. "I do. I'm forgiving Rosie. I'll love her whether she is innocent or guilty. Love is wanting to save her when it looks impossible. That's love. Rosaleen was lying to me all along. But I still love her."

He started to get to his feet.

Kay saw it then. His bare wrist. "Where is your watch?" she asked.

Stephen straightened. "I don't know. I lost it." His gaze narrowed. "You haven't seen it, have you?"

"No. I would have given it to you. Where did you lose it?"

"If I knew that, it wouldn't be lost."

Kay watched him leave, then she got up, rolled her stockings back on and slipped her feet back into her pumps. She had an idea. She went into the lobby—she didn't want to waste time on the elevator. She chose an outside line on the lobby telephone and asked for the Police Department. When the line connected, she asked to speak to Detective Mike Connor.

"Hello, Miss Thompson," he said. "To what do I owe the pleasure?"

She said softly, "Do you know anyone in the Overtown Police Department? I want to find out if they found a man's army watch in Stella Hilton's apartment."

"I know a couple of guys. Give me a few minutes."

"Can you call back to Mrs. Roosevelt's suite?" She gave him the telephone number of the Delano Hotel.

Mike Connor was as good as his word. Not long after she had reached the suite, the telephone rang. Mike Connor was put through. Breathlessly, Kay greeted him.

"They did find an A-11 army watch, Miss Thompson. At first I thought you were asking because it belongs to Tim—"

"It doesn't," Kay interrupted. "It belongs to Stephen Roberts."

Her heart pounded. She added, "I mean, I don't know it does, but Stephen's watch is missing. It seems too much coincidence that his watch got lost and the same watch turned up at the crime scene."

"You think it's Roberts's watch and he and Rosaleen are in this together?"

"No!" she exclaimed. "That isn't what I mean—"

"Roberts could not have killed his stepfather," Mike Connor said, interrupting her. "But he could have planned it with Rosaleen Davis, and she killed Miller. But here's the thing . . ."

He paused. Kay finally gasped, "What? Stop with the pregnant pause."

"There was a name engraved on the back of the watch. That was how I knew it didn't belong to Tim. It reads O'HARA. U.S. 1ST ARMY. It doesn't belong to Roberts either. It looks like Miss Hilton had a gentleman friend."

"Okay," Kay said slowly. "What will happen to Rosaleen? This watch is evidence that someone else went to Stella Hilton's apartment."

"That's for the Overtown Police to investigate, not us. As far as I'm concerned, she is still out on bail."

"Thank you, Detective," Kay said. At least Rosaleen would have her freedom for now.

As Kay hung up, she frowned. Stephen lost his army A-11 watch. One turned up in Stella's room. But it wasn't Stephen's watch.

It seemed an impossible, unbelievable coincidence.

What would Mrs. Roosevelt think?

CHAPTER 30

I had almost forgotten the different hues, ranging from dark purple to light green, that color the ocean along the Florida coast.

—Eleanor Roosevelt, My Day, May 2, 1949

Kay raced up to the suite to talk to Mrs. Roosevelt. "Detective Connor found the same type of watch—the A-11 watch issued to men in the army—in Stella's apartment. The name engraved on the back of the watch is 'O'Hara.' Not Stephen's name. But it seems too strange a coincidence that Stephen lost his watch at the same time another man named O'Hara lost his watch at Stella's home. While murdering her."

Mrs. Roosevelt held up her hands. "Repeat that again. Just a little slower."

Kay had been trying for concise. She had achieved incomprehensible. She told Mrs. R what she had learned. With more care. Mrs. Roosevelt caught on immediately.

Mrs. R went to the telephone and called Tim's room.

She related the findings of the Overtown police over the telephone. Then listened. Kay heard Tim's voice, with his soft Irish lilt, through the receiver. After she hung up, Mrs. R said, "Tim stated that the First Army did indeed land on Omaha Beach. He said it was possible Stephen picked up the watch from a deceased comrade-in-arms. Or sometimes soldiers traded personal items for luck. Like a promise to look out for each other. I suppose the best way to get to the bottom of it would be to ask Stephen."

"We need to ask him right away," Kay said. "But if he denies it, how can we prove the watch was the one he wore?"

"I do not know," Mrs. Roosevelt said. She looked thoughtful. "But this is the last day of our stay in Miami. We must travel to New York tomorrow in the early morning so that we can embark tomorrow night for Paris."

"I have the airline tickets," Kay said, trying to look efficient, when her mind was struggling with worry. "But we don't know who the murderer is. Rosaleen has been released from prison, but she has been charged with two murders and may be charged with Stella's murder. If we leave, what will happen to her?"

Tomorrow was the last day of December. They would be flying to Paris on New Year's Eve. Kay hadn't even thought there would be flights on New Year's Eve.

Before Christmas Eve day, Kay had dreamed of dancing with Tim on New Year's Eve. She had dreamed of a kiss at midnight. In all honesty, she had dreamed of a marriage proposal at midnight.

Instead, she had broken up with Tim and she would be in an airplane when the clock struck twelve on New Year's Eve. She would be doing her job, heading to Paris for the continuance of the United Nations session.

But what mattered now was Rosaleen.

"I would like to go for a walk along the beach," Mrs. Roosevelt said.

"The beach?"

"You haven't spent any time at the beach. Perhaps, during the walk, we can put our thoughts in order."

Mrs. R wanted to discuss the mystery.

Excited, Kay hurried to her room, and pulled on the Marilyn Monroe bikini and her wrap. She sighed as she slipped her feet in her flat sneakers and grabbed her sun hat, the one that barely survived her trip in the suitcase.

Mrs. R changed into white linen trousers and a loose white blouse. A large white straw hat shaded her face, but did not hide her trademark smile. Together, they walked through the gardens, past the pool. The deck had been scrubbed clean, and there was an empty space where the chaise longue had been.

Mrs. Roosevelt stopped and studied the spot thoughtfully.

"Do you see any clues?"

"Oh, no. I was thinking. But we should do that at the beach," Mrs. Roosevelt said, then led the way to the back gate, and out onto South Beach.

Kay let out a soft sigh as her shoes sank into the warm sand. And no one was chasing her in a car this time.

"I love water," Mrs. Roosevelt commented. "I always adored being on Campobello. But it was a little chillier than this."

Kay remembered what Tommy had told her about the summer home on Campobello Island, part of the Canadian province of New Brunswick. It had been a wedding gift from FDR's mother, Sara Delano Roosevelt.

"Franklin loved to sail," Mrs. Roosevelt said, her eyes softening with remembrance. "He liked the ocean from the deck of a ship, even when the vessel rolled and pitched so much that most people retired to bed. My own appreciation of the ocean is enhanced by being on dry land. But do I like to swim."

"Aunt Tommy told me that you use the swimming pool at Hyde Park every day in the summer."

Kay had begun working for Mrs. Roosevelt this year in the fall, after the swimming season at Mrs. Roosevelt's home in Hyde Park, New York, had ended.

"My many grandchildren make that activity enjoyable. The first plunge of the year at Hyde Park is extremely cold. Only the knowledge that my grandchildren enjoy it keeps me in long enough to enjoy it also."

"I like my swimming to be in warm water," Kay said. It touched her heart how fond Mrs. Roosevelt was of all her grandchildren—Kay had seen the photograph of FDR and ER at the White House with thirteen grandchildren. She had wondered if she would ever have such a large family. Or a family of her own at all.

She wanted her job. She wanted to travel and learn with Mrs. Roosevelt. But she wanted children too.

Yet it seemed it couldn't be done, because she needed to find an open-minded, modern man.

"I like the ocean up north, but it's awfully cold," Kay said.

"You will find it is quite balmy here."

At this time of day—midmorning—the beach was becoming busy. Families set up blankets and beach umbrellas. Men strolled along the beach, gazing toward pretty women in bathing suits who posed attractively on towels and blankets.

At the water's edge, Mrs. Roosevelt kicked off her shoes. Kay stared in astonishment as Mrs. Roosevelt rolled her trouser legs up to her knees.

"Perfect for paddling," Mrs. R declared.

Kay still could not get over how natural and ordinary Mrs. R was. Even though she was a former First Lady and grew up in high society.

Mrs. R was as warm and welcoming to ordinary families as she was to presidents. She was as comfortable arguing for human rights at the U.N. as she was walking barefoot through the waves crashing on South Beach.

Mrs. R waded out so deep that the bottom of her rolled trousers got wet. "I do enjoy the feel of squishy sand between my toes."

Everything interested Mrs. R, Kay thought. She loved to explore. To experience. To try. In her mind and heart, she was like a young person, eager to learn about the world.

"You look surprised," Mrs. Roosevelt observed.

"I never dreamed I'd see you splashing through the water on the beach," Kay admitted.

"I thought we could reflect while we walk. You don't need to cover your bathing suit with the wrap if you wish to get some sun."

Kay hesitated. Then she slipped off the wrap. The sun was warm on her shoulders and her bare arms. She paddled barefoot beside Mrs. R, the wrap lying over her arm.

Mrs. R's first question startled her. "What did you feel when you met with Mr. Petrov?"

"H-how do you know?" Kay gulped. What had she felt? Right now, she felt guilt.

"Tim knew. He followed you. He said it was for your protection. He left when he saw Mr. Petrov pick you up in his convertible. Tim didn't want to spy on you."

"It sounds like he did." Kay looked down. "I'm sorry I did it. Dmitri sent me a note, and I was just so curious to see what happened to him." Her heart raced. She had made a huge mistake.

"What has happened to him?"

"Dmitri is successful and happy. He owns a new car dealership. I am happy for him. And proud of him. Also, I felt . . . envy. He started with nothing—not even his own name—and he is building his own business. I wish I had his courage."

"You have a great deal of courage."

A wave crashed into Kay's legs. She squealed. "Are there jellyfish in here?"

"They are not usually in the water this late in the year. And if they are, they are small ones. It does not hurt very much when you are stung."

"Stung!" Kay realized she didn't sound courageous at all.

Mrs. Roosevelt began walking along the firmer sand, at the edges of the rolling waves. With her height and long legs, Mrs. Roosevelt was a fast walker.

"We should speak about what we know about the murders," Mrs. R said.

"We don't know who murdered Franz Müller—at least, *I* have no idea," Kay admitted. "I don't know who stabbed Reynolds. Or who killed poor Stella Hilton. Did the watch belong to Stephen? Did he drop it at Stella's apartment? Did he silence Stella to protect Rosaleen?"

"He belongs to the CIA," Mrs. R said.

"You mean, he wouldn't kill someone?"

"I think he would have been more careful about dropping his watch."

Kay stopped. The waves rolled up to the ends of her toes, then ebbed away. "You think it was planted. Just like Rosaleen's ring and bracelet."

"It is a possibility. We must consider who had means and motives," Mrs. Roosevelt said.

"The night of the party, everyone we met seemed to have a motive to murder Josephine Baker. But that wasn't real. The letters were fake and there was no threat to Josephine."

"That is true. And interesting, I think," Mrs. R said.

Kay thought about it. "The same people who had motives to hurt Josephine Baker have even more motive to murder Franz Müller. It's funny, isn't it?"

"That is true." Mrs. Roosevelt stopped. She shaded her eyes with her hand and looked out over the ocean. "Would you like an ice cream cone?" she asked.

"Oh! I mean, yes. Of course."

Kay knew she should refuse an ice cream cone because this little bathing suit wouldn't hide the results of eating ice cream. It barely hid anything. But she didn't want to spoil the treat.

Mrs. R purchased two cones from a small shack on the beach.

As Mrs. R licked her vanilla ice cream, Kay said, "Stephen and Rosaleen have the most obvious motive. Money. An inheritance worth fifty million dollars. And Müller threatened to disinherit Stephen over his engagement."

"Yes."

Kay's ice cream began to melt. She licked it quickly.

Mrs. Roosevelt observed, "It was impossible for Stephen to have murdered his stepfather. As for Rosaleen, despite the police opinion that the test was inconclusive, I do not think she fired the gun. I cannot picture her stabbing Eulie Reynolds either. He was an enormous man, and she is tall but slender. Nor can I envision her murdering Stella. Tim said her throat was cut with precision. A particularly ruthless act."

"I don't want it to be Rosaleen," Kay said, passionately. "If she had to shoot Müller to protect herself, I could accept that. It was self-defense. But I don't want her to have killed him for money. And I don't want to think she killed Stella."

"Yes, I do not want to think Rosaleen could commit a premeditated murder," Mrs. R agreed.

"I guess it could be Mr. Gros," Kay said. "His motive is vengeance against a Nazi death camp commandant." She sighed. "I don't *want* it to be Mr. Gros. And he doesn't have a motive to have murdered Stella Hilton."

"We must be impartial," ER observed. "Especially here, while we are reviewing facts. There is Rosaleen's mother, Flora. If she feared Rosaleen was in danger from Mr. Müller, it is possible she shot him to protect her daughter."

Kay nodded. "And maybe she did the same thing to Eulie Reynolds. Josephine invited her to the Delano. She was *there*, at the hotel. Maybe she overheard Stella at the Copa City Club, and feared Stella's story would incriminate Rosaleen."

"She was on the spot," Mrs. Roosevelt said. "But Flora would not have implicated her daughter."

Shielding her eyes against the sun, Kay added, "I hoped that

Eulie Reynolds shot Franz Müller. He had motive—if he was involved with the KKK bombings, he could have feared Müller was going to identify him. Also, he wanted to take over Müller's position in the organization. But he is a victim, so he can't be the murderer."

"We are assuming the same murderer killed both men. It is possible there was more than one murderer," Mrs. Roosevelt observed.

Kay groaned. "I hope not. I haven't been able to figure out the first one, never mind two. Or three."

Kay watched a tiny rivulet of melted cream inch toward her fingers. She had made a promise . . . but she must break it. They were running out of time. "There is something I have to tell you, Mrs. Roosevelt . . ."

Mrs. R looked so startled Kay wondered what she had expected Kay to confess.

She related everything she had learned on the night when she and Tim followed Reynolds and Mains to the cross burning. "I promised Claude Mains I would tell no one he is a reporter. But now I fear he is also a killer. He had motive if Franz Müller knew who he really was. He also had motive to murder Eulie Reynolds, if Reynolds discovered he is a journalist. Reynolds might have wanted to shut him up permanently and Mains had to stab him in self-defense."

Mrs. Roosevelt nodded. "Yes, Mr. Mains does have a strong motive. But we do not know if anyone had blown his cover."

"But what motive did he have to murder Stella?" Kay asked. "Stella insisted she saw Rosaleen shoot Müller. We think Stella lied to extort money, but why would Mains kill her . . ." The idea dawned. "The person who murdered Stella is the person who paid her to lie, of course. Because that person was afraid that she would admit the truth and reveal the real killer's name."

"That is a sound theory," ER said.

For a few minutes, they walked in silence along the water's edge. Kay looked out over the ocean, to ships passing by. Waves broke over their feet.

"There are two things I find curious," Mrs. Roosevelt said.

Kay waited. When Mrs. R said such a thing, something startling was coming. Something that would tie Kay's brain into knots, trying to figure out exactly what it explained.

"It is interesting that Rosaleen's ring was found near Eulie Reynolds's body," Mrs. Roosevelt said. "If the murderer was Mr. Mains or Mr. Gros, how would they know about the engagement ring? How would they have access to it?"

Kay had not seen that point. "That means it was . . . one of the people in Josephine's suite. Someone close to Rosaleen."

"The fact that the ring was taken meant the murder of Eulie Reynolds was planned. It also means the murderer intended Rosaleen to be the scapegoat."

"Stephen knew Rosaleen had taken off the ring. He was the only one, other than Rosaleen," Kay said thoughtfully. "And his watch was in Stella's apartment."

"We do not know either of those things for certain yet," Mrs. Roosevelt cautioned. "We don't know if he was the only person who knew about the ring. We don't know if that is his watch. I think it is very likely. But the name on it, O'Hara, gives one to think."

"It does? I guess I don't know why Stephen was wearing someone else's watch."

"I wonder exactly why the ring was planted. The murderer stabbed Reynolds and escaped undetected. The false clue was not necessary," Mrs. Roosevelt said.

"I guess the killer hoped that pointing the finger at Rosaleen might keep the police from really investigating. Again," Kay added sardonically.

"That seems the most likely answer." Mrs. Roosevelt deviated around three children building a sandcastle.

"When I learned Detective Connor found the A-11 watch, I thought immediately it was like *Towards Zero*," Kay said impetuously.

In their previous investigation, she had seen similarities to Alfred Hitchcock movies. She was a lover of thriller movies and whodunnit books. "The book by Agatha Christie," Kay explained. "All the clues pointed to Rosaleen's guilt for both murders. Well, for the first murder, it was mostly that she was there.

"In *Towards Zero*, one person plants fake evidence against himself to look guilty. But the police realize it's all faked and they dig deeper. They find more subtle clues that point to someone else. But it was a double bluff. The murderer was the first man after all. He was trying to set up someone innocent. It was a woman he loved, but after she rejected him, he hated her. He made it look like she had planted the fake clues against him. He wanted to see her convicted of murder; he wanted to watch her hang."

Kay knew her explanation had been confused and messy. But Mrs. Roosevelt was accustomed to getting to the core of the Soviets' wordy speeches at the United Nations.

To her surprise, Mrs. Roosevelt stopped suddenly. "Do you believe Stephen does not truly love Rosaleen?"

"I accused him of that," Kay said, blushing. "He seems determined to say she is guilty—oh!"

Was it possible Stephen was setting up Rosaleen?

But Stephen had the perfect alibi for Frank Miller's murder.

"What are you thinking, Kay?"

Kay flushed again with embarrassment. "I wondered if there was a way Stephen could have faked his alibi. If it wasn't for Tim, I would have suspected he faked it."

"But he could not," Mrs. R said.

Two men walking by let out wolf whistles. Kay knew she should have expected it, wearing this bathing suit. Suddenly she felt exposed. Vulnerable.

If she wanted to be taken seriously, should she be dressing this way?

When she started working for Mrs. R, she had worn dull dresses. Mrs. Roosevelt encouraged her to be herself. But could she be pretty and flirtatious as well as serious? Men never thought that was possible in a woman—that her mind could be more complex than what her clothes were saying.

She threw on her wrap.

"Do not let those men bother you," Mrs. Roosevelt said.

"It's not that. It's the . . . uh . . . breeze off the water," Kay said lamely.

"There is another thing I found curious," Mrs. Roosevelt said. "Josephine said she did not follow Rosaleen to the dressing room. Rosaleen told her not to come, and she had to insist on that, because she had secretly arranged to meet Stephen's stepfather. Rosaleen also knew the letters were fake and there was no threat to Josephine.

"But I felt it was unlike Josephine to allow Rosaleen to return to her dressing room alone, regardless of what Rosaleen said. However, it was not so strange if Josephine knew the letters were a hoax."

"What?" Kay asked.

"I believe Josephine suspected Rosaleen was behind the letters all along. It would explain why she did not want me to see them."

"But what about the party? I thought Josephine hoped to find out who wrote the letters."

"That is what Rosaleen claimed Josephine said. Perhaps by saying that to Rosaleen, Josephine hoped Rosaleen would take the chance to be honest and confess to writing them."

"She gave Rosaleen the chance to be noble."

"I believe so. And I think she did so because she believes in Rosaleen."

"It was kind of her to forgive Rosaleen," Kay said. "Josephine is a truly great woman. I feel very privileged to know her. And you, Mrs. Roosevelt."

Kay was sure she detected a blush on Mrs. R's cheeks.

"We should return to the hotel," Mrs. Roosevelt said. "Tim gave me an idea. He was curious about the soldier named O'Hara. I will telephone Sandy and ask him to investigate."

Mrs. Roosevelt turned and began striding along the sand in the other direction. "I also wonder if Josephine was not entirely truthful. Maybe Josephine did follow Rosaleen to the dressing room. She did not believe Stella's story. If she had followed Rosaleen, she knew Stella was not truthful."

Kay panted a little as she took long, fast strides to keep up.

She thought of something.

If Josephine had followed Rosaleen, was it possible . . . that Josephine had done it?

Was Stella trying to blackmail Josephine because it was Josephine she saw with the gun, not Rosaleen?

CHAPTER 31

One can fight danger only when one is armed with solid facts and spurred on by an unwavering faith and determination.

—Eleanor Roosevelt, *The Autobiography of Eleanor Roosevelt*, 1961

"I am sorry, Stephen, but Rosaleen has been brought in for questioning by the Overtown police," Josephine said softly. "The lawyer has said he fears Rosaleen's bail will be revoked."

"Did you fire the lawyer?" Stephen asked. His face looked carved from stone.

Josephine cocked her head to the side and looked vulnerable, Kay thought.

"It will be the decision of the judge, of course," Josephine said. "But Monsieur Schwartz fears that if Rosaleen is charged with three murders, the DA will insist she be kept in jail for public safety. When she was released before, the lawyer argued long and hard. So long and hard that the judge threatened to hold him in contempt. His performance was admirable."

They were all in Josephine's dressing room. *All* meant Mrs. R, Tim, Stephen, Josephine, Flora Davis, and herself. But as Jacques Abtey arrived, Stephen said, "I'm going out into the theatre."

"No, stay," Josephine implored. "There is something I wish to tell you all."

"All right," Stephen muttered. He leaned against the wall behind the chairs which were arranged in a circle.

Josephine nodded with satisfaction. "Good. But first, I was told that you have been fired, Flora. Is it true?"

"I missed my shift and was fired on the spot," Flora said sadly.

"Of course you could not work! You are distraught over your daughter's plight! How could there be no sympathy?" Outraged, Josephine waved her hands expressively. "You will never sweep a floor again. Come with me, back to Les Milandes, my home in France. There is work to be done, and I need a friend to help me. You will receive a salary, of course."

"I won't accept your charity." Flora dabbed her eyes with a thin handkerchief.

"It is not charity," Josephine said. "But that gives me *une idée magnifique*. When I am working with my charitable organizations, they get a lot of work done. But when I leave to tour, suddenly nothing happens. They slow to a crawl."

"It's your energy, Josephine," Jacques remarked, taking a seat. "The force of it inspires everyone."

"I need a friend I can trust," Josephine insisted. "A friend to make them work just as hard when I am not there. And I would like you to sing again in shows at Les Milandes."

"How can you trust me, after what I did?"

"I trust and admire Rosaleen, so I believe you have the same qualities."

Josephine sighed. "My fight against segregation has cost me many performing contracts here in the United States. I needed the money to do more than repair Les Milandes. I wish to build a community that will prove to the world that all people can live in harmony. My husband, Jo, and I have talked about adopting children from all over the world. Orphans from different races and religions, living together as brothers and sisters."

"I would be honored to go to France with you," Flora Davis said.

Kay was pleased to see the two friends had reunited and made up their differences. "But unless Rosaleen is freed," Kay asked sadly, "will you be able to carry out these wonderful dreams?"

"You are right. I have asked you all to be here tonight for a special reason. Eleanor knows what it is. I am going to end this once and for all," Josephine stated. "I am holding a final gathering after my performance. A special late-night spectacle."

"What are you doing, Josephine?" Stephen asked suspiciously.

"I believe I know," Jacques Abtey said. "It's dangerous. I think Josephine intends to reveal the murderer."

"Jo, there is no point in it," Stephen groaned. "You're going to make accusations toward innocent people. You'll get yourself sued. Or worse, you will incite someone to attack you, like that KKK man, Claude Mains."

"I won't stand by and remain silent in the face of grave injustice. And I know Eleanor agrees with me. She would not do so either."

"Who do you think is the murderer?" Stephen asked.

"That would be telling. Everyone is not here yet."

"Jo, this isn't a game," Stephen said warningly.

"I know. It is not. But I feel this will be the most important performance of my life. And there will be three important guests. You will see when you go to the theatre."

The three important guests were already seated when they reached the Copa City Club and went to the table reserved for Josephine's party. They were Detective Connor, a detective from Overtown who Mike introduced as Detective Gus Hayes, and Rosaleen.

When she saw Rosaleen, Kay felt utter dismay. Rosaleen sat at the table, looking tired and defeated. Nothing like the sassy, spirited young woman Kay first met.

"How is Rosaleen here?" Stephen asked Josephine. "Isn't she under arrest?"

Was he happy to see Rosaleen? Kay could only see shock in his expression, not joy.

"Detective Connor helped to arrange it. It is important that Rosaleen is here, and the detectives will be getting evidence for their cases."

People began taking their seats. Rosaleen's arrest for the murder of Stella Hilton had not been in the news. The crowd did not know about it. They would in the morning, when it was reported in the newspapers. Or broadcast on their radios. People with televisions would see it on WTVJ, Miami.

The sell-out crowd packed the lounge. Applause was deafening as the spotlights picked out Josephine, walking out on stage. The diamonds in her hair and on her white gown dazzled under the lights.

Kay expected her to call out for justice for Rosaleen. But she didn't.

Kay watched the stage, but she barely registered Josephine's brilliant performance. She sensed tension in the three men—Tim, Stephen, and Jacques. Stephen drank three Cuba Libres.

At the end of the performance a waiter came to their table. He informed them that they were to stay after the other guests left. Josephine Baker had requested that specifically.

Kay watched him go to two other tables. Once the lights came up, she saw Claude Mains had stayed at one table and Isaac Gros at the other.

Her heart gave a pang. Both of those men appeared to have noble motives—Mr. Gros in his fight against discrimination and Mr. Mains in his work to expose the criminality of the KKK. Could one of them be a murderer?

Flora Davis sat beside her daughter, holding Rosaleen's hand. She looked haggard, as if she had aged twenty years during tonight's performance. Why was she so afraid?

"Mademoiselle Kay." Jacques Abtey leaned to her. "You do not drink your drink? Is it not to your liking? I will have it replaced."

Kay glanced down at her daiquiri, with rum. "I'm worried," she admitted. "Mrs. Roosevelt unmasked a murderer once and put herself in danger to do it. I'm afraid Josephine doesn't know how much of a risk she is taking."

"I think she does. And I would never let harm come to Josephine."

"You could do no more against a loaded gun than Franz Müller could. I'm sure he had no intention of dying that night."

"Touché. But this is important to Josephine."

"I'm afraid for Rosaleen," Kay said. "I am afraid because of Stephen."

"I don't understand," Mr. Abtey said.

"I don't want to believe that they plotted this together," she whispered. "And if they did, why would Stephen keep saying that Rosaleen is guilty? It scares me that Rosaleen is the one who got arrested, and Stephen is the one who gets all the money."

"You think they planned it, and he doubled-crossed her?"

"I don't want to think that," Kay said. "I don't want to believe it is true."

A woman entered the lounge, which was empty except for the people at Josephine's table, and Mr. Gros and Mr. Mains. The woman walked toward the empty table between Gros and Mains. Her gait was elegant and sensual, like a runway model. Kay's eyes widened—it was Anna Lane. Anna Lane looked like a movie star, wearing a formfitting dark blue suit, towering navy blue stiletto pumps. Her lips were colored with Fire and Ice, and her platinum hair was pulled back into a smooth chignon.

"Miss Lane, thank you so much for coming. I felt you would

want to be here when the truth is revealed," Josephine said. "There are two gentlemen here who have not had the privilege to meet you. One is Jacques Abtey, a close friend of mine."

Mr. Abtey bowed. "Enchanté." Kay felt he was exaggerating the exoticness of being from Alsace.

Anna Lane nodded to him.

"That man is—"

"I know who he is." Anna Lane coldly stared at Stephen. "Why is he here and not in jail?"

"Because he could not have murdered Monsieur Miller," Josephine said. "Please be seated. It is time you know the truth. Rosaleen Davis must be freed. The real killer must pay."

"The real killer is in prison," Anna Lane declared. "But her accomplice needs to be in there too."

"Anna, I didn't kill my stepfather," Stephen said. "I'm a lawman. And I walked away from my stepfather because he was an evil man."

"Fortunately," Josephine said, "Mrs. Roosevelt knows who is guilty."

"Mrs. Roosevelt does?" Stephen repeated, startled.

Kay felt just as startled.

"Eleanor had better tell you what she has deduced." Josephine moved to the end of the stage. Tim got up. He intercepted Josephine. Holding her hand, he helped her descend the steps in her last costume, a towering headdress and figure-hugging scarlet gown.

Before taking her seat, she implored, "Tell us, Eleanor. There is a room full of witnesses. The killer is not going to get away with it."

Kay was nervous and impressed as Mrs. Roosevelt stood and cleared her throat. "Josephine wished for you to come here tonight because you were guests at her gathering on the night Frank Miller was murdered." Mrs. R nodded toward Flora. "You were there also, Flora. You were outside, in the hallway."

"Working as a cleaner," Flora said.

"Are you saying the *cleaner* did it?" Anna Lane demanded. "Why else would she be here?"

"No, I am not saying that Flora Davis is responsible," Mrs. Roosevelt responded firmly. "I wish to go through my thoughts, step by step."

"Why?" Anna cried. "Just say the name! I-I cared for Frank. I want to know who took him from me."

"Anyone could have accessed the club to murder Müller," Mains protested. "It doesn't have to be 'one of us' like in a detective story. I'm innocent. I didn't shoot Frank Miller, or stab Eulie Reynolds, or that girl Stella Hilton. I should be leaving—"

As he stood, Stephen got to his feet. "As an operative of the CIA, I have to ask you to remain seated, Mr. Mains."

"Under what authority? Am I under arrest?"

"I'd like to know how you knew that Stella Hilton was stabbed. As for being under arrest, if you would like to eliminate any confusion, I can arrest you," Stephen said coolly.

"On what charges?"

"Your involvement with the Klan gives me enough reason to hold you for twenty-four hours and interview you about any involvement in the bombings and murders that have taken place in Florida."

Kay saw Mains flinch. Panic flashed in his eyes. Kay saw he was afraid the truth could come out.

"Why don't you cool your heels here, in this comfortable lounge, while we find out what in blazes is going on," Stephen finished.

Stephen didn't like this. But wouldn't he *want* to prove Rosaleen innocent?

"I want another damn cocktail then." Mains snapped his fingers aggressively.

When no one appeared, Mrs. Roosevelt stated, "The waitstaff has gone home, Mr. Mains."

"There's my champagne," Josephine said. "If that keeps you in your seat, I can open a bottle."

There was silence while Stephen went to fetch the champagne and returned with four bottles tucked under his arms. He popped one and filled a glass for Claude Mains.

"Why's everyone looking at me?" Mains demanded nervously. "I had no reason to kill anyone."

Kay realized he was playing a part. He was pretending to be an arrogant member of the KKK. But was his nervousness due to his fear of a misstep in his part, or due to guilt? Had he learned about Stella from his contacts as a reporter, or because he had silenced her himself?

"We all know who is responsible for the death of Mr. Miller," Anna Lane said mulishly.

Mrs. Roosevelt continued. "Mr. Mains, you say you had no reason to murder Mr. Miller or Mr. Reynolds. But you do have a motive," Mrs. R said.

Kay saw Mr. Mains turn his head toward her. He knew she had revealed his secret. He looked scared. And angry.

"You know what that motive is. In truth, everyone had a motive," Mrs. R said softly.

Mr. Gros stood swiftly. He held out a hand imploringly. "You think it is me. You know I recognized Miller as the Nazi commandant of Buchenwald death camp, Franz Müller. You believe I made him pay for his crimes. I stayed behind at the club to confront him when he left. But, as I told you, I did not shoot Franz Müller."

"The story you told me is not completely true, is it?"

"It is, Mrs. Roosevelt."

"You said you saw Mr. Miller get into a taxi. Mr. O'Malley found the first cab driver who came to pick you up, but no one remembered picking up Frank Miller. You wanted to make it look as if you left because you felt Josephine was safe. Josephine was waiting outside for Rosaleen—you should have seen her. I think you returned to the club to confront the person who had sent her threatening letters. You went back to confront Rosaleen Davis. You did it because you were afraid for Josephine."

"What the—?" Stephen sputtered.

"It is true," Mr. Gros said. "Josephine told me about the letters. On the previous night, the night before the party and murder of Müller, I remained in the club after Josephine left. Rosaleen Davis was the last to leave the dressing room. From the closet, I saw her lock the door, then stoop down and push an envelope under the door. I was shocked and appalled.

"The next night—the night Franz Müller was killed—I heard the shot as I was taking the stairs down to the dressing rooms. When I reached the dressing room, the door was closed. I heard Rosaleen Davis rattle the door, then bang on it. I heard the racing footsteps of the security guard. I panicked. It was a moment to have courage, but I did not."

Flora Davis looked terrified. "You mean, this was all over those terrible letters? I convinced Rosaleen to help me. And I never meant to harm Josephine."

"You did not see who fired the shot, Mr. Gros?" Mrs. Roosevelt asked.

"I saw no one else in the hallway. No one passed by me."

"You should have seen Stella Hilton. She claimed that she saw Rosaleen fire the gun, then she ran away with her male friend. Of course, she might have run into her dressing room. Or she might have lied—and she didn't see anything at all."

"I was dishonest with you, Mrs. Roosevelt. I am sorry because I respect you. I would not have killed Müller."

"We only have your word for that," Claude Mains said. "You had a big motive. Revenge against a Nazi death camp officer. And you thought Josephine Baker was in danger."

"But I knew Müller did not send the threatening letters."

Mains considered. "Maybe you thought they were working together. Or Miller was paying Rosaleen Davis. Or—"

"Be quiet!" Anna Lane cried. "You do not know the truth,

but you insist on flapping your lips. You have interrupted Mrs. Roosevelt. Didn't you hear what Mr. Gros just said? He didn't see anyone in the hallway. Rosaleen Davis must be guilty!"

"The person could have hidden," Mrs. Roosevelt said. "Flora Davis admitted she was there and hid in the supply closet—so the killer could not have hidden there. Stella Hilton claimed she left her dressing room. That meant her dressing room was empty. The killer could have slipped into there."

"But wouldn't Stella Hilton have seen the killer?"

"Yes, I believe she did," Mrs. Roosevelt said. "I believe that is why she was murdered."

"Or it was Rosaleen Davis," Anna Lane repeated.

"It was discovered that Jacques Abtey was not truthful about the date he arrived in Miami," Mrs. Roosevelt continued. "Mr. O'Malley and Miss Thompson spoke with the airline at the airport counter and discovered he arrived earlier."

Abtey said, "That is true."

"Miss Thompson suggested you were here, tracking down the 'Ghost,'" Mrs. Roosevelt said.

"Yes," Jacques said. "A few weeks ago, a friend sent me a clipping from the *Miami Herald*. It was a photograph of Frank Miller at a ribbon-cutting ceremony for his latest hotel development. I recognized him as Franz Müller. I remembered him as a Nazi officer stationed in Algiers in the early 1940s. He was sent to oversee Buchenwald in 1943. When I studied that photograph of the small group with Müller in the center as he wielded the scissors, I knew I had found my Ghost."

Kay felt satisfaction. Her hunch had been correct . . . Franz Müller was the Ghost.

Mrs. Roosevelt said, "Miss Lane, you insist Stephen is guilty, but as he was in an airplane traveling to Miami at the time of the murder, he could not have done it. So you have insisted it was his fiancée, Miss Davis."

She turned to Stephen. "If it were not for your alibi, Stephen, you would be the prime suspect, I fear. You had two motives. We know you are innocent. May I speak hypothetically?"

Stephen looked hunted, but he nodded. "Go ahead. Say anything you like. You're right. On the face of it, I had a motive."

"But he did not do it," Rosaleen breathed softly, from her place by the two detectives and her mother.

"Franz Müller opposed his marriage to Rosaleen and threatened to disinherit him," Mrs. R continued. "Hypothetically, the murder could have been cold-bloodedly plotted. Franz Müller was told by Stephen to meet him after the party and the murder was carried out to smooth the path of his marriage and to inherit millions. But why would Stephen allow blame to fall upon the woman he loves?

"Or Stephen might have planned to meet his stepfather and insist he was going to marry Rosaleen. When he saw Müller alone in the room with Rosaleen, he might have shot his stepfather because he feared for her safety. But even if Stephen could have been both on an airplane and backstage at the Copa City Club, he would surely not have locked Rosaleen in with the body.

"For the same reason, Flora Davis must be innocent. She also had two motives. She might have acted to protect Rosaleen if she feared Miller would harm her daughter. Or she might have felt that removing Miller would ensure Rosaleen could marry a wealthy man."

"But I would have ensured Rosaleen got away," Flora declared.

Mrs. R nodded. "A mother would have grabbed her daughter by the hand and raced her out of there."

"I am a suspect, of course," Josephine said, her voice rich and strong, ringing out. "What if I had followed Rosaleen back to the dressing room because I was worried about her?"

Jacques Abtey shook his head. "You are not a killer, Josephine."

"I had motive. I wished to protect Rosaleen. I knew Müller was a guard at Buchenwald."

Josephine stood, gazing around the small audience. "I learned in wartime that sometimes risk and danger are required for good. I had two motives—to protect Rosaleen and to punish Müller for his cruelty."

"When Rosaleen was arrested, you immediately rushed to help her, demanding her release and paying for a prestigious defense lawyer," Mrs. Roosevelt said gently.

There was silence.

"You are right. I probably have the strongest motive of all. Is that the solution? That I'm the one who did it," Josephine said.

CHAPTER 32

In my own case, it was not a sign of courage . . . it was simply that, like most human beings, I am not given to seeing myself disappear off the face of the earth.
—Eleanor Roosevelt, *This I Remember*, Circa 1949

Eleanor knew she must tread with care. Revealing a killer was a grave risk.

To Josephine's exclamation, she responded solemnly, "At first, I believed you could not be a suspect."

Josephine, dressed in a scarlet dress and towering headdress of red feathers—all three feet of it—shook her head. That headdress made Eleanor's neck ache, and she wasn't wearing it.

"Everyone should be a suspect," Josephine said.

"That is true. But I believed you would never have locked the door, trapping Rosaleen in with the body. That must have been done to ensure her arrest. The murderer assumed the police would look no further than the other person in the locked room with the victim, Rosaleen, despite Rosaleen's story."

"But you suspected Josephine knew Rosaleen and I sent the letters to scare her," Flora said suddenly. "That could mean Josephine wanted to hurt Rosaleen. Or at least scare her."

Eleanor shook her head. "I did not believe that. I considered what Jacques Abtey and Isaac Gros had told us about Josephine. She risked her life as a spy for the Allies. She gave many concerts during the war, even while ill, and accepted no fee. She had been willing to perform on makeshift stages at the front lines for the troops. She had braved the typhus wards at Buchenwald. Josephine is far too noble to do such a thing to Rosaleen. Josephine never would have been underhanded."

Eleanor added firmly, "I believe she would not commit murder."

She saw relief on Kay's face—she knew her secretary greatly admired Josephine.

"You are beating around a bush!" Anna Lane broke in, in a nasally, grating tone. "Stephen and Rosaleen are guilty. You have eliminated everyone else who is a suspect. Stephen planned the murders and Rosaleen carried them out. Stephen inherits millions from his stepfather. When he learned Franz was going to change his will, Stephen had to act fast. They decided to kill him here in Miami, so Stephen had an alibi."

Anna very much wanted the finger pointed at Stephen. Perhaps Anna had wanted to marry Mr. Miller and be a millionaire's wife, but that did not explain her unwavering belief in Stephen's guilt.

"That singer said she *saw* Rosaleen Davis do it!" Anna snapped.

"But did she?" Eleanor asked.

Anna Lane looked startled. "She said that she did. Why would she lie?"

"I believe I know why. I do know for certain that she did lie. Mr. Gros did not see her, of course, but that did not mean her story was untrue. It *was* possible that Stella saw the shooting then ran back to her dressing room instead of trying to escape down the hallway. That way she could have witnessed the shooting, but Mr. Gros did not see her.

"Stella Hilton revealed that she was lying," Eleanor said. "She said Rosaleen entered the room and took out the gun from her purse. But Rosaleen did not have her purse. She corrected her story and said Rosaleen took the gun from the folds of her skirt. I do not think she could have hidden a gun there. So, did Stella make up the story? Did she want to extort money from Josephine?"

"She was lying," Stephen muttered.

"She was," Rosaleen whispered.

"Her memory was faulty," Anna declared. "That proves nothing."

Eleanor took a breath. She liked to be brief in her public speaking. But she needed to go over this, piece by piece.

"There is another possibility. Stella was paid to point the finger at Rosaleen. But Stella muddled her lines. What the poor young woman didn't realize is that the murderer planned to silence her too. Her murder served to provide clues pointing to Stephen. Miss Thompson discovered that an army watch like Stephen's was found at the scene. You were questioned by the Overtown Police, am I correct?"

"I went in voluntarily to help with the investigation. I don't know how the watch got in Miss Hilton's apartment," Stephen spoke tersely.

"I expect they obtained a search warrant for your room at the Delano, based on finding your watch at the scene." Eleanor looked to Detective Hayes.

"We found a knife hidden under the mattress of his room," the detective said. "There were traces of blood on the blade."

"It's not mine. I didn't kill that singer!" Stephen shouted. "Those 'clues' were planted, just like there were clues planted that pointed to Rosaleen."

"Yes. There were clues pointing to Rosaleen. Clues that you insisted proved Rosaleen was guilty, just as you insisted she was forced to kill in self-defense. Miss Thompson has felt that you have insisted Rosaleen is guilty just a few times too many," Eleanor said, disapprovingly.

Stephen swung around, facing Rosaleen. "Rosie, that's not true. I believe in you. I was scared you killed to protect yourself."

"You tried to set up Rosaleen," Eleanor said. "You wanted her to take the fall for your crime. Your accomplice murdered Frank Miller, giving you an alibi. One of you stabbed Eulie Reynolds, but your accomplice *must* have murdered Stella Hilton. Your accomplice was supposed to plant clues that pointed to Rosaleen. What you did not know was that your accomplice intended to double-cross you."

"This is insane. I don't have an accomplice. And why would I want to murder Eulie Reynolds?"

"Blackmail."

"Over *what*?" Stephen demanded.

"I believe you are involved with the Florida Terror."

"That is ridiculous. I work with the CIA."

"Stephen Roberts is not your real name," Eleanor said. "The name engraved on your army watch is O'Hara."

"So? O'Hara was a good friend. We traded watches on the boat as we arrived at Omaha Beach. We did it for luck."

"That is not the truth. Tim made telephone calls to the Department of Defense, aided by my friend Sandy Sandiston. The soldier who owned that watch died in a POW camp. He did not land at Omaha Beach."

"What do you mean?" Rosaleen cried. She was trembling.

"The person who murdered Franz Müller is Stephen's wife. I am so very sorry, Rosaleen."

A keening cry pierced the sudden, deafening silence. Eleanor's heart lurched—it was the sound of an innocent person's heart utterly breaking.

"His *what*?" Rosaleen cried.

The poor child. That sort of betrayal changed a woman. A woman never forgot it. She never—fully—trusted again.

"You were correct, Kay," Eleanor said. "You felt Stephen's

behavior was wrong for a devoted fiancé. He was pretending to love Rosaleen while he was planting clues that pointed to her."

"But who is his wife?" Josephine asked.

"The same person who is Mr. Abtey's 'Ghost.' Frank Miller's secretary, Anna Lane."

"The secretary?" Claude Mains exclaimed, shocked.

Kay bristled at his tone. As if a secretary couldn't be anything more than a pretty woman with an empty head and a full steno pad.

Even though it was over murder, Kay still bristled.

She also wanted to smack herself in the head. All the signs had been there. She had sensed Stephen was a bad fiancé. Jacques Abtey said he saw the Ghost in a photograph of Frank Miller cutting a ribbon. He must have seen Anna Lane in the photo with her boss, and he recognized her.

But if Anna Lane was Stephen's wife, why double-cross him?

"Stephen, I believe your real surname is Müller," Mrs. R explained. "From my contacts in the State Department, I learned that a German POW officer, captured by the Allies, revealed that Private O'Hara, the American soldier who owned that A-11 watch, was murdered by one of the other officers in the camp. That officer took the watch as a trophy. I remembered that Josephine spoke of how Jacques had changed his name and adopted an American accent. I realized Stephen could have done the same. Were you the German officer who killed Private O'Hara?"

"No. I don't even know what you are talking about," Stephen declared. His expression was one of disbelief, as if he thought Mrs. R had lost her mind. But Kay knew Mrs. R knew exactly what she was talking about.

"I suspected Anna Lane after a conversation she had with Miss Thompson," Mrs. Roosevelt continued. "Miss Lane referred to Frank Miller as Franz Müller in one instance. It was a slip, and she used the name naturally, as if she knew very well who he really was. She used the name 'Franz' again tonight. If she had just learned his true identity and it had come as a shock to her, I am certain she would have told my secretary she'd had no idea she was working for a Nazi, an enemy."

"Very clever, Mrs. Roosevelt." The sultry voice rang through the lounge. Anna Lane had dropped the nasal voice. She now spoke with an accent that sounded German.

"Clever? It's fiction. I'm not a Nazi," Stephen sputtered. He pointed at Anna. "This woman is my father's secretary. I've never seen her before I saw her in my father's office. I figured *she* was planning to marry him for his money."

Kay noticed Stephen made the same mistake as Anna Lane—he had instinctively referred to Müller as his father, not *step*-father.

"That was the illusion you both constructed," Mrs. Roosevelt said. "You thought she was working with you to obtain those millions. You needed a scapegoat for your crimes. An engagement to a Black woman appealed to you. I assume that you are accustomed to manipulating women, Stephen," Mrs. R said.

"This can't be true." Rosaleen stood slowly. She looked down helplessly at Stephen.

"Of course it isn't true." He gazed hopefully at Rosaleen. "Mrs. Roosevelt is old. She imagines things that are not real."

"He loves me," Rosaleen said, as if in a daze. "He can't have a wife."

"Oh!" Kay exclaimed. "The tall 'man' in a trench coat was really Anna Lane. The lipstick I found must have been dropped by Anna."

"If Ursula shot my stepfather and killed those other two people, I had nothing to do with it," Stephen said. "I thought she was dead. That's why I asked you to marry me, Rosaleen. It's true. I was conscripted into the army in Germany. But I wasn't a Nazi. I didn't kill anyone in a POW camp. I came to

America after the war to make a fresh start. Just like my *step*father."

"You slipped up just now," Kay said. "You called him your father. And you called Anna 'Ursula.'"

His face contorted into a sneer. Then he softened his expression. "Yes, he was my father. I hadn't seen him for years until I saw his picture in an American newspaper. I came and told him he owed me. He came up with the story that he was my stepfather so no one would question his story about his past. I went along with it to keep my past secret. My real mother had died long before in Germany. My stepmother pretended I was her son. Her actual son was listed as missing, presumed dead in the war. When my father asked her to go along with the ruse, she agreed. She would do anything to please my rich father. So many records were lost and destroyed in the war, it was easy to assume a new identity. Getting into the CIA while keeping my past secret was a challenge, I admit, but I pulled it off. My father got into America with his past, but I didn't want mine hounding me."

Anna Lane, whom Stephen had called Ursula, took a step closer to Stephen. "You said you thought I was dead. What you mean is that you left me for dead in Casablanca."

Her smile was ice-cold as she explained, "We worked in sabotage for Abwehr. The counter to Churchill's SOE, the Special Operations Executive. You sank our ships. We, in retaliation, sank ferries. Stephen and I worked together. But on our last mission, I ended up trapped belowdecks in the engine room. Stephen fled, knowing the bomb was about to go off. I managed to get out of the room and to the upper deck just as the explosion tore the ferry to pieces. I was plucked out of the water. As a precaution, I always carried false papers. I was treated in the very clinic where Josephine Baker was fighting the illness that almost killed her."

Anna turned to Josephine. "I knew that you were carrying out intelligence operations from your hospital room, Miss Baker. I knew your room became a safe place for Allied spies to meet. I thought of killing you. But I was weak. I was barely touched on the outside, but on the inside, I was greatly damaged. The blast damaged my lungs and one of my kidneys. To protect myself, I convinced the doctors I had amnesia. Ironically, I did not remember the explosion. I only remembered going belowdecks with my husband. For a long time, I did not remember that he bolted for the stairs, without trying to free me.

"While I slowly recovered, I waited for my husband to come. Even though he was an Abwehr agent, I was certain he would risk everything to see me."

"When I was released from the hospital, months later, I went searching for my husband. He was gone. He had left Casablanca, reputedly for France. He had not gone alone. A French woman accompanied him."

Anna gazed at Stephen as if he were gum on her elegant heel.

"For six years, I traced him. I followed a trail of money. A Frenchwoman collaborator in Paris. Blondes in Austria. After the war, there was a horsey-faced English girl in London. That foolish girl was so much in love, she let him rob her blind to pay for his passage to America.

"He knew his father was here. His father, a camp officer at Buchenwald, was invited to settle by the American CIA, who wanted him to hunt Communists for them. It was ironic that Stephen had managed to secure work with the CIA, also to hunt Communists."

Kay stood up from her seat, facing Anna Lane. "Why did Stephen trust you? He betrayed you by leaving you to die. Did he really think you just forgave and forgot? How could he still believe he could trust you?"

Anna lifted her head, looking down disdainfully. "As a man, his condescension for women is his blind spot. When I told him

I had no memory of the explosion, he bought completely into my lie. He thought he'd gotten away with leaving me for dead. He knew I wanted to share in his father's fortune, which would come to him through Franz's will. Franz had no idea I was married to his son. I learned that Stephen had never told his father he had made a wartime marriage.

"And . . ." Anna arched a brow. "Stephen honestly believes he can manipulate any woman."

Kay almost sympathized with Anna Lane.

But this woman was a killer.

"While I was working for Franz, he confided that he was worried about Stephen's engagement to Rosaleen. Not for the reason you would think. Despite his vow to protect the Aryan race, Franz greatly admired Josephine Baker. He planned to warn Rosaleen that she could not trust Stephen."

Her laughter filled the room. "That was quite delicious. Franz was a murderer. And he was going to protect this poor, silly girl? I suspected Stephen was up to something. I was right. Stephen arranged for his stepmother's car accident. He was waiting for the moment to murder Franz. I convinced him that if I did it while he was flying to Miami, he would have the perfect alibi. I knew Franz planned to speak to Rosaleen after Josephine's performance. I told him to suggest to her a meeting in the dressing room. I followed them. I disposed of Stella Hilton and planted clues that pointed to Stephen. I knew it would be too subtle a plot to make it look like he planned the killing of his father with Rosaleen. I needed the police to believe he had committed a murder. I needed to get him executed. I am still his legal wife. His inheritance would be *mine*."

"But Stephen didn't kill anyone," Rosaleen whispered, her voice barely heard. "*She* did."

Kay drew in a sharp breath. Rosaleen was struggling to fool herself. She was trying desperately to cling to an image of a man she loved.

"She's right," Stephen said. "I didn't kill anyone. Ursula is the killer. I learned what kind of ruthless, vicious killer she was in the war. She enjoyed sabotage work. It was carte blanche for her to kill. I was afraid of her. When I thought she had died in that explosion, I felt free."

Kay knew the churning in her heart was horror. And outrage. Stephen had planned his father's murder with Ursula, but he might get away with it.

Stephen turned to Rosaleen. "I found true love with *you*."

He was trying to look genuine.

But he couldn't hide it. Not anymore. He couldn't prevent a smug smile from showing for a moment as he saw Rosaleen gazing at him, obviously hanging on his words.

"Look at his smug smile, Rosaleen. Please don't believe him," Kay cried. "The only person he loves is himself. That is the smile of a man who believes he has you in the palm of his hand! You deserve so much more!"

Rosaleen hesitated.

"The redhead is jealous," Stephen said. "She's an old maid."

"Rosaleen, you know the truth in your heart," Kay said. "You are a smart woman. You planned to be a lawyer. Could Anna Lane have taken your ring and bracelet from your room? Stephen took them."

"I-I believe you," Rosaleen said. "And I believe Mrs. Roosevelt."

"Put the weapon down!"

The command startled Kay. It came from Tim.

She had been looking at Rosaleen. Now she saw Anna Lane was holding a gun. Pointed at Mrs. Roosevelt.

The two police detectives reached for their weapons, but Kay moved instantly. She jumped in front of Mrs. R as the shot exploded, ringing in the confines of the theatre. Kay almost gagged on the stench of burning powder. But there was no pain.

Anna Lane staggered back. Blood had splattered her neck. Stephen held his service revolver.

She took her hand away and the palm of her white glove was smeared with red blood. "My shoulder? You always were a bad shot."

The second shot stunned them all.

Dark red spread across Stephen's white shirt. Despite the direct hit to the middle of his chest, he lunged toward Anna, but she stepped back quickly, out of his reach.

Anna Lane's beautiful face glowed with triumph as she watched Stephen collapse to his knees, then slither to the floor.

Tim O'Malley, heedless of the weapon, jumped to his feet. Kay knew he wanted to help Stephen even though the man had shot Anna Lane right in front of them.

But another shot whistled beside his head and Kay knew Anna had deliberately missed.

"Put your gun down," Detective Connor barked.

Anna smirked. "Stay where you are. Do not move. Any of you. If anyone tries to save that *man*, I will shoot you in the head."

"Nonsense," Mrs. Roosevelt declared. "You must allow us to go to his aid. It is what is *right*."

"What is *right* is that Stephen—he is really Fritz Müller—is now experiencing the justice he deserves."

"No!" Rosaleen shouted.

Anna swung the gun around to point at Rosaleen.

Rosaleen stuck out her chin. "I'm not afraid of you," she cried.

Kay stood at Rosaleen's side. To her horror, Mrs. Roosevelt joined them. "Miss Lane, stop now," Mrs. Roosevelt said.

"I don't think you can stop me." Anna leveled her gun, pointing toward Rosaleen. "And Stephen deserves to be known as a *murderer*. I didn't kill that KKK man. Stephen did. Stephen was the man behind some of the KKK's bombings. A man on the inside at the CIA, using his Abwehr skills to keep his activities hidden from his American bosses. There were other former Nazis involved with Reynolds. One of them recognized Stephen. Reynolds threatened blackmail, knowing Stephen was going to inherit millions.

"Stephen tried to stop the two of you from investigating—" She gestured to Kay and Tim. "He followed you and cut the brakes on your car. Of course, there are no mountains in Miami, so you were not at great risk. It was stupid of Stephen . . .

"But now that you know everything . . ."

Anna cocked the pistol.

Kay desperately tried to think of a way to distract Anna. To disarm her—

A flash of scarlet flew toward Anna. It was like a big, exotic bird. Anna swung toward it, screaming in surprise as Josephine's tall, feathered headdress landed on her. She writhed, trying to throw it off, but the thick, long feathers tangled around her arms. The gun went off and Claude Mains cried out.

Tim made a sound too. A guttural grunt. It was exactly the sound he would make if a bullet hit him, and Kay's knees went wobbly. But she saw Tim had made it to Anna's side. He had his hand clamped on Anna's arm and forced her hand down. Kay began to approach.

"Give it up, Anna. Ursula. Whoever you really are." To Kay, he said, his eyes filled with worry, "Stay back from her, Kay."

"You're being too chivalrous with her," Kay exclaimed. As Anna wrenched away from Tim's grasp because he was weakened by being *shot*, Kay swung the chair she had picked up. The seats at the Copa Club were light, stacking-style chairs. The chair caught Anna in the chest and sent her reeling back. Using the advantage of Anna's stumble, Tim pulled the gun from her grasp.

"Chivalrous?" Tim pulled Anna's arm behind her back. In a swift motion, he pressed the murderess's face down on the table. "There. Not so chivalrous." He secured Anna against the table with his right hand and held her weapon in his left hand.

"That other shot—?"

Kay looked around, heart in her throat. "It shattered Mr. Mains's champagne glass. And scared him." Claude Mains was sitting back in his seat, fanning himself with a napkin.

"You know, I thought he was the killer," Tim said.

"Mr. Mains is not what he appears," Kay said. "I think he is one of the good guys. But you were hit. Where?"

"I'm fine." He put his hand to his leg. And she knew he was not fine. She helped him sit down.

Mrs. Roosevelt and Jacques Abtey were by Stephen's side. Rosaleen was also on her knees beside him.

Detective Connor guarded Anna Lane.

"Detective Hayes, would you telephone for an ambulance?" Mrs. R asked. "Two? For Stephen and Tim O'Malley."

Always calm. The detective took off at a run to do so.

Minutes later, Stephen was loaded into the ambulance on a stretcher. Tim insisted the ambulance attendants bandage Anna's shoulder before they took him on a stretcher. Detective Connor moved Anna Lane's wounded arm behind her gently to put on handcuffs. Anna gave a sharp, angry laugh. "What do you care? Are you afraid I'll have a sore shoulder when they execute me?"

With a clink that resounded in the quiet, Mike Connor snapped the cuffs on Anna's slender wrists. She was led away to a squad car by two uniformed officers.

"We need to get statements," Detective Connor said. "Sorry folks, but I need them before we let you go. I think this will take a while."

"Can I go to the hospital with Tim?" Kay asked.

Mike Connor hesitated. Then he said, "Yeah. Go. Tell him to get better."

As she was leaving, Kay heard Josephine say, "There is plenty of champagne in my dressing room, to calm our nerves. It is over. Brave Mr. O'Malley must be okay. Thank you, Eleanor, for finding the truth. For saving Rosaleen from marrying that awful man. For bringing about justice."

"You would have made a fine secret agent, Mrs. Roosevelt," Jacques Abtey said.

"Yes!" Josephine exclaimed. "Though, like me, she would have had to hide in plain sight. For the whole world knows Eleanor Roosevelt."

CHAPTER 33

Person after person has said to me in these last few days that this new world we face terrifies them. I can understand how that feeling would arise unless one believes that men are capable of greatness beyond their past achievements . . . The time now calls for mankind as a whole to rise to great heights.

—Eleanor Roosevelt, My Day, August 10, 1945

The hospital ward contained several beds. Curtains were drawn around them. The lights were dim, casting deep shadows in the room and the hallway beyond. Kay shifted in her chair beside Tim's bed. The most uncomfortable chair she had ever sat in.

Kay knew she looked terrible. She had dozed on this terrible chair and knew her hair was tangled and her makeup smeared. She had spent hours by Tim's bedside. After surgery for the wound on his leg, he slept, still under the effect of the anesthetic.

He was going to be all right. The bullet had grazed him, the wound was not serious.

"Will he walk again?" she had asked the doctor.

The doctor, whose name was Petrie, had stared at her in amazement. "Why wouldn't he?"

She wanted to be there when Tim woke up, to reassure him that everything was going to be okay.

Mrs. Roosevelt came to see him before leaving for the airport, only to find him fast asleep. She updated Kay.

"Do stay with him if you want, Kay," she urged. "I must take the flight now to arrive tomorrow morning and collect my luggage to take to Paris. But you can fly later and join me."

"Won't you need a secretary?"

"I can manage for a few days. I know you feel your place is here."

Kay nodded. "It is."

Or she assumed it was. Maybe, when Tim woke up, he would feel differently.

She was asleep when he woke up. She knew because she was awakened by the sound of nurses asking questions and Tim answering in his Irish lilt. As she struggled to sit up in the uncomfortable armchair, he looked at her and said, "Your snoring sounds like a chainsaw."

"I've slept in a chair to watch over you. Thanks very much."

She went to get up.

"No, don't. I'm sorry. Please stay, Kay."

A young nurse came with a food tray.

"Can I get an extra one for my friend?" Tim asked.

"I don't think so. I don't think she would want it." The nurse hurried away.

Tim tasted the food, covered in a thick layer of gravy. "Yeah, you wouldn't want it."

Kay smiled. "I had food at the cafeteria."

"A lot of good-looking doctors?"

"Didn't notice." Then she added, "You risked your life again. Don't do it anymore. I don't know if the third time will be lucky."

"Didn't have a choice," he said.

"I know."

"I get it," he said. "You don't want me standing in front of bullets, but I feel the need to do so. I miss you when you travel, but you need to do it. I understand how you feel. You have to do what you feel the need to do. And I'll wait for you. I'll wait as long it takes to have you in my life, Kay."

He settled back and slurped his juice through a straw. "I hear I'm going to heal okay. Tell me what happened after they shipped me out on a stretcher. Get yourself a coffee first. Gentlemanly of me, isn't it? I'd grab you one if I could."

"I know." Kay hurried off, brought back a coffee that was both weak and bitter, and settled in the chair beside Tim's hospital bed. The curtain was drawn to give privacy.

"I came with you, but Mrs. R told me that she and Josephine comforted Rosaleen. Rosaleen blamed herself for being fooled by Stephen. Mrs. Roosevelt assured her that she is not to blame, and that a woman does not have to shoulder responsibility when she is fooled by a bad man."

"True," Tim said, and slurped.

"Josephine insisted that Rosaleen must return to school and Josephine will help pay the tuition. I don't know if it's fortunate or not, but Stephen did not survive. He died en route to the hospital. I think Josephine is going to see to his burial. I don't know where Franz Müller's fortune will go, but not to Anna Lane, because she shot him. Jacques Abtey is determined that Anna Lane—whose real name is Ursula Müller—will pay for her war crimes, as well as the three murders she committed."

"How is Josephine taking it all?"

"Josephine is strong," Kay said. "Her fight against racism has led to the rest of her American contracts being canceled. She plans to travel south, to Cuba."

"That will thrill the CIA."

Kay smiled. "I guess it will give them a thicker file on her."

"I pity the poor secretary who has to carry those fat files for the CIA and J. Edgar Hoover of the FBI." Tim paused. "Who was Claude Mains really? I know you figured it out."

"I promised I wouldn't say. But I think you will have the answer to that mystery soon. You'll be able to read about it."

"Got it," Tim said. "And Isaac Gros?"

"He is returning home and working for justice for the Florida Terror. I hope it happens."

"Is it the thirty-first of December today, or did I sleep through it?" Tim asked.

"It is indeed the last day of the year."

"Aren't you supposed to be on your way to Paris?"

"Mrs. Roosevelt said I could fly later to join her. I wanted to stay with you."

A slow smile lifted his lips. Kay could feel her heart melting. "Not your dream, I bet," he said, "to spend New Year's Eve in a hospital."

"Spending it with you makes it perfect," she said.

"Wish I could take you dancing."

"We will. Some day."

"I will wait," he said. "Forever if I have to."

"I don't think it will be that long," Kay said. She added softly, "I envied Rosaleen because she had a big dream—to become a lawyer and fight segregation."

"You'll find your dream, Kay," he said. "I want to be there to help you make it come true."

"Happy New Year!" shouted a man in the seat in front of Eleanor. He toasted his fellow airline passengers with his drink, spilling a lot of it.

"Happy New Year," Eleanor echoed. She gazed out of the window of the airplane. It was pitch dark, indicating they were over the Atlantic Ocean.

She was celebrating the stroke of midnight en route to Paris. She hoped Kay and Tim had found a way to celebrate together.

Exposing the two murderers had been harrowing and dangerous. Tim could have been badly wounded. But Rosaleen Davis had been proven innocent. Eleanor felt satisfied with that ending.

Josephine would be traveling to Cuba, and Eleanor hoped she was able to realize her dream of peace and diversity at her home of Les Milandes.

Eleanor had decided on a plan for her own future.

If she could no longer work toward world peace at the United Nations, she intended to volunteer with the AAUN.

The thing obviously to do was to strengthen the one organization in America which was solely devoted to information on the United Nations and evaluation of programs and work that was done. It was important, for the UN was the one organization that had the machinery to bring together all nations to maintain world peace.

A glass of tonic water rested on her tray table. She raised that to toast the New Year.

As people on the airplane got up and hugged each other, filled with joy and hope, Eleanor put the final touches on her My Day column—she was writing the one for January second. Kay had wired the one for tomorrow before Eleanor left.

She thought of the one she had written for January first . . .

EN ROUTE TO PARIS, Tuesday—Today another year will begin—1952.

On New Year's Eve it's customary to look back over the past year. We have much to be proud of. . . .

There is a story told of two men who belonged to a nation that was almost financially bankrupt, and one was overheard to say to the other, "Let's attack America and land on her shores. We will be overwhelmed, she will occupy us, put our country back on its feet and then leave us alone." When such jokes are told about a nation, that nation has made an enviable record for herself. . . .

A Happy New Year to all of you, but may it carry serious reflection for each and every one of us.

New adventures awaited, Eleanor thought. But she would never forget this last week at Miami's South Beach.

AUTHOR'S NOTE

This book, the second in Eleanor Roosevelt and Kay Thompson's investigations, is a product of my imagination though some of the characters in its pages are based upon real people. Once more, I hope that my depiction of Eleanor Roosevelt does justice to the remarkable woman she was.

In my early stages of research, I learned that Josephine Baker performed in Miami around 1951. This led me to read more about the talented singer who also worked to end discrimination. When I decided to base my story around Josephine Baker's Miami performances, I discovered she was in Miami at the end of 1950. Since my story is fictional, I added a return visit to Miami toward the end of her tour.

Josephine Baker did work as an honorable correspondent for the Allies during the Second World War. Her courage was inspiring. Jacques Abtey, the man who recruited her for espionage work, is a real person. I humbly hope my depiction of these real people reflects their strength, courage, and honor. Her impassioned words to Jacques Abtey that she was prepared to give her life for France came from a translated version of her autobiography, written by herself and Jo Bouillon.

My character of Isaac Gros was inspired by the stories of real survivors of the Holocaust and from Eleanor Roosevelt's own words published in her My Day column. Rosaleen Davis, Franz Müller and Stephen Roberts/Fritz Müller, Eulie Reynolds, Claude Mains, Stella Hilton, Flora Davis, Anna Lane, and "Sandy" Sandiston are fictional.

Kay Thompson is a fictional character and is not related to Mrs. Roosevelt's secretary Malvina Thompson, but Malvina

"Tommy" Thompson was indeed Mrs. Roosevelt's secretary for several decades.

Tragically, Harriette Moore, the wife of Harry T. Moore, passed away in hospital on January 3, 1952, due to the injuries she sustained in the bombing attack.

In the text, I have included other writings and dialogue attributed to historical figures.

In Chapter 2, Kay references a passage written by Eleanor Roosevelt in "Keepers of Democracy," published by the *Virginia Quarterly Review* in 1939. The words attributed to Albert Einstein came from a pdf of his letter, from the online site *The Eyes of Willie McGee*, mcgeebook.wordpress.com.

Eleanor Roosevelt's responses to the questions posed by the young people at the American Association for the United Nations conference come from her autobiography and her My Day column of May 4, 1953. For the latter response, I took artistic liberty in attributing the thought to Eleanor Roosevelt before she put it in her column.

Eleanor Roosevelt's reflection on the words in her My Day column are from her January 1, 1952 My Day column, accessed online through The Eleanor Roosevelt Papers Project, Columbian College of Arts and Sciences, The George Washington University. Having the opportunity to learn about Eleanor Roosevelt and Josephine Baker, two remarkable women who were both champions of human rights and women with great empathy, courage, and understanding, was an honor for me.

CHAPTER OPENING NOTES

1. Michele Wehrwein Albion, *The Quotable Eleanor Roosevelt*. Gainsville, FL: University Press of Florida, 2013, 174. (Original source: Blanche Wiesen Cook, *Eleanor Roosevelt*. Vol. 1, *1884–1933*. New York, Viking, 1992, 250.)
2. Michele Wehrwein Albion, *The Quotable Eleanor Roosevelt*. Gainsville, FL: University Press of Florida, 2013, 211. (Original source: Eleanor R. Wotkyns, *With Love, Aunt Eleanor: Stories of My Life with the First Lady of the World*. Petaluma, Calif.: Scrapbook Press, 2004, 91.)
3. Eleanor Roosevelt, My Day, July 4, 1944, *The Eleanor Roosevelt Papers Digital Edition* (2017), accessed 3/6/2025, https://www2.gwu.edu/~erpapers/myday/displaydoc.cfm?_y=1944&_f=md056838.
4. Eleanor Roosevelt, My Day, August 3, 1945, *The Eleanor Roosevelt Papers Digital Edition* (2017), accessed 3/6/2025, https://www2.gwu.edu/~erpapers/myday/displaydoc.cfm?_y=1945&_f=md000093.
5. Eleanor Roosevelt, My Day, November 30, 1960, *The Eleanor Roosevelt Papers Digital Edition* (2017), accessed 3/9/2025, https://www2.gwu.edu/~erpapers/myday/displaydoc.cfm?_y=1960&_f=md004883.
6. Michele Wehrwein Albion, *The Quotable Eleanor Roosevelt*. Gainsville, FL: University Press of Florida, 2013, 197. (Original source: Blanche Wiesen Cook, *Eleanor Roosevelt*. Vol. 1, *1884–1933*. New York, Viking, 1992, 491.)

7. Michele Wehrwein Albion, *The Quotable Eleanor Roosevelt*. Gainsville, FL: University Press of Florida, 2013, 129. (Original source: Eleanor Roosevelt, *Tomorrow is Now*. New York: Harper and Row, 1963, 62.)
8. Michele Wehrwein Albion, *The Quotable Eleanor Roosevelt*. Gainsville, FL: University Press of Florida, 2013, 154. (Original source: Eleanor Roosevelt, "Should Wives Work?", *Good Housekeeping*, Dec. 1937, 29.)
9. Eleanor Roosevelt, My Day, July 14, 1945, *The Eleanor Roosevelt Papers Digital Edition* (2017), accessed 3/9/2025, https://www2.gwu.edu/~erpapers/myday/displaydoc.cfm?_y=1945&_f=md000076.
10. Michele Wehrwein Albion, *The Quotable Eleanor Roosevelt*. Gainsville, FL: University Press of Florida, 2013, 154. (Original source: Eleanor Roosevelt, My Day, November 6, 1942, *The Eleanor Roosevelt Papers Digital Edition* [2017], accessed 3/6/2025, https://www2.gwu.edu/~erpapers/myday/displaydoc.cfm?_y=1942&_f=md056335.)
11. Eleanor Roosevelt, My Day, June 18, 1946, *The Eleanor Roosevelt Papers Digital Edition* (2017), accessed 3/9/2025, https://www2.gwu.edu/~erpapers/myday/displaydoc.cfm?_y=1946&_f=md000368.
12. Eleanor Roosevelt, *Tomorrow is Now*. New York: Harper and Row, 1963, 6.
13. Eleanor Roosevelt, My Day, January 21, 1947, *The Eleanor Roosevelt Papers Digital Edition* (2017), accessed 3/9/2025, https://www2.gwu.edu/~erpapers/myday/displaydoc.cfm?_y=1947&_f=md000553.
14. Eleanor Roosevelt, My Day, December 29, 1951, *The Eleanor Roosevelt Papers Digital Edition* (2017), accessed 3/9/2025, https://www2.gwu.edu/~erpapers/myday/displaydoc.cfm?_y=1951&_f=md002104.
15. Michele Wehrwein Albion, *The Quotable Eleanor Roosevelt*. Gainsville, FL: University Press of Florida, 2013, 114.

(Original source: Eleanor Roosevelt, *Courage in a Dangerous World: The Political Writings of Eleanor Roosevelt*. Edited by Allida M. Black. New York: Columbia University Press, 1999, 258.)

16. Eleanor Roosevelt, My Day, November 13, 1946, *The Eleanor Roosevelt Papers Digital Edition* (2017), accessed 3/9/2025, https://www2.gwu.edu/~erpapers/myday/displaydoc.cfm?_y=1946&_f=md000494.
17. Eleanor Roosevelt, My Day, April 1, 1939, *The Eleanor Roosevelt Papers Digital Edition* (2017), accessed 3/9/2025, https://www2.gwu.edu/~erpapers/myday/displaydoc.cfm?_y=1939&_f=md055229.
18. Michele Wehrwein Albion, *The Quotable Eleanor Roosevelt*. Gainsville, FL: University Press of Florida, 2013, 145. (Original source: Eleanor Roosevelt, January 21, 1944, letter to Joseph P. Lash.)
19. Eleanor Roosevelt, My Day, December 28, 1951, *The Eleanor Roosevelt Papers Digital Edition* (2017), accessed 3/6/2025, https://www2.gwu.edu/~erpapers/myday/displaydoc.cfm?_y=1951&_f=md002103.
20. Eleanor Roosevelt, My Day, February 16, 1946, *The Eleanor Roosevelt Papers Digital Edition* (2017), accessed 3/6/2025, https://www2.gwu.edu/~erpapers/myday/displaydoc.cfm?_y=1946&_f=md000264.
21. Eleanor Roosevelt, Remarks at the United Nations, March 27, 1958, The Eleanor Papers Project, https://erpapers.columbian.gwu.edu/quotations-eleanor-roosevelt.
22. Eleanor Roosevelt, My Day, January 5, 1946, *The Eleanor Roosevelt Papers Digital Edition* (2017), accessed 3/6/2025, https://www2.gwu.edu/~erpapers/myday/displaydoc.cfm?_y=1946&_f=md000228.
23. Eleanor Roosevelt, My Day, April 6, 1949, *The Eleanor Roosevelt Papers Digital Edition* (2017), accessed 3/6/2025,

https://www2.gwu.edu/~erpapers/myday/displaydoc.cfm?_y=1949&_f=md001246.

24. Michele Wehrwein Albion, *The Quotable Eleanor Roosevelt*. Gainsville, FL: University Press of Florida, 2013, 142. (Original source: Eleanor Roosevelt, *You Learn By Living: Eleven Keys for a More Fulfilling Life*. 1st Harper Perennial ed. New York: Harper Perennial, 2011.)
25. Eleanor Roosevelt, My Day, January 27, 1948, *The Eleanor Roosevelt Papers Digital Edition* (2017), accessed 3/20/2025, https://www2.gwu.edu/~erpapers/myday/displaydoc.cfm?_ y=1948&_f=md000873.
26. Eleanor Roosevelt, *You Learn By Living: Eleven Keys for a More Fulfilling Life*. 1st Harper Perennial ed. New York: Harper Perennial, 2011.
27. Eleanor Roosevelt, My Day, December 10, 1952, *The Eleanor Roosevelt Papers Digital Edition* (2017), accessed 3/9/2025, https://www2.gwu.edu/~erpapers/myday/displaydoc.cfm?_y=1952&_f=md002401.
28. Eleanor Roosevelt, If You Ask Me, *Ladies' Home Journal*, Volume 65 October 1948. Digital Edition: The Eleanor Roosevelt Papers Project, 2014–2016.
29. Eleanor Roosevelt, My Day, August 16, 1941, *The Eleanor Roosevelt Papers Digital Edition* (2017), accessed 3/6/2025, https://www2.gwu.edu/~erpapers/myday/displaydoc.cfm?_y=1941&_f=md055966.
30. Eleanor Roosevelt, My Day, May 2, 1949, *The Eleanor Roosevelt Papers Digital Edition* (2017), accessed 3/6/2025, https://www2.gwu.edu/~erpapers/myday/displaydoc.cfm?_y=1949&_f=md001268.
31. Michele Wehrwein Albion, *The Quotable Eleanor Roosevelt*. Gainsville, FL: University Press of Florida, 2013, 166. (Original source: Eleanor Roosevelt, *The Autobiography of Eleanor Roosevelt*. New York: Harper and Brothers, 1961, 390.)

32. Michele Wehrwein Albion, *The Quotable Eleanor Roosevelt*. Gainsville, FL: University Press of Florida, 2013, 166. (Original source: Eleanor Roosevelt, *This I Remember*. New York: Harper and Brothers, 1949, 261.)
33. Eleanor Roosevelt, My Day, August 10, 1945, *The Eleanor Roosevelt Papers Digital Edition* (2017), accessed 3/6/2025, https://www2.gwu.edu/~erpapers/myday/displaydoc.cfm?_y=1945&_f=md000099.

BIBLIOGRAPHY

Albion, Michele Wehrwein. *The Quotable Eleanor Roosevelt*. Gainsville, Florida: University Press of Florida, 2013.

Baker, Josephine, and Bouillon, Jo. *Josephine*. Translated by Mariana Fitzpatrick. New York: Paragon House Publishers, 1977.

Bell-Scott, Patricia. *The Firebrand and the First Lady: Portrait of a friendship: Pauli Murray, Eleanor Roosevelt, and the struggle for social justice*. New York: Alfred A. Knopf, 2016.

Bocquet, José-Louis, and Muller, Catel. *Josephine Baker*. London: SelfMadeHero, 2017.

Caravantes, Peggy. *The Many Faces of Josephine Baker: Dancer, singer, activist, spy*. Chicago, Illinois, Chicago Review Press, 2015.

Lewis, Damien. *Agent Josephine*. New York: PublicAffairs, 2022.

Lichtblau, Eric. *The Nazis Next Door: How America became a safe haven for Hitler's men*. New York: Houghton Mifflin Harcourt Publishing Company, 2014.

Michaelis, David. *Eleanor*. New York: Simon & Schuster, 2020.

Roosevelt, Eleanor. *The Autobiography of Eleanor Roosevelt*. New York: Harper and Brothers, 1961.

The Eleanor Roosevelt Papers Project, The George Washington University, 312 Academic Building, 2100 Foxhall Road, NW Washington, DC 20007, Digital edition published 2008, 2017 by The Eleanor Roosevelt Papers Project.

Winter, Jonah, and Priceman, Marjorie. *Jazz Age Josephine*. New York: Atheneum Books for Young Readers, 2012

Wood, Ean. *The Josephine Baker Story*. London: Sanctuary, 2000.